'A beautifully written story of love, friendship, beliefs, fear, passion and I'm not embarrassed to say I cried at the end . . . each page is a literal work of art'
COMPULSIVE READERS

'Comes to a dramatic and totally unexpected conclusion'
IT TAKES A WOMAN

'You seriously have to read this book'
LIPSTICK & LACE

'This was a fun and cleverly written book, and I would recommend it to anyone who enjoys a good mystery with a hint of humour!'
EMMA'S BOOKERY

'The characters are skilfully written, so easy to get lost in their lives'
LINDA STRONG REVIEWS

'I couldn't let go, I read it from cover to cover because there was no way I could leave it without knowing . . . This is an exceptional piece of work'
EMMA, GoodReads Reviewer

'Set in a small-town America and filled with some of the most exciting characters I have seen in fiction for ages'
READING ROOM WITH A VIEW

'I thoroughly enjoyed reading this; there are so many delightfully comic touches along the way, but all supported by a deeper sentiment and characters you can't help but feel for'
BURIED UNDER BOOKS

ALL THE WICKED GIRLS

CHRIS WHITAKER

ZAFFRE

First published in Great Britain in 2017 by

ZAFFRE PUBLISHING
80-81 Wimpole St, London W1G 9RE
www.zaffrebooks.co.uk

A CIP catalogue record for this book is
available from the British Library.

ISBN: 978–1–78576–152–2
Trade Paperback ISBN: 978–1–78576–379–3

also available as an ebook

1 3 5 7 9 10 8 6 4 2

Typeset by IDSUK (Data Connection) Ltd
Printed and bound by Clays Ltd, St Ives Plc

Zaffre Publishing is an imprint of Bonnier Zaffre,
a Bonnier Publishing company
www.bonnierzaffre.co.uk
www.bonnierpublishing.co.uk

For Charlie and George, my boys.
And for Ayisha Malik (because I honour my bets).

1

Summer

There ain't no meaning.

That's where the fear lay all along. That's what they didn't get, all those people yellin' and screamin' on the television, those preening pastors crossing the air, those parents lockin' down their teens like they could keep grip on their wanderin' souls.

And when it was over they couldn't take it—that discovery. They went on mourning, they spoke of before like before was real or somethin'. The death of ideals.

I get it though—the need for good and evil—but that endless stretch of gray between, that's where you'll find me and Raine, and maybe Pastor Bobby too.

Raine's my sister. I got a photo of us on my nightstand, in a sparkly frame shaped like a heart; gaudy as hell but my daddy bought it for me. We're young in that shot, arms linked, bubble-gum smiles and eyes squint 'cause we never did keep our sunhats on. We were camping up by the Red River, the part where the bank runs low and the water breaks for brown rocks so slick we weren't never allowed to wade out. That's the best spot for fishin'.

Daddy reckons he's pulled out striped bass just as big as the kind Uncle Tommy caught when he fished the Coosa.

That's also the very same spot where Chief Black found a penis in the fall of 1985, back when the whole country was hot with talk of the McMartin preschool case and the couple hundred kids they reckoned was ritually abused there.

It's far and away the most excitin' thing that's ever happened in the town of Grace so we all know the story by heart.

The penis belonged to Richie Reams. Richie was a high school football stud—big arms and light eyes and fingers that smelled of pussy most days. He lived with his momma in a single-wide over in the scratch-ass town of Haskell, though she spent her nights with a hard-drinkin' trucker she met at the bar she tended.

Coach said Richie was destined for greatness if he could stay outta trouble, but that weren't Richie's way. Too much of a weakness for girls. Supply was dwindling though, especially being as Richie had a leanin' toward blond-haired, blue-eyed innocents. There weren't many of those left in Haskell. 'Course they still had the hair and the eyes, but Richie had fucked the innocence right outta them. That's why he'd ventured into Grace. Virgin huntin'.

He set his sights on Mandy Deamer. She went to Westview, same high school I do. I've seen her photo: Farrah hair and dimpled smile, the kinda pure that turned Richie's insides out.

He made sure to bump into Mandy outside Mae's Diner on the first day of summer break. Might've made his move straight off but she kept a bull of a girl as her sidekick: Franny Vestal. Franny was the cruel kinda big; six two and wide, and dressed head to toe in black most days. She had her eyes set hard on Richie from the get-go, like she could see through the smoke in his mind. He'd tried to soften her with a couple throwaways—*nice eyes, tall like a model, had a friend for her*— the kinda lines Richie thought a fat girl should've swallowed whole. Not Franny. Richie told Black he'd reckoned she was a dyke.

Mandy caved two weeks later. Realized her mistake after Richie's gold promises died hard in the blessed light of day. He was safely back in Haskell by the time she found out she was carryin' his baby.

Four months into the pregnancy Mandy took her own life. The shame got to her; hot stares and cold whispers and holy judgment.

Her brother Harvey found her hangin' from the long beam in the barn behind their place. Messed him up bad enough for the Deamers to pull their kids from Westview and school them at home from then on.

Franny came for Richie in the dead of night. Black later told the *Briar County News* she'd held chloroform over his mouth, so he didn't wake when she stripped him naked, though he did when his cock came off.

She left him bleedin' and screamin' but called 911 'cause she weren't no murderer, she was just rightin' a wrong. She tossed his dick into the Red on her way home. A few hours later it washed up on the bank.

Lottie Stimson's dog found it, picked it up in his slobberin' mouth. Lottie wrestled it from him, screamed, then fetched Black, and Mitch Wild, who was Black's partner back then.

They sent Lottie on her way, she was cryin' bad. Black told her he'd stop by her place to take a statement, also told her to keep her mouth shut till then. 'Course she'd been straight on the telephone; said she'd heard noises in Hell's Gate, probably the killer gettin' a good look at her. She dressed it up nice enough for my momma to head straight over with a bottle of Barton.

Lottie also called her husband, Jasper, home from the logs; gave him an excuse to sit out front with his shotgun, his retarded brothers and more than a couple beers too. Itchy fingers. Now Jasper was known 'cause he'd just served a five bid in Fountain Correctional Facility for beatin' a cop, so Black made a mental note to call ahead before he walked up their track. Though he forgot to pass that note on to his partner.

Mitch Wild was shot dead when he stopped by the Stimson place after dark that evenin'.

Franny handed herself in once she'd cooled. Talk was the cops found all kinds of dark at her house: wicker pentagrams hanging from the trees in her yard, sketches of Babylon and evil eyes, and that LaVeyan book on her nightstand. Black said it was bullshit but that didn't stop it from burnin', and the kids at school reckoned the flames fired blue and the smoke twisted into the face of Mandy as it rose.

I've heard that tale maybe fifty times, each a little different, but at the end I ain't in no doubt who the devil in that story is, and it ain't Franny.

Mandy is buried in a pretty spot in the cemetery beside St. Luke's. She was my age when she died. Fifteen. That's a long way short of a decent life.

I'd stop by her grave when I went to church and Momma would always say to me, "*Keep clear of boys, Summer. They ain't got nothin' to give you but trouble.*"

Raine sometimes complains that nothin' excitin' is ever gonna happen in Grace again.

Daddy told her careful what you wish for.

2

A Cautionary Tale

Summer Ryan went missing in the night hours of May 26. Her daddy called his boys before the cops 'cause he reckoned they'd move quicker. And also 'cause Joe Ryan had spent the better years of his life keeping far from law enforcement.

The group fanned out and moved slow. Flashlights cut stuttered lines beneath ink sky and moonlight fell blue between longleaf pines that rose tall in the distance.

Most had kids of their own so knew that cold fear that was rolling over Joe and Ava. Having a daughter loose all night, fifteen, smart or not, their part of the world rarely saw mistakes go unpunished, prizes unclaimed.

Tommy Ryan led them, the missing girl's uncle, and he carried a gun and a bow and was handy enough with both.

They walked the flat fields behind the girl's house 'cause that's the way she might've gone. There were rumblings she'd packed a bag before she ran, which meant they were probably wasting their time; that she was probably holed up with a friend or a boy or was laying low till whatever caused her to flee worked itself out. Still, the land weren't safe and hadn't been for a long time. Not since the first girl was taken.

That nightmare had stretched for over a year then stopped sudden. Five girls: all from Briar County, all young, and all church girls. They reckoned it was over 'cause thinking anything but meant they'd go on holding their breath, and they were tired of that terror that saw them wake at all hours and creep down their hallways to check on their own.

They were ten in number. They'd run with Joe back when he was young and did bad things. They'd straightened out when Joe went down 'cause eight years was sobering. They lived in Grace and the close surround, their wives talked, their kids hung out. Most weekends they drank beer together, ate barbecue, watched football, and joked and laughed.

When the sun rose, those with jobs would break for work of different kinds—a couple in construction, a couple hauled freight, one fixed air-conditioning units—then they'd come right back. They'd listen out for the telephone. They'd get tight on their own kids; tell them to be home before dark, to stick to the streets and not even glance at Hell's Gate National Forest.

If they caught the guy—newspapers called him the Bird—they'd kill him before calling the cops. It weren't said but they knew that's what they'd do.

*

The Grace heat got up early. By eight, the streets baked and kids stood by sprinklers, screaming on each pass.

Noah Wild wore his father's badge on a length of twine he looped twice over his head. He'd polished it till sunlight bounced from the eagle's wings.

Stores crept to life; A-frames were hauled to the street by slow-moving keepers, most a decade past retirement but clinging to purpose with iron grips.

He stopped outside the Whiskey Barrel. Purv was hosing the sidewalk, his worn sneakers deep in a puddle as the spray pooled.

Purv saw him and grinned, then reached out and thumbed the badge. "You look mean, like a real cop."

Noah wanted to return the compliment but Purv wore an apron that fell low, the shirt beneath drowning him. Purv was a funny kinda small given his father stood a tough six three. He flicked his hair up to give him inches but weren't fooling nobody, especially when the wind blew. He had one eyebrow, thumb thick and running the width of both eyes. They'd once tried to split it, with some duct tape and a whole lot of cussin'.

"I still reckon it's missin' somethin'. The badge alone ain't enough," Noah said.

Purv studied him careful. "How about a toothpick? Just let it hang, like Cobretti. I'll pick some up."

"I'll need a gun belt too."

"You reckon you'll get a gun on your first day?"

"Yeah . . . probably low caliber though, just till I show Black I know how to handle a Koch."

Purv looked away, bit his lip hard.

Noah sighed. "K-o-c-h."

"I saw your grandmother pass by just now," Purv said. "She was wearin' a housecoat and rollers, talking to herself. I tried calling out but she looked at me like she ain't never seen me before."

"Thanks for tryin'."

Purv nodded then yawned.

"Rough night?" Noah said.

"Someone stole my father's truck. He weren't happy, had to walk it back from Merle's place."

"Shit," Noah said, 'cause he knew what that would've meant for Purv.

Purv's father was a bully, not the misunderstood kind that cowered beneath, just the misshapen kind that'd be stone through if you sliced him in half. If Purv knew a beating was due, Noah would crouch at the end of his yard and wait for the signal that he was still living before he headed home. One flip of the lights, on and off.

Noah reached a hand out and gripped Purv's shoulder tight. "We're brave."

"We're fierce."

"Catch you later," Noah said.

"Good luck."

Purv went back to hosing.

Noah headed for the center of the square, for the stretch of Bermuda grass watered day and night during the hot months.

He found a bench and reached for his sunglasses, a birthday gift from Purv a year back, expertly lifted from the drugstore in Brookdale, along with two packs of Marlboros. Smoking and stealing were just about Purv's favorite pastimes.

They'd been friends since Noah could remember. They spent summers in the Kinleys' fields, racing down lines of corn and firing stick guns at the shiny twin-engines that buzzed low, then stopping by the Red to try and glimpse the senior girls in their bathing suits. They spent winters trampling through white woods, trying to follow buck tracks but making so much noise they never caught sight of one.

Noah watched a couple old guys amble into Mae's Diner and take a seat by the misted glass. Noah liked Grace before it got up. He'd once worked a paper route, rising at dawn and pedaling his rusting bicycle down the pretty streets with the tall houses and the watercolor yards. Each Christmas he walked that same route with Purv, and they stared in warm windows at distant scenes.

He sat back, breathed deep, and thought of summer break rolled out ahead. He was about to enter junior year; his grades were shit but that was all right, he'd worked out long ago that school weren't for him. Purv was faring worse, but then it weren't no secret that God took with both hands when he created Purvis Bowdoin.

They didn't complain 'cause they were brave and they were fierce and they never forgot that.

*

Raine Ryan moved fast. She followed the snaking line of the Red River, shooting a glance at the water, dark and rushing right alongside her. There were breaks farther upstream, calm enough to swim but skimmed with algae and fifty deep if you believed the rumors.

There was a tree by Abby Farley's place that hung right out over the bank, Abby's brother had slung a rope over it and tied an old tire to the end. Their momma said it weren't safe, like that'd stop them. Summer wouldn't ever take a turn, she just sat on the bank reading a book and smiling every time Raine hollered at her to watch.

Raine caught her foot on a cypress root and went sprawling in the dirt. She lay still for a moment, her breath coming short, her head over the edge. She wondered what would happen if she fell in. She could swim good but the Red was quick. She'd be claimed, sucked beneath as the water roared louder than her screams.

She kept tight hold of the note, hauled herself up, and saw a deep cut on her knee. Blood rolled steady down her shin and she leaned down and wiped it with her finger then brought it to her lips. The taste of blood never bothered her all that much.

She set off in the direction of town, the trees clustered tight as she looked down and ran.

When she reached the square she slowed and calmed and wiped sweat from her head. She glanced up at the Grace Police Department. It occupied a grand building at the head of the square, stone and painted a shade of parchment that dulled a month after it was done.

Inside she asked for Chief Black and was swept into his office by Rusty, with his heavy stomach and half limp. He was eating a sandwich, ketchup by his mouth and a spot of grease on his necktie.

He left her and she sat, pressed her hands flat against the table; fingers splayed, nails bit short. They weren't allowed to wear varnish. Their momma said they were too young, said it like a lick of red on their nails would part their legs for the boys.

She crossed the room and rifled through the desk drawers, saw empty bottles before she found Black's wallet and slipped a twenty from it. She moved quick back to her chair and sat still.

The door opened and Trix stuck her head in. "You okay, Raine?" Trix worked the front desk, had her hair cropped boy-short and dyed dark.

Raine nodded.

"Is it important? Lot of shit goin' on this mornin'."

"Like what?"

"Ray Bowdoin. Someone stole his truck last night and he ain't happy."

"I gotta talk to Black. My daddy sent me."

"I'll grab him soon as I can."

For the most part Raine did as she pleased, and what pleased her were acts that saw her in shit, so she weren't no stranger to Trix, Black, and the others.

She reached into her pocket and pulled out a crumpled photo of Summer. Twins, similar once, though nature had other plans as they grew. Summer was quiet and smart and all kinda other things Raine weren't.

She leaned down and checked the cut on her knee, licked a finger and cleaned the blood from it.

Black came into the room and she caught the smell of booze that trailed him.

He sat down and rubbed his eyes before he spoke, maybe to show he was busy or tired, or maybe just tired of her.

"What did you do this time, Raine? If you've been messin' with those Kirkland boys again it's on you. Ain't my business to go meddling in family matters, got enough on."

"It's Summer," she said, a trace of heat in her voice. She had her daddy's temper, her nose turning up in a snarl.

He looked up.

"She's gone missin'."

He tried to keep level but she saw the color drain right from him. He made to speak but fumbled his words.

She watched him close, the creased shirt and the dry lips.

"Since when?" he said.

"Last night. She left a note." Raine slid it across the table.

He picked it up with a shaking hand. "*I'm sorry.*"

She nodded.

"So she ran," he said, the color returning.

"Looks that way."

"What's she sorry about?"

Raine shrugged.

"Where's your daddy?"

"Out lookin'. Said he'd walk the flat fields then follow the Red to Hell's Gate. He wants you to send Rusty and Milk and anyone else you can spare."

"Milk's out sorting the mess from last night. Ray Bowdoin's truck –"

"I know," she cut in.

"You tell your daddy I'll put a call out, but I need him to keep a cool head. Reckon you can do that?"

"Why don't you tell him yourself?" she said, bait in her tone.

"Summer left a note. She probably just needed some space . . . like you do sometimes."

He stood and made for the door.

"Black."

He turned.

"It still ain't safe out there. Y'all didn't catch him."

*

The station ran silent as Ray Bowdoin filled out the papers. Noah watched him close, the way he stood and the gold rings jutting from fists so big Purv didn't ever stand a chance.

When Ray was done he tossed the pen at Trix.

"I ain't holdin' much hope you'll find it," he said as he drew a cigarette and pressed it to his lips.

"You can't smoke in here," Trix said.

Ray lit his cigarette and Rusty stood, a hand on his gun.

Ray walked to the door then turned. "The dog, that fuckin' mutt my neighbor got. I told Purv to come tell y'all 'cause it won't shut up."

"He told us," Rusty said.

"And?"

"Dogs bark, Ray. That's what they do. You tried petting it?"

Ray smiled, winked at Trix, then headed out.

"You should've shot him," Trix said.

Rusty nodded 'cause he knew she weren't kidding.

"When do I get my gun, Trix? I'll need two . . . crossfire. I ain't gonna be a house mouse like Rusty," Noah said.

"Remind me again why he's here?" Rusty said.

Trix ignored him. She'd arranged for Noah to spend the summer with them, a couple shifts each week, answering the phone and working the file room. Trix had been friends with Noah's momma since they were small. She'd sat with her through the last days, then held Noah's hand at the funeral as he stared at the casket but wouldn't let no tears fall. Tough like his daddy was.

Noah pulled out a chair, spun it round, and straddled it. "Can we talk about my powers?"

"You got the power to answer the phone. Nothin' more."

They fell quiet as Raine walked through. Noah felt her look over, their eyes meeting for a moment which stretched till his knees shook and his gaze dropped. There was something wild there, some kinda draw that went beyond the obvious and got the boys dreaming and drooling. He'd pass her by at school, back when she used to show up, but they ran in different circles—Noah's consisting of Purv alone, and Raine's just about every senior with access to a car and booze.

Black followed a minute after she left.

"What's up?" Rusty said.

"Summer took off last night," Black said.

"Summer?"

Black nodded.

Trix looked up, worry in her eyes. "Summer ran?"

"And?" Rusty said.

"Probably ain't nothin'. She left a note," Black said, rubbing his temples. He looked over at Noah, eyes settling on the badge he wore.

The phone rang. Rusty glanced at Noah then pointed to it.

Noah reached across the desk, brought the receiver to his ear, and took a breath. "Detective Noah Wild. Homicide."

Rusty shook his head. "What is it?"

"Smoke comin' from Hell's Gate last night," Noah said, the phone against his ear.

"Another fire. Fuckin' holy rollers from White Mountain, hollerin' at the devil again. I'll take it," Rusty said, reaching for the handset.

Black parted the slats and watched Raine cross the square. She passed a couple guys but they kept their eyes low. Even with Joe Ryan outta sight they wouldn't risk a glance at one of his daughters.

His mind slipped from Summer to the missing girls from Briar County, then to the sketch of the Bird that'd run in the newspapers. Big and feathered and frightening. A cautionary tale about heading lone into the woods at night.

3

Summer

There was moments so pure and perfect I almost can't bear them. Maybe a sunrise so stark that line between us and the heavens blurs to nothin' but a smudge.

I dreamed in stills, in frozen time and melted clocks, but 'stead of desert there was the steady turns of the Red River 'cause that was my constant.

I saw us sittin' by the bank. We were camping with Daddy and we snuck out after he was sleepin' and laid back and held hands. The sky was stretched so deep and dark and heavy it might've smothered us had the stars not pinned it high. We saw one tumble and Raine reckoned it was a firework, but in the mornin' Daddy told us it was a fallin' star and we should've made a wish on it.

I reckon that's my moment: the point so high life can't do nothin' but pivot and fail. Maybe it came too young but that's all right 'cause at least I got it.

The first time I told that to Bobby he asked me if I knew what a nihilist was and said it with a straight face 'cause that's how Bobby makes jokes. Like they ain't jokes. But that's bullshit 'cause morality don't come into it. Maybe he meant pessimist. Or realist.

I once heard Daddy say faith is reliance and reliance is weak, and Momma got real mad at him 'cause he weren't long out and we hung on his words.

Not long after Richie Reams lost his cock, the Etowah County Sheriff's Office were on the news talkin' about a site they found out in Walnut Grove. I looked it up in the Maidenville library and there's grainy photographs of dead dogs and flipped crosses still standin' in the dirt. They made routine inquiries but never got nowhere.

I grew up with the Panic; with evangelical Christianity askin' questions and Mötley Crüe providing the answers. The propagators' message was simple, a vast network of Satanists lived amongst us, and they were claimin' young souls and the country was goin' to shit 'cause of it. These Satanists, they hid their message in music and books and video games, they rippled the still waters of suburbia till Washington Wives began to fight back with Parental Advisory stickers and conservative hysteria.

There was a big sign hammered into the grass in Mick Kinley's sixth acre, showin' a cartoon devil holding a scythe and promisin' to "come get you" if you don't go to church. It's that kinda thinkin' that lit the touch paper and fanned the flames till the whole of Grace was molten with fear.

I spent a lot of time in church. Momma said it was my second home and she said it with more than a lick of pride.

St. Luke's is the fifth-oldest church in the whole state. It's stone and tall, with a bell tower that chimes every hour till late. I'd sit on the bench by the colored glass, and in the summer months, if I timed it right, the sunlight would spill through and paint me with a rainbow. It's beautiful. I mean, I know people say that a lot, especially about grand old buildings, but St. Luke's is so beautiful it's hard to breathe when you're inside.

Isaiah Lumen was the pastor for a lifetime and more, then he had a stroke right in the middle of a sermon. He was renouncin' and burnin' and he just fell back and kicked his legs up. People were gasping, but a part of them was wonderin' if it was part of the show, 'cause Pastor Lumen can turn it on sometimes. Now, he was mad like that since I can remember, but it got worse after Deely White's cattle got slaughtered, 'cause up till that point the devil was just circling Grace, he hadn't come inside. Black reckoned it was kids but he didn't say it with no conviction 'cause takin' a blade to animals like that, it ain't what kids do.

Folk reckoned it weren't all that bad, that Pastor Lumen would be back preachin' in no time, but that first stroke was followed by another. And that's when Pastor Bobby came to town. Bobby Ritter. Momma said she ain't never heard of a pastor callin' themselves by a nickname. Said he oughta call himself Pastor Robert or somethin' decent. She likes to go on like she's high cotton but she ain't never lived nowhere but Grace.

Now if Pastor Lumen was be-angry-and-do-not-sin Jesus, then Pastor Bobby was love-endures Jesus. He carries himself with this quiet confidence, like shit don't bother him; even if Merle rolls into service lit and loud, Bobby don't pay him no mind. And he's real young too, and he's got a nice smile but he don't smile much, so when he does you kinda feel like you're special or somethin'.

Yeah, Bobby's popular in Grace.

By his second service the church was heavy with sweet perfume and flutterin' hearts.

4

Alabama Pink

There were trucks parked out front of the Ryan house; old pickups with big tires, mud sprayed up the doors and rifles on the seats.

Raine heard voices in the kitchen. She looked in and saw men standing over the table and maps spread all over. Her momma was on the telephone and she was talking and her eyes were sunk and swollen.

She saw her uncle Tommy take a beer from the refrigerator. He wore his hair long and had the kinda smile that kept the ladies lining up. He'd sweeten his drawl, then drop them quick after. Said he only had eyes for his nieces. That was true for a long time while their daddy was away. She and Summer would go on begging each weekend to stay in his cabin. He'd teach them to lay snares, to track and shoot.

Raine turned and stepped out onto the porch. She sat on the top step, by the spot where she'd carved their names with a hunting knife when they were seven and got in major shit for it. She traced her finger over the curves.

Rusty had stopped by their place at noon, reckoned Summer was safe 'cause she'd packed a bag first. Not like the missing girls from Briar County. They got snatched up, plucked from their lives so sudden and random the cops didn't piece it together till number three.

She heard the engine before she saw the truck. It barrelled round the corner and stopped right in front of her. Four guys got out, Tommy's friends, their doors slamming together.

One was young; she tried a smile as they walked into the house but he wouldn't meet her eye.

Raine walked over to the truck, reached in through the window, and took a half-empty pack of Marlboros from the seat. She stuffed it in her pocket quick as she heard her daddy call.

"Can I come out with y'all? I want to help search," Raine said straight off when she reached the door.

Joe shook his head. "Head out on your bicycle, maybe get up with the neighbors. Don't go near Hell's Gate."

Raine nodded, knew they reckoned she was holding out 'cause that's why he was sending her out alone.

"I don't know where she is, swear I don't." She felt his eyes on her 'cause he knew her tells.

"You cut your knee," he said, looking at her leg.

"Ain't nothin'."

She got in scraps and scrapes since she was small but she didn't cry so they never knew if she was hurt bad or not.

He opened his arms, she stepped into them and he kissed her head and held her awhile. He was tall and strong and she loved him more than she did her momma, which she didn't find a hard truth to swallow. Daddy's girl, that's what folk said, so when they couldn't keep her straight no more they talked about apples and trees and smiled, for a while.

"Bring her back, Raine."

She picked up her yellow bicycle from where it lay in the yard. She pedaled to the end of her street, dumped it in the tall grass, then doubled back for her momma's truck. The keys were in the visor but she let it roll the slope before she fired it. A cross hung from the rearview mirror, swinging back and forth as she bumped along the road.

The engine quit as Raine was gunning it down one of the long tracks by the Kinley farm. Steam ran from the hood and fogged the windshield. She climbed out and walked round to the tailgate, cussin' when she saw the empty water bottles in the bed. She stared around. The corn stood tall and green on both sides, clustered so tight she couldn't make out much beyond the high sun. She knew there was a breeze 'cause the crops moved but it weren't strong enough to trouble the heat.

She paced the track awhile, kicked out and watched dust spread as she reached a hand up and dragged it through her hair. Her daddy would be pissed. She weren't supposed to take the pickup, not just 'cause the engine was fucked but 'cause she was a year shy of getting her license and Black's patience had worn long back.

She wondered what time Summer would break, no way she'd stay out all night. She was soft like that, had been since they were small and the Spanish moss painted shadow faces on her bedroom wall. She wouldn't catch shit for it neither. Their momma would be full of worry 'cause it was Summer this time.

CHRIS WHITAKER | 25

She might even sleep beside her, like she used to when they were young and got sick, stroking their hair with cigarette fingers and telling them stories about their grandparents, and cotton and soybeans, and the boll weevils that choked their land and their lives.

She leaned back, the metal hot on her thighs. She brought her knee up, ran her finger over the scab and licked salty sweat from her lips.

Noah drove slow down his street then turned onto Hickory Glen, following it till he passed by the square and the town began to thin in his rear-view. He rolled the window, glanced up, and saw a thundercloud over the canopy of Hell's Gate. His grandmother had been waiting on a storm. She spent her days on the front porch, rocking and switching her gaze between their yard and the sky, her mouth turned down like the weight of what had come and gone dragged on it. She spoke of death with an evenness that came from outliving her only daughter. Some days she rode him about his grades, and others she stared straight through him. Social Services had paid a visit four months back when she fell and bruised her hip so bad it turned black.

She went to bed early each night, closed the drapes long before the sun dropped. He'd wait an hour, then take the key from the brass hook, start the Buick, and sit patient while it shuddered and smoked. The Buick was black and rusted and long as a boat. It had the wire wheels that Purv reckoned girls would like, but then Purv reckoned lots of shit Noah had a hard time buying.

It'd been his grandfather's car. She wouldn't sell it, said she could still smell the old man in it. Noah took it out most nights, had done so for six months now, the thrill an even match for the fear of getting caught.

He kept the speed down as he drove along Elba, passing the barren fields. A scarecrow stood, head bowed and dropping a shadow of crucifixion.

He turned off, passed the Kinley place, and ducked low in case Rita was looking out, then drove the track for half a mile before he saw a pickup in the distance, parked lazy in the red dirt.

He caught sight of Raine; recognized the light hair and the long legs. For a moment he sat still, searching for courage, then he eased the gas pedal down and trundled toward her. He drew up short, killed the engine, and got out.

She had her eyes closed, her head tilted up as the sky turned iron above. She wore shorts cut high on her thigh, the last smoke from a cigarette rose from the dirt by her foot.

"Raine."

Her eyes snapped open and she turned to look at him.

"I'm sorry, I didn't mean to scare you," he said.

"You didn't. I ain't the type that scares easy." She had a rough edge to her voice, maybe 'cause she smoked and drank.

"Do you need help?"

She met his eye, cocked her head, and stared so long he wanted to say something else, anything else.

"Storm . . . she's a comin'." Anything but that.

She smoothed her vest down, pulling it tight over her chest.

He swallowed dry.

"I need water," she said. "For the truck."

"I could fill you up –"

"I doubt that."

His eyes widened. "Shit, that came out . . . I could get you some water."

She wore a half smile that rolled his stomach. She tucked her hair behind her ear then spit her gum in the dirt.

"You know who my sister is?"

He nodded.

"You seen her about?"

He shook his head.

"I gotta find her. I was headed for the houses on Chapel Lake Drive. I figured she might've headed that way . . . everyone reckons she followed the Red."

"I could drive you there? Right now, wherever you need to go." He tried to keep the eager from his voice.

She looked around like she was weighing options, then walked at him.

He stepped to the side and she got in the Buick and he followed.

"Smells like old man in this car," she said.

"That'll be my dead grandfather."

"He ain't in the trunk is he?"

She reached for the radio and found something loud and angry. She kicked off her sandals and put her bare feet on the dash, then pulled a bottle of Barton from her bag and drank. Vodka and smoke and cheap perfume, Noah's head was light.

They drove down roads with arched trees that cut the sky to nothing but a dying strip. They passed a couple double-wides and they saw the blue green of television light blinking in the box windows. He made a right onto Chapel Lake Drive, took it wide, and ran the grass but she didn't say nothing and he was glad.

"I can't see a lake," he said.

"Ain't no chapel neither."

Chapel Lake Drive was once grand, maybe fifty years back when the land was rich with cotton and Grace was something more than run out.

He pulled up. The gate was wrought iron, hanging loose at the top hinge. There was a long driveway that wound its way up to a big house. The fascia was carved and might've been beautiful but for the dark mold crawling from the soffits. The roof was half covered in tarp and steel scaffolding rose to it. A sign hung, the lettering fancy but faded. BOWDOIN CONSTRUCTION.

Both knew it was the Lumen house.

They left the Buick by the gate and followed the gravel, thinned and torn with broadleaf weed.

"It's gettin' dark," Noah said, looking up. "And Pastor Lumen scares the shit outta me."

"Maybe you'll get lucky and the Angel will come to the door," she said.

The Angel. Everybody knew him 'cause he had fluffy white hair and snow-white skin and eyes ringed with the lightest pink. Most knew he was albino, 'cept for Samson's momma and the pastor, who were quick to declare him an angel when he was born. Raine's momma said they didn't ever take him to the doctor.

She banged the door with a closed fist, shaking the timber frame and loosening citrine paint.

She pressed her head against the window beside. There were paintings on the wall, winged women with their tits showing and horses with ringlets of white hair. She saw a bowed shelf and a photo frame with a pressed pink flower behind the glass.

Raine reckoned it looked like an Alabama Pink even though you weren't supposed to pick them. The flowers were so rare no one knew where to find them. Rumor was, if you held them to the light they'd cast a colored glow.

She stood there a long time, then felt dark crawl the roofline and snatch daylight away. She turned and saw Noah standing in the grass watching her and he jerked his head away quick like he'd been checking out her ass or something.

They moved on to Merle's place next door. The farmhouse roof bowed so bad that Merle slept in the barn behind. Nobody answered at either when Raine banged the doors. Merle ran the auto shop on Sayer Street, and he ran poker games and sold jars of moonshine.

Merle's 'shine was known far 'cause it was so charged that lighting a smoke within fifty yards of it would likely start a fire. It happened once before. Wilbur Orr and his part-timers put it out before it reached the barrels, otherwise half the town would've been buttered on the fumes.

They tried another couple houses but didn't get nothing.

*

Samson Lumen dressed the same no matter the season; pale skin covered, hat pulled low and dark shelled glasses that shielded his eyes from a sun too ruthless. His momma once said he was an angel and angels flew at night, like that explained away the questions he asked.

He worked at the school and the church and at both he did those background jobs most reckoned beneath them.

Sometimes the kids pissed on the floor then hollered for him and laughed.

With his daddy, the pastor, in the hospital he lay with fearful eyes each night, thinking every noise was the noise he'd been waiting on. He locked the doors and windows but the roof of the old house was open to the night and to dark creatures like Ray Bowdoin.

Ray looked at him like he was soft and strange and ripe for picking. At first it was money, the money Ray said the pastor owed for the work he was doing, but now it was more.

Ray had a gun in his truck and a switchblade in his pocket and the kinda eyes that told Samson he was close with both. Samson was afraid of death and of Ray Bowdoin, but most of all Samson was afraid of his daddy, of the damnation the pastor said would visit them if Samson didn't prove himself worthy and right of the Lumen name. Though his daddy was sick with an ailment that drooped his eye and his arm like they were being tugged from beneath, the hatred still burned. The pastor didn't care for his only son, not since he was born and not since he'd found the pornographic magazines Samson bought from Lucky Delfray when he was fifteen. He remembered that day clear; the heat of his daddy's hand and the cold ache of the Red River, and his momma's panic as she ran for the house and the telephone.

There were worse things than sins of the flesh his momma had said, but she didn't get it, not none of it 'cause his daddy saw to that. Sweep it away and bury it deep.

Samson had his head pressed to the window when the girl knocked at the door, the pretty ghost girl that stole all his breath.

He wanted to answer, to call her in and maybe talk to her and the boy, the boy with the cop badge. Samson didn't have no friends. But then he'd seen what they brought, the heavy dark cloud that ate the Alabama sky like summer weren't ever coming back. So he dropped to his bed and he curled fetal, his head beneath the pillow 'cause that's how cowards hid.

*

Raine rolled down the window, hung her arm out, and opened her hand to the breeze. "You ever pretend your hand is a bird?" she said.

Noah shook his head.

"When I'm in my daddy's truck I put my hand out the window and pretend it's a bird. I sweep it up and down in the wind. You try it."

"I ain't sure I should take my hand off the wheel."

"You always such a pussy?"

He rolled his window and stuck his arm out, and he swept his hand up and down and cupped slate air between his fingers.

The Buick veered across the double lines and knocked down a mailbox.

"Shit," he said, jerking the wheel.

She laughed, so he smiled like his heart weren't pounding out.

He pulled into the gas station on Highway 125 and filled a container with water, then drove back toward the Kinleys' fields.

"I don't see you at school no more," he said.

"You go to my school?"

He took the hit well.

She rubbed her eyes 'cause she'd got in late the night before. She'd seen the note straight off, then climbed the stairs and changed her clothes, woke her parents and watched their world dim.

"She'll be okay," he said.

"I ain't worried."

She threw the empty vodka bottle out the window and heard it smash. She liked the sound, so high and jarring.

The Buick bumped along the track and she frowned like Noah should've known how to ride the ditches better.

He popped the hood of her truck and filled the empty coolant tank.

She stood by the tall crops and thought about her sister, and though she didn't believe as Summer did, she said a quick and quiet prayer that when she got home things would be right, 'cause she couldn't handle her momma getting on her over nothing else.

"I could drive you again," he said, head under the hood. "If you need help, come find me at the station."

"So you're a cop?" she said, glancing at the badge, an eyebrow raised.

"Yeah," he said, straight. Then added, "kinda."

She laughed and he blushed, then she climbed into the truck and pulled away.

She saw him in the mirror standing still and watching her go till dust ghosted his face. She kept the window down. Her hand was a bird and she made it fly as the crickets sang their night songs.

*

The sweats came and went but sleep did not. Chief Black sat in a high-backed chair in the center of the living room and stared at a large map of Briar County and at the faces of the stolen girls. The Briar girls.

Home was a small clapboard close to one of the many backwaters that fed the Red River. The walls were papered with all they had on the Bird. The link was there, the churches of Briar County, but of them there were many and second-guessing weren't even close to possible.

He'd worked murders in his years as a trooper, domestics and rapes and men that touched kids. They left prints on him so deep he knew he weren't cut out for the job. Mitch Wild used to tell him a good cop was a cop with heart, but then Mitch could say that 'cause purpose fit him like a second skin, a skin he'd slip from as he headed home each night. Noah looked so much like Mitch it carried Black back every time he saw the kid.

The Briar girls case was unmatched in scale, from Briar County Sheriff Ernie Redell to the state cops, and they'd turned up nothing.

"The Bird." He said it loud with a slight slur.

The press cooked that one up. The only sighting with girl number four, Coralee Simmons. Twenty minutes after she got taken, by a track she used as a shortcut to the Green Acres Baptist Church, a couple kids playing soldier had seen someone walking through Hell's Gate. He was big they said, big like a monster and feathered like a bird. He had a girl on his shoulder, hanging limp like she was sleeping. And the bird smiled at them, then brought a finger to his lips.

It was well outta Grace but Black was nearest, got there and headed in lone. He backed Ernie and Ernie backed him, there was a lot of land in Briar and not nearly enough cops. He'd been walking maybe a mile when he glimpsed something. He'd drawn, called, and followed. The shape, that's all it was, was big and moved quick. The ground was leaves and mud, the trees tight and close. Black was sloppy, drunk, but he'd gained a little before he fell hard. The shape turned and Black had raised his gun 'cause the shot was clear no matter what he'd told Ernie and the state cops. He'd missed by a head. That miss . . . sleep didn't come, the blood on his hands wouldn't ever dry.

He poured a measure of Evan Williams. He had pills— Phrenilin and Nembutal and Halcion. When he mixed them with booze they guided him to lucid dreams where he aimed a little left and took the shadow off its feet. And where he made the call to Jasper Stimson, and Mitch Wild didn't walk that dark trail alone and take that bullet to the chest and leave a widow and a child to claw at Black's soul.

He weren't old but felt tired, weren't fat but weight dragged on him. Sometimes he was amazed what the human body could endure. He surfed close to the divide, never more so than when girl five got taken.

He wouldn't chase that Baphomet shadow again, not a chance. No, he wouldn't chalk up another loss. She'd show up soon. Summer Ryan would be all right.

5

Summer

When Raine's done somethin' bad she stands there, hand on hip and nose turned up like she's about ready to bare her teeth. Same every time, don't matter if she's been caught with a boy or caught smokin' or caught stealin' liquor from Ginny's, she's always ready to throw first.

Daddy was sent to Holman for eight years a month before we were born. We ain't never allowed to speak of it 'cause Momma said the past is just that, but from what I got he could've served just a couple but wouldn't roll on nobody. Maybe an ounce of loyalty is really worth a pound of cleverness, but then maybe Elbert didn't have to raise twin daughters alone like Momma did. So I forgive her sins, and they ain't really sins, she's just tough on us 'cause the fear kept pace with her every night without Daddy.

Momma looked at Raine and saw the long road of age-old mistakes, saw missed periods and clandestine trips to the hook doctor somewhere outside Mobile so he could claw at her womb, and an eternity of that frantic kinda prayer to keep everyone involved from burnin'.

That kinda worry all day and all night from this life to the after. Kids. Best case is they make you proud, but pride comes before a fall so you're fucked either way.

Momma worked two cleanin' jobs and she didn't never complain. Raising girls, especially a girl like Raine, it takes the patience of Jude just to keep her aimed right. Some days Raine would dress all black and loop *Stained Glass* till Momma shut the power off.

I always saw Raine though. The shit she did, the trouble, it didn't make her grow up fast, that ain't how it works. Innocence lost ain't lost at all, it's just buried down in some people. She's got her own fears, that she's headed someplace that ain't never gonna be different to where she's been, just more and more of the same. Grace and boys that don't care, grocery store jobs and three kids by three different deadbeats.

Welfare checks, cigarettes, and booze, and soft looks that harden with each knock.

And faith.

There'll be faith. And there'll be me, 'cause loyalty, like faith, is blind. I'd do it though, I always knew that, no matter what talent they reckoned I got I wouldn't never leave my sister behind. And when I said that once to Momma, she slapped me hard across my cheek. My hair fell and my eyes blurred 'cause I hadn't never been hit before. Scared as she was for Raine, maybe her biggest fear was me livin' a life empty of all that might've been.

Bobby lives in a house at the top of Jackson Ranch Road. It's a nice place with a big yard and wood shutters that get painted every couple years. I ain't sure if the church owns the place or if they bought it, but cost ain't a worry for them 'cause Bobby's wife is the oldest of money. Savannah. She wears flower dresses and pearls even when she ain't going out nowhere. She's beautiful in the kinda way that can't be denied—ain't my type don't apply.

The first time I went to their place it was spring and the mandevillas were that shade of blush that only lasts a blink. The pretty streets in Grace, they're a sight come spring.

I was nervous 'cause it was Bobby and Savannah and I'd only seen them at church, and they had this glow about them. Savannah told Momma how she used to teach cello back in Maidenville but stopped once she fell pregnant. They ain't got children, though. Momma told her how the school said I was smart and that I oughta try playin' an instrument, so Savannah said she'd teach me for free.

Momma made me bring a bunch of asters and I held them tight as I stood on the porch. I peered through the window and saw a vase filled with a big bunch of fancy flowers so was about to toss the asters when Bobby opened the door.

"You bought me flowers," he said, face straight.

"They ain't for you."

He stepped to the side.

The floor was cherrywood, polished so I could see sunlight bouncin' off. Bobby was wearin' a T-shirt; he looked different without his collar, kinda like he was naked or somethin'.

"Where should I go?" I said.

He gently took hold of my shoulders, turned me the opposite way, and pointed.

"That's Savannah's room. I'm not allowed in there in case I break somethin'," he said into my ear.

He patted me on the butt.

I smiled. My cheeks were hot.

I could feel Bobby's eyes on me as I walked the hallway, my footsteps tappin' the kinda echo that stripped the place bare.

I knocked and Savannah opened the door, led me inside, and closed it behind. She took the flowers and set them down and said I was sweet.

"Have you ever played the cello before?" Savannah said.

"I ain't never *seen* a cello before," I said.

6

Smiling at Boys

Raine found her daddy at the kitchen table, head dipped and red-eyed. He'd been out the whole night.

The kitchen light was burning. She glanced out the window and saw nothing but night. The storm would break soon. The last one had run north of them, hit Huntsville so hard it turned out houses.

Raine made herself a bowl of cereal and sat.

"Anything?"

Joe shook his head and thumbed his eyes. He wore an old plaid shirt, the sleeves rolled to his biceps. He had a tattoo, just one, a dove swooping down from his elbow. It faded more each year, like it knew it no longer fit. He got it in Holman. Raine never did manage to figure out what her daddy had done, but eight years was time enough for her to know it weren't nothing petty.

Escambia County was a couple hundred miles from Grace but they'd made the trip every month. Raine had dying memories of the visitation room, of tight smiles and sitting on her daddy's knee, of screaming herself tired on the long drive back while Summer read stories beside her.

"I need you to talk to the other kids in town. Maybe she's staying with one of her friends," Joe said.

She nodded. Sometimes she caught her daddy watching her. She didn't dwell on what she'd lost, on what he'd lost, but it was there in his eyes. Uncle Tommy had helped with money and filled the role as best he could. Summer got pushed down at school one time and Raine had sorted the bully, a fat kid named Charlie Hicks. She'd broke his nose with a stick then caught a lashing from her momma. Tommy took her for ice cream after and told her she was right to protect her sister.

"You want me to fix you somethin'?" Ava said as she walked into the kitchen.

He shook his head.

"Your sister's in for it when she shows her face again," Ava said, tried to smile but couldn't quite.

"You sure there's nothin' you ain't tellin', Raine?" Joe said.

"Shit, I already said all I know."

"And you're sticking to that," Ava said, sharpening.

Raine pushed her bowl away and glared at both of them.

She heard a knock at the door, then her momma led Black into the kitchen and poured him a coffee.

Black sat. He slipped the gun from his belt and set it on the table.

"Took your time," Joe said.

"Rusty came," Black said.

"Rusty ain't Chief."

"I take it you've not heard nothin'."

Joe shook his head.

Black kept his face even. "Milk's been making calls. We'll knock doors. I need to take a look in her bedroom."

"Waste of fuckin' time," Raine said, glaring at Black. "All of you out there and you ain't found her yet."

"Watch your mouth," Ava said.

Joe raised a hand and Raine quietened but didn't draw her eyes from Black. He'd sent her daddy to prison all those years back and she hated him accordingly.

"Could be she's hidin' out in Hell's Gate –"

"She wouldn't go there," Raine said, waving him off. "In case you forgot y'all never caught the Bird. Ain't no one dumb enough to go into Hell's Gate now."

"Well then she's with someone. Maybe she's staying with a friend."

"Raine's gonna ask round today."

"You'll catch most of 'em at church this mornin'," Black said.

"I'm headin' out again. I'll drive up Hallow Road then cut in by the yellow fields, see if I can get Tommy to round up some more men to walk the trails with me," Joe said.

"You'll need flashlights, I got a couple in the trunk. And keep watch for the storm, you don't wanna get caught," Black said, glancing out the window.

Black stood, Ava stood with him.

"Y'all should be treating this like another one," Raine said. "Summer could be girl six and you ain't doin' shit. I'll have to find her myself 'cause Black's a gutless –"

"Enough," Joe said, warning in his tone though his eyes never left Black.

*

"She's got a lot of books," Milk said. "Ain't just stories, there's reference and art history and all kinda shit."

There weren't much to go through 'cause the room was all function. There was a bed and a desk and a closet. Nothing on the walls but paint in a shade of lace that called reservation. Summer Ryan was not a wild child, not even close.

"There's boxes full of 'em in the garage too," Black said. "Ava said they wanted to throw 'em but Summer kicked up about it."

Black found a bottle of perfume buried under clothes and studied it. It was expensive looking, some kinda French name he wouldn't even try to pronounce.

He saw a white dress on the rail, the dress she wore that day she played for them at St. Luke's. He lingered for a second then turned when he heard Ava by the door. Milk went over and put a hand on her shoulder and told her shit she wanted to hear. Milk was black, he was big and he acted tough, a decent front for the kindness beneath.

"I ain't liking this," Milk said, as Ava went to fetch coffee. Milk lowered his voice. "It's him again."

Black waved him off. "More likely she's run off with some boy her daddy wouldn't approve of."

Milk saw through it too easy. "You know that ain't what happened. She's young . . . she's a church girl. She's pretty. Sound familiar?"

Black rubbed his eyes. "It's been six months since Olive Braymer got taken."

"Don't mean shit. And it's ours this time," Milk said, an edge there. "This ain't a runaway, Black, much as you might want it to be. Summer is a Grace girl. You gotta get on this again. Ernie ain't got the men to chase everythin'."

Black ignored him, turned back to the task till Ava returned. He stood, walked over, and handed Ava the fancy perfume.

"But Summer don't wear perfume . . ." Ava said.

He saw the heat there so he followed her down the hallway into Raine's bedroom.

There was music playing loud, Manson singing about cake and sodomy, till Ava walked over and cut it. The room was a long way different to Summer's; a mess of color and posters. He saw makeup on the dresser, body glitter, and clothes strewn.

"What?" Raine said, glaring at her momma.

Ava held up the perfume bottle.

Raine took a moment then shrugged.

"You tellin' me your sister took this?" Ava said.

Raine glanced at Black, then at her momma.

"Well?"

Black left them to it, heard the yelling as he stepped back into Summer's bedroom.

"Anything?" Black said.

"What's that?" Milk said, glancing over in the corner, at the black case.

"Cello," Black said.

Milk nodded.

". . . kinda like a big guitar."

"I know what a fuckin' cello is."

Ava appeared at the door, cheeks hot like she was mad. "It's Raine's, the perfume."

"She said that?" Black said.

"Didn't have to. I know my daughters, Black."

*

Purv was wearing his church clothes, slacks that were rolled at the feet and belted tight at the waist, and a shirt so large he could get his head through the buttoned collar.

"Mayland tonight," Purv said.

"You comin'?" Noah said.

" 'Course."

They turned at the corner of Greenwood and fell into step with the nine thirty crowd. The air was sweet with tobacco and perfume. Some of the men had been laying out at the Whiskey Barrel so Noah could see more than a few red eyes. He overheard some muttering about the storm cloud that shadowed the town, some were grateful the heat had broke a little, others were scared of what was coming and glanced at the sky like it was about ready to fall.

Noah saw young boys with slicked hair and hand-me-down shirts, and girls wearing flowered dresses and pretty pins like it was 1950. Noah liked Grace on a Sunday. He'd been dragged along his whole life on account of his needing the Lord more than most.

They crossed the cut grass, dodging gravestones as they got the drop on the line forming.

"I see Ricky Brannon sitting front row again," Purv said.

Noah craned his neck and looked. Ricky's momma had brought him every week for a month 'cause he got busted playing *Dungeons and Dragons* with his cousin. Rumor was she asked Pastor Bobby to come bless the house in case any of the harpies got out.

They stood when Pastor Lumen drove in, even though he weren't the pastor no more. The first stroke had been minor, just enough to thicken his tongue and drop a shoulder. The second near killed him. The docs said he wouldn't pull through, but a year on and he was riding the streets on his scooter. The scooter was all white 'cept for one side, which was wrapped with *The Creation of Adam*. Painted intricate and beautiful, it was a gift from the people of Grace to their own savior.

Noah heard church funds were lifted to pay for it.

Even in the scooter and slumped a little, Pastor Lumen still cut the church silent with his watery gray stare. He'd kept a tight grip on St. Luke's and its people, passing merciless judgment like it was his to serve, partiality limited only to those that bowed low enough for him.

The scooter whined as it passed them.

"Engine's fucked," Purv whispered.

Noah nodded.

Bobby stood and he cleared his throat and stared out at them awhile. He spoke of Summer Ryan, how her family were worried about her. He asked people to bow their heads or kneel, pray for Summer to come back safe and to give her parents and sister the courage to stay strong. Then he spoke of the Briar girls, like he did every week.

When the service was done, Bobby told them to stay well and take care, and to be mindful of the storm 'cause he reckoned it was gonna be a bad one.

*

Raine was standing at the end of Jackson Ranch Road, which was about as near to the church as she'd been in a while. Her momma had tired of getting on her about it.

She moved under a tall oak as folk spilled out, the men walking with Sunday football purpose while the women fell back into talk. There were lanterns on the wood fence, usually lit during winter months, but they flickered flamelight against the cloud cover.

She saw a group of girls she might've known once, arms linked as they talked Madonna and Courtney and diet pills. They glanced over, whispered, and laughed.

"Fuck are you lookin' at?" Raine said, drawing death stares from a couple old ladies that passed.

The girls fell silent and turned away 'cause even three on one they wouldn't like the odds.

She'd called a couple guys she knew, the kind that'd take her out in their muscle cars to watch their dumb friends muddin' in the hill by Lossmon Lake, then go on to park and try and slip a hand up her skirt. They said they'd keep an eye out but wouldn't take her driving the streets 'cause they knew the town would be hot with Joe and Tommy turning over stones, and they sure as shit didn't wanna be found hiding under one.

Raine saw Noah and smiled. She smiled at boys all the time 'cause she liked watching their insides turn to mush.

She pulled her top down a little and arched her back.

"Hi, Raine," Noah said. "This is Purv." He motioned in Purv's direction.

"Seriously?" she said.

"Purv with a *u*," Purv said.

She chewed cinnamon gum. "Well that's somethin', I guess."

Purv looked down.

"Can you take the car out tonight?" she said.

Purv glanced at Noah. Raine caught it.

"What else you gotta do? You two got dates or somethin'?" she said.

Purv started: "Noah's got –"

"Nothin'," Noah cut in. "I can get the car, I ain't got nothin' to do."

"Pick me up at nine."

Noah nodded quick. "All right. There ain't much gas in it though."

"We're only headed to Hell's Gate, ain't far."

"Hell's Gate? Tonight, in the dark?" Purv said.

"Yeah," Raine said. "You ain't scared, are you?"

Noah shook his head. "We ain't scared of nothin'."

"All right then."

The Buick was grumbling, the idle dipping so low Noah worried it'd quit altogether. He kept the lights off, like she'd told him. She lived on All Saints Road, though he couldn't make out her place from where he was sitting 'cause the trees were thick and vines hung low.

He jumped when the car door opened.

"Didn't mean to scare you," Raine said, climbing in.

"I ain't the type to scare easy," he tried.

"That line'll work better once you've stopped shakin'."

He drove slow, sticking to the narrow tracks of red dirt 'cause they were safer than the asphalt roads.

She shifted in her seat, her shorts riding high on her thigh. He kept his eyes pinned hard ahead. She had a bag; it was canvas and old and he wondered what was inside. She wore a ring with a stone the same blue as her eyes, and chewed gum—he could just about smell the cinnamon over the leather.

He wanted to talk but didn't know what to say.

"Do you have a spare stick?"

She stared at him.

"Of gum. I wondered if you had some gum for me." He sighed. It was bad.

"This one's still got a little flavor." She spit the gum into her hand and leaned across. "Open your mouth."

He opened his mouth and she popped the gum in. Then she laughed. And he blushed.

He brought them the Lott Road way, passing the half-finished house the Laffoons owned. The bank said they were on the hook for twenty thousand, and maybe into Ray Bowdoin for even more 'cause he'd started work, though Rhett said they didn't ever give Ray the work, he just showed with his men.

He stopped a couple houses down from Purv's. Glenhurst was a road no one was proud to live on, so far from the pretty streets it felt like they'd crossed the town line. He could hear screen doors tapping and a baby screaming itself raw.

"I thought the Bowdoins had money?" Raine said. "I see the signs all over town."

"They used to. They had a big place up by the Dennison house, land with it too. Me and Purv used to camp out under the cypress there. You seen it? It's the biggest tree in the whole county. They sent scouts once but they reckoned it was hollow so they left it be."

"So how come they ain't still livin' there?"

"Purv's father lost his money, he built too many houses or somethin'."

They watched Purv creep down the side of his house. He cut across the neighbor's front yard, and then climbed into the back of the Buick.

Raine pulled a map from her bag and spread it across her knees. Purv leaned forward between the seats as Noah drove.

"I was lookin' back at the Briar girls," Raine said.

"Why?" Purv said.

" 'Cause ain't no one else doin' it. It's easier for Black if there ain't a link 'cause him and Sheriff Redell couldn't find none of 'em. But what if there is?"

Purv dropped his eyes.

"I remember the first girl was taken up near Standing Oak," Raine said, drawing a red circle on the map. "And the second girl was taken by Highway 225." She drew another circle, the pen jogging as the Buick rode a ditch. "Shit, keep the fuckin' wheel straight."

"Sorry," Noah said quiet.

"Everyone knows the only thing linking where those girls was taken is Hell's Gate National Forest. So that's where we're headin'," Raine said.

"At night. Three of us, in the woods lookin' for some kinda monster that looks like a giant bird," Purv said. He tried a laugh but it had a tremble to it.

Hell's Gate whistled and groaned, the trees making dark faces that Purv wondered if the others could see. Raine knew the tracks, reckoned her and Summer used to walk them with their uncle 'cause he had a cabin.

Purv was scared but tried to keep his mind on the task. He knew Summer a little. He'd been there when she played her cello at St. Luke's. Near enough the whole town had.

"You got that twin thing?" Purv said. "You know, supernatural, where you can feel your sister?"

" 'Course," Raine said, and he didn't know if she was messing or not.

"That's amazing," Noah said.

Purv could tell Noah had it bad. He didn't blame him. Raine was fiery and blond, and her tits were big and her ass was small and that was a killer combo in anyone's world.

Raine lit a cigarette then sat on a fallen oak.

"That's some cologne you've got on, Noah," she said.

Purv could tell Noah was blushing.

"That's why we keep hearing the white-tails. You got yourself a following."

"I like it," Purv said. "What's that scent? No, don't tell me . . . top note of mandarin . . . little tonka bean creeping beneath?"

"The nose on this kid," Noah said, shaking his head as they bumped fists.

Raine stared at them.

"What'll we do if we come across the Bird?" Noah said.

Raine blew a jet of smoke from pursed lips. "You really believe that bullshit? Ain't no fuckin' bird monster, just some sick guy taking what he wants. Always is."

"What about all the fires, and the white-tails they found all cut up and strung from the trees?" Purv said.

"Dumb kids. Probably Windale kids, or maybe from White Mountain."

"Purv's got a knife. Big knife for huntin'," Noah said.

"Bring it next time," Raine said to Purv.

"You reckon Black will start searchin' for him again?" Purv said.

It'd been on the local news. Volunteers manned, college kids and church people, out-of-towners. They'd swept the fields nearest the spots where the girls were taken, found nothing every time but ran the same process again and again. Noah and Purv had rode their bikes all the way to Calder Creek to watch, and they were excited about the action till they got there and saw the parents of the missing girl huddled tight together and clutching a soft toy. They rode back in silence 'cause the shit they saw on TV was real and it was hard.

"Black is a drunk, he ain't lookin' for my sister." She pulled her hair back, tied it, and spit on the leaves.

*

There weren't no lights on when Purv got home, which either meant his parents were sleeping or his father hadn't paid Southern Pine again. He jumped when he heard the neighbor's dog start up.

He stepped onto the rear porch and reached for the kitchen door, cursing when he saw it'd been locked. He didn't have a key, used to but lost it somewhere out by the Red.

He turned and headed in the direction of the copse by the Dennison place, by his old house with his old bedroom and maybe his old life inside. A life that'd been easy 'cause his father had money and worked hard and mostly let him and his momma be.

There was a new family living there now. They had a couple kids and sometimes Purv saw them climbing the big old cypress that used to be his.

When he reached the tree he curled himself up small and pulled his coat up over his head, and then he said a silent prayer that the storm would hold off till morning.

*

Noah pulled the Buick to a stop. Raine didn't move to get out.

"We can look again tomorrow," he said.

"She'll probably show by then."

"Won't your parents worry you ain't home?"

"They reckon I'm in bed."

"Oh."

"Purv," she said. "I heard shit about his daddy."

"What did you hear?"

She rubbed her hand over the leather seat. "That he's a cunt. Likes to beat on his wife."

"I told Purv he can come live with me but he won't."

She brought her legs up and rested her chin on her knee. The soles of her feet were dark with dirt. Her arms were gold and scratched and the hairs were so fine and so white.

" 'Cause of his momma?"

"He pretends like he don't give a shit about her. I mean, she takes her beatin', which is one thing, but watchin' Purv take 'em . . . sometimes she just runs, don't even call no one. But it's his mom, you know."

She stared out the windshield and saw little but night unbroken.

"It's funny," he said. "Grace. It's a funny kinda town. People go to church every Sunday, reekin' of booze and the sins of the weekend. They pray it away then do it again, same each and every. I saw Purv's father there today, hidin' in the back where the Angel sits. What business has he got there, man like that?"

"Maybe he's feelin' bad about what a cunt he is."

"Maybe. But what's the point? Surely someone that evil ain't got no place in heaven. I mean, if God lets him in then what does that say about God?"

She opened the door and climbed out.

He watched her go, easing the Buick forward till she was lost to the dark. Then he headed in the direction of the big old cypress tree, just in case Purv was camping out again.

*

Raine opened her sister's bedroom door and slipped in, careful to close it quiet behind her. She walked across the dark room to the lone bookshelf where Summer stacked her worn favorites. On the nightstand was a photo in a sparkly frame that Raine thought was pretty and maybe wanted for herself. She reached for it, carried it to the bed, and laid down.

She held it tight, there weren't the light to make out more than the outline, but when she closed her eyes she saw it clear: the two of them up by the Red, holding hands 'cause that was their thing they did since they were tiny. They held hands. Even now, if they were sad or mad or happy, they held hands.

7

Summer

Briar girl number one was Della Palmer. Della was sixteen and lived in Standing Oak, which is an hour from Grace. Della's momma is Peach, Peach Palmer, and she's the kinda lady that lets men fuck her if they can scrape together fifty bucks, 'cause she's got a drug problem to pay for and Della's daddy walked out before she was born.

We heard about Della on the local news. We were eatin' supper and watchin' *Melrose* when she flashed up missin' and Momma said Standing Oak girls are trouble so that was that. No one thought she was taken 'cause no one believed Della was decent. Even though she went regular to the West End Mission and she made good grades and didn't get in shit at school.

Della was walkin' home from church on a Sunday mornin' and she cut down Willowbrook Drive; the cops know this 'cause she walked part of the way with the Lewis family. That was the last time anyone saw Della. According to the *Briar County News* there weren't no tire tracks and nobody saw nothin'. There ain't many houses on Willowbrook and the folk that live there ain't the type that'll spill to cops. They chalked it that she'd run 'cause that was easiest. Maybe she had a boyfriend that drove a Chevy 'cause one of Peach's neighbors saw it stop by late a couple times. Peach couldn't say if it was a john 'cause she was too strung out to notice much of anything back then.

Later, once they finally got that Della was the first and not just another runaway, I saw Peach again. This time there were shots of her at the Briar County Sheriff's Office, sittin' by Sheriff Ernie Redell as he made a plea to the camera. When he said Della's name Peach got up and stood and looked around like she didn't know where she was. And then she dropped her head and cried into her hands.

"Do you have any friends, Summer?" Bobby said.

"You," I said.

"Friends your own age."

"No."

"How come?"

"I'm odd, they're even."

He smiled. "What are you reading?"

I glanced at my book. "*A Tree Grows in Brooklyn*."

"I liked Francie."

"Those immigrants," I said. "They reckoned education was all it took to rise up and find a place, like that was the key to the kingdom, like it was that simple. Why do people want to fit so bad? Don't matter where, they just need a place."

His sleeves were rolled back. He's got the kinda eyes where you ain't never sure what's goin' on behind them. He's sad sometimes. When he thinks no one is watchin' he looks real sad.

"Education is important."

He said it flat so I laughed.

"Raine's in trouble again," I said.

"How come?"

" 'Cause she don't fit. She's not smart enough to keep her head down . . . 'cause it ain't forever. The real world, it's comin' for us."

"And you?"

"I'm smart enough to know better. I do what I need to do but I can see it for what it is—a means to an end. I see them. They tell lies like that's the right thing to do."

"What kinda lies?"

"They say be all you can be. They tell tales about makin' a difference in a world where difference ain't exactly tolerated."

He stretched his legs out and looked at me. It was hot and his collar was loose. Sometimes it was too quiet in St. Luke's so I'd stamp my foot down and make an echo.

"What should they be tellin' you?"

"Keep low and let life run steady through your fingers while you plan for the ever after. That'd be one kinda truth. Raine . . . they know she's cuttin' but they don't even call the house. It's like they've given up or somethin'. She ain't ready."

"For what?" he said.

"Life. Momma reckons it's comin'. I know she's expectin' Raine to just take off one day, leave a note or somethin'. Maybe she'll get pregnant, take that route to nowhere."

"She's just struggling to find her way."

I set my book down and turned to face him. "What does that even mean? Her way to where exactly? To the other side?"

He shrugged. "That makes life nothin' more than a test."

"I guess that's why Momma worries so much, 'cause she believes."

"It's hard not to in a town like Grace," he said.

"If there ain't nothin' to this life then it's a wonder more kids ain't reachin' for guns and swallowing the barrel. Actually, that might've been a viable shortcut, but the church has got that base covered. Purgatory—the holdin' cell between life and eternal life. God's own drunk tank, where sinners sober up to the horrors of a life without sin."

He laughed.

"Don't anyone go to hell no more? I think about murderers and rapists repenting at the gates, tossing a Hail Mary toward the light, eyes wide when it lands. And it always lands."

"It seems that way."

"If that's all there is to this, an eighty-year dry run, then surely now is the time to make mistakes, to let loose and do whatever you want, to get it outta your system."

"That's somethin' to take comfort in at least."

"However much of a mess you've made, whatever you've done wrong or whatever wrong's been done to you, just take a breath and dust yourself off. You're just practicing. You'll nail it on the next try."

"Exactly," he said.

"Shit. When you think about it that way it's no wonder religion is big business. You'd have to be crazy not to believe."

8

Peach Palmer, the Prostitute

Across the town, the people of Grace readied themselves for the storm. They made such precautions a couple times a year 'cause folk still remembered the lives lost in the Super Outbreak in April '74. They checked the news for weather reports but the rest of Briar County was clear and the front had come up outta nowhere. Trix took calls and sent Rusty out to check on the widows and make sure they were ready with shutters and shelters and flashlights. Sometimes they asked him to check their roofs, so Rusty walked a fair way back and nodded and squinted 'cause there weren't no chance at all he'd climb a ladder.

Ginny Adams stocked the shelves in her convenience store and prepared for a run, same as always.

Black stood by the window and watched the main square. It was early but dark as night with the cloud above, quiet 'cept for a couple lights burning in Mae's Diner and Benny's Butcher Shop. Only five years back it'd been a hive, dawn till night, with folk riding the Transit to work at the Kinley Mill. That was till they shuttered it. No one blamed them. The Kinleys held it longer than they might've; gave work to shortwooders and mule-loggers and paid double to keep it local. Couldn't run that loss forever though.

With so many outta work they lost stores quick; half gone in a matter of months and homes foreclosed. There was anger, especially being as they couldn't switch on a television without seeing the moneymen grinning gleeful as they talked of booms, steady job creation, and golden times ahead in the rest of the country.

Milk walked into the station carrying a couple coffees.

"Fifty bucks," Black said, hand out.

"Already said I ain't paying till it's done," Milk said.

"All that DNA, ain't a jury alive that'd let him free."

"But it's O. J. The Juice. Two thousand yards, fourteen games." Milk whistled.

Black sighed.

"Anything on Summer Ryan yet?"

"Nothin'." Black said.

"Three days. Still reckon she ran?"

Black turned back to the window and the dark sky and didn't say nothing.

*

Savannah kept his photos in a shoebox in the closet. They brought his things when they moved 'cause it wasn't up for discussion. Bobby packed them, wrapped all his toys, books, and clothes, then unpacked them careful in what would've been his bedroom. Bobby liked it contained 'cause they had guests often and he didn't like them asking about Michael. She understood why but it didn't make it any easier.

When she was home alone she'd take the shoebox out and she'd smile at the photographs 'cause she found that once she started crying it was tough to stop.

She walked to the window and looked out at dark sky despite the early hour. Her mind ran to Summer. When she hadn't shown for her cello lesson on Saturday night, Savannah had called the Ryan house and Ava answered on the first ring.

She's missing. She's gone.

Savannah had left the house and run the length of Jackson Ranch, through the cemetery and into the old church where she'd found Bobby and had told him. Bobby had stood and turned pale and they'd driven straight over to the Ryan house. It'd been busy with pickups all over and big men looking out from the porch like they were expecting trouble.

She'd seen Joe and Tommy with maps and shotguns.

Ava had cut through the cluster and hugged both of them and said she was gonna kill Summer when she showed. But she'd said it with a smile like it'd keep the sharp edge from what was playing.

Bobby had driven the Grace streets till late while Savannah sat with Ava and watched the big men's wives come with plates, and worry and tears, then leave again.

When the house was quiet, Ava had asked Savannah if Bobby would pray for her daughter to come home safe, and Savannah said *of course* like that was nearly enough.

Bobby had been out searching every night since.

*

Purv hid out in the alleyway behind Mae's Diner. There was a low wall beside a Dumpster, and though the smell weren't pretty, it offered him a place to sit when he grew tired of standing. He lit a cigarette and rolled it between his fingers as it smoked.

He'd bolted that morning, before Noah's grandmother could get up and see him sleeping on their couch and give Noah shit for it.

He glanced up at the storm cloud and reckoned maybe it'd fallen lower overnight. He didn't notice Roy and Rex till it was too late.

They were cousins, seniors; both a little affected but by what Purv didn't know. There were rumors that Rex had once tried to fuck a stray cat.

"Purvis," Roy said. Roy was the brains of the operation on account of the fact he could belch the alphabet.

Purv eyed them nervous.

"I heard you got a job," Roy said. He was carrying a stick, leaning on it, and drinking a red Snapple. "Good timing, 'cause I'm comin' up a little short this month."

Rex tipped his head back and laughed, cutting an ugly shadow into the strip of light that fell from Mae's kitchen. His T-shirt was a size too small and slivers of his pale gut hung from beneath.

"I ain't been paid yet," Purv said, his voice holding steady.

"You can pay up, or you can catch a beatin' then pay up. It's your choice."

Roy laughed and made a show of clenching his fist.

Purv glanced down and saw an empty Sam Adams bottle but didn't have the nerve to reach for it. Any case, it'd be the kinda show they'd look straight past. And then he saw Noah at the top of the alleyway beneath the streetlight. He quickly grabbed ten bucks from his pocket and thrust it at Rex, but not in time 'cause Noah saw what was going down and quickened his step toward them.

"Roy and Rex," Noah said, flashing his badge.

"That ain't even yours," Roy said, laughing.

"I saw a stray just now, Rex. Maybe wrap up this time, there's a litter been born in Brookdale that look an awful lot like you," Noah said.

Purv clenched his fists and tried to swallow back the nerves 'cause he knew what was coming.

"We're brave," Noah said, loud and mighty like a call of the wild.

Purv couldn't get the words out 'cause Noah threw the first punch. Always did no matter who they were up against. It was a hard right that connected nice with Rex's forehead and dropped him, but that was all he managed 'cause Roy was still holding the stick.

When it was over, when Mae heard the noise and stopped it before it got bad, blood dripped steady from Noah's nose and he blotted it with paper towels.

Purv was breathing hard. They'd mostly left him be, just pushed him to the ground, but that was all it took 'cause his ribs were still black from the last time his father got mad.

They walked slow.

"Almost had 'em," Noah said.

"Yeah," Purv said. They hadn't ever won a fight so Noah reckoned they were due.

"I was thinkin' about Summer last night. And then I was thinkin' about those girls again. The Briar girls."

Noah nodded. "Yeah, but Summer ran. The Briar girls were just out, taken without warning. Black ain't linking it."

"Could be he don't want to. Maybe it's on him a little . . . that sighting. My father said Black could've taken the shot. That was the talk anyhow."

Noah shrugged 'cause no one really knew what went down.

"I ain't sure what we're doin' with Raine," Purv said.

"Helpin'. I'm a cop."

"That make me your partner?"

" 'Course. You can be Tubbs."

"I ain't black though."

"You're more black than I am," Noah said, tossing the paper towels in the trash.

"How'd you figure that?"

"Halbert."

"Oh. Yeah."

Halbert was Purv's uncle who lived over in Gattman and married a black lady.

"You think you got a shot with Raine?"

"Not in a million years. She did give me her gum though," Noah said, smiling.

"That don't sound like much."

Noah raised an eyebrow. "From her mouth."

Purv looked over. "She gave you the gum from her mouth?"

"She did."

"That's practically like makin' out with her."

They rounded the end of the alley and heard yelling. They saw Raine outside the station and Trix trying to calm her while Black looked on from the doorway.

Raine walked down the stone steps, her eyes hard. She crossed over to the bench and sat, glaring up at Black.

Purv followed Noah over.

Raine glanced at Noah. "What happened to your face?"

Noah brought a hand up to his cheek. "You should see the other guy."

"Ain't a scratch on him," Purv said.

Noah sighed.

Purv looked out across the dark square, streetlights burning despite the hour. There'd soon be a run at Ginny's.

"Black ain't doin' shit about Summer," she said.

"We can go out again later . . . if you want," Noah said.

They watched as an '85 Camaro roared up and Raine stood. "No offense, boys, but I got a better ride tonight."

Noah followed her a couple steps and felt the engine rumble right through him.

The window rolled down. "You been babysitting?" the jock said. He was older, Purv recognized him. Danny Tremane.

"She's fifteen, pervert," Noah fired back.

The jock made to get out but Raine said something to him.

She got in and stared out the window at Noah, half smiling as the Camaro tore through the square.

*

Noah and Purv caught the Transit bus all the way to Mayland. It was an hour late but Noah couldn't risk taking the Buick out during light hours.

He sat on the torn seat and watched the trees slip by in the gray dark of the storm cloud.

Purv sat opposite. He caught a break getting a job at the Whiskey Barrel during the summer. He was too young to tend but Hank Frailey let him mop up the beer and piss and puke for a couple bucks an hour.

Sounded rough but it beat being at home.

Purv needed looking out for, always had done. When they were ten years old Noah hadn't seen him for a whole day so he stopped by his place and found him beaten bloody. He'd fetched Trix and she'd driven them to Mayland in her orange Maverick, Purv laid out on the backseat and Noah holding his hand tight and telling him he was brave and fierce. Black had hauled Purv's father in but Purv and his momma wouldn't say nothing so they couldn't hold him. Milk and Rusty knocked a shade of shit outta him then dumped him in the center of the square. But that didn't fix nothing.

Noah pressed his face to the glass as the bus rumbled outta Grace. The sky cleared as they crossed the border into Windale.

Noah stood and walked to the back, looked up and saw a stark line that contoured the town. Dark then light like God had forgot to flip the switch in Grace. The storm cloud rose high toward the heavens; a sheer wall of gunmetal that looked about ready to unleash hell.

"Jesus," Purv said, from beside him. "I ain't never seen nothin' like that before."

"You're late," Missy said, as Noah sat in his chair. Missy was old and black and liked to tease Noah about how pale he was. She'd place her arm beside his and call him a ghost, but she only did that to keep him from staring at the blue machine. She knew he still had nightmares about it. He flinched a little as she threaded the needles into the large scarlike vein that rose from his bicep.

"The Transit was late," Noah said.

"You were in for yesterday, Noah. And no one answers your phone."

Noah shrugged. "I was working on real police business."

"That's right," Purv said.

"Shut up, Purv," Missy fired back, then turned to Noah. "Three days is too long, Noah. You dumb or somethin'? You could die –"

He tried to wave her off.

"You want me to call Social Services? If you can't remember, and your grandmother can't remember –"

"Sorry," he said, glancing up and meeting her eye.

Purv fell quiet beside.

Missy reached down and laid a hand on his cheek. "I'm just lookin' out for you. You remember what happened to Landon –"

"Noah's tough. And Landon was old," Purv said.

"And would've lived to be older," Missy said.

Noah nodded and Missy smiled at him.

"Television's still fucked," Purv said, nodding toward the screen.

"You got the video player," Missy said, as she made notes on the board.

"Yeah, but we're at the mercy of that bastard Goodwill lady and she keeps bringing us shit. I reckon she's fuckin' someone in Chemo. They got *Alien 3* last week."

Missy sighed.

"Ain't never at the start neither. She never heard of *be kind, please rewind*?"

Purv had been a fixture at the dialysis ward ever since he turned eight and Noah's momma said he could ride the Transit with them. He tried to give Noah his kidney at least once a year, the last time being a couple months back, when they'd seen Dr. Leggette walking his pinscher by the Red. Purv had been lit at the time, he'd taken his shirt off and demanded Leggette remove it there and then.

Noah had laughed too hard to try and stop him.

They kept the lights low. Paintings lined the walls, mostly local scenes; a cotton field, a blur of color that Noah guessed was Main Street.

Purv flipped his collar up then turned it down again. Purv didn't ever sit still.

Noah glanced at the blue machine. "*Think of it like a washer*," his momma had said to him back when he was small. "*It won't be forever, and I'll always be here if you get scared.*" She'd been wrong on both counts.

"All right?" Purv said.

Noah nodded. "Yeah, I'm all right."

Purv asked him that a lot. Noah didn't ever give another answer, even when it was all getting on him. Purv knew though. Sometimes he reached over and put a hand on Noah's shoulder, other times he told him a fact so random it distracted for a little while. Noah loved him for it.

"Everyone in the world has a unique tongue print," Purv said.

Noah smiled then turned to Missy. "We're ready for the movie now, thanks."

She walked over to the television carrying the tape.

"Dare I ask what we got today?" Purv said.

She checked the case. "*Babes in Toyland.*"

"Finally, she's sent somethin' blue," Purv said, rubbing his hands together. "What kinda toys? Double-ended –"

"It's Disney."

"Oh, for fuck's sake."

*

Peach Palmer lived out in Standing Oak. The drive took a dead hour, from Highway 125 through Tessner and into the pines. It was the kinda haunting drive that kept Black swigging from his flask the whole way. He kept a hand on the wheel and used the other to rub the tired from his eyes. He passed blurred houses, metal and ugly, low-wide churches, and Briar girl ghosts. He slowed the car and cruised mile after mile till he sobered, then he took another drink and hit the gas. His jaw was tight and he caught a glimpse of his eyes in the mirror so he reached up and angled it away.

He killed the engine at the top of her street and let the cruiser roll the gentle slope to her place. He sat outside, waited for the last of the orange sky to die, and saw Peach watching him from the window, pulling the drape back just so and staring.

She met him at the screen door, a hand on her hip, then stepped aside as he passed.

Her place: three beds, a bath and small den, the kitchen opening up right into it. She kept it well enough but money was tight and the men that called regular couldn't be trusted around nothing of value.

"You look tired," she said.

"Always."

"I can fix you somethin' to eat."

"I ain't here to eat." It came out bad and he caught it. "Sorry."

"How do you want me?" she said with a glare that made him smile.

"I ain't here for that, either."

He moved a stack of newspapers, sat on the old couch and sunk low.

She passed him a can of Lone Star and he took it and drank half down.

"You seen him again? That tall guy that gave you a hard time?" he said.

"No."

"You call me if he shows."

She nodded.

"Serious," he said.

"I called the cops last time, they didn't show for an hour. Those cops . . . they know what I do."

"So you call me, or call Trix and she'll put you straight through to me."

She lit a cigarette. He looked at her hands, at the lines that gave her age a decade older than her face; acrylic nails, one broke at the bed. She was still pretty.

"We don't talk about what I do," she said. "You get all funny and make me feel bad about myself. You want me to cry, Black?"

"I hate it when you cry."

She nodded, her eyes sad.

"A girl's gone missin'."

She drew a long breath.

"She ran. Left a note."

She breathed out slow.

"Time is passing . . . the family ain't strangers to me."

"But you're worried."

He nodded.

"He's still out there."

"He is."

He held up a hand and it shook and he took another drink.

"It's hot here," he said.

She picked up a magazine and fanned him with it.

"And it's so dark in Grace. So fuckin' dark."

"I heard," she said. "Big storm headed your way."

"This family. They got another daughter, troublemaker, she stops by the station, looks at me like I got answers to questions she ain't even thought of yet. I locked up her daddy . . . in another life. She burns with it, you know?"

"It's your job to bring her sister back."

She moved over and sat next to him, close.

"It's comin' back."

"What is?" she said gently.

"Him. Della. The trouble; devils and all that was. I can feel it, creeping slow enough that most people ain't even seen it yet."

They had a small service for Della, 'cause Peach couldn't cope no more. Just her and him in the backyard beneath an apple tree that Peach said didn't ever bear fruit. A service to keep her alive, Peach said.

"The Bird."

He nodded.

"Maybe it weren't him that time."

"It was."

"You didn't have a clear shot," she said, repeating what he'd told her.

"There's no one lookin' for Della no more," she said.

"There is."

"You?"

He didn't say nothing.

Peach handed him another beer, then unbuttoned his fly. He moved to stop her but she pushed his hand away.

He opened the can as she went down. Closed his eyes and blinked back tears.

"Peach, I didn't –"

She hushed him, then did what she did to make him forget awhile.

When she was done she wiped her mouth, grabbed his beer and took a long sip, then rested her head on his chest, her cheek on his badge.

"You ever feel like you're not here?" he said.

"I spend most of my life wishing I was someplace else, if that's what you mean."

There was a photo on the sill, parting the drapes. Peach when she was seventeen, wearing the kinda firebrand smile that told him she'd slipped late, that there'd once been another path.

"I mean sometimes I really feel like I ain't in the room. Maybe I float outside, but I can't see myself, my body. I ain't part of the world. The world that other people live in . . . I shoot the shit with Milk and Rusty, I keep at the bad men." He rubbed his eyes.

She brought her face up, rubbed her cheek against his, her lips on his ear. "When I ask why, what do you say?"

"That y's got a curl in its tail."

She smiled. "Guilt."

"For the things I've done and the things I should've done. Is that easy enough?"

She kissed him hard.

"Will you take me somewhere one day?"

"Where?" he said.

He was fading now. It was late.

"Away from this house. I hate it here."

He took her hand, squeezed it tight then rested back.

She walked outta the room and came back with an envelope and handed it to him.

"What is it?"

"I found photos of Della."

He had more than he'd ever need.

"She has her hair different . . . it ain't . . . there's some photos and she looks different. Maybe you need them. Maybe you could show them round."

This was how it was. She rode him to keep him looking for her daughter. He rode her 'cause sometimes he forgot there was feeling beyond nothing.

"You can crash here."

He shook his head like he could drive.

"You can sleep with me. Just sleep, in the bed, Black."

He nodded, let her help him to his feet and felt her arm tight around him as she guided him to her bedroom. It was different, not where she took the men. There was something soft about it. He saw an ashtray, a pipe she'd used to chase night into day. She said she was getting clean. She had a long record.

She undressed him slow. She ran a hand over the long scar on his stomach then pushed him back onto the bed.

He feigned sleep till she was breathing heavy beside him. He reached into the drawer and took out what he needed and did what he did, and when he was ready he parted his toes and stuck the needle between, and he swam to the place where hands held him high above.

He listened to the lopsided sounds outside her house. He saw a Bible on the floor, the wind blowing in and fluttering the pages. He wondered if he was dreaming and what kinda dream it was, but knew in his heart it wouldn't end good.

He stared at Peach, at the curve of her spine and the flare of her hips, and he thought about the cruelty and randomness of life.

"I love you," she said, and he wondered how she could.

He closed his eyes like he hadn't heard it.

9

Summer

Briar girl number two was Bonnie Hinds. She lived in a trailer park off Highway 225, which runs straight as an arrow and crosses three rivers till it meets Heathville and the strip malls. Bonnie and her daddy were members of Christ the Saviour Lutheran Church, which ain't nearly as grand as it sounds. Bonnie's daddy went where the work was, though the newspapers didn't say exactly what kinda work, maybe 'cause it weren't nothin' legal. He'd be gone weeks at a time so Bonnie mostly took care of herself. She didn't show for church one Sunday mornin' so the pastor, Bryson Dailey, stopped by their trailer. He liked to check on Bonnie 'cause he knew her situation and had conducted her momma's funeral a year earlier. He knocked at the door, came back in the evenin' and knocked it again, then called the cops 'cause he was worried. She didn't lead much of a life outside of school and the church but the cops still chalked her up as a runaway. It took them a day to locate her daddy. He told them he was comin' straight back but didn't arrive in Haskell till three days after that. He said he didn't know if Bonnie had a boyfriend or who her friends were or nothin' at all they could use. They didn't link her to Della Palmer.

"You ever feel sad?" I said.

"Everyone feels sad, Summer," Bobby said.

"For no reason? Just so sad you could shut the world out and cry and cry till all that's left of you is a pile of clothes on the floor."

"Sad enough to cry yourself outta this life."

I watched them, Bobby and Savannah. I was at their place four nights a week while Savannah taught me. I'd say I had to go to the bathroom but I'd just walk through their house and look at their things. There was a kid's bedroom. It had a race-car bed and toys and a small closet in it.

"Savannah said you're the most talented student she's ever worked with. And that she gets the feelin' you're not even tryin'."

"She tell you about the school? The fancy one in Maidenville?"

"Yes," Bobby said.

"We couldn't never afford a school like that."

"You'll get a scholarship. Savannah wants you to sit for the entrance exam and write the paper."

"I ain't leavin' my sister."

"Just write it, see what happens. It's good to have options, Summer."

There was silence awhile.

"I thought I'd write about the Briar girls," I said. "I been lookin' into them."

I'd put on my best dress and ride the Transit to Maidenville, then walk the bright streets and pass the shiny stores with the shiny ladies inside. Sometimes they'd smile and I'd feel so new I reckoned maybe I could see the kingdom for what it could be. I'd sit in the grand library among the towering masters and I'd trawl the archives.

"I think Savannah was hopin' you'd write about literature, or maybe art seeing as you have an interest."

I looked down. "How about Thackeray then? Maybe I could be Becky; fix hard enough on the endgame so the rest don't even matter no more."

He smiled. "Keepin' an open mind isn't sellin' out, Summer."

"So then I'll write about the Briar girls, 'cause that's what's real to me and to my sister. That fear and that kinda wonder."

We sat on a bench in the cemetery, the sun was high and strong but a willow shaded us. I had a book beside me. Bobby wore the kinda light cologne you could only smell if you were real close to him. I'd borrowed some of Raine's sickly shit that stung my neck and I was wearin' a dress and didn't tug it down when it rode.

I thought I saw Bobby glance at my thigh.

"Your level of faith is somethin' special, Bobby. I was thinkin' about it last night. I couldn't sleep; it's gettin' too hot. I keep my window open even though the crickets are so loud they make their way into my dreams."

I was talkin' up a blue streak, which happened a lot when I was around Bobby. It's funny, I didn't really know what I was doin' at first, always stoppin' by the church hopin' he'd give me the light. I sat there readin' and fixin' my hair and stealin' looks when his head was turned.

"Faith is confidence in what we hope for," he said quiet.

"And assurance about what we do not see."

He stared at me like he hadn't never seen me, and I wondered about Francesca and Paolo and that eternal whirlwind. I closed my eyes to the sun but felt the second circle so hot and so close.

10

Light Walls and White Ghosts

The lawyer's office was fancy and spoke of the five hundred an hour her daddy was paying. Savannah's mother sat beside her, clutching her hand like she might flee at any moment.

The lawyer's name was Donald something and she stared right past his bloated face at Fairline Park behind. Savannah was born and raised in Maidenville, rich by anyone's standards but her own. She never cared a dime about money and all that it brought.

"*They don't even speak anymore*," she heard her mother say as Donald nodded, his eyes suitably compassioned.

Her mother had some kinda surgery to pin up her face but it left her looking shiny and startled instead of young and fresh.

"*After Michael passed . . .*" her mother reached into her big bag and pulled out a tissue.

Savannah tuned them out awhile. She thought back to the first time she'd brought Bobby to her family home, with the sweeping driveway, the sprawling estate, the lake and the boat-house. He'd stood back, hands in pockets and shy eyes. He'd worn a borrowed jacket a size too big. She'd watched him as her daddy gave him the tour, boasted about wine in the cellar and the costs of resurfacing the tennis court like he didn't know nothing of his audience.

They weren't impressed. After Bobby left they'd told her just that. There was a line of boys, from college and her daddy's office, all of them better 'cause they had blood the right shade of blue.

"Bobby's an orphan, see. And he came to her with no assets to speak of, not a single thing. Can you believe that?"

She saw Donald nod then shake his head like he didn't know what response her mother was seeking out.

When Bobby trained it was a little easier. Her parents were active at St. Margaret's so that gave them something, at least. Then Michael came and they let it slide, how quiet Bobby was, how much work it took just to get him to let them help their only daughter out. Bobby didn't care nothing for money neither, but pride had its own price.

They'd met in Yellow Valley Park, by the water. She'd been on a date with some jackass who made the right noises when her mother put the gold feelers out. His name was Bryant and he went to Harvard Law and had bad manners. He'd drunk too much, tried to kiss her then grabbed her arm when she turned her head. She'd cried out. Bobby had appeared from nowhere and dropped Bryant with a vicious punch then walked off before she had the chance to call after him.

She'd seen him the next day, tending bar in a dive on Pool Street. She made all the moves 'cause she'd never been with a boy like him before. She was soft and she was beautiful. He was handsome but there was a troubled edge clear as day. They'd eaten burgers and she'd made jokes about knights and saviors.

She'd taken him to her bed that same night and was deep in love by morning.

"*There's a trust—he won't contest, right, Savannah?*"

She drew her eyes from the window.

"Bobby," her mother said. "What will he want?"

"Nothing," Savannah said.

Her mother went back to talking while Donald passed her the papers.

"I just need you both to sign."

Savannah held the divorce papers in her hand and she thought of their son and their life, and how sometimes endings came long before the story was told.

"It's for the best, sweetheart," her mother said. "You can come back here now, where you belong."

*

They took the Buick out early 'cause day was night in Grace. Noah worked an early shift at the station, Trix trying to find something for him to do. But he was just happy to sit there and watch the cops awhile; watch the hustle as the phone rang and they headed out to catch the bad guys. There was a photo of his father in Black's office.

He'd got home tired, 'cause sometimes he just felt real tired. The dialysis, even on the off days, it was a lot for his body to take. Draining blood, filling blood. He didn't ever let it show.

Raine had shown at his door, a cigarette behind her ear and the canvas bag slung over her shoulder. The bag was big and she was small. She'd told him to get the keys to the Buick and he'd nodded 'cause he was fairly certain there weren't a thing in the world he wouldn't do for her.

They drove down the pretty streets and they stared at the tall houses. They passed kids their age on roller skates, laughing and smiling despite the darkness. They ran low on gas so they scraped together what they could and drove the back roads to the gas station on Cane Creek Road. It cost more but they couldn't risk getting pulled 'cause the Buick was all they had.

There were only four pumps, but the Lincoln Gas Station was popular 'cause they sold porn magazines. The owner was Lucky Delfray, and Lucky weren't the type of guy to turn away paying customers, so he sold whatever they demanded and turned blind to age. Noah filled the Buick with twelve dollars' worth of gas.

They knocked on doors along Cassidy Avenue and looked on as mothers shook their heads slow: *sorry, I ain't seen her.* Behind them their kids watched *Double Dare* and ate ice cream like all was right.

*

They sat in the office and spoke of Summer. Black glanced past Pastor Bobby at the print behind, *The Wedding at Cana*, the curved clouds and the monuments and the wine that was water.

Bobby looked bad: eyes heavy and three days' worth of stubble.

"She was worried about the Briar girls," Bobby said. He'd told Black about the paper she was writing for the fancy school in Maidenville.

"Why do you reckon that was?"

"She's sensitive, maybe. I'm not entirely sure, Black. I worried about it, how she fixated on them. She asked me questions, about where I thought they might've got to."

"What did you tell her?"

Bobby leaned his head down and ran a strong hand through his cropped hair. "That I thought they were in heaven."

Maybe the moment stretched a little 'cause Bobby was quick to follow it. "I told her that 'cause I didn't know what else to say." Black felt Bobby watching him close. "You any closer to findin' this guy?"

"She spends a lot of time here, in St. Luke's," Black said, ignoring it.

"She's a fixture, alongside Samson and the dust. Savannah has been over to see Ava a couple of times."

"Good. She needs her friends close."

"I hear people talk about the Ryan girls and about Ava and Joe. I mean, when we first got to town I was expectin' somethin' else when I met them."

"What were you expectin'?"

"I had Joe fitted as someone to avoid. And there's a lot said about Raine, that she's trouble."

"And Summer?"

Bobby rubbed the muscles in his neck like they were tight. "They were right about her. That she's sweet. But we went there, for dinner with the Ryans, and I saw them, I watched them and the way they were with each other, and maybe Raine is havin' a tough time but Joe and Ava, they're good parents."

Black glanced at the painting again and saw the line of birds and wondered how he'd missed them the first time. He rubbed his eyes 'cause nothing was clear.

"Jesus, in that painting, he's got that glow. He's lookin' at the guy with the viola," Black said.

"That's the artist, Veronese."

"He put himself in the painting?"

"According to Summer it was tradition," Bobby said. "She used to stand there and stare at it. I'd find her in here and then she'd ask me about morality, and vanity and status. She'd ask about the lamb and the hourglass. She didn't miss a thing." Bobby cleared his throat. "I'm worried about her."

"She ran," Black said, eyes still on the painting. "We're doin' background but she'll show up."

*

Late afternoon they sat in the dark under a canopy of wide leaves, and they shared sandwiches Raine had bought from Mae's with money she'd taken from her momma's bag. They passed round a beer Purv had stolen from the convenience store while Noah flashed his police badge and distracted Ginny Adams, who worked the counter. Noah let the bottle touch his lips then passed it to Raine.

"Have your share," she said.

He shook his head. "Pure of body, pure of mind."

"So fuckin' weird," she said.

Purv's face was streaked with green, brown, and black war paint. He'd stolen the makeup from the drugstore on Beachwood

Avenue, then pissed Raine off something awful when he spent fifteen minutes applying it to himself and Noah.

They had a couple heavy flashlights and they set them side by side in the dirt, pointed at the treetops. Purv reached forward and passed the bottle to Raine. His shirt rode and Noah caught sight of a welt, thick and angry looking, maybe a belt buckle or something.

"What do we do when the Buick quits?" Noah said. The car had started smoking bad when they pulled off Hallow Road.

"We'll take it to Merle. He won't say nothin'. Last I heard he's in the hole a grand to my uncle Tommy," Raine said.

Purv nodded. "He owes to near everyone in town. No way he'll turn down cash."

"We don't have cash."

"Merle's always checkin' me out, old pervert. I'll figure somethin' out, might have to flash my tits or somethin'," Raine said.

Noah swallowed.

Raine lay back along the fallen oak and stared up at the dark cloud. "How much longer can it sit there? It's like night now, all day long ain't nothin' but night."

Noah reached for the map and aimed the flashlight at it. "We need a system. We can't cover the same ground, we gotta mark it off or somethin'."

"My uncle Tommy's got detailed maps of Hell's Gate, every inch from the Red all the way through to the Brookdale side."

"I bet it don't cover the north, that's Deamer land," Purv said.

Since all that went on with Mandy, Franny, and Richie Reams, the Deamers had become part of Grace folklore, a band of as few as three or as many as fifty depending on who you spoke to. They owned about a hundred acres of land that ran deep into Hell's Gate.

"I'll keep movin', go deeper than the cops did," Raine said, and they stood and they packed their shit and moved again.

They hiked on for another hour, Raine navigating and Noah falling back. He licked his lips; they felt dry. He had to carefully ration what he drank throughout the day, his kidneys unable to process the amount his body craved. It was worse when the heat got up. He chewed gum and sucked ice cubes, but they were small in the way of distraction.

"Why the fuck are you so slow?" Raine said, glancing back.

Purv went to speak but Noah shot him a look and quickened his step.

At points the tracks grew too dark and thick so they doubled back and looked for another way through. The forest floor dipped and rose and before long their shirts clung to their backs.

Noah almost walked straight into Raine, not realizing she'd stopped dead in front.

"What's up?" he said.

She pointed.

They stood in a straight line, stunned into silence.

Noah was the first to stick his arm through and watch the sunlight crawl up it. He made a fist, like he could grab hold of the rays and drag them into Grace.

"This is the Grace border," Raine said, looking at the map. "Another step and we're in Windale."

The wall of bright light rose from the leaves straight up to beyond and Purv took a step back 'cause it looked like the screen in the Picture House; like they were standing in the dark staring out at a world painted so rich there weren't a way it could be real.

Noah stepped forward, sliced in half, then turned back to reach out and pull Raine into the light. She squinted.

"Come on, Purv."

Purv crossed the border slowly, feeling the heat on his arm so sudden and hot he drew it back.

"I ain't never seen nothin' like it," he said.

They stood together and stared from the light of Windale into the dark of Grace.

Purv took out a small penknife and carved his initials into the wide bark of a cedar, then Noah's and Raine's.

"And Summer's," Raine said, so Purv did that too.

Noah was lying on the leaves, his head in the sun, his legs cut by the shade.

They jumped to their feet when they heard voices. Raine ushered them deep into Grace cover where they kept low and watched.

There were three boys, older.

Raine stood first and walked out, so Noah and Purv followed.

The boys stopped when they saw them, locking eyes with Raine.

"Danny," Raine said.

Danny walked over, his friends falling in behind him. They were tall and broad, tan and polished like they were cut from some kinda jock mold.

"We came to see it," Danny said, staring at the wall.

"You hiked it from 45?" Raine said.

"Nah, parked by Route 43 and followed the creek. We ain't dumb enough to hike with the Bird and all that." He glanced at Noah. "Nice makeup. You kids playin' dress-up?"

Noah glared at him.

"Did you ask round about my sister?" Raine said.

"Maybe," Danny said. He held a bottle of beer and his eyes were a little glassed.

Raine took a step forward. "You hear anything?"

"What's it worth to you?"

Danny was smirking now, his friends laughing. One of them glanced over at Purv, said something quiet, and they all laughed again.

"You hear anything or not?" Raine said sharpening.

"Come back with us, leave the kids to play," Danny said. "I got booze. Maybe you'll be more fun than you were the other night."

"Danny, serious, you heard anything about Summer?"

"Come on, we'll work somethin' out. A trade."

"Just tell her what she needs to know then fuck off," Noah said, feeling Purv flinch beside him.

Danny stared at Noah.

Noah stared hard at Danny.

"That's the second time you run your mouth, ain't gonna be a third," Danny said, taking a step nearer, sticks cracking under his feet, the echo falling wide.

Danny looked over at Purv. "Ain't you that kid that gets beat by his dad?"

"Shut the fuck up, cunt face," Noah said.

Danny took another step. "What did you say, little boy?"

"I called you a cunt face. 'Cause your face looks like a cunt," Noah said.

Purv swallowed.

Raine was watching Noah, an eyebrow raised.

Danny flushed, clenched his teeth, and handed his beer to one of his friends.

Purv took a step back, Noah, a step forward.

Danny's friend put a hand on his shoulder, said something about Noah being a kid and Danny smirked. "How would you even know what a cunt looks like anyhow?" He winked at Raine.

"Your momma showed me," Noah said.

"Shit," Purv said under his breath.

Raine bit her lip and wanted to laugh but didn't wanna make it worse.

That tipped Danny. He charged, swung at Noah, and caught him high on the cheek. Noah fell to the leaves.

Danny stood over him, breathless and grinning.

"What you gotta say now, boy?"

Noah looked up as the sun caught his father's badge. "You punch like a cunt."

Danny moved again but Raine walked over. "Come on, Danny."

Danny shrugged her off. "I ain't done with him."

"Yeah, well, I was just gettin' warmed up," Noah said.

Raine grabbed Danny's face and made him see her. "Let's go. I'll come back with you." Then she leaned in and kissed him hard, pushed her tongue into his mouth and reached down there and grabbed him till he went with it. When they broke she shoved him back till he turned.

The group moved off.

"Raine," Noah said.

She turned back. "Go home, Noah."

They disappeared into Grace darkness like they weren't ever there.

Purv held out a hand, pulled Noah to his feet, and dusted him down.

"I had him," Noah said.

"I know you did," Purv said. "I had your back."

"I know you did."

*

Savannah kneeled on the stone floor of the dark church. She didn't use a cushion because sometimes she felt it ought to hurt. As acts of penance went, it was a small offering, and it paled beside what she had done, but she stayed that way till her bones ached.

Bobby was driving the streets again, looking for Summer.

Savannah had a key to the old church and she used it when she needed to. She'd hid the divorce papers in her closet. Her mother called asking when they could expect her home again.

She closed her eyes tight because the sin was so vivid and so sublime, the formidable shape that lurked beneath the trees and reminded her that paradise lost could never be found again.

She was done when she cried, for all that had happened the tears fell heavy and dripped from her jaw. This was what he wanted, true remorse.

She turned when the door opened and wiped her eyes hard enough to blur the white ghost that appeared beneath the carved wood.

"I was lookin' for Pastor Bobby," Samson said.

"He's not here," she said, managing to smile.

"Oh," he said then turned.

"Are you okay, Samson?"

He stopped and then he stepped into the church and walked over to her, shoulders hunched and head bowed. Savannah had been a church girl her whole life yet she'd never seen anyone pray as often or as hard as Samson Lumen. Whatever it was, whatever he carried, it was something crippling.

"I wanted to pray," he spoke quiet. "I need to."

"You can pray."

"I can wait till mornin' and come back."

She could see little but the white of his hair, his face featureless in the shadow. She reached out and touched his arm and tried not to feel him flinch a little.

"It's okay. I was praying, that's why I'm here."

"Really?"

"Yes."

He sat on the front bench beneath the shadow of Jesus and at that moment Savannah thought maybe they were right to call him an angel.

He raised his hands in prayer and before she turned away she saw them shaking so bad he could barely keep them pressed.

11

Summer

I fall in and out of myself. Who I think I am ain't always who I am. I can go weeks where I slip from one person into another. It's like gettin' lost in the woods. I'll pass by somethin' I know maybe three or four times, but it don't lead me out, it don't show me the way.

I went to that fancy school with Savannah. The Maidenville Academy. It was ugly how much they had; the music room and the shined floors, the robot kids that slow-stepped with their hands neat behind their backs. Part of me ached for them. And for me.

I told Savannah I'd spoke to Momma about it, that she knew, but she didn't 'cause pipe dreams are just that. They ain't got no groundin' beyond.

I met an old man in a dark-wood office with all kinda certificates on the wall behind, like they meant somethin' more than vanity. He spoke and I smiled polite and Savannah put a hand on my shoulder. She told him I was special like that was somethin' good, and then she smiled the whole drive back. That smile though, it was so much like Bobby's . . . so much missin' from it.

I found an article in the *Maidenville Herald* from three years back. Bobby and Savannah's boy was named Michael, and he died in a car wreck when he was four years old 'cause a drunk ran a stop sign and his car seat hadn't been fitted right. There was a small shot of them, the three before, so happy I cried right there in the library, till the old lady came over and handed me a glass of water and asked if I was all right. *I don't know*, that's what I told her, 'cause I didn't.

I ain't that big, anywhere. I ain't tall, my tits ain't as big as Raine's. By the age of two you could tell us apart easy—her face seems to fit together in a way that mine don't. It's all right that she's prettier, I ain't jealous. She gets a lot of attention from the boys, always has, and not just 'cause she's willin'. I saw the teachers look at her sometimes, the older men who carried that stain of pathetic about them; divorced 'cause they reckoned there was greener pastures waitin' on them, skinny arms and potbellies and thinnin' hair. They'd gawk for a few seconds then catch themselves, file the sight, and call on it later, when they reasoned away the guilt 'cause she was so much a woman.

I guess I looked pretty funny playin' the cello, what with it bein' so big. I felt like I was some kinda experiment—give the Ryan girl an instrument and see what kinda sound she makes. It came so easy. The first time Savannah settled behind me, her hand over mine, her head over my shoulder. I took a deep breath and played a note. I liked the sound; it was soft but strong.

Before long I could play *Kalinka,* and Bach's second suite, and then his *Arioso from Cantata 156.* The music, the notes, I heard them full and rich and I let them run together. It's hard to explain, it just is. Sittin' behind it like it was armor, my mouth shut so no one could hear how I talk.

Savannah would look at me when I was playin' and I'd see her throat move as she swallowed. Sometimes she'd close her eyes and hold her breath so long. Other times she'd breathe real fast and shallow.

There was a photograph of Michael on her desk; sand hair and brown eyes and a straight mouth, like maybe you had to earn his smile with more than an ask and a lens. I could see both of them in him. Savannah glanced at it sometimes when she thought I weren't lookin', and I caught that sharp kinda pain that told of what was wrong with her and with Bobby and what was wrong with them together. The gloss so thick, I saw it drip and run.

I could've cried and died for them.

I was playin' and we had the door open. It was summer and the heat was heady and Savannah had switched the fan off 'cause it was noisy. She was sittin' in front of me, her eyes closed as I played a cello arrangement of *Étude Op. 25, No. 7 in E* 'cause I loved it. Chopin. I would've been one of them ladies that fainted in his room come the end.

I saw Bobby stop by the doorway. He met my eye and smiled at me and I smiled back.

It felt different havin' somebody else watch—havin' Bobby watch. He'd come from the yard so his shirt was dark with sweat. He'd cropped his hair short and Savannah was gettin' on him about it, sayin' he looked more like a soldier than a pastor, and he'd rolled his eyes and winked at me and I'd laughed.

I played for him, held the bow tighter and sat straighter while he watched. That piece, sometimes Savannah played along on the grand they had by the window, and that piece stole her away someplace far.

Bobby had that same look, and for a while he was lost till he found me and nodded. And then he dropped his eyes down.

My legs were open, the cello between them; it ain't the most ladylike way to sit. My skirt was high, bunched up at the waist.

Bobby followed my leg from my foot up higher.

I played and watched Savannah as she breathed in time with each note, her chest risin' and fallin' and risin'.

Bobby's gaze at the top of my thighs. I saw him but he didn't look away, he just stood there starin' like I was a sight. And then he took a step forward and leaned to the side, his shoulder against the doorframe like he couldn't hold himself up no more. That sad in them, in both of them.

He leaned and drew breath as the notes rose high above the three of us, and the room and the house and town.

I kept playin'. My throat ran dry and my heart raced and my cheeks were hot. That was a moment, right then, where I floated up and watched myself and watched Bobby watchin' me. A crossroads where both paths lead you someplace where light and dark ain't nothin' but shades of the same gray.

And though my hands were startin' to shake and I was strugglin' to grip the bow, I knew what I was doing so I did it. I pushed my leg out a little farther. I saw Bobby dip his head an inch, so I pushed out more, and I could tell by the way he was focused, and by the way he swallowed, that he could see up my skirt.

We held that way froze, just me and Bobby and his wife with her eyes closed. The pain of what it was I hadn't yet known; the evolving tragedy that was and would be our lives.

12

Clara Stokes and the Demon Hunters

A week had passed since the people of Grace had seen the sun above their town, or the moon or the stars, or anything but the heavy cloud that kept them buried in dark. It was the first sight that greeted them in the morning, when they rose early and pulled open drapes, and the last at night, when they dropped to aching knees and said goodnight prayers.

They kept a half-eye on the horizon, on the wall of blazing sunlight that ran the town line and baked the surroundings hard.

It dropped each day, that's what folk reckoned, so low that neighborhood kids threw baseballs at it and climbed on flat roofs and stood on toes to try and touch it. Sometimes it moved, swirled and twisted till a crowd drew and spread word it was time.

The widow Beauregard told a frowning group in Mae's Diner that she reckoned it was the Bird, that he was back and summoning something so dark she didn't sleep no more, just prayed and prayed 'cause prayer was the only weapon of the righteous. She'd been waved down when her back was turned but the Panic still gripped throats, so while the smoke was still just that, people began a slow search for the flame.

A couple small pieces had started showing up in the *Brookdale Chronicle* and the *Maidenville Herald*. Word did spread of the sights that could be seen on Hallow Road, that long straight stretch of road that led from Grace to beyond. Cars had been spotted, left lazy in the dirt halfway to the line, people littering the green fields, heads tilted and mouths hung as they moved between Grace and Windale, dark and light.

Raine rose with a sharp pain in her gut and first thought maybe it was the booze 'cause she'd snuck out with Danny Tremane again, but when she gulped water straight from the faucet the pain got worse. It was Summer; she had to get her sister back. The week had passed so quick and jagged, the fear climbing every morning she woke and saw her daddy beat at the kitchen table after another night of empty searching. And so she slipped from the house onto the dark streets of town and she walked them fast till her head pounded and her shirt clung damp to her back.

She called Danny from the pay phone on Jackson Ranch Road and he told her he was busy. She told him please and he cut the line, and she slammed the receiver down so hard it broke.

*

When Noah opened the door, Raine pushed past him and walked into the kitchen like she'd been there before. It was tired and the cabinet doors were falling off and he looked embarrassed.

"Are you okay?" Noah said.

She ran a hand up and tousled her hair. Her eyes were blackened 'cause she'd slept in her makeup. She saw his worry and it pissed her off 'cause he didn't know nothing about her.

She pulled herself onto the kitchen counter, then crossed her legs and rubbed a hand along her bare thigh like the muscle was tight.

"Can I fix you somethin'? A drink?"

She shook her head, then she stared at him till he wilted. "I can't sleep, Noah. I'm scared now."

"We'll keep lookin', later, after I finish at the station."

She rubbed her eyes like she might cry and he walked over. He put a hand on her shoulder and she slipped from the counter and laid her head on his chest, made a noise like she was sobbing but there weren't no tears at all.

"I have to find her," she said. "It's been too long."

She wondered how far he'd strayed from his depth. She could smell her own perfume, so sweet it made her gag, and beneath it the sweat and the fear and all that was turning real.

"Will you do somethin' for me?" she said.

" 'Course, anything you need," he said.

*

Black drove down Lott Road, passing by Glenhurst and shooting a look in the rearview. He kept the speed down and flashed the lights at a couple dead turns. With the sky so dark they'd already had a couple of accidents to deal with.

Trix had taken the call. It'd come from Clara Stokes and it was about the Ryan girl. Clara wouldn't give no details to Trix, wouldn't talk to no one but Black, which weren't all that surprising. Black knew Clara, knew she was the raw kinda lonely that meant it'd take an hour of iced tea and small talk before she got round to what it was. He'd left Noah behind, though he'd wanted to come. Black knew Noah was getting close with Raine so he'd told Trix to keep a lid on the call. That way he could stop the Ryans heading to Clara's place and getting worked up on the drive.

Clara lived in a small house by a pocket of swampland that bled down to the Red. He'd been to her place five years back, when they had a long week of biblical rain that flooded most of the area.

He'd slept three hours the night before, woke in the dead night and reached for a bottle of whiskey. A week. The Ryans were more than anxious. Joe and Tommy had rolled through the square that morning in a fiery mood, stopping only to pick up coffee at Mae's and shoot hard glances at everyone inside. Black had passed Summer's details to Sheriff Ernie Redell but they were all working the assumption she'd run. That long year, girl after girl, it'd driven them all to the brink and none were keen to revisit. Ernie had a theory the Bird was dead, the reason behind it little more than wishful. The doubt was there though, it kept Black in his chair instead of bed each night, running over a copy of the thick file with a whole lot of nothing in it.

He pulled the cruiser into a patch of mud right outside Clara's place. She was sitting out front on the porch. The house was low and old, every board needed replacing. There was a pile of soiled sheets and some engine parts strewn. Clara had a deadbeat son who was serving time over in Pickensville for some misdemeanor or another.

Black got out. There weren't neighbors; it was quiet 'cept for the sound of a low branch scraping the roof of the house.

Clara stood when Black reached her, filled a pitcher with iced tea for him, and then sat again.

"This cloud," she said, by way of a greeting.

He nodded, sat opposite and sipped his tea, pleased to find it was laced with rum. He glanced at her, at the baked lines in her face and the thinning white hair and the coal-black eyes.

"I kept sayin' the storm was comin' but so far ain't nothin'." she said.

She'd lit a kerosene lamp. It flickered on the wood between them.

"I got a call about the cloud from –"

"Bailey from the church?" she cut in.

He nodded.

"He said he was gonna call. I told him there ain't no point but he's a stubborn old sumbitch."

She rolled a cigarette, her fingers thin and shaking bad.

"How's Carson doin'?" Carson was her grandson, lived over in Sweet Water with his momma.

She shrugged. "Reckon they call me?"

"Trix said you might know somethin' about Summer Ryan."

She licked the paper, stuck it down, then took a good while to get it lit.

"She left a note," Clara said, squinting up at him, a grain of tobacco stuck to her lip.

"She did."

"So she ran?"

"Looks that way."

"But you're gettin' worried, right?"

He took a long drink and looked on silent as she topped it off.

"Joe and Ava?"

"As you'd reckon. So what've you got to tell me, Clara?"

"I saw her a couple times."

"When?"

"Maybe a month back. Maybe two or three. I got pills, I can't remember things too good when I'm taking 'em."

"Right."

"She weren't alone. That's why I called. I thought it was strange . . . I ain't the type to meddle but it played on my mind. And then I heard she was missin' and I thought I'd better call you."

"Who was it you saw with her?"

"It was raining, both times. That kinda falling rain that damn near washed me outta my home. So I was standing out front those days, just in case it crept up on me."

"Who did you see with Summer?" he said, gentle.

She dropped her cigarette to the floor and stamped it with her shoe. He saw blue veins on the top of her foot, pumped up high like they were trying to split.

"Didn't seem right being as he's much older than her . . . ain't kin or nothin'. And he was holding an umbrella so I almost couldn't make him out, but he's got that hair."

"Who?" Black said, this time pushing.

"Samson, from the church. Samson Lumen. The Angel."

Black drew a breath, his mind running to Pastor Lumen. "You sure?"

"Yeah, I'm sure."

*

Noah and Purv laid back in the soft grass by the cypress tree, staring straight up at the dark sky and sharing a cigarette.

"You reckon we should pick up some silver bullets?" Purv said.

"Why?"

"For the Bird. In case we find him."

"I think silver bullets are for werewolves."

"A stake, then."

"That's vampires."

"Well, what kills birds?"

"Rice."

"I'll pick some up from Ginny's."

"You realize he ain't an actual bird?"

"We're huntin' motherfuckin' demons," Purv said, holding the hunting knife out in front. "I'll slay the Bird. I'll cut his fuckin' wings off so he can't fly no more."

Noah laughed.

Purv traced the blade with his finger.

"I was thinkin' about that temple they found in Hell's Gate, by Hartville. All them bones. Some of 'em was human, that's the way I heard it. A skull, maybe it was from a kid or somethin'."

"Probably bullshit."

"Probably."

"Are you worried about what we're doin'?" Purv said.

"Yeah. You?"

"Yeah. I like stealin', you know that –"

"I do."

"But I take shit people ain't even gonna miss. Stealin' files from a police station . . ."

Noah had a copy of the file in the trunk of the Buick. Raine asked and he did it. She said if he could get Black's file—the file on the Briar girls—the file with the names of the bad men, then they'd have a place to start. She said they wouldn't do nothing but stop by the houses and watch awhile to see if there was any sign of Summer, 'cause she needed to do something, and time weren't on their side no more. He got that.

So when Black was out on a call and Trix was busy and Rusty was sleeping in his chair, Noah had gone into the file room and searched. And he'd seen shit he had no business seeing, photos that'd keep him awake this life and the next.

"What you reckon we'll do when we get to New Orleans?" Purv said.

Noah closed his eyes and smiled. It never took Purv long to swing talk to New Orleans. They'd made the plan when they were ten, on a day when Purv took a royal hiding and had turned up on Noah's doorstep in the early hours looking for a place to hole up while he tried to figure out if anything more than his life was broke. They'd settled on New Orleans for no other reason than they'd heard about the women at Mardi Gras, and that was a sight both were keen to witness.

"I reckon we'll find a cheap apartment to rent, nothin' fancy. Then we'll find work, maybe in a bar or somethin'."

"Good thing I got the job at the Whiskey Barrel. I can say I got experience," Purv said.

"That's right."

"I was checkin' for the hospitals. There's a couple units down there. We'll take a look, choose the one with the prettiest nurses."

Noah smiled.

Purv cleared his throat. "I was thinkin' as well, I know we don't never talk about it, but what Missy said . . . You can't skip no more sessions."

"I know. It's just with Raine needing us, and I got this badge on. I kinda forget awhile, you know?"

"Yeah. I know."

They got to their feet when they heard steps. Noah saw it was Raine 'cause her hair was so light against the dark. When she got near she nodded at him, he nodded back and the three made for the Buick.

They spread out the file on the backseat.

"Shit, there's a lot here," Raine said.

"That ain't even half of it. I flipped through the rest but it didn't have no names in it."

A couple of the guys were on parole, a couple had been arrested more than once but never held for long. Noah guessed Black would've run them down already.

When Raine was done she laid out the map and circled fifteen houses, stretching across six towns and three unincorporated communities.

"We'll start at the nearest and work our way out," Raine said.

They set off slow, heading toward the kinda darkness that made Grace seem light.

*

It was getting late when Savannah answered the door and for a minute her face fell. The fear, it was irrational, but she caught it quick and stepped aside.

Their house was lit, every room warm white, soft throws on the sofas and dark wood pieces her parents had gifted them over the years.

She led Black into the kitchen.

"Bobby around?"

"He's out searching with the other men. Every night now. Is it important?"

"It can wait, just wanted to run somethin' by him. I'll leave you, you're eating."

She saw him glance at the microwave carton and she felt shame creep into her cheeks.

"I was at Pinegrove, I volunteer there. I was late getting back and I didn't know what time Bobby was coming in, but he called and said he was stopping out –"

"I love mac 'n' cheese too," he said.

"Would you like some? There's another carton."

"Sure."

They ate in the den and she poured them wine and Black drank it slow, which she guessed was an ask. She knew about him; there was talk as soon as they moved to Grace.

They'd already spoke a little about Summer and Ava and Joe, about the worry and the fear that Black was fighting hard to play down.

"Bobby loves her," she said. "I mean, he loves having her around, talking to her and listening to her play."

"Ava reckons she dotes on the two of you."

Savannah laughed. "She follows Bobby around almost as much as Samson. But she's a sweetheart, Black. I remember when we first met her."

"She bring you cookies?"

"Oatmeal raisin."

"She drops a batch at the station every Christmas, has done since she was ten. I don't get near 'em 'cause Rusty's desk is nearest the door."

She laughed.

"She's missin' her lessons," he said.

"I'll make her catch up."

He smiled.

"I once gave her a composition, by Dvořák. It was difficult and she slipped up like I knew she would, and I realized I'd rushed her, and after I felt awful, because I forgot, Black. I forgot she was fifteen and she hadn't been playing all that long." She sipped her wine. "A month or so later she sat down and played it again; I didn't ask, she just played, and she played it near perfect. And she didn't say anything after, she just got up and bowed and smiled."

He finished his drink and she offered him another and he took it.

"It's so dark outside. When Bobby opens the door and leaves each morning, it's just so dark. He works late too."

"Must be hard on you," he said.

She shrugged like it was nothing, but truth was Bobby didn't spend his time home with her, not just since Summer ran but since they got to Grace. It was supposed to be a fresh start for them, they drove the fifty miles in his old Honda because he was proud and she loved that about him. For a while it worked, she dressed nice every day, pearls and an apron, hand on hip and a southern smile. She could project like no other.

"He looked tired when I saw him," Black said.

"He's been out every night, helping Joe Ryan."

"That's decent of him."

"He's a decent man." She said it flat.

"Are you all right, Savannah?"

She stared awhile, not at him. "We live Bobby's life." She cleared her throat. "He needed that, after –"

"I heard about your boy," Black said, eyes down on his empty glass. "Sorry."

"Thank you." She said it rote. "It's tough on Bobby . . . his son, you know."

"Same for you."

"Yes, same for me. Did you ever want children?"

"I got two; daughters."

She looked up. "Oh –"

"They live with their mother, long way north. She married again."

"What happened?" she said, then caught herself. "Sorry."

"Life. Sometimes there's turns you don't see comin', you know?"

"I do."

There was something in his face, more than tortured, more than broke.

"We make our way, heads bowed 'cause that's the way it is, and by the time we look up ain't nothin' the same. I don't sleep well."

"Bobby doesn't."

"We both took roles where good ain't even in question, or shouldn't be. We wear masks; what's under though, it ain't –" He looked up, met her eye like he forgot he weren't alone. "It's just hard."

"What is?"

He smiled. "Being human."

She thought of Bobby, of what she had done and how redemption was no longer an offer he could extend. The papers burned hot in the closet. It might ruin him and her but it might not. She couldn't go on.

Black finished his drink and he held it like water. He stood and said goodnight.

When he'd gone she prayed on the flagstones in the kitchen, makeup running lines from her eyes like tears so dark.

13

Summer

Briar girl number three was Lissa Pinson. Lissa was the girl
that turned things, the girl that got the state cops down and
Briar County cold with fear. Lissa lived in Whiteport, around
sixteen miles from where Della Palmer was taken. Lissa's
house was wide but metal, the yard tended but the grass brown
and dry. Lissa's daddy was a deacon at St. Thomas Episcopal
Church, which'd been on the news when the Panic began
'cause two of their members were arrested. Peter Falcon and
Derry Malcolm—both were seventeen when they broke into
their high school and sprayed the word "satin" in big red letters
on the gymnasium walls. *Satin*.

Lissa was reported missin' on a Thursday afternoon after she
failed to show at school. Her parents spent the mornin' searchin'
before they called in Ernie Redell, sheriff of Briar County. I saw
Ernie on the news that night; he's got the kinda silver hair that
works for him. That's when Black came into school and we sat and
listened as he told us about the Briar girls and how they was just

like us. We got letters sent home with us and were told to be inside before the sun dropped and to keep an eye out for each other.

Ernie couldn't narrow down where exactly Lissa was taken, but we saw a map of Whiteport with the route she walked marked out in red like a trail of blood. Lissa's daddy remembered seein' a white van idling outside the church a couple weeks prior, but when he'd crossed the street the van had driven off quick.

Lissa had a boyfriend who went to the Maidenville Academy, but he was church good and had it that all they did was catch a movie and grab a milkshake and hold hands. "*Yeah, 'cause that's why he went with a girl from Whiteport,*" Raine had said, rollin' her eyes.

Daddy bought books for me. I ain't exactly sure where he got them but he'd come back from the road with a heavy stack and leave them by the stairs. I'd carry them up in batches, real careful, 'cause books are somethin' precious. They thought it was funny, my parents. They watched me readin' like they couldn't figure me out, especially when Raine was sat beside me watchin' a movie.

Bobby and Savannah had a room in their place with book-shelves on every wall like it was a library.

Daddy didn't check they were right for me. I had a couple *Encyclopaedia Britannica*s and would go on beggin' for more whenever that commercial ran.

When I was ten years old I read about Emma Bovary and all that shit she got up to 'cause she was bored of her place in life.

I ain't sure if Flaubert found that precise word he was lookin' for but it's a book I've read maybe fifty times.

"What's this one?" Raine said. She was pullin' out books from under my bed, her butt in the air.

I looked down. "*Tess of the d'Urbervilles.*"

"She's got a set like Anna Nicole," Raine said, smilin'. "And she's smokin' a pipe. *She's No Angel.* Does Daddy know you got this one? It looks filthy."

I laughed.

"Can I read it?"

"Yeah," I said, knowin' she wouldn't.

"Five hundred pages. Did you fold 'em at the good bits?"

"No."

She slid it back, disappointed.

She climbed up on the bed and lay beside me, her head on my shoulder.

"You nervous about the math test?"

"I ain't even thought about it," I said.

"I wish we didn't have to go. We could be like them Deamers, homeschooled. Abby reckons there's thirty kids on their land, all kin. They even built 'em a classroom so they can learn together."

"You want Momma as your teacher?" I said.

"Fuck, no. I'd get in more shit than I do at school."

"I ain't sure that's possible."

She laughed. She's got the sweetest laugh, but then Pastor Lumen said the devil takes many forms.

"I made out with the Tenahaw boy, with the light hair. I don't remember his name," she said.

"Judson?"

"What kinda name is that?" she said, wrinkling her brow.

"Why'd you make out with him?"

"He asked."

"Oh."

"I saw you after school, carryin' Mrs. Kindell's groceries for her," Raine said.

"She's old."

"I heard Momma tellin' her about you the other day, about how good you was at playin' the cello. She's so proud, Sum."

"She's proud of you too."

Raine shrugged.

"You reckon I'm smart like you? I was thinkin' maybe I just ain't found nothin' I like to do yet."

"You and me are the same," I said.

She pressed her face close to mine.

"Don't leave me behind, Sum," she said.

"Never," I said.

She kissed my cheek, and smiled.

14

Men Don't Cry

They'd struck out at the first three places. Two were empty, no sign of anyone having been there for a long time, and the third was home to a young family who must've moved in recent 'cause there were boxes stacked by the garage and a U-Haul parked in the driveway. But this house, on Mullin, it gave Noah the creeps. They'd seen movement half an hour back: a shadow through the drapes. The mailbox had fallen, there was paint cans by the steps, and a wide hole in the roof had been patched with sheet metal.

"Zeb Joseph Fortner," Raine said again.

They'd already run through Zeb's file. He'd been in and outta jail since he turned nineteen and got charged with petit larceny after he stole cash from his momma, though that was kicked up to a felony grand when Zeb tried to pawn her wedding ring a week later.

At first glance Zeb weren't nothing more than a career thief, but he'd been accused of following a local girl named Cassidy Meyers to and from the high school in Colfax a couple times. Sheriff Redell had spoke to him a year back.

"Stakeout," Noah said, leaning back. "Cop life, ain't all glamour."

"Should've brought coffee and donuts," Purv said.

Noah reached under the seat and pulled out a pair of binoculars.

"Shit, how big are those," Raine said.

"They're my grandfather's. I found 'em in the attic."

"Good sight on 'em I bet," Purv said.

Noah held them to his face and his arms started shaking. "I should've brought the stand."

"I reckon we should go take a look," Raine said.

"No," Purv said.

"Yeah. Maybe we should," Noah said. "The guy's dumb but if he's got Summer in there I don't reckon he's dumb enough to let her up by the window for us to get a look."

"You sure we ain't better waitin' it out? I mean, he could have a gun or somethin'. Or a knife maybe. Or there could be other bad guys in there," Purv said.

"All the more reason to go get her out," Raine said.

They left the doors to the Buick open in case they needed to get in quick. The road weren't more than slivers of tar laid thin and driven on before it'd set. Purv nearly fell, so Noah reached out and held his skinny arm.

Noah looked up at the sky and realized how much he'd been missing the starlight. The bad dreams he had when he was small, about the blue machine, he'd wake stricken and cry out and his momma would come in, open his drapes wide, and lay beside him. She'd point and tell him the names of the constellations and he'd say he could see them too but couldn't ever.

"Let's go up the side, get a look through the window," Raine said.

They kept low and moved slow, each step measured and light. They pressed themselves close to clapboards that hung loose and splintered. They didn't speak of fear but knew, dumb or not, if Zeb saw them there weren't no telling what he'd do.

"Can you hear anything?"

Raine shook her head, and then just like that all hell broke out.

The Bronco swung up through the chain-link fence and into the front yard, engine roaring loud. They barely had a chance to duck into the back before the doors opened and four men piled out. Raine pulled Noah and Purv to the ground and they stopped still, their chins in the dirt, breathing hard.

The men were big and they ripped the screen from its hinges and began kicking the front door till it split.

Noah felt Purv trembling beside him. He reached out and put a hand on his friend's shoulder. Purv had his eyes closed like he was praying, breath held so long his chest burned.

The guy with the long beard hollered for Zeb to come outside.

Noah was the first to see the back door open and a scrawny guy step out, head low like he was about to break for the trees behind.

Noah stood without thought. "He's there," he yelled.

The guys stopped kicking the door and moved toward Noah, who pointed at Zeb as he broke into a run and stumbled. They caught him quick.

The big guy with the long beard grabbed hold of Noah's shoulder and pulled him forward into the moonlight. The guy had thick arms and the kinda stare that held Noah even while Zeb cried out and scrambled behind him.

"What you doin' hidin' out here, boy?"

The other three looked to him to see what was gonna happen next. He nodded toward Zeb and they rained punches that landed hard and clean, and it weren't long before Zeb was calling on God like he was the one clenching his fists.

"I'm lookin' for someone," Noah said.

"Out here in the middle of nowhere?"

"I figured maybe this guy knew where she was."

The man took a moment. He smelled of whiskey but looked like the kinda man that could handle his liquor.

"We're lookin' for my sister."

The man spun, a hand going to the gun on his belt, but maybe for show 'cause he didn't draw.

The other guys stopped, caught sight of Raine, and came over while Zeb slumped against the porch.

"What've we got here?" the younger guy said.

"My sister's missin'," Raine said, glaring at them, not a trace of fear in her.

"She as pretty as you are?" the young guy said, the other two laughing.

Raine pulled the hunting knife from her bag and held it loose by her side. "Yeah, she's as pretty as I am. But I'm better with a knife."

There was some laughing but maybe there was an edge to it.

The big guy put a hand up and they stopped just like that. "You're Joe Ryan's girl."

Noah saw a flicker, a change as they lost interest.

"Yeah," Raine said.

"I heard about your sister. You reckon Zeb might've had somethin' to do with it?"

"Maybe," she said, still holding the knife and glancing at the men.

"I got a daughter. Zeb's been following her round. I'd sooner cut off his dick than let him anywhere near her. I guess Joe would feel the same way."

Raine nodded.

"I wanna take a look inside," Raine said.

"All right. While you're in there we'll find out if he's got any inkling where your sister might've got to."

Noah followed Raine up onto the porch, Purv following close behind.

They entered through the back door. The kitchen was a stinking mess. There were take-out cartons piled high, plates thick with some kinda black, and maybe a dozen empty glass jars. Noah watched his step, angling Raine away from a pile of needles on the carpet. They moved through the house quick, trying not to breathe as they went into the bedroom. There were old magazines on the floor, girls lewd and spreading inside.

"Summer ain't been here," Raine said, her voice firm like she was certain.

There were only four rooms so they were back outside within minutes, but that was all it took for Zeb's face to have changed into something Purv had to turn from.

"He don't know nothin' about your sister."

The big guy was breathing hard, blood up his shirt and on his hands and arms.

"You kids all right gettin' back to Grace?"

Raine nodded.

They turned and left the yard, trying not to hear the sound of Zeb whimpering and muttering and blowing blood bubbles from his mouth.

They drove back to Grace in silence. It was late, they were tired but all three knew sleep wouldn't come easy that night. Raine was anxious. She was thinking about what might've happened, what they could've found in Zeb's house.

"We gotta find her," she said.

Noah glanced over. The Buick bounced along Hallow Road.

"We gotta find her now."

"See all those jars in the kitchen back there?" Noah said.

Raine nodded.

"The kind Merle sells his shine in," Purv said.

"Don't mean nothin', but if that's the sort of guy Merle knows –"

"Then we should go see Merle," Raine said.

The dark was total by Merle's barn, not even slips from Windale made it out to them.

They stood in a close line, shoulder to shoulder. Raine had banged the door till they were sure Merle weren't inside.

The barn was tall and burnt and thin trees lined each side. Noah took a couple steps back and aimed a flashlight up at the windows. They were high and square, five holes cut in the wood with plastic sheeting keeping the weather out.

"He's probably at the Whiskey Barrel," Purv said. "He's there most nights. Ain't got money to drink so he's into Hank Frailey for a couple hundred bucks. Hank tried calling it in a few times but Merle said he'd look at the Trans Am for him."

"So, what, we head back?" Noah said.

"What about next door?" Raine said.

Purv flinched. "You wanna call on Pastor Lumen and the Angel at this hour?"

Raine glanced over at the Lumen house and saw a light burning downstairs. "Momma wants Pastor Lumen to get up with the White Mountain people, and the Windale churches. They still reckon he's some kinda savior."

"Pastor Lumen's back in the hospital," Noah said. He'd seen him at Mayland the last time he'd been in for dialysis, the pastor was sitting out by the parking lot smoking a thin cigarette. Noah hated the old man, had done since the pastor told his momma Noah was being punished for past sins. He told her about right-eousness and transgression and the consequence of absolution till she fled St. Luke's in a fit of tears.

Raine shrugged. "So we'll ask the Angel to help."

They crossed the rough ground, passed Merle's farmhouse, and walked onto Lumen land. Noah and Purv hung back a little as Raine walked along the wood porch and pressed her face to the window. She straightened up fast and took a step back.

"What?" Noah said. "You see somethin'?"

The situation went bad real quick.

Raine gripped the gun in two hands. Noah and Purv stood to the side and watched, both breathing hard. She held it level, eyes down the sight and pointed straight at Samson's chest. It was a .48; from this kinda range it'd tear a messy hole in him, and from the look in Samson's eyes he knew that too.

Her hands weren't shaking, which was something. The only way the gun would fire was if she meant it to. She'd pulled it from her bag the second he'd opened the door.

The light was bad in the Lumen place, just one lamp, the glow nothing but a smudge on the gloom. The floor was oak and might've been polished and grand once but that was a long time back.

Noah looked around and saw a flower pressed in a frame, and black-and-white photos of the pastor.

"Raine," Noah said, gentle as he could.

She ignored him, eyes locked on Samson.

"Where'd you get the book, Samson?"

Samson swallowed. He had his palms up like he was being robbed. His hands shook and his pink eyes blinked fast. The skin on his cheek was mottled red like he'd been slapped or burned. His mouth was tight, blush lips pulled like he was hurtin'.

"That's Summer's book you was reading. Purv, open the cover."

Purv picked the book up from the side table and opened the cover. His breath caught when he saw *Summer Ryan* scrawled across the top.

The front door was still open. Noah could hear a chorus of crickets going on like there was something normal about the night.

"Summer writes her name inside all her books. It's a habit she got when we was young and we got bought two of every-thing. See, I'd always make a mess of my things, but she didn't. Ain't in her to make a mess."

Purv set the book down.

"I'll ask you one more time, Samson. Then I'll pull the trigger. And you shouldn't be thinkin' I won't, 'cause everyone knows I'm my daddy's daughter."

"She gave it to me," Samson said.

"Why?"

He dropped his head.

"Why?" she said again.

"I walked her back from school, it was raining. We were talking. She brought the book to church one day. She said I'd like it."

Noah glanced from Raine's eyes to Samson.

"Why'd she say that?"

"I don't . . . I can't understand but she talked about compassion and humanity. And the title and the Lord's Prayer."

"Liar," Raine said.

Samson blinked and tears fell. His hair was bowl cut and blinding white.

Noah hadn't ever seen a man cry before. It was different to a child's cry, maybe like it came from someplace deeper.

"Where is she?"

Samson shook his head.

"You've done somethin' to her."

Samson looked at Noah, his eyes wild. "I wouldn't hurt nobody."

"You've done somethin' to my sister."

"I'm scared," he cried.

"Where is she?"

"I don't know what's happening. I was tryin' to read the book, but it's tough 'cause there's long words and then you bust in here and now I don't know what's happening," Samson said, frantic. "It's not right, none of it."

She cocked the hammer back.

Samson dropped to his knees and he placed his palms on the wood and a dark patch spread on his pants.

"Raine," Noah said.

"He's done somethin' to her."

"Raine," Noah said again.

He took a step toward her.

Her eyes darted to Noah then back to Samson.

Noah reached a hand out slow, inch by inch. He pushed down on Raine's hand and she lowered the gun. He slipped it from her and passed it to Purv, who clutched it nervous, not knowing whether to aim it at the Angel or not.

"We'll tell Black. Right now, we'll go tell Black that Samson's got Summer's book," Noah said.

She took a step back. "He won't do shit. He don't care. Summer's a Ryan and that means she don't count for nothin'."

Noah shook his head. "He'll find out, I promise."

He grabbed Purv and the three headed for the Buick.

They left the Angel on the floor, wet with piss and tears.

*

Black knocked a glass over when he heard the door, stood sloppy, and walked the hallway.

Raine stood there small and tough, the low lights of a Buick shone from the end of his street.

She pushed past him and he followed her.

"Samson Lumen," she said, breathless. "The Angel."

"How'd you hear about that?" he said, sobering but she caught the slur.

"You know? Why ain't you taken him in? Why ain't you out there all night like my daddy and the other men?" she said.

"Raine –"

She saw the gun on the table, and the bottles and the pills. She stared at him and then she stared at the wall, at the girls and the maps and the newspaper clippings going back eighteen months.

"You reckon he took Summer don't you? That's why you ain't pressin' nothin', 'cause you're such a fuckin' mess and you can't catch him –"

"That's enough, Raine."

"You owe me," she said, pointing a finger at him. "You owe me and you owe my sister."

He felt her anger so hot it warmed the dark room.

"You know that's not right, Raine. Your daddy . . . he knew what he was into."

"You went harder 'cause he wouldn't cut a deal. Daddy's got honor and you made him pay for it."

"That ain't fair . . . that ain't the way it works."

"Don't matter what's fair. You broke up Momma's heart till there weren't enough to go round. Is that fair, Black? Daddy said all of us is lookin' for a way out or a way back. You gotta bring Samson in. He might know where she is."

"I will," he nodded. "I'm just working –"

"You're scared of what they'll say. Pastor Lumen and the church."

"I need to talk to Bobby and then –"

"Bullshit. Find my sister. Get out there and find her."

He saw her tears but they didn't fall.

She held a bag and it was big; her hand trembled and it hurt him 'cause sometimes she looked small like a child.

"You're the only one that got close to the Bird."

"I didn't. I was nearest when the call –"

"Could be it's Samson, could be it ain't. But do somethin' now. It's been too long. Find Summer. I need her."

She walked for the door and then turned. "I was gonna take this to my daddy but Noah said you'd listen, that you'd help me. He goes on like you and his father was somethin' back then . . ." Raine paused to look at him, maybe to see if he'd say something, to see if there was fight left in him.

Black dropped his eyes to the floor.

Raine shook her head. "I knew he was wrong."

15

Summer

I gave Samson Lumen a book once. I reckoned he might've liked it 'cause of the whiskey priest and the Judas mestizo and that eternal power. The church can't be destroyed, it lies outside our dawn and our death and there's comfort to be had in that. And Samson needed comfort maybe more than anyone I ever met.

It was fall and we were late gettin' to class when we saw the boys clustered round. They were seniors, tall and tough-lookin' to us.

"Let's see what's goin' on," Raine said, tuggin' my hand.

We heard laughin' and hollerin' and Raine reckoned it was just another scuffle, but then we saw the man standin' there. He had white hair but he weren't all that old. He was tall and skinny and his skin was a shade so light.

The boys were tossin' a sunhat round.

"He's Samson. The janitor," I said.

They tossed it high and it landed near Samson's foot and he stooped to pick it up, but when he did one of the boys, Jesse

Cole, kicked him and he fell to the dirt. Another boy grabbed the sunhat and the game began all over.

"I feel bad for him," I said, and Raine turned to look at me. "He's sweet, he's always smilin' at me."

She saw I was gettin' upset and she walked into the middle. She ain't got fear, never had it.

"Give it back," she said to Jesse.

Samson was watchin', his eyes squint like he couldn't even bear the light.

Jesse was smirkin' till he caught a look from one of his friends. I'd seen that look before, said they knew who our daddy was and who our uncle was.

Raine handed the sunhat to Samson and he took it and nodded but didn't say nothin'.

A couple days later Jesse was beat so bad his momma called Black. Black came up to the school but no one said shit and Jesse couldn't remember nothin' neither.

I like the notion of karma, the causality and purity of deeds.

Sometimes I saw Bobby as a father, holdin' his boy in strong arms. I imagined I was his and I ain't even sure what role I wanted, the wife or the child. Wants and needs—the line that divides ain't nearly bold enough.

I never saw them kiss—Bobby and Savannah—they didn't kiss or hug or touch each other the way my parents did. And it made me so sad and so glad.

Sometimes he'd reach out and touch my shoulder and my body would burn. Sometimes I walked real slow when he was behind me 'cause once when I did that he patted me on the butt to hurry me.

I wondered if it was love, or someplace south of love, where sin ain't nothin' but a threat, so empty we'd laugh at it while he anointed my body with his blessed hands.

I wore a coat 'cause there was chill, then took it off when I got to church. I sat in the back, by the carving of the two saints locked in pained surprise, like they'd just discovered mortality was a state far beneath them.

It felt strange not wearin' a bra.

I saw Mary and her baby; her head to the side, a bird in the baby's hand, its wings up like it wanted to fly.

I watched Bobby glance, then set his papers down and start the slow walk over.

I took a deep breath and straightened my back, pushin' my chest out a little. I was wearin' a shirt so sheer I might as well have screamed dark verse at him. Maybe somethin' about vital existence and undefiled wisdom, 'cause I was grateful for his love, it wouldn't go wasted.

"What are you reading today?" Bobby said, smilin' that smile he saved for me.

"*The Catcher in the Rye*. Again."

Bobby sat down on the bench in front then turned to face me. "I used to want to be Holden Caulfield."

I tried to concentrate on my breathin' when he glanced at my shirt. I tried to stop my heart chargin' ahead of me. Nothin' was happenin'. When you took a step back there weren't nothin' happenin'.

"You don't even know how he ended up. Could be he got married and had kids, worked in a bank all his life," I said.

He glanced at my chest again. I arched my back a little more. That scream; it shattered the colored glass and I saw the saints and Mary and her baby cryin' for my lost virtue.

"Sometimes I miss my younger self. I look back like I was somebody else," he said.

"Is that what I'll do?"

"Depends on the choices you make. Good or bad."

"How will I know?"

"You won't know what you're gonna do until you do it."

I smiled.

"Are you a good person, Bobby?"

I ain't sure why I asked that. Maybe if there was a spell, I was seein' if it could be broken.

"In my experience good isn't always good, bad isn't always bad. But sometimes people do things that cast such a far-reaching shadow it's not possible to escape. Do I want to be one of those people? No. Have I done bad in my life? Yeah. Am I a bad man? I'm not sure how to answer that."

"Try."

"Only God can judge me," he said, a half smile on his face like he suddenly realized where he was.

"I don't want to be judged," I said.

"You're right to feel like that."

"What did you do that was bad?"

He looked down, maybe to see if the stone was opening.

"You can tell me," I said.

"There was a girl in Tallassee. She came to me and she was pregnant and I sent her to a clinic in Dayette."

"Why?"

"She was fourteen . . . her father."

"Oh."

"It weren't the baby's fault. Is it murder?"

"No."

"'*Before I formed you in the womb I knew you.*'"

I looked far into his eyes. "Are you okay, Bobby?"

"What is okay?"

"Maybe the golden mean."

"We crave the extremes, like some fatal flaw."

"I worry about you."

"You shouldn't."

"I know."

He met my eye. I dropped my shoulders. He reached forward and tucked my hair behind my ear. He kept his hand there, warm against my cheek. I looked up and saw Samson by the doorway and he was starin' at me with eyes so sad.

16

Faith

Black came for Samson early and without fuss. No sirens, no flashing lights, no cavalry. Black thought he might've had to get him outta bed, but weren't all that surprised when he saw Samson sitting on the front step. Especially seeing as what went down the night before.

Black pulled the cruiser through the gates, followed the curved driveway halfway up, and rolled to a stop beneath tendrils of Spanish moss.

A light burned inside, just bright enough to throw a glow over Samson.

Samson stood. "Mornin'."

Black checked the sky as he walked over. It didn't feel too much like morning, but weren't long after six. There was a light breeze, just enough to lift the tarp on the roof. Black heard Ray Bowdoin was working on the old house, also heard he hadn't been paid since the pastor got sick so had pulled his men from the job.

"Still up there," Samson said, eyeing the cloud.

"You an early riser, Samson?" Black watched him and saw an angry burn across his cheek. He remembered when Samson was a boy, always marked.

"Yes, sir."

"You know I was comin' for you?"

"I reckoned so. I couldn't sleep, Black. Not the whole night."

"What happened to your cheek?"

Samson brought a hand up and held it to his face but didn't say nothing.

Black took a step forward, eyes glancing at the shuttered windows, at the rotted beams with the swing seat hanging crooked.

Samson smiled, swallowed, and rubbed his eyes. "I'm scared, Black."

Black looked down and pressed his shoe into the dirt like he was stubbing out a cigarette.

"I didn't do nothin' like they think, you know that." Samson began pacing, rubbing his thumb along his fingertips over and over. His pants were high at the ankle, pale skin flashing with each step. "I want to go down to Mae's. I want to order my biscuits and drink my coffee. I want to walk to St. Luke's and pray. Been starting my day that way for a long time now. Reckon I can do that again, Black?"

"Sure, Samson."

Samson blew out a heavy breath, then stopped still and tucked his hands into his corduroy pockets.

"Mind if I ask you a couple questions first?"

Samson fixed his eyes on the cloud again, then on the darkened acres that rolled out across the street. "Okay, Black."

"Go on and get what you need from the house. I'll take a seat out here."

Black wondered if he could get Samson to the station without a soul catching sight of them. Maybe he'd dip the lights, roll the cruiser into the lot out back, and hustle him in under cloud cover. He thought of Pastor Lumen, of Joe Ryan, and the storm that was circling above them.

He glanced into the house and saw the television on, Pat Robertson preaching and begging like salvation was his alone to peddle.

"Have I got time to brush my teeth, Black?" he called from inside.

"Sure, Samson."

Black liked him, didn't have reason not to. He reckoned he'd had it rough, growing up in a house so close to God's less redemptive side. *Drown the children 'cause there ain't no one truly innocent.* Black had seen Pastor Lumen berate the boy in front of a church crowd. Looked at him like he saw nothing but the frailty of mankind in the kid's pink eyes. Before she passed, Mary doted on him like she really believed her boy was an angel. She'd called in once, something bad had happened with Samson and the pastor but when Black got to the house they wouldn't say shit.

When he was done Black led him to the cruiser. Samson put his belt on and glanced up at the cloud again. "I reckon today will be the day when the storm comes."

Black nodded, though didn't know which kinda storm Samson was talking about.

They rode in silence. Black was expecting the radio to go off any second; he was surprised it hadn't already. He'd sent Milk over to watch the Ryan house as soon as Raine left. There weren't no way Joe was gonna sit on information like that. More likely they were planning something.

Black drove on, rolled down the window, and listened hard as they headed for the square. He saw lights on in Mae's.

Then he saw the pickups. Three of them, outside the station, beneath streetlights that burned all the hours now.

He cursed, slammed on the brakes, then crunched the transmission into reverse. Another truck pulled up close behind.

He stopped the cruiser, dipped the lights, then reached for the radio. "Four trucks here, Milk."

"Shit. I been watching, ain't nobody left the place, the lights are still out."

There was another way outta the Ryan place, along the north field and down onto West Pine. It was rough ground but could be driven slow.

"Get back here," Black said.

There were a couple guys in the station. Black radioed in and told them not to come out just yet but to ready themselves.

He could make out Joe Ryan in the truck behind.

Black let the engine idle, waited a three count, then told Samson to stay put as he got out. Samson didn't say nothing, just looked around all wild-eyed.

Black kept a hand on his gun as he looked across the square and saw Mae at the window, watching with her big glasses and her mouth set tight, eyes flipping from Joe to the station.

Joe walked toward him slow and easy. Black glanced over his shoulder and saw John Brunel, one of the junior officers, standing on the front porch outside the station.

"I just want to talk to him," Joe said, palms out like he couldn't make a fist with them.

Joe was carrying though, Black knew that. So were all his boys. It'd be over quick if that's the way Joe decided to play it.

"Well, that ain't your job, Joe. You know I can't let you take him."

"Does he know where my girl is?"

"Tell your boys to stand down and I'll find out."

"He'll talk quick if I'm askin' the questions."

Black eyed the road behind, waiting on Milk.

"I could take him, you know that, Black."

"Yeah, I know."

"Tommy wants to."

Black glanced back and saw Samson looking on.

"You gotta let me do my job, Joe."

"You don't want to do it, Black. Everyone sees it. Over a week now. Might be different it was another girl gone missin', didn't have my name."

"Ain't the way I work."

"You're lost, Black. Out too deep now."

Joe stared at him and Black could see him running options. He'd calmed, Joe, years back they wouldn't have been having this conversation. Joe had worked for the Kitcheners, a known family in Birmingham. They were into everything and Joe was a rising star before he got picked up. Mitch Wild, Noah's father, had led it, took him down for a host of charges after some guy that owned a distillery up in Brayton had rolled. Black was the one that cuffed him, the one that made the front pages. Joe pleaded guilty, mouth shut as was custom. Joe was known and Joe was liked.

"She's fifteen. And she ain't like her sister . . . and you got the Briar girls. Ain't nobody done shit about 'em lately. Not even made the newspapers. They're ghosts already."

Black watched him careful.

"You lost your taste for this, Black, ain't no fight in you. Way I heard it you let him ride once before. It was bad, all that happened with Mitch back then. You ain't sharp no more, just runnin' the clock. I ain't blaming you for wanting to hide out. But you need to step aside, don't want no more blood on your hands."

Black swallowed and he felt the sweat on his collar as the truth stung at him. "I got people out there, askin' questions. I got Ernie Redell, he's got her photo now so he'll get up with Mayersville and before long we'll circle far."

Black heard a truck door opening behind him, and then he glanced back and saw Tommy Ryan, and Tommy was looking up at John and running numbers in his head and thinking how easy it'd be to take Samson. Black's falling hope was that Joe wouldn't give word.

"You take Samson and then we got a whole lot of different problems to work through, and that ain't gonna help us find Summer. You need to give me time to talk to Samson, find out what he knows. Could be nothin'."

"A grown man walking my fifteen-year-old daughter home from school ain't nothin', Black. I know people reckon he's slow or somethin', but that don't mean shit. Call him an angel but what's in words and names? Don't matter who his parents are, divine rights and select few and bullshit."

"*Hey.*"

Black spun and saw John had drawn on Tommy but now had three guns pointing back at him.

"Call 'em off, Joe. Now. Please."

Joe glanced over at his brother, then up at John, then back to the cruiser with Samson inside.

"Please, Joe. Give me some time."

Black saw Milk's cruiser turn into the square then come to a quick stop. Milk opened the door, pulled his gun, and knelt behind.

"You give me your word you'll go hard on Samson, make him tell you what he needs to and then you come tell me. No more waitin' on this."

Black nodded. "I'll get into it. I'll find your daughter."

"Your word, Black. You'll straighten up and search for her."

"I give you my word."

"All we got is our word, Black. Ain't nothin' else but that."

*

Raine hadn't slept the whole night. She'd told her momma what had happened and they'd sat together in silence, watching out the window for her daddy to come back from the search. He'd made her go over it slow, then he'd called

Tommy, but that was all she got 'cause her momma told her to get some sleep. She'd laid on Summer's bed and buried her face in her sister's pillow so hard she couldn't find her breath no more.

She walked past the square and stopped under a streetlight for a while. It didn't scare her, that cloud that people kept talking about. She didn't believe the shit she heard about the Bird summoning it, the sin and the great transgressions, the punishment or the fury. Her momma was praying more. Watching the sky and praying.

Raine walked up Jackson, found herself in the cemetery on the grounds of the old church that Summer loved so much. She saw gravestones, leaning and scored with old names and old dates. Some were newer, people passed. One shone, even in the dark it shone 'cause it was tended so often. Mandy Deamer, the pregnant girl who took so many lives when she tied that rope and wobbled that stool.

Raine walked into the church. She liked the smell, candles and books, and she liked the light that flickered warm. She looked up at the high ceiling, at the carved beams and the history.

She saw Bobby and he was stood still and staring at the big cross like his mind was far.

"I ain't even sure what I'm doin' here," she said as he turned.

He looked like he hadn't slept much neither. He wore it well, that pain in his eyes suited him, made it like he knew what suffering was.

"Do you want me to leave you?"

She stared at the cross like she was seeing it for the first time. "I had to get outta the house. You know what happened to Samson? I heard Momma on the telephone, reckons Black's taken him in."

"Black called me early."

"It might be him," she said.

"I don't –"

"You ain't gotta say, Pastor Bobby, that ain't why I'm here. I'll keep lookin', case I'm wrong."

She walked over to the cushioned bench and sat at the far end, reached into her bag and pulled out a book she'd taken from Summer's bedroom.

She didn't know Bobby all that well but she liked him 'cause Summer did.

"You reckon the cloud is anything to do with God?" she said, her voice carving up the silence.

He took a step nearer, his hands deep in his pockets. "I don't. I think there'll be a storm and it'll go."

"That ain't what some folk are sayin'. Not just the crazies."

"I reckon some people have too much time on their hands."

She nodded, holding her book in her lap and flipping the pages.

"This is Summer's book."

"Which is it?"

"I picked it up 'cause it's called *The Color Purple*."

"Do you like it?"

"I ain't sure purple is my favorite color no more."

He smiled.

"You reckon God reads those letters from Celie?" She swallowed. "I'm being careful not to bend the pages," she spoke quiet. " 'Cause she'll be pissed if I do." She rubbed her eye with the back of her fist. She weren't a girl who cried, not in front of people, but that first tear cut her resolve so deep she dropped the book to the floor. The sound was close and harsh and a light dust rose in the air around it.

She didn't kick or struggle when she felt his arm on her shoulder, and she didn't feel the shame of leaning into him.

She cried for a long time.

Bobby took his arm from her when she calmed. She wiped tears with the palms of her hands.

"Fuck," she said, real quiet.

"It's okay, Raine. To come here, to read your book, or break down in tears. All of it. It's all okay."

She wiped her hands on her cutoffs, her tears streaking the blue dark. She looked up toward the ceiling again, wondered how many had knelt and cried before her. Church was a place where tears fell, happy and sad. It was also a place of hope and despair. A first call and a last resort. She wondered how Bobby lived through the extremes. It must've been something to do with faith. She struggled with her understanding of faith, what drove it, what caused it to desert you. And she wondered how some could cling to it so hard they'd base a life on it.

"I need Summer to come back now, it's been too long. And we got this fuckin' cloud so Grace is dark now." She bent to pick up the book and saw Summer's library card had fallen from the pages. "But it ain't all that different, 'cause it's always been dark to me."

*

Purv listened to the heavy thump on the front door. His momma locked the bolt when his father went out drinking. She'd soon slide it in case he splintered the wood, then she'd have to paint another line of Elmer's down it come winter, when ice stole through the gap and goosed her skin.

The neighbor's dog was yapping loud.

Purv stared at a map of New Orleans up close. There was a lot of water: lakes and the Gulf. Purv liked the idea of living by the water. He still enjoyed walking the line of the Red, watching the river flow and spit as it headed out far across the state. He wondered what the Mississippi would look like, if the water would be any clearer or flow any faster.

The storm cloud darkened the window. There'd once been drapes but they got ripped down when the Tide missed a kick and lost his father fifty bucks.

He heard the front door open and he folded the map away quick.

There was yelling, then he heard the creak of the stairs.

He stood just in time to see his father at the door, a bottle of Lawson's in his hand.

"You do your schoolwork?"

"Yes, sir," Purv said, wondering if his father knew it was summer break.

Purv switched between meeting his father's eye and staring at the ground, either of the two could piss the old man off depending on which way the wind was blowing.

Ray stood there a long while.

"You keepin' outta trouble?"

"Yes, sir."

Purv kept the hunting knife on top of his closet, behind a football his father had bought for him when he was six. There'd been vague promises to teach him how to throw it, but they died when Purv didn't grow big and strong.

"Your momma saw you with the Ryan girl the other day, in the square."

"Her sister's gone missin'."

"You ain't spendin' time with that girl. I don't care what she looks like. Ryan business ain't ours."

Ray had fallen out with Tommy Ryan a long time back. Purv didn't know why. Maybe it was over gambling or business.

Purv stayed silent, sometimes that was the right move and sometimes it weren't.

He swallowed down a big lump of fear when his father stepped into the room and slammed the door closed behind him.

"I'm sorry," Purv said.

It was a reach. Weakness got him beat just as much as strength.

Ray stared at him with soulless eyes then walked at him.

Purv flinched but Ray pushed past and stared out the window.

"Fuckin' dog," Ray said, and he hammered the window so hard Purv thought it might break. And then Ray barrelled from the room and took the stairs fast.

Purv stood at the window and heard the back door open. And then he saw his father step into the dark with a kitchen knife in hand. Purv watched him hop the fence but then turned his back when the yapping stopped, and the night fell death silent.

17

Summer

I saw them shinin' in their broken life. I breathed dawn air when I stepped into their house like it was the place new days were born.

There's a willow at the end of Bobby's yard growin' tight to the picket fence so its limbs hang over the land behind. It was late in the night and I snuck out, sat beneath it and parted the tendrils.

They had nice things; I imagined they collected them from places I only read about in books. I saw their photographs on the side table by the front door: them on white beaches pullin' faces; their wedding day. Some small chapel and hardly any guests 'cause Bobby didn't have no family and wouldn't want a show. I stare at that one like it ain't real; a sepia dream of a life so pretty it could've been staged. Maybe that's what God saw and maybe that's why he stepped in, in case they forgot who was pullin' strings. I wondered if complacency was a sin.

Bobby was watchin' television in the den while Savannah sat in their library and read. Their lives side by side yet separate.

Bobby slept in Michael's bedroom. I saw him by the window, lookin' out but he couldn't have seen me 'cause my eyes ain't bright like Savannah's.

I lay down in the grass and let the leaves fall back and I caught snatched glimpses of starlight through the cover.

When I woke it was cold. I heard a noise and got scared so I climbed to my feet. I saw her straight off. Savannah. She was wearin' runnin' pants but she didn't run, just walked slow down Jackson Ranch Road.

I followed from a long way back, down the pretty streets where folks left porch lights burnin' all night like they'd welcome callin' strangers.

We weren't supposed to be out after dark, none of the kids, that's what our parents said.

When she got to the edge of town, and she crossed the last street and walked the last field I almost called out to her 'cause I reckoned she must've been lost. 'Cause with all the shit goin' on, all that fear and that panic, why else would she walk into Hell's Gate in the terror of night.

"You stay together. Your momma will come get you from school for the next couple weeks," Daddy said.

We were watchin' the television. Coralee Simmons had just gone missin'. Briar girl number four. Sheriff Ernie Redell was on the news again. He gave a quick statement where he said enough, but nothin' we hadn't heard before.

They cut to the reporter and his name was Chuck Cash and he wore a necktie and cowboy hat.

Chuck was standin' in front of the Green Acres Baptist Church out on Route 84. There was a crowd behind and they had flashlights and Chuck said they was gettin' ready to head out, but he didn't say where they was headed.

They flashed up a photograph of Coralee and she looked real young with braces on her teeth.

"Shit," Daddy said, shakin' his head.

"You goin'?" Momma said.

Daddy nodded. "I'll call Tommy and we'll head up there, see if we can help out. They need numbers, lot of nothin' over by Gin Creek."

The newspapers ran the Briar girls on the front page the next day. And then that sighting leaked, the boys playin' soldier in Hell's Gate who saw the monster with the girl draped over his shoulder. In a breath the whole area was hot with talk of the Bird. The kids at school drew cartoon birds and made jokes to cover the fact that they was sleepin' with one eye open from then on. We didn't go nowhere near Hell's Gate, not even to the best sun spots along the Red 'cause that was close to the trees and we were worried about some monster comin' out and draggin' us away. Raine stayed home each night, lay in my bed with me, and we looked out the window and saw the tops of the oaks and we wondered what was goin' on in those woods.

There was a couple boys at school who dressed in black each day, even painted their nails and faces. The other kids used to rip them. The day after the Coralee news broke those boys got beat bad and tied naked to a bench in the square. We all knew it was Danny Tremane and some of the other jocks but no one said shit. Handin' out beatings in the name of Jesus, Danny glided down the halls from then on.

Abby Farley reckoned she heard screamin' comin' from the copse by her place, so her folks called Black and he went in with Milk but they didn't find nothin'. Black was run ragged those weeks after Coralee was taken. He came to school and spoke to us again but this time there was somethin' desperate about him. His hands were shakin' and he locked us with a dead stare and told us it weren't for jokin', that there was somebody takin' children away and doin' God knows what with them. He pointed a finger out and told us to be scared 'cause that kept us sharp. And then he told us not to go to church no more, and that's when the principal came over and they had words we couldn't hear.

I believe that they do. I can't prove that they do.

I heard that, on the television and the radio. I read that in every newspaper, local and national. That belief was its own kinda faith, they just never saw that.

The devil ran riot and righteous, and those two-bit pastors and those Lidocaine lies, those intelligence officers and those fuckin' former satanic priests who suddenly saw the light (it weren't the light of God, it was the light of television cameras), they all played their parts so perfect. They bathed in the Panic 'cause it gave them such purpose. Religion needs fear, that ain't never been a secret.

We watched that episode of *Geraldo* where he talks about the boys who got killed in Arkansas, and he's sayin' those three did it 'cause it was part of a satanic ritual. He kept askin' the parents to describe the marks on the body like they weren't talkin' about their own child just been murdered. We all knew about that case, we all followed it 'cause it felt like it weren't smoke and mirrors no more.

It was real and it was comin' for us.

18

Those Shiny Maidenville People

Pastor Lumen sat in his hospital bed, bent forward, a tube running from his back and draining fluid from his lungs. His longtime friend Deely White sat beside him while the doctor worked. Deely's wife, Carvelle, kept a hand on the pastor's arm while they told him what had gone on.

The old man straightened. Hollow cheeks, white hair now, like his boy's, and a thin mustache that traced an eternal frown. He was tall when he stood, still mighty and imposing despite the hanging arm. "Black's a drunk," he said cold.

Deely nodded 'cause he always did.

"He's fearful of the Ryans, Joe and his brother, and their band of transgressors."

"He's just askin' him questions," Carvelle said. "Samson's helping 'em find the Ryan girl."

"She was lost at birth. And Bobby?"

"I reckon he'll sit with Samson and see him through."

Pastor Lumen fixed hard eyes on the monitor beside him, the quickened beep a scant reminder of where he was. Mentally he was strong. He believed he was strong.

"Bobby don't got the heart for it, it ain't his fight. You heard about his boy? He should be lookin' up for the answers 'stead of down."

Carvelle reached up and patted his shoulder.

"You want me to go and see him?" Deely said.

Pastor Lumen nodded. "I don't want Black talking to the boy."

*

Samson Lumen was sick. The first time they tried talking to him he'd panted like a dog, sweating so bad Black had stopped awhile till he calmed. The second time Samson puked right there on the table between them.

They'd called a doctor who didn't give them nothing more than saying maybe the man was anxious.

They'd put Samson in a cell for the night 'cause Joe and Tommy Ryan had parked up out front of the station and stayed there.

The room was small so they kept the A/C on and left the door open.

Samson sat on a hard chair and kept his hands in his lap and his eyes on the table.

"So you walked Summer home from school. Where'd you see her?" Black said.

Samson swallowed. He was sweating again. "I saw her comin' out the school gate."

"Where were you?"

"I was finished for the day. She was out late. She was carryin' her music case. It was big and she was strugglin' with it 'cause the handle was broke."

Samson glanced up at Milk.

"And then?"

"It was raining, then it turned heavy. So I caught up with her and asked her if she needed any help."

"You ever do that before? Help out one of the kids?"

He shook his head.

"So why then?"

"I ain't exactly sure. I just felt bad for her. She's small and she was strugglin'. I see her at church."

"You were being a gentleman," Milk said.

Samson looked down. "I ain't sure about that."

"So you walked her back. Which way?"

"Along Beeson Road."

"Why not just stay on Riverway to All Saints? That's the easiest way back to the Ryan house."

Samson cleared his throat, glanced at his empty glass of water but didn't ask for no more. "I just followed Summer. I didn't know where she lived. She cut through Rushing –"

"Into the woods?" Milk said, surprised. "A fifteen-year-old girl led you, pretty much a stranger, into the woods."

Samson nodded, glanced at the Bible Bobby had dropped off, then looked up. "Yeah, she did."

Black sighed, stretched his hands up, and fanned his shirt. They'd told Samson he was entitled to a lawyer. He'd just shook his head.

"Then where?"

"We came out by the Red, near to her house."

"You said you didn't know where she lived."

"She said . . . she said that her house was near, and thanked me, then grabbed the case and took off quick."

"And what did you do?"

"I stood there awhile."

Black looked over at Milk. Milk was big in his chair, hunched over like he'd split the thing if he straightened.

"You watched her?" Milk said.

Samson nodded. "It was raining hard and the Red flows fast. My momma used to tell me the Red would reach out and grab me if I got too near."

"You think Summer's pretty?" Milk said.

Samson looked at Black, then down at the Bible.

"It's okay, Samson," Black said.

"I don't look at girls like that," Samson said.

"You like guys?"

Black shot Milk a look.

"Summer's just a child," Samson said quiet, looking like he might puke again.

"So this was the first time you walked her home. What about the second?"

"It was maybe a month later. Same again, it was raining and I walked her back."

Black poured Samson a glass of water and told him he was doing good and they were nearly done.

"What did you and Summer talk about?"

"It was raining so loud I couldn't hear much."

"Not in the woods though, it's sheltered pretty well in there so maybe you spoke to her when you were cutting through?" Black said.

"I ain't sure."

"Come on, Samson. Summer's missin' and we're tryin' to find her. She might be in trouble, and she'd need your help again."

"She said she was sad."

"Why?"

"She said she didn't think life would be so tough. And she looked upset, like maybe somethin' had happened at school, or at home. I didn't know what to tell her. I ain't good with words. I'm tired, Black. I want to go now. I need to check on my daddy 'cause he's sick."

"You're doin' well, Samson. We're nearly done, I just need to make sure we ain't missed somethin', otherwise we'll have to bring you back in and do this all again, and then you'd miss breakfast at Mae's again, and your mornin' prayer in St. Luke's."

Samson dipped his head, then brushed something from his shoulder. Black wondered how right he was in the head, and how much they should press him.

"The book?" Black said.

"She gave it to me at St. Luke's one time when I was cutting the grass 'cause she said she read it and thought of me."

"Can you think of anything else she said? Anything at all that might help us find her? Even if it's somethin' you reckon ain't worth mentioning."

Samson picked up his Bible, rubbed his thumb over the embossed letters, then set it down again. Then he shook his head, kinda like a kid might when they don't want to eat no more greens.

They'd left Samson in one of the empty offices and sent Trix out to fetch him a sandwich and a Coke from Mae's. Black and Milk ate together out back.

"What's that?" Black said.

Milk glanced at the glass. "Protein."

"You can get that from meat you know, don't have to drink the shit."

Milk took a sip, smacked his lips, and leaned back heavy in his chair. "Noah in today?"

"Don't think so. Why?"

"Seen the badge he wears?"

Black nodded.

"I remember that funeral, his daddy," Milk said. "All those people on the streets, must've been a thousand. He wore a suit, Noah, you remember that? Small little suit and necktie. Didn't cry neither. Then his momma passed, and he's still sick. It don't rain but it pours."

Black remembered it clear, the procession drove long and slow down Hallow Road, eight motorcycles passing a blur of stars and stripes and those tight faces of kindly strangers from towns far and wide. State police wore full dress; Black had stood silent among them. Noah's mother wouldn't look at him.

"Still, sometimes I reckon he's got it better than the Bowdoin boy. It ain't gonna end well, not with Ray like he is."

"I stop by there now and then, just sit outside awhile, hope maybe Ray sees me and knows that we're watching."

Milk shrugged. "Temper like he's got, ain't nothin' gonna stop him."

Black sighed.

"What do you reckon on Samson?" Milk said.

"Not much so far."

"He's odd."

"Ain't a crime."

"I reckon he's hidin' somethin' big. And that skin all burned up on his cheek like that, it's strange."

"What we got is her book at his house, and he walked her home twice. What's the motive for more?"

"Sexual, like always. She's pretty, he ain't."

"That simple?"

"Yeah, that simple. He made a play, she knocked him back, he couldn't take it. We should check out the Lumen house."

"Won't get a warrant."

"Samson will let us, he's scared, just word it right. Do it while the old man's still at Mayland."

Black nodded.

"Let's say he did somethin' to Summer, he definitely ain't smart enough to cover his tracks. We'll find somethin' that puts her at his house and then we can get heavy. He ain't got the money for a lawyer so he'll get stuck with Forbes."

Forbes L. Dillinger. That weren't his real name, it was something he cooked up to make himself sound hot when the truth
was he was about as useless a lawyer as you could find. They
threw him state bones every now and again, no-wins he could
try and plead out.

"You know we can't send Samson back out there."

"I know."

"So what then?"

"I ain't figured it yet." Black looked down at his burger and
pushed it away.

"You got anyone else for all this?"

Black shrugged. "Just waitin' on a break."

"We're due."

"We are."

They looked up when Trix stopped by the door. "You need to
come see this," she said.

They walked through to the front, bent the blinds low, and
looked out into the square. Five trucks. Joe Ryan's boys. They
sat on the hoods, smoking and dealing cards and sipping beer.

"Looks like they're settling in," Milk said.

*

Main Street in Maidenville was redbrick and beautiful. They left
the Buick a quarter mile away and walked along, side by side. The
stores were fancy; each streetlight had a basket of purple daisies
hanging from it. There was a small hotel, restaurants, and banks.
Even the hardware store had a shine to the window. At the far

end they could see the back of Fairline Park, the trees sweeping from green to gold like they'd been given a lick of paint.

Purv glanced around. "Fuckin' Starbucks, ruinin' small towns."

Noah frowned at him.

They passed Maidenville moms sitting outside a bakery, eating pastries and sipping from wide cups while their kids tangled beside them. They passed the Fountain Record Store, the first in the state to stick labels on the front of certain albums warning of occult references.

Raine spat her gum out onto the sidewalk. A passing man shook his head.

"What the fuck's his problem?" Raine said.

Purv shrugged.

"I reckon I could live someplace like this," Noah said, looking around, a smile on his face.

Raine waved him off. "Everywhere looks better in sunshine."

"I could live here too," Purv said, eyeing the fancy convenience store. "Man left the counter to help a lady load her groceries. I could strip the shelves bare in that time."

They found it at the north end of Main, by the crossroads, behind a steep bank of grass. Maidenville Public Library. The building was old and grand. There were banners, one told of a bake sale that coming weekend, the other of a drive to collect books for the local elementary school.

"Place is huge," Purv said. "How many books you reckon they got in there?"

It was bright inside, smart carpets and bold paint and towering shelves. Raine picked out a book, thumbed the pages and looked around. There was clusters of kids reading at long tables.

"All these people in here," Purv said. "Ain't they got televisions in Maidenville?"

There was a boy working the desk, maybe college age, thick frames and cheeks fired with acne.

"Over there," Noah said, nodding in the direction of an empty terminal.

They walked over and sat at the computer. Raine took Summer's library card from her bag and typed in the membership number.

"Password?" Purv said.

Raine tried their date of birth. It didn't work. "Shit," she said.

The boy glanced over then stood.

"He's comin'," Noah said.

"I haven't seen you here before," the boy said. He wore a nameplate: Henry.

Raine smiled, arched her back a little, and pushed her tits out.

"You need any help?"

"I can't remember my password," Raine said. "Such a ditz. It's this heat." She pulled her top down a little and blew. "Some days I even forget to put my panties on."

Noah glanced at Purv and Purv glanced at Henry, who was blushing bad and fiddling with his glasses.

"You reckon you can help me out?" she said, voice loaded with sweet.

Henry nodded quick, leaned down and tapped a couple keys, then smiled as the screen lit.

Raine scooted forward and saw a couple of files.

The boy cleared his throat. "So, can I show you how to –"

"Fuck off now," Raine said.

"Excuse me?"

Raine waved him away with her hand.

Henry walked off slow and sad.

"Brutal," Purv said.

Noah nodded.

"Either of you know how to print these files?" Raine said.

Noah and Purv shook their heads.

"Jesus," Raine said, standing and turning and hollering for Henry. She pulled her top down again as he came running.

Raine flipped the pages, articles from the locals and nationals going back a couple years. She sat in the back of the Buick while Noah drove the dirt roads toward Grace.

Purv turned from the front seat. "Maybe Summer was doin' a project on the Briar girls. Did she talk about them?"

"Maybe. We watched the news, she got upset, she used to ask my daddy about it when he got back from the searches."

"Anything there?" Noah said, glancing in the mirror.

Raine scanned the pages, didn't find nothing new till she got to the end. "There's a ton of shit about the Maidenville Academy."

"That fancy school," Purv said. "Why?"

Raine read as they drove. "Briar girl three, Lissa Pinson, went with a boy from that school."

"You reckon Summer talked to him?" Noah said.

Raine stared at the pages, and she thought of her sister looking for the Briar girls, and maybe looking for the Bird, and she got a pain in her stomach so bad she couldn't barely breathe.

*

Joe and Tommy Ryan sat outside the gates to the Lumen house, the engine idling but the lights cut. Joe had just got off the phone with one of his boys, Austin Ray Chalmers, who was sat out front of the police station with a couple men.

Tommy lit a cigarette, took a long sip from the flask he was carrying, then offered it to Joe, who shook his head.

"We goin' in?" Tommy said.

"No. Cops will. We don't want to fuck anything up. If Summer was in there they'll know about it."

Tommy rolled down his window and leaned an arm out.

Joe eased the truck along to get a look down the side of the house.

"Where were you last night?" Joe said.

Tommy shrugged. "In the square with you."

"I woke early hours and your truck weren't there. We ain't movin' till she's found. Austin Ray and the boys, we'll do shifts. We gotta stay on Black."

Tommy glanced at his brother, then back out the window. "Ran home to take a shower is all."

Joe nodded, then he looked out, saw a bottle of William Lawson's in the weeds and wondered if Samson was the type that liked to drink. Like Black. He'd known Black a lifetime. Before he'd gone inside Black had been slick with purpose, a drinker, always, but tough and smart. Him and Mitch Wild made a tight pairing. Joe had seen it on the night news, on the small black-and-white in his cell. They didn't say but he knew Black had fucked up 'cause Mitch was a pro to the bone, no way he would've walked up to that house without cover.

"You heard anything more from Black?" Tommy said.

"He ain't got nothin' yet, reckons Samson was sick yesterday. If this drags, if she don't show . . . we'll have to pull him out."

"The Angel? How?" Tommy looked over at him.

"Just go in and take him."

"All right."

"I was thinkin' we wait for the storm. Do it when the cops are busy, when people ain't lookin' down."

Tommy nodded. "Move on the storm, I like that."

Tommy opened the glove compartment, saw a SIG and a Smith & Wesson inside. He carried a knife, always had since they were boys and got caught out by a couple guys from Windale who did a number on Joe 'cause he was the bigger of the two. It'd been Tommy they were after; he'd fucked one of their girls. Joe said it was him.

"You know much about this guy?"

"No. The Angel was like a ghost till recent. He worked at the school but outside of that, nothin'. I got it the old man was shamed of him, never saw Samson at church or nothin', like he was locked down with his momma."

"I saw him recent, at St. Luke's, when we dropped the girls there," Tommy said.

Joe nodded. "That's what Ava reckons. He started goin' to church again, every day she said."

"How come?"

"Could be when his momma died. Could be when the old man got sick he wanted to go pray for him."

"Could be 'cause Summer was there," Tommy said quiet.

Joe put his foot on the gas, wondering what was to come, hoping it'd be over soon and Summer would come home safe, and that he wouldn't have to hurt nobody for that to happen.

19

Summer

The bell tower at St. Luke's is somethin' special. It chimes on the hour. Don't matter if I'm readin' or watchin' Raine swing out over the Red, I always hear it and I always notice 'cause it's kinda like the heartbeat of Grace.

Daddy said when he was a little boy he got a job workin' the cotton fields by Carolina Road. It was tough work and he couldn't slack 'cause Ezra Kinley had a line of boys by his place each mornin' and only the need for half of them. Ezra would let them break at midday when the sun was gettin' fierce, and he'd get Cass to bring out a pitcher of lemonade. Ezra kept a ball and a mitt and a couple bats by the house and they'd play an hour before they worked on. Daddy said the boys would count the chimes off, waitin' till it was time, then pray the bell would break so they could get longer out.

It was tight, the stairway windin' dark and dusty circles. Bobby asked if I wanted to help him, he had to check the workings every month. I felt Bobby close behind me. I walked slow, countin' each step. I dressed for him. I took clothes from Raine's closet then left the house early. The skirt was short and I wore underwear that went right up my butt. I almost slipped once. I ain't even sure if I did it on purpose but Bobby reached out and placed a hand on my hip.

"All right?" he said.

"Yeah."

We passed the room where the ringers used to sit. I've been in there before, there's a line of photos on the wall and they show the church after Hurricane Camille swept through. There was a hole in the roof but it could've been worse 'cause there weren't much that still stood along the Mississippi coast.

I was already deep outta breath. Bobby helped me as we crossed the beam. I focused on my feet. It was hot and sunlight crisscrossed the tower through gaps in the stone. I had a fine sweat on by the time we reached the ladder. I was hopin' I didn't have patches under my arms 'cause I hadn't never seen Savannah a shade off perfect.

I glanced up and saw the wooden wheel and the cogs and the dull steel bell. Dust rose like glitter and I reached out and tried to grasp it.

"We can go back. It's hot in here," Bobby said, wiping his forehead.

His arms are a kinda gold color 'cause he spends a lot of his time outside, walkin' to visit people and helpin' Samson with the grounds.

"I want to see the top," I said.

"It's high, if you get dizzy on the ladder just stop climbing, don't look down and hold on tight. I'll be right behind you."

"Catch me if I fall," I said.

"You'll take me down with you."

I laughed.

I climbed slow, keepin' my head up. I felt the ladder move as Bobby climbed beneath me. At one point I glanced down and saw him lookin' straight up, his cheeks colored with shame.

I stopped near the top.

"All right, Summer?"

"Just need a minute," I said.

I glanced down again, his face by my ankles, his eyes strippin' me bare. I wanted him to touch me, to reach up and do ungodly things to me in the church tower.

I thought of my momma, if she could see me, her shinin' star flashin' her ass to a pastor.

When we got out the air hit me hard and I gulped it down 'cause I didn't realize I hadn't been breathin' for the longest time. That was the thing with Bobby, around him I forgot I was mortal, I went to a place where his gaze pumped my blood and his smile filled my lungs.

I walked to the edge and saw Grace below, and I saw across Briar County to the rise and the fall of the country beyond. It was so long and so wide and so deep and so endless. Maybe I liked that feelin', like I was a dot on a canvas so vast you could lift me out and nobody would notice. That insignificance that people fear, I sought it 'cause it made it all right, those acts that were so small.

"Where's my house?"

He leaned close to me, his cheek almost brushin' mine. He put an arm round my waist and pointed. I stared off, tryin' not to breathe when his hand moved lower.

We stayed that way a long time. There ain't a sound up there but the lightest whistle of the breeze. I could see trucks hurtlin' down Highway 125 and I thought of the men in them like my daddy, with their family livin' lives so lonely. That was me and my momma and my sister.

I leaned forward, my elbows comin' to rest on the stone. My skirt pulled high, his hand drifted lower till it rested on my ass. My mouth ran dry.

I shifted slightly, moved my feet farther apart. I saw a cluster of birds shoot high from Hell's Gate, then scatter and come together in some kinda dance.

Bobby took his hand away and I wondered what I'd done wrong. It was a game I didn't know how to play or what it meant to win.

My hair fell. I counted to fifty.

I almost jumped when I felt Bobby's hand on my thigh, at the top, under my skirt. His touch was hot, sweat on his palms.

I breathed ragged.

His hand rose higher, resting on my bare ass.

"Sometimes I want to go home," he said.

I was damp through.

"But there was never home."

I kicked my foot out a little more, arched my back, and brought my chin down to rest on my fingers like I was watchin' the flames below.

I flexed my toes.

He moved his hand across my ass, my underwear against his palm.

"I can see the whole of Briar County," I said.

I counted to fifty again, this time fast, then I dared to push back.

I felt the pressure soft at first.

He pressed harder, I pushed back just as hard. He slowly worked his hand lower, tracin' his finger down.

I closed my eyes.

The bell sounded and I jumped and he took his hand away.

And maybe that one time I wished it was broke too.

20

Working Rich Boys

The first reporters gathered early at the border on Hallow Road. Sun had risen in the rest of Briar County so the line was stark like usual and they fired off shots. They were local, most had friends who lived in Grace, and they were still chalking it to a storm, but there'd been rumblings of the missing girl and the Bird and a churchman. They couldn't link to the Briar girls 'cause the Grace girl had run, and Black and Ernie Redell had played it low, but when you added everything there was a flavor getting stronger.

Tib Tyler, from the *Briar County News*, had dressed smart, yellow corduroy suit, bolo tie, and black Panama, and he'd tried to get a meeting with Black but kept getting stonewalled. Tib had a friend who worked as a cameraman over at WXFB and he was en route with a van and a pretty face and they were planning on running something light, just about the dark town.

"I ain't liking it," Tib said. "I ain't liking it not one bit."

The man beside was Brent Mann and he worked for the *Maidenville Herald*. "There isn't much to like. It'll be a bad one."

"I ain't talkin' about the storm. The girls. You heard about the Ryan girl?"

Brent nodded. "Heard she ran, maybe with a boyfriend. Nothin' in that."

Tib chewed the end of his pen and stared high at the sky. "The Bird's back, and he's brought the devil with him."

Brent shook his head. "You run with that and Ernie will lynch you."

*

Savannah kneeled on the grass and fussed with the flowers. The stone seemed too big to mark a child's grave, hard when it should've been soft. St. Margaret's was a simple church, white boards and pretty steeple, acres of rolling Maidenville green framed it.

She'd bought him a gift. It was a toy car and she'd wrapped it careful in teddy bear paper. He would have been seven and she worried the paper was too babyish because she didn't know what seven-year-old boys were like.

Bobby hadn't fitted the car seat correctly. The strap should have been looped through at the shoulder, that way when the truck hit, Michael might have escaped with nothing more than bruises. She tried to imagine carrying what Bobby had to, she tried to imagine hurt beyond her own but it was too much.

"What did you get him?"

She turned and saw Bobby and smiled. "I didn't know if you'd come. You were out all night again."

"Summer."

"Anything?"

He shook his head and kneeled beside her.

"I bought him a car, the kind you pull back and let go. Is the paper too babyish?"

"No." He took it from her and placed it by the grave. There were carved doves, an angel and a scroll and a photo where Michael smiled so wide.

She wished the birds would stop singing a while.

"I thought it might get easier, because that's what they say," she said.

He wore dark glasses that hid his thoughts.

When he reached forward and laid a hand on the stone she cried, and when she cried her eyes swelled and her nose ran.

"I miss him," she said.

"Yes."

She reached out and he took her hand. There was so much to say but nothing that would change much of anything.

*

"You're quiet," Peach said.

Black held a cigarette in his hand but didn't light it.

She'd fixed him something to eat, though he said he didn't want nothing. She'd cleaned her place, always did if she knew he was stopping by. He smelled some kinda lemon cleaner, bleach like it'd strip the sin back.

She fluffed cushions on the sofa then sat down and smiled at him. It was the kinda nervous smile that almost kept him from showing up.

She kept clippings in a box beneath her bed. It'd crossed his mind she knew the Bird. That he was one of her men, those silent men that showed and came and left. The dark side of nature but nature all the same.

"Drink?" she said.

"No."

"No?"

"No."

"Anything on Summer Ryan?" she said. No one called her no more; not Ernie Redell, not the state cops. There weren't no one keeping in touch and he knew it killed her.

"Nothin' at all."

"You're holdin' that guy from the church though."

"It'll go off, I can feel it. People are angry, lookin' for somethin' to fight about. Could be it's me holdin' on to a pastor's son."

She came over and perched so close he could smell her perfume. There was a new photo of Della by the window. She was a quiet kid. Peach would entertain and do what she did and Della would stay locked in her bedroom. The men didn't know she was there; it was safer that way. She'd called once, they found it, when she was eleven and heard her momma taking a beating. She'd called 911 like Peach had taught her.

"You reckon he's back and he's taken Summer Ryan?"

He said nothing, just stared at the television set.

She leaned in and kissed him. That's how it started between them. She couldn't bear it, all the waiting around, the tension. There was much unsaid, about how the state cops were with her, what they said about Della and Peach in the newspapers. They wrote Della off quick: knocked up and ran. Opinion turned as time rolled by, Peach drew something from that. She gave an interview to a hack from a national, showed him Della's report cards and he was fair when he ran it, painted her as the rose that grew in weeds, mother a whore but daughter canonized. That was the first time Black saw Peach, her real smile, and it was beautiful.

"That guy ain't stopped by?" he said.

"Told you I'd call you, didn't I."

He nodded, making certain. There were times he wanted her to call, just so he could do something more than nothing for her.

"Those photos you gave me," he said. He'd sat with them and studied them while Milk looked on.

He took the photo out of the envelope he brought and held it to the light.

It was a clear shot, the face behind Della looking straight at the camera. There weren't no doubt it was Tommy Ryan.

"You know this guy?" Black said.

Peach stared at the photo, glanced at Black then back at the photo.

"How long?" Black said.

"Once, maybe. Long time back."

Black rubbed his eyes.

Peach reached a hand out and looked so sad he couldn't help but take it in his.

"He weren't with us that day. I ain't seen him in a long time."

"Was Della home that time he stopped by?"

She shrugged. "I guess."

"I know Tommy Ryan," he said. "He's got a reputation."

"He got a temper on him?"

"Yeah, but more a reputation with the ladies. He's popular."

"Ain't just the losers that pay for it, Black."

"I'm sorry, I didn't mean nothin' by that."

"I know."

He wondered if she did.

"I better get goin'," he said.

He saw the look again. "Thanks for supper."

"You didn't eat much."

He leaned forward and kissed her, keeping it brisk, but she held him after and wouldn't let go. He felt her spine, her ribs, like they were outside her skin. She was getting clean. Some kinda program they ran over at the Pinegrove Center, handing out prayers and methadone like they had equal worth.

She held him close. "You'll keep lookin' for Della won't you, Black?"

He nodded, eyes closed in case she saw it, that he was all she had and he pitied her for it.

Black took the Coyette way back, passing Gin Creek and the big houses along Route 29, by the state line. He opened the window and let night in. He passed the Green Acres Baptist Church on

84, heard they had some trouble a few months back, kids with spray cans. He pulled over.

His mind ran to the Ryan girls. He'd see them in the square when they were small, pretty dresses and holding their momma's hands, gussied up like they were headed to a party 'stead of the grueling run to Holman to visit their daddy. They'd be smiling, chatty, full of all things innocent and right. They'd arrive back at dusk, dresses wrinkled like their eyes.

He sighed and looked out the windshield and thought of all that Raine had said to him, all that hurt and anger in her eyes.

The church was white, lit up bright but quiet. He could see the faint outline of the Bird, sprayed on the wall, by the picket. Briar girl number four had gone to that church. He could see her face clear; brown hair that touched red and that shy kinda smile they all shared.

He got out and stood on the sidewalk awhile, then walked the curved path to the church.

The front was grand and pillared and stucco smooth. He walked along the side, past the arched windows ten feet high and stained yellow and red and green.

"Can I help you, Officer?"

Black turned. The girl was young but carried a godly confidence, like she'd smile at a perfect stranger and not worry about the return.

"I'm Chief Black, from over in Grace."

She reached out and spoke while he shook her hand gently. "Eliza McKissack, my daddy is the pastor here. We were just finishing up inside if you want to speak with him."

Black shook his head.

She looked down. "I thought maybe you were here about Coralee."

"I guess I was. I am. Not to speak with nobody, just to see the church. Did you know Coralee?"

They walked slow, she fell into step beside him. The church grounds were large and lit and tended.

"Yes, sir. She was in my class, and she came to church every week. I spoke to Sheriff Redell back then. You still haven't heard nothin'?"

Black shook his head. They stopped by a cedar, mighty and beautiful, its branches swaying gentle.

"We pray for her every week."

Black nodded.

"We were close. She was good, you know that? Not that the others weren't, but she was so sweet. Why'd he pick her?"

"I don't know."

"My momma said it's the devil's work. I hate when she talks like that. Makes it like there ain't no one to blame, just blanket evil, faceless, like that's somethin' real, somethin' we all have to live with. Why's he choosin' church girls?"

"I don't know." Black reached up, ran a hand over his badge and felt the shine coming off.

"But you're still lookin' for him?"

"Yes."

He glanced at the girl. She wore a dress that fell to her ankles.

"You reckon she's somewhere out there alive, Chief Black?"

He thought about lying, but her eyes, they were so wide he just smiled and she read the smile well 'cause she took it and nodded like she was disappointed in him.

They started toward the church.

"Me and my friends went over to Grace. We got as far as the dark wall. It's somethin' else."

"It is."

"I went back with my parents 'cause they didn't believe it. And then they saw it and Momma was cryin'. And I don't even know why. Daddy was quiet, and he was lookin' up and he said he didn't know where the sky began. The sky and the earth, Chief Black. That's our world. The sun and the stars. I worry that it's changin', since I was small it ain't the same. Are people gettin' crueler?"

"People have always been cruel," Black said.

"Daddy says we have to fight harder to keep principled. I see kids in my class dressin' black and listenin' to hard metal, but that time's passing us now, they don't even know what they're rebelling against."

Eliza walked him all the way back to the cruiser.

"You take care," she said. "Keep lookin' for my friend."

He got in and started the engine. She motioned for him to roll down the window.

"God's darkened Grace, Chief Black. It's important you realize that and you do somethin' about it. The clouds pour down their moisture, and abundant showers fall on mankind."

"Eliza, will you do somethin' for me?"

"Yes, sir."

"Stay away from church for a while. Just till we catch him," Black said.

She smiled. "I don't have a fearful heart, Chief Black. God will come with vengeance and divine retribution. You'll see. But I will pray for you."

"Thank you, Eliza."

She gave him a warm smile and was about to wave him off when she looked past him, at the photograph on the seat beside.

"Is that Della Palmer?" she said.

He passed it to her.

"You know that man behind?" he said.

She stared for a long time before she nodded slowly.

*

It didn't take long to find it. There was a bar on Dallas Court Road, a honky-tonk with sawdust floors, a dead neon sign, and Confederate flags tacked to the siding.

Raine had gone back to the Maidenville library, spent a couple minutes flirting with Henry, and found out all she could about Walden Lauder, the boy that'd dated Briar girl number three, Lissa Pinson. Walden was the Maidenville Academy's golden god, smart and good at football and good looking; a total prick was the way Henry told it. Henry told her about the bar too, the Bowery, served kids from Maidenville and Brookdale and Whiteport, didn't ask for proof so long as they paid over. Maybe Raine had been there once before, with Danny, but she'd been so lit it could just as well've been any shithole five towns wide.

"Sure you don't want us to come in?" Noah said. "I could flash the badge, watch those rich kids shit it when a lawman rolls –"

She got out while he was still talking.

It was hot and crowded; smoke blurred a lone man on a small stage playing bluegrass that just about cut above the talking and laughter. Raine wore cutoffs and boots and drew hungry stares from men her daddy's age.

She found him in the corner, a head taller than the group he was with, brown hair and golden skin just like the photo in the *Maidenville Herald*. There was a long line of empty bottles on the table. She moved slow, watching a couple hard-faced women dancing, asses jutting like bait as burly men gazed on.

When she was near she stood beneath purple light that fell from spots so low she felt the heat. Took him two songs before he caught her eye and smiled. He gestured her over but she just grinned and turned her back. He came to her a minute later.

"You're pretty," he said, cheeks red and hair matted, tongue thick with booze.

"I am," she said.

"Where you from? I haven't seen you here before. I'd remember you."

"Whiteport," she said.

He smiled. "Whiteport girls are fun."

She took his beer from him and drained it. He fetched another bottle from the table, made eyes at his friends like he was onto something good.

They sat in a shiny SUV in the lot, Raine straddling him, her tongue in his mouth, his hands on her ass. Music thumped heavy from the bar, light spilling as people came and went. He'd already told her shit he thought would impress her, something about his father's boat in Orange Beach. She'd made him order tequila, matched him till his legs wobbled then led him out.

She broke the kiss, pulled back a little, and was about to start working him when the door opened. She saw the badge first then sighed.

"Hands where I can see 'em."

"What the fuck . . ." Walden said as Noah and Purv climbed into the backseat.

Raine moved over to the passenger side.

"I'm lookin' for my sister," Raine said. She pulled the photo outta her bag.

Walden glanced at it quick. "I haven't seen her."

He made to get out but Raine took the gun from her bag.

"Jesus Christ," Walden said, sobering fast.

"Show him again," Noah said.

"She might've been lookin' for you," Raine said. "She might've been lookin' for Lissa Pinson."

Walden reached for the door again. Raine pressed the gun into his side.

"Fuck," he said. "You fucking crazy bitch."

"Shoot him," Noah said.

"All right."

"Shit . . . Jesus. I don't know anything. I took Lissa out a couple times, I already told the police. I don't know where she is. He took her, the Bird."

"Where'd you meet her?"

"Here." Walden watched the gun as he spoke. "I met her here."

"I need to find the Bird," Raine said.

"The cops can't find him, what chance have you got?"

"You said Whiteport girls are fun," Raine said. "What did you mean?"

He shook his head.

She slapped him hard across the cheek.

"Fuck," he said.

She aimed the gun high, pressing the barrel into his chest. He was sweating, eyes darting across the lot.

"Tell me. I'm just tryin' to find my sister. You tell me everything and I'll go. I won't say nothin' to no one else," Raine said.

He stared at her awhile. "Lissa was wild, not like they said in the newspapers. Church girl . . . she dragged me out back . . . against the fence, we did it against the fence. She told her friends, that's why the cops came to me." Walden's hands were shaking, his eyes red and sad. "I couldn't tell them that. My mother was sitting there. She would've found out. My father . . . I'm heading to college. I have a future."

"Ain't a big deal, you fucked some girl," Raine said. "So what?"

Walden looked through the windshield, at the heavy moon and the low stars. "Lissa came here, maybe a month later. Showed me the test . . . I wasn't buying it at first."

Noah listened silent.

"What test?" Purv said.

Walden just stared out.

"She was pregnant," Raine said, gripping the gun tighter. "Lissa Pinson was pregnant."

21

Summer

I lay awake each night thinkin' about Bobby. It's funny how it creeps up on you. Is there a difference between adoration and infatuation? If there is it can't be much.

I read *Lolita*. So Humbert was a monster and you ain't gotta have noble wings to see that. But it was Lo I dreamed of. Lo and Lola and Dolly, but never Dolores 'cause she was bare of all that was human. I thought about solipsism and the world around, and I wondered if an audience of one was the best I could ever hope for.

Bobby was a man, and me, I was just a girl.

I watched my sister work; the way she stood, hand on hip, head cocked, sweet smile and tousled hair. Her skirts were short but never showed too much, her tops were cut low but managed to hide her bra. She stirred feelings in her smile, tightened pants by the way she walked. It was effortless and exhausting.

There was a funeral at St. Luke's during the fall of 1994. I thought of the Briar girls 'cause by then there weren't no one not thinkin' of them. We sat down every night and saw Briar County on the news; reporters filling with rumor, interviewing kids who probably hadn't never spoke to the girls, talkin' to neighbors in blue overalls with slick hair standin' in front of single-wides. They cut to a man wearin' wire-rimmed glasses and he reckoned the Bird was a loner, maybe religious and maybe worked with his hands and maybe socially awkward. Daddy said maybe that man was full of shit.

The coffin was small, some old lady, maybe she weighed less than a child 'cause the bearers didn't break a sweat.

I watched them lower her, then I scattered petals like they wouldn't age and die too. I was a fixture; no one questioned why I showed at these things. Maybe I was lonely, that's what I heard when they spoke to me, some kinda soft pity I bathed in.

After it was done we sat by the cast-iron heater.

"You okay?"

"Thinkin' about the girls," I said.

"The paper you're writing?"

I hadn't written nothin' down. Savannah kept on askin'.

"I'm scared about it all."

"Be careful, Summer."

He took my hand and held it tight, fingers interlinked in that intimate way. Funerals looked like they robbed somethin' from Bobby.

"I think about that first girl most of all. Della. She's got the same birthday as me. Where do you reckon she is?"

"In heaven."

"That's all right, if she is. She's safe up there."

He brought my hand to his lips and breathed it warm.

"How come there's a man like the Bird out there? You reckon it's somethin' to do with the devil."

"We are each our own devil and we make this world our hell."

"He might've been lit when he wrote that."

Bobby smiled.

"I was reading that book, *Michelle Remembers*," I said.

"I'm not sure any of that is true."

"She believed it was."

"Or maybe she believed she could make a fast buck. Didn't she write it with her psychiatrist, and then marry him?"

"What those people did to her, evil is a spiritual being. I think about Della and what she might've gone through, at the end, if the end has come."

"Try not to think about that, Summer."

He pulled me close and hugged me tight. I wore a white hat, fluffy and pulled down over my ears.

When he touched me my heart beat too fast. I worried it'd break out my chest and drench him in my blood.

"Grace is beautiful in the fall," he said.

I wanted to climb on top of him, bite off his tongue and keep it for me so no one else could ever hear the sound of his voice again.

"What would you do if I got taken away like those Briar girls?" I said.

"I'd save you."

22

To Live Perfect

They got Tommy early, when Joe had run home to wash up and check in with Ava.

The men watched Milk as he strolled over, calm and slow, a cup of coffee in his hand.

Tommy was sitting on the middle bench, lacing his boots, an unlit cigarette hanging from his lips.

Each day brought the tension a little closer to the surface, the men a little more eager to act. Some hadn't worked steady in years. They were skilled in dying practice, a lifetime wasted watching their fathers haul timber and working up a proud sweat.

Now they picked up odd jobs in towns far from Grace. They'd ride a hundred miles to spend a day laboring, back breaking, but worth it for the feel on the drive back. They were focused on Summer, on helping Joe and holding a line against the cops, and maybe against the church 'cause their wives' prayers had gone unanswered for so long. That dead feeling that came when their purpose was snuffed out by faceless outfits with smiling shareholders was turning to something like anger. So they didn't grouse about sitting in darkness night and day, they were doing something, they were ready to move and fight.

"Mornin'," Milk said.

"Is it?" Tommy said.

"A couple miles out maybe."

He finished lacing his boots and stood. He was tall, not as broad as Joe but he had the height to look big and scary to a kid seeking monsters in Hell's Gate.

"Black wants a word."

"Joe's gone home for an hour. I'll send him over when he gets back."

"With you, not Joe."

Tommy glanced around, nodded at one of his boys, then took the cigarette from his mouth and slipped it behind his ear.

*

They sat on East Pine Road and watched the clinic. It was built into the trees, one story, and painted a shade like moss that saw it blend nice. The Dayette Women's Clinic. There weren't no signs, they'd had trouble since the day it opened. Raine remembered the news reports, the placards: WOMEN DO REGRET ABORTION; AMERICA'S SHAME; CHOOSE LIFE. The center was run by a lady name Cara Delaney. A few years back the news was hot with her 'cause she was prosecuted for helping desperate young girls the state said she had no business helping.

Raine rolled the window down. It was early but there were cars in the lot beside.

"So this is where he sent her," Noah said.

Raine nodded, her mind running to Lissa Pinson. Walden spilled all of it. He'd given Lissa five hundred bucks and driven her to Dayette himself. He said it cold and flat and she almost slapped his pretty face again.

"Wait here," Raine said.

"You want me to come in? We could pretend it's mine," Noah said.

"I ain't sure they'd believe that."

She opened the door and crossed the street, squinting against the morning light 'cause she weren't used to it no more. She carried her pack with her gun and her maps and she felt Noah's eyes on her as she walked up to the glass doors.

Inside it was cool with central air that pricked her skin. There was a line of plastic chairs facing an old television that rolled CNN without sound; just a talking head and a background of O. J. looking on as doctors and lawyers clashed.

Raine saw a girl sitting opposite. She was young and she kept her head down so her hair fell, eyes locked tight on a magazine. She shuffled her feet, rolling toe to heel and back like she was anxious, which weren't all that surprising.

An old lady came out and she was carrying a file. "Amber King?"

The nervous girl nodded and stood and followed her back.

"Can I help you?"

Raine turned and there was a lady with fire-red hair wearing a kind smile.

"I'm pregnant," Raine said.

*

"Raine said you're close with her and Summer. She said there ain't nothin' you wouldn't do for 'em," Black said.

Tommy softened at that, sank back a little in his seat, and finally took a sip of the coffee Trix had brought in.

"Yeah. That's about the size of it."

"You're closer with Raine though?"

"Not always, just when she started gettin' in shit. Summer's got a head on her, she can take care of herself."

"You see yourself in Raine?"

"She's got that Ryan fire, you know? And she's more into the woods, the huntin' and trackin'; she's got talent for it. But that don't mean I play favorites. Summer's a kid to be proud of. If I knew she was comin' to stay with Raine then I'd go the extra . . . maybe rent a movie she'd like or somethin'."

"You stepped up when Joe went to Holman."

Tommy shrugged like it weren't nothing but Black remembered well. Tommy taking the girls to Mae's every Sunday after church. They'd sit by the window, the girls sharing a sundae while Tommy watched them, a smile on his face.

Black heard Milk out front, on the telephone, maybe another call about the storm cloud.

"You ever met a lady named Peach Palmer?"

Something flickered in Tommy's eyes, some kinda realization, like he could see the snare.

"Could've."

Black slid the photograph over.

Tommy picked it up.

"That the Briar girl?"

Black nodded.

"You tryin' to blindside me, Black?" He stood quick, the chair fell back and clattered to the floor.

"I'm tryin' to find your niece. Bring her back safe. If I gotta upset you to do that then I ain't got no problem with that."

Tommy eyeballed him awhile.

"I can make this formal if you want, Tommy. Start recording. Lock you down while you wait on your lawyer to get over from Maidenville, charge you a couple hundred bucks just for the miles. I don't care either way."

Tommy picked up his chair and sat down again. "You gone tough again, Black?"

"It's what y'all want. I gave Joe my word, and Raine."

Tommy watched him awhile, maybe looking for a change but there weren't none, not outside. "You figure me for this? This shit with the Briar girls. Hell, Black, what the fuck would I be doin' sittin' outside a police station if I had shit to hide?"

"Peach Palmer?" Black showed him a photo of Peach, a file shot from a few years back when she'd got charged with possession.

"Maybe she looks familiar. Could be I took her out one time. I take out a lot of ladies."

"You got an alibi for the day Della went missin'?"

Tommy took a moment. "I was fishin' the Wheeler Lake for a few days, best spot below the Guntersville Dam. I caught it on the radio on the drive back."

"Anyone see you fishin'?"

"I went with Merle."

"And that is you with Della Palmer."

Tommy looked at the photo again. "I ain't with her. That's the rodeo at Red Oak Mountain. I go every year, ask round."

"How about the Green Acres Baptist Church, you ever been there?"

Tommy stared at Black and Black stared back.

"Well?" Black said.

"There's a lady there, lives off Route 80. I was seeing her, now I ain't."

"And she dragged you to church?"

"Not just church, down to Pinegrove where she volunteers."

"You did all that just for a lady?"

"Sucker for a pretty face."

"Write down her name and address."

"How desperate you gettin' here, Black? How worried should we be about Summer? I mean, I figured she'd show, that she'd fought with a boy or one of her friends, or maybe Ava was riding her too hard or somethin'. I thought that guy was done. The Bird."

Black handed him a pen and watched as he wrote.

After he was done with Tommy Ryan, Black found Deely White waiting in his office. Black sighed and sat heavy in his chair.

Deely sat across from him, fingers steepled across his gut like he was mulling something casual. He was old, red faced with white brows and a chin that weren't more than a puddle of fat.

"Let me guess . . . Pastor Lumen sent you to do his bidding," Black said, tired and in no kinda mood.

"You ain't to talk to the boy again, not unless you're bringing charges."

"He ain't a boy. He can speak for himself."

Deely closed his eyes like he was pained and Black was dumb. "The family have a lawyer, Milt Kroll –"

"I know Milt, he's older than the pastor. Tell him to come down, I'll talk with him."

"Well, he's on vacation, but his office –"

"More like he knows what's playin' with the Ryans and he don't want to touch it."

"The pastor was clear, ain't nobody to talk to the boy. You can't ask him nothin'."

"Why not, is he hidin' somethin'?"

The eyes closed again.

"Open your fuckin' eyes," Black said.

Deely startled.

Black raised a hand. "I'm busy, Deely. We got a missin' girl, that's all anyone should be worried about. If Samson ain't got nothin' to hide then I don't see the problem, do you?"

"I . . . I just –"

"You tell the old man I'll do what I like. Samson knows the deal, he said he don't want to talk to a lawyer. I got that on record now."

Deely stood with a face so red Black worried it'd burst. "You shouldn't think the pastor is weak, Black. That's a mistake."

Black sighed and watched him leave. He reached into his drawer and pulled out a bottle of Crown. He opened it, inhaled deep, then closed the cap and put it away.

*

"I can't take much more Disney," Noah said, frowning at the television set.

Purv hushed him. "Turn it up. I wanna see how this plays out. I get that she's a lady and all, but that tramp ain't taking no for an answer. Should've been fixed long ago, fuckin' mongrel."

Noah licked his lips then rubbed his eyes. He shifted in his seat, battling the urge to rip the tubes from his arm and walk away. He got like this now and again, felt the weight of his troubles so heavy on his lungs he couldn't squeeze a breath. He hated coming to Mayland. When he was younger they'd set up the machine at his house, showed his momma how to use it. It was loud though, so loud it ran into his dreams, twisting hot dreams where the machine keeping him alive turned into some kinda monster, locked onto him, claws in his veins.

"If the earth spun the other way then the rain forests would turn to deserts and the deserts to rain forests," Purv said.

"Fascinating," Noah said.

Noah glanced over at Missy and smiled but she just frowned 'cause he'd skipped another session. The hospital had written his grandmother but he'd tossed the letter in the trash.

"They brought in Tommy Ryan this mornin'," Noah said.

"Why?"

Noah shrugged. "Probably nothin'. Maybe they wanted to ask him some more about Summer. I tried to get near the room but Milk was hanging by the door."

"You gonna tell Raine?"

"No, don't seem worth tellin'."

"How'd it go at the clinic?" Purv said.

Noah shrugged 'cause Raine had been quiet on the drive back to Grace. "We're goin' back tonight."

"It's open at night?"

Noah shook his head and Purv sighed.

"You comin'?"

" 'Course. Y'all know how to pick a lock?"

They sat in the Buick till midnight, when the lot and the street were empty. Raine told them what had happened, how the lady with the fire-red hair had taken her to a room and asked her a bunch of questions while she sipped sweet tea.

Raine gave a fake name and a Haskell address. She asked if Raine had told her parents, asked her that three times, even asked if she'd told her friends 'cause she was worried Raine didn't have no support.

The lady's name was Dolores and she said she'd check the diary and give her a call, that she could come back and talk to somebody but by law they couldn't carry out the procedure without parental consent.

Raine didn't get a chance to look around 'cause she weren't left for a moment.

"We should take it to Black," Noah said. "What Walden told us, we should tell Black all of it."

"He'll sit on it, or kick it to Briar and they'll sit on it. Black don't want to see Summer linked, he's too drunk and too scared."

"I don't like this," Purv said as they got outta the car. "What if they got an alarm?"

"Then we'll have to move quick," Raine said.

They skirted to the back of the building, across the short grass. There was an American flag tangled in a tree branch, and maybe there was some words on it but they were too dark to make out.

Purv crouched by the door, slipped a thin wire from his pocket, and got to work on the lock.

Raine watched as the minutes ticked by. "Does he know what he's doin'?"

"Hush, baby girl," Noah said.

Raine shook her head, pained.

"I'll tell you a little somethin' about Purvis Bowdoin. When it comes to locks, the guy's a technician –"

They both jumped as Purv smashed the glass pane with a rock.

"What happened?" Noah said.

Purv shook his head and looked down. "Must be a foreign lock."

Noah put a hand on his shoulder. "Don't beat yourself up."

"Jesus," Raine said, frowning at them.

"No alarm," Noah said.

"Wait outside," Raine said.

"If we had the time I could dust for prints, see if Summer was here," Noah said. "Just need some talc and a little jojoba oil."

"MacGyver?" Purv said.

Noah nodded and they bumped fists.

Raine slipped through careful and crunched shards under her sneakers, Noah followed close behind. They moved along the hallway in darkness, checked three offices before they found the file cabinets. There was a bank of them, eight, wide and tall but they were in order. Raine switched on the flashlight.

"What are we lookin' for?" Noah said.

Raine pulled the paper from her pocket. "Briar girls. You look for Braymer and Hinds, I'll check for the others."

They searched fast, thumbing files. They didn't find the Briar girls.

They moved into another room and they saw a bed and a screen and trays of equipment. There were paintings on the wall of fall trees with orange leaves, and desert beaches more than a world away.

"This is where they bring the ladies," Raine said.

"Yeah," Noah said.

The smell was chemical and harsh.

"I see 'em on the news, those people that stood out front," she said.

"I remember."

"They got that look in their eyes, like they got God on their side, you know. Nobody knows what he'd say though ... not really. Sometimes I think about Mandy Deamer." Raine put her hand on the bed, on the cloth. "I used to think it was wild, that story. But imagine her, how desperate she must've been to take her own life. Surely that ain't right, feeling that way, or being made to."

"It's not," Noah said, his eyes on the painted sea, on the folding white waves.

"And Momma said Mandy had a head on her, that the Deamers was tough people. Mandy and her brother used to show at church . . . but everyone sins, right? Even those folk that lay judging. You can't live perfect, it ain't . . ." She looked through the slats at the shape of the night sky. "I ain't even sure what I'm sayin'. It's just sad is all."

When they were back in the Buick and driving up Highway 72 they saw a cruiser pass, lights flashing as it turned down Kenton Road toward the clinic.

"Shit," Purv said. "Must've had a silent alarm. Took their time though."

Raine followed the lights till they went to nothing. Her mind ran to David Gunn, the doctor that'd offered abortion services in the boondocks. He was shot dead 'cause pro-life was restricted to the unborn. "Probably the cops don't give a shit about the Dayette Women's Clinic."

*

Savannah crossed the hallway and watched Bobby sleep. He wore only shorts and she followed the contours of his chest as he breathed shallow breaths. He ran, there was a bench in the garage, he lifted weights so heavy the bar bent as it rose. It wasn't vanity that drove him.

They didn't sleep together, not since Michael. She missed sex, which was a truth that came hard in the wake of burying their only child. It was as much the physical act as the emotion that came with it, and that was a feeling far too indulgent to speak of.

She tried, sometimes she wore her hair up because he liked it that way, and she wore the French perfume, but she fell far short of brazen because she knew her husband. She still loved him, which was as troubling as it was comforting.

Her mother had called again. She'd made small talk awhile: the trip to Bermuda, the housekeeper that was stealing, and then she'd pressed hard. She told Savannah of the Patterson boy, of how he was going through a difficult divorce but how he was handsome and about to be made partner. Savannah had slammed the phone down.

She could still protect Bobby, to keep him from suffering further. Despite what was coming she could still right one wrong. And so she crept from the house and into the heavy night, and she walked toward Hell's Gate National Forest. For him, she told herself. This was for him now.

23

Summer

Sometimes I caught Savannah watchin' me play, and she'd get this look on her face like she'd seen God and she couldn't understand why he looked so fuckin' normal.

"Have you written that paper yet?" Bobby said.

"No."

"Savannah asked me to tell you to get on it."

"Why does she care so much?"

"You ever think maybe she sees what you don't?"

"Imagine me at that school. I'll be like some monkey using a tool. Heads will turn. *Come see the redneck girl play cello*. They'll listen so hard they'll reckon they hear my pain in every piece . . . echoes of my tainted life."

"You worry too much."

"It ain't worryin', Bobby."

"So what is it?"

I shrugged. "I'll die young. I won't have to make these decisions."

"That's not a good plan."

"People don't plan to die young, it just happens. Some people ain't made for this world."

"Oh."

"You reckon music can take you someplace else?" I said.

"Like to a fancy school in Maidenville?"

"No. I mean someplace you ain't never heard of. You just catch a ride on the notes and let 'em carry you away."

"Is that how you feel when you're playin'?"

"Maybe. Maybe that's how Savannah feels, when she closes her eyes, and when she opens them and they're full of tears. Maybe she went somewhere during my piece. Maybe during *Elgar* it's worse. The tears I mean."

I glanced over and Bobby looked so sad, like he'd gone to that same place.

"Are you okay? You and Savannah, are the both of you doin' all right?" I wanted him to tell me.

He rubbed his eyes. I put my hand on his shoulder.

I snatched it away when I saw Samson walk out of the office. He shot us a glance, looked away quick, then went out the main door.

"Marriage isn't easy."

"No."

"Two people and one union."

He put a hand on my knee.

I glanced at the sainted wall, at Madonna and her fat kid, rolls on his knees and ringlet hair. She's got a hand up to the saints like she's tryin' to stop them from doin' somethin' bad. They're saints though, they don't do nothin' bad.

I glanced down at his hand of glory so bold against my skin.

"Savannah is suffering," he said.

He squeezed my thigh gently.

I was calm; I'd learned to slow my breathin'. I counted in my head.

"Marriage ... the imbalance of rights and obligations. I watch them, the brides and the grooms, their faces and their unknowin' smiles as I join them together. Imagine if you could hold on to that."

I nodded and wondered if there was a difference between innocence and naivety.

"You're not supposed to hinder ... the children, they belong in the kingdom of heaven. I try to believe again. I do the Christian Youth thing. I drive out to the churches and talk to the teens. The Green Acres Baptists, the Mission, Valedale."

I swallowed.

He shook his head, like he was sad or mad. He inched his hand higher and glanced at the door. I never thought about kissin' him, or holdin' him, it went beyond touch and feel and feelin'. There's another level, below, so much of life piled on top I reckon most don't even know it exists.

"Does being a pastor mean I don't belong to me anymore?" he said.

I wanted to give the right answer, the one that wouldn't see him snatch his hand away.

There's a piece of music, Bach, his *Cello Suite No. 1*, there's a point at the end of the prelude where it climbs so high I know what death feels like, so acute and so delicate, that end to a life so ordinary it barely exists.

"I count days that are short and endless."

Another inch, under my skirt now. Then he stopped for a long while.

I reached for my book and held it up over my lap. *The Call of the Wild.* I thought of Buck and turnin' feral, and I thought maybe civility should've been on that list beside envy and pride.

"You ever wonder where life is being lived?" he said.

"Yeah."

Another inch. I held my breath till I saw light but no dark.

I stared at the pages. Words turn funny if you look at them long enough. Sticks and curves and dots.

"I don't want to be sorry. I see sorrow. I see it in the broke faces. They're so lost. They come to me thinkin' they're found again."

"You ain't got nothin' to be sorry for."

"What I did and what I'll do."

I held the book steady as he moved his hand across and rested it firm between my legs. I thought I was cool but I was hot. He had to feel it. My heart drummed loud enough to shake the walls of the old church. I saw it crumble and I saw it ruin, and I wondered about Augustine and hereditary guilt 'cause there was comfort in knowin' we'd burn before we even took breath.

"I think about never meetin' you," he said. "If I hadn't come to Grace. You find your own crossroads out there, or it finds you."

"I don't want to be sad," I said, my throat so dry.

"The lows make the highs."

"So it's important to make the highs count."

The lightest rub. I could've died. That edge I'd always been scared of, that edge where my sister lived her life.

"We're supposed to set our minds on things above."

"That means there's no one watchin' below."

Back and forth and light and strong. The book was shakin', I did my best to grip it tight.

"Stone and wood. Sometimes that's all this is. This place. Human hands sculpting somethin'. What do you see?"

He didn't know how hard it was to form words. "I see stone and wood and nothin' more."

The book hid me, when I felt my underwear slide and when I felt his skin against mine, I kept it in place. He traced a path across light hair, gently feelin' around, like he was lost.

"I see life in differing shades of sunken color. There's no red or yellow. Maybe there was before but before has happened. Sometimes I wish I was dead but I know it will come."

I dipped the book as he found me.

I swallowed a cry. I tried not to move but couldn't.

He didn't stop, just kept the same stroke over and over, like he didn't know that he was killin' all that went before.

"It is beautiful though, the stone and wood. Whatever they meant, whoever they built it for, they achieved somethin' in a world of nothin'."

"Bobby," I said, breathless.

I didn't know why I was sayin' his name.

"They made a thing of beauty."

He pushed.

"Bobby."

I looked at Abraham and the three angels, and I saw Sarah laughin' 'cause she don't believe it's real.

"Bobby," I couldn't barely speak.

I tipped over. I leaned into him, stifling a cry in his shoulder. He didn't stop. I shook, my whole body from my toes to my halo.

"So beautiful I can't even bear it sometimes."

24

Church Street Blues

Black rolled the cruiser through white ranch gates that hinted at something grander than the beat-down building at the top of the drive. There weren't no one in sight but the flag flew high in afternoon sun as he parked beside a short line of cars.

The Pinegrove Center relied on state handouts and donations from churches across Briar County. It was the place Peach came sometimes. She flirted with sobriety, let it think she was interested then flipped it off in a haze so thick she lost days.

Black pushed the heavy door and felt stale air rush out. There weren't no one at the front desk so he strolled the hallway. The doors were closed, signs tacked on each ready for meetings of different kinds. Sometimes Peach asked him to go with her but the thought of strangers baring their souls like that made him want to drink.

He found Greta Gray out back, sitting beneath a tall tree catching a smoke and watching the light clouds.

She stood when he came, smiled the kinda smile that'd floor a man.

They made small talk awhile, she lived in a house off Route 80, had a sick father, and worked two jobs to try and keep up with the bills.

"Tommy fed me lines," she said, more amused than bitter. "I seen his kind, all that talk so smooth he must've reckoned I was dumb."

Black smiled.

"He's nice lookin' and all, but I reckoned I played him right. He took me to dinner, I brought him here. He took me to the movies, I made him come to Green Acres with me. It weren't a test so much . . . or maybe it was. There's another side to him, softer and kind, maybe I wanted to see where it'd go."

She stubbed out her cigarette and licked pillow lips.

"But you tired of him."

She looked at him with eyes too blue, like they'd been painted on. "Other way round. I reckoned maybe he was tirin' 'cause I didn't invite him to my bed or nothin'."

"He weren't?"

She shrugged. "He turned up here a couple times after we was done."

"To see you?"

She shook her head. "Days he knew I weren't working."

"Why?"

She smiled a little. "Maybe 'cause he ain't like you think. He saw the work we was doin', the people we help. It got to him; he wanted to make a difference too. So it was worth it, our time together. I took that from it and that's worth somethin'."

Black reckoned he knew Tommy better but didn't say nothing 'cause Greta spoke so warm.

"You had trouble here a few years back," Black said.

"We did. He's gone now and we've moved from it."

The *he* she spoke about was Ken Kelly. Ken led the New Christian Governance and Pinegrove became an outlet for some of his miracle men to heal and cleanse in exchange for eye-watering donations. Talk of embezzlement led to an FBI investigation and last Black heard Ken was looking at a long and broken fall from favor.

" 'Course we struggle for funding, but now I leave work with a clear mind. We look beyond religion, we help anyone who needs us. We have doctors visit every Tuesday, that's when we're busiest."

Black nodded, and then he stood when she did and they began to walk back toward the building.

"Do you have records?" he said.

"Yeah, but you're wasting your time. Tommy ain't your Bird, Chief Black."

He followed her into the hallway, into a room with a desk, a file cabinet, and a jar filled with plastic sunflowers.

She pulled open a drawer and took out a stack of guest books.

"We make people sign in. Most of 'em give fake names but it's somethin' over nothin'."

Black sat at the desk and began flipping pages and checking names. He found Tommy Ryan five times, consecutive weekends.

"Got what you need?" she said.

He sighed like he'd lost something, then he stood, but not before he caught another name, at the bottom of the page, in delicate scrawl. Samson Lumen.

*

Noah and Raine and Purv sat fifty yards from the house, which stood lone on a slip of road that ran from Route 45 through a splinter of trees toward the limit of Briar County.

There was a wire fence that ran far in either direction, the barbs on it rusty and sharp, and a hand-painted sign that read KEEP OUT in blood lettering.

The file listed his name as James Quintell Mayors but he went by "Popp." Popp had the kinda rap sheet that made Raine wonder why they didn't just put him down. He'd spent thirty of his sixty-five years in the St. Clair Correctional Facility. Popp liked them young.

"I ain't sure how to play this one," Raine said.

"Ain't no playin'," Purv said, reading the file in the backseat. "We don't go in there 'cause there ain't a way in."

Raine glanced in the mirror and saw Purv's hands shaking as he gripped the papers.

"Get closer," she said, and Purv went to say something but didn't.

The Buick coasted, the windows down and the heat up. There was a truck and a van parked by the house, both tired with flats and cracked windshields.

She could see television light in the window and liquor bottles lined up on the porch.

"I need to go in," Raine said. "Same as before, leave the Buick doors open and we run if there's a hint of trouble."

" 'Cause that worked so well last time," Purv said, climbing out.

Raine brought her bag, which had the gun inside, and she held the hunting knife too 'cause she didn't know if Purv or Noah would have what was needed. Maybe Noah was brave, but sticking someone, shooting someone, it was something altogether different.

She led them; she kept low and ran the line of the tangled weeds and the long grass. The wire was trodden down to knee height in a couple spots and she climbed over then turned back and helped Noah and Purv.

They were used to the dark now, to moving under moonlight and treading cautious. They stayed with the trees till there weren't nothing but open space between them and the house. Raine could see it better now, the porch and the bottles and garbage. She could smell something bad, like rotting meat.

They ran across open land and passed a dug trench filled with trash bags. When they got to the house they stuck close to the wall.

Raine could hear music, and Purv breathing close behind her. She was sweating, her hair streaked dark. She moved slow and pressed her face to the glass but couldn't see shit 'cause it was thick with a haze of dirt.

Raine glanced back at Purv and mouthed at him to keep watch as she handed him the hunting knife.

She walked up the steps to the rear porch, Noah beside, and as he reached for the screen door she pulled the gun from her bag and flipped the safety off.

The house was dark and the smell was bad. Raine looked around for signs of her sister but couldn't see nothing beyond the mess. They moved along the hallway, ducked their heads into both bedrooms and saw they were mostly empty 'cept for stained mattresses on the floor.

The music was loud, *Church Street Blues*, so loud she felt every note rattle her. They saw a shadow moving and she pulled Noah quick into the bathroom, the window was boarded and the smell so thick they couldn't barely breathe.

She reached into her bag and pulled out the flashlight and when she switched it on she couldn't do nothing but scream.

The sink was blocked and filled with blood and meat. Noah stared at her wild-eyed as they listened. Her chest rose and fell. She gripped the gun so tight.

Noah flicked his head in the direction of the bathtub and she saw a buck, slit open and laying there. She breathed hard and felt the sweat rolling from her.

She didn't know how loud she'd screamed, if it'd made it above the music, so they moved fast into the living room but there weren't no one there.

And then the song died and they heard it. Yelling.

"Purv," Noah said, grabbing her arm.

"We ain't checked the last room," Raine said, shrugging him off.

Noah grabbed her hard and pushed her out the front door. And then Purv was hollering at them to run, and he was beside them still clutching the hunting knife. They made for the trees, their legs blurring and chests burning. Purv stumbled when the first shot rang out and Noah pulled him to his feet. Noah caught his arm on the wire then wrenched his shirt free.

Raine turned and fired once into the black and she hoped she'd hit Popp right between the eyes 'cause all that shit she'd seen in the file kept the rage hot in her mind.

When they got to the Buick, Noah fumbled for the keys. Raine watched the house and yelled when she saw the truck lights as it pulled outta the woodland beside. She rolled the window and kept the gun trained out.

Purv ducked low on the backseat, the rear door wide open behind him.

"He's comin'," she said. "Close the fuckin' door, Purv."

Purv was lost, fingers in his ears and eyes shut tight.

The truck barrelled down and she squeezed the trigger again and again. Maybe she heard Purv crying out, and maybe she saw him shaking, but then Noah fired the engine and he crunched the Buick into gear and turned the wheel just as the truck veered into them. The Buick door came clean off and they watched it spark and drag along the road beneath the fender of the truck.

"*Go*," Raine yelled. She released the clip and fumbled in her bag for more bullets.

Noah hit the gas and they heard the tires scream for grip.

He turned down tight lanes and wove a path through the wilds he reckoned nobody could follow.

*

Black watched Samson as he shifted in his seat. He weren't eating, no matter what they brought back from Mae's.

Milk stuck his head in. "You need me?"

"No, we're just talking."

"I'll head home, get some sleep."

Black nodded.

Everyone was pulling long shifts; it was taking its toll. They talked at length about what could be done, maybe posting men at Samson's place or keeping a tail on Joe, but neither gave surety like holding on to him. He was free to leave, but Black couldn't protect him if he did.

"I ain't been sleepin'," Samson said.

"You'll get home soon enough. It's just till things cool and Summer Ryan shows up again."

"I know."

Black wondered how much he understood.

"I was lyin' awake last night, and I was thinkin' about Summer."

"What about her?" Black said.

"I was thinkin' of all those people out lookin'. That means they care, right? She's got people who love her. And I was thinkin' maybe they shouldn't be worried 'cause we ain't never really lost, not if you believe. God has a plan, you believe that, Black?"

"Sure, Samson."

"You remember being a teenager, Black?"

"Yeah."

"What was it like for you?"

"I was a quiet kid, weren't smart enough or dumb enough to be anything but."

"Did you always want to be a policeman?"

"I grew up with Mitch Wild, you remember him?"

Samson nodded.

"We were close like brothers . . . and he wanted to be a cop 'cause his daddy was a cop. So I went with him, we trained together and worked Briar. He got married and I got married and we settled in Grace and that was life and it was all right."

"Sounds nice," Samson said.

Black nodded. "He would've been Chief, no doubt. He was a tough cop."

Samson sipped water.

"How about you?" Black said.

"I was quiet too. I mean, I still am."

Black waited for him to go on.

"I used to reckon maybe I was blessed . . . the way I look. I know people call me the Angel 'cause my momma said that, but she only said it so they wouldn't get on me. But I'm scared, Black. The Lord won't fight for me. I'm not like them, my daddy, the others."

"I went to Pinegrove, Samson."

Black saw his hands tremble. He couldn't figure what Samson had been doing there 'cause Greta Gray wouldn't say shit and he respected that. He was fishing now.

Samson brought a hand up and held it flat against his forehead, then he started shaking real bad.

"I thought they could help me."

Samson cried. Black watched him.

"They couldn't help, not really. Don't matter what they say, those things they did, hands and cleansin'."

Samson cried and cried, and he bent forward and he coughed and retched. Black hadn't ever seen fear so pure and so consuming.

"It's all right, Samson –"

"It ain't. What I did, Black, it ain't never gonna be right again. There ain't a way back, I'm so scared."

"What, Samson? What did you do?"

They heard a noise. They saw the door open and then Deely White standing there, and Trix beside, cheeks hot like she was mad.

An hour later Samson retained Milt Kroll and Black's hopes of finding the truth died a quick and painful death. Milt called them and agreed it was safest for Samson to stay put, but in the meantime his office would ramp the pressure on Black and Ernie Redell to bring this mess to a close.

*

Noah pulled the Buick over 'cause he couldn't slow his breath and was still seeing spots.

They got out and the three stood and looked at the damage to the car.

"Shit," Raine said. Then she turned to Noah. "What the fuck were you doin' back there? There was another room."

"He was on us. He had a gun," Noah said, still struggling for breath. He was pale and dizzy so Purv came over and put a hand on his shoulder. He got like this sometimes, his blood pressure dipping too low.

"You okay?" Purv said.

"Just need a minute," Noah said.

Raine stared at him and shook her head. "You shouldn't have pulled me outta there. I can take care of myself. Summer could've been in there, we don't know. She could've been hurt. I got the gun, I ain't scared to shoot."

"There weren't nothin' in that room. I saw through the window," Purv said.

Noah straightened up and wobbled once but Purv kept a hand on him.

"I didn't want nothin' to happen to you," Noah said quiet.

"Why the fuck do you even care, Noah? Is it 'cause of the way I look? You wanna fuck me? Is that it?" She walked toward him till she stood so close she could smell that cheap cologne he wore.

He looked down and shook his head. "I just like you . . . and I wanna be a cop . . . I'm helpin' Black."

She laughed. "You're a fuckin' joke, carryin' that badge. I don't get it with you, why you're so fuckin' weird like that. Maybe you reckon it's real or somethin'. I see you sittin' in the station, not doin' nothin', just watchin' the cops." She wiped sweat from her head and spit in the dirt. "I gotta go to Black now, give him somethin', sell my sister out. I thought you could help me, 'cause you got the file for me, but that's it now. You hold me up. I could walk the trails fast but you hold me back 'cause you're slow. And look at you now, bit of trouble and you go to pieces. Too fuckin' scared."

"He ain't scared," Purv said. "He's –"

"Shut up, Purv," Noah said.

She might've pressed him but they heard the noise start up sudden and loud. A voice that soared.

They climbed the bank and stared out across the fields. Noah and Purv fell in behind her as she walked toward the lights.

They reckoned they were someplace east of Haskell, maybe ten miles from White Mountain. The group was fifty deep but they stayed far enough back 'cause they weren't exactly sure what was going on.

There was a wood stage, just ply strips and paint cans propping them. The pastor was hard faced but showy. Raine could tell by his voice and the way he swept it high with the cries that he knew how to work them.

"It's the Mission," Noah said.

Raine nodded. The West End Mission, they were hard-liners; a whisker short of fanatical, they set up where they could after their church burned, just after Della Palmer got taken.

There were others like them, by White Mountain, folk that preached to their own God in their own way. The kids at school used to talk about a lot near Cold Leaf Creek where they had a healer, the proper kind that'd spit and froth and shake before he brought out the snakes.

"He's talking about Grace," Purv said.

They heard mention of the cloud and dissension and idolatry, and the folk nodded and hollered.

"If your right eye causes you to sin, tear it out and throw it away. For it is better that you lose one of your members than that your whole body be thrown into hell."

"I could see these folk tearing out their eyes," Purv said.

Noah nodded.

They were about to turn when Raine saw her. She moved nearer and heard Noah calling but she had to see.

"Who is it?" Purv said.

Raine lost sight of her before the group cleared. And then there she was, fire-red hair and hands clasped and eyes clenched tight in prayer.

"The lady from the Dayette Women's Clinic."

25

Summer

"You don't talk much," I said.

Samson smiled and kinda looked embarrassed. He held the umbrella in one hand and my cello case in the other.

We walked slow. We passed cars drivin' careful as their wipers swept and their wheels sprayed an arc of the fall toward us.

Up close Samson had the pinkest lips I ever saw. He helped Bobby out, he was at St. Luke's almost as much as me 'cept Samson had purer purpose. He tended the building like he does at school, and he looked at Bobby with somethin' like awe in his eyes.

"Rainin' cats and dogs," I said, and he smiled again.

I led him the Beeson way so we could cut through to the Red. I liked watchin' the Red when it was rainin', seein' it rise up like it'd burst.

Grace hadn't felt right since Coralee Simmons got taken. The streets had an edge to them I can't really explain, maybe like we were just waitin' on our turn and glancin' at each other and wonderin' who it was gonna be. Daddy had a talk with us about not goin' to church till the Bird was caught and I nodded like I was listenin' but my mind was on Bobby. I sat out again and watched Savannah as she took that same route toward Hell's Gate but there weren't no way I was gonna follow her in there. I pictured her runnin' the trails with a flashlight, her heart poundin' out while she taunted the devil. That veneer so perfect she was desperate to crack it.

"You like to read, Sam?" I said.

"No one ever called me Sam," he said, kinda smiling again. "I ain't never really read a book."

"I sit by the window and read and drink tea and Momma says she ain't even sure I'm her daughter."

We cut into the woods. The rain died with the trees holdin' it from us and I could hear the creaks and groans and the snaps under our feet.

"Is it hard being so white?" I said, and it sounded funny and Samson started laughin'.

"Sometimes it is . . . lookin' like this."

"I like it, your hair, it's nice."

He blushed.

We stood on the edge of the woods and watched the rain land and I told Samson how I wished it'd flood Grace. He made a joke about an ark and I thought of Noah, who's a kid in my school and he's on dialysis 'cause his body don't work right. I wondered about evolution and independence, if people like the Bird were just angels in a different guise, sent down to dent the numbers and hold the fear. Two birds and one stone and a whole lot of ripples. God's work can't always be clean 'cause he knows better than anyone about the science of suffering. Lessons learned and forgot.

"How's your daddy doin'?" I said.

"He don't say much to me . . . I mean about his sickness, he don't tell me. We have nurses stop by, but sometimes I have to help, lift him out the tub and all. He gets mad at me, he yells a lot."

"Maybe 'cause he's embarrassed."

Samson nodded but I knew, everyone knew about the pastor. He was mean and crazy and folk were shit scared of him. He'd look at me like I was somethin' bad, even though I was at the church more than the other kids.

"It's good that you go to church, Summer. Most of the kids only go 'cause their parents drag 'em."

"I always liked St. Luke's. When I was small I'd stare at the colored glass, the pink that falls. It's so pretty."

"It's nice talking to you, Summer."

I smiled. "It's decent of you to walk me back."

I took my cello from him. It weren't really mine but Savannah had a couple and said I could keep one so I could practice at home and school.

"Summer," he said.

I turned.

"You're nice. The other girls ain't, but you're nice."

"You're nice too, Sam."

I felt him watchin' me as I walked away.

I asked Momma to tie my hair up pretty. I walked the even mile to Bobby's place just before sunset. I like that time, that perfect hour when orange day turns to blue night, when you glimpse the first lightnin' bug and crickets drown the birds.

I played Debussy but felt far from innocent and far from naive. I reckon innocence is overrated, we've all fallen short, it's what he expects and I weren't gonna disappoint.

Savannah clapped once when I was done.

"What color is flaxen anyhow?" I said, layin' the bow down.

"The same color as your hair," Savannah said.

Sometimes she didn't speak for the longest time. At first I thought it was some kinda test, like maybe I was supposed to hear somethin' in the acres of silence.

"You want me to play it again?"

"No. Not yet."

I looked over to the corner of the room. "What's that?"

She followed my eye. "A lute."

"Who busted the end?"

She smiled. "It's supposed to be like that."

"Yeah?"

She nodded.

"I think I saw one. Maybe it was in a painting, Orpheus or somethin'. That sound right?"

She cocked her head a little. "Yes, that sounds right. There's a play I like, *The Honest Whore* . . . the heroine is a lutenist."

"*The Honest Whore*, is it blue?"

She laughed. She's got the kinda laugh that's on reins, like laughin' 'cause it's needed but ain't wanted.

"No, it's not blue."

"What's it about?"

"A lady named Viola, she's married to Candido. He's mild-mannered, and it bothers Viola, so she comes up with ways to provoke him, to see his temper lost."

"She wants to piss him off on purpose?"

"Yes, basically. It's humorous."

"How does she do it?"

"Various ways. She gets her brother to help."

"Does it work?"

"Candido doesn't lose his temper, but he ends up being incarcerated as people think he's mad."

"So she's happy about that?"

"Devastated, actually."

I looked at the lute again, at the polished wood and the golden strings and how much it said about Savannah and the distance between us.

"She wouldn't have done that if she was married to my daddy. But maybe my uncle Tommy, 'cause he don't care enough to get riled."

Savannah laughed again, like she knew him and she knew us.

"Have you finished your paper yet?"

"You reckon the other kids won't like me 'cause I'm a Grace girl?"

She reached forward and took my hand. "I think you're strong, Summer."

I kept glancin' at the door.

"Bobby's not home," she said.

I got it then, that she knew somethin'. I was thinkin' maybe she reckoned I had a crush on him, like all the girls in Grace did. That was all right if she thought that. Maybe she thought it was sweet, that I doted on the golden pastor, maybe I drew hearts in my schoolbooks and stuck his initials inside. Maybe I dreamed of marryin' him, virgin in white walkin' the aisle in St. Luke's.

She cried then. It was so sudden I didn't know what to do. So I sat there and watched, and then I told her I needed the bathroom and she told me she was sorry.

They had a grandfather clock as tall as me. It was dark wood and glass and ticked so loud I reckoned they could hear it from their bedroom.

Their bedroom. I pushed the door open, soft light and cream carpet, neat and ordered and glossy. I looked at the bed. They had five throw pillows on it. The sheets were cool, maybe silk or something like it.

I walked over to the dresser. I opened the middle drawer, smelled somethin' floral and spiced. I pulled out one of her bras; it was lace and fancy and made me feel like a child.

There was a bottle of perfume. It was French and I took it and put it in my bag.

That night when I lay in bed I held it to my nose and closed my eyes. I reached down there and moved between lives.

26

Perfumed Girls

There was a backwater behind the church, a mirror of rippled sky that twisted and wound miles through woodland till it met with the Red somewhere near the county line.

The church was burned till just a skeleton of the building remained.

The West End Mission.

It was Della Palmer's church, 'cause if you cut through the pines it was only ten minutes to Standing Oak.

They'd had trouble after, when someone decorated it with a pile of dead squirrels and a large pentagram. Rumor was their own pastor lit the match, maybe 'cause he wanted to see if it would burn and not consume. The Mission took a hard line; their faith was unflinching.

A year back, when the case was red hot, Black had been called to a party that got outta hand at a rental near Brookdale. They'd got there and found the usual; high school kids getting lit and getting high, music loud. But then he'd gone round the back and seen the girls, three of them, scared white. They were pointing in the direction of the woods. Black had called for backup, gone in with Milk, locked and aiming. They'd nearly blown the kid's head off. A jock, big and dumb, as was the custom. He'd made the feathered suit himself, thought it'd be funny to scare his girlfriend.

That was the first of the hoaxes.

The newspapers had been first to speak of the devil. There weren't no grounds for it. Folk lapped it up, what with the Panic looking for kindling. Some idiot at the *Briar County News* cooked up a cover sketch of Baphomet with feathers, said they sold out in every town so ran it again week after week till it was burned in the minds of every kid in the area. It kept them outta Hell's Gate, though into Ouija boards and other nonsense that freaked them out enough to call in every weekend.

Black walked over to the church and ran his hand along a piece of charred timber twenty foot long.

"You lookin' for a rabbit at the altar? Or was it a parakeet?" Milk said.

"It was bullshit, that's what it was."

Black looked down and saw a BOWDOIN CONSTRUCTION sign in the dirt.

"Don't look like Ray's done nothin' at all," Milk said.

Pastor Roberts had made the complaint. He reckoned the church had paid Ray Bowdoin five grand to begin clearing the site ready to rebuild it. Ray had taken the cash months back. Hadn't done shit yet.

"You still friendly with the mother? That girl that came here, I forget her name."

"Peach Palmer," Black said. "Her name's Peach Palmer and her daughter's name is Della."

"Della was the first," Milk said, his tone softening.

"Yeah."

Black rubbed his eyes.

"They made the link already. Connected dots that ain't there."

Milk was talking about the hacks. The Bird was back, God sent the cloud 'cause the devil was at work in Hell's Gate.

"So now we're back chasin' shadows," Milk said.

"This guy ain't even got a shadow."

"There's somethin' we're missin'."

"Maybe. We're tryin' to see what others couldn't. But maybe there ain't nothin' out there."

Milk glanced at him.

"Could be some guy, no record, just started up and can't stop. The only hope we got is that he makes a mistake. But how many girls go before he does that?"

Black sighed.

"How about Tommy Ryan? Anything on that?" Milk said.

"I found the lady he was seeing, Greta Gray, she confirmed it. Dates line up too, she dragged him to Pinegrove, then he dropped her cold."

"Tommy Ryan goin' to church and volunteerin' at Pinegrove. What did she look like?"

"The kinda lady worth findin' God for."

Milk laughed.

"Funny thing was he visited the place a couple times after he'd canned her, when he knew she weren't workin'."

"Jesus," Milk said. "Tommy Ryan helpin' others, what's the world comin' to?"

They were about to get in the cruiser when they heard a car pull up. The track was deep so they couldn't make out who it was. They walked the leaves till they reached the clearing and Chason Road and they saw an old Taurus, wheels in the hard mud, engine running but no one inside.

Black glanced around, and then he saw her. She was coming outta the trees, young-looking redhead with tired eyes and a sweep of freckles across her nose.

She was startled when she glanced up, took a step back and nearly tumbled.

"Sorry, didn't mean to scare you," Milk said.

She licked her lips like they were dry. "I don't see nobody out here, that's all."

"You part of the Mission?"

"Yes," she said, glancing about like they weren't alone. "The mail . . . I collect the mail, some of the folk in White Mountain still send letters to this address. It's overgrown now, I have to wade through just to find the box."

"Where you guys at now?"

"Wherever Pastor Roberts can get, sometimes the hall in Ayling, sometimes in the fields. Don't matter, God hears us wherever."

"Right," Milk said, throwing a glance at Black.

"You here about the money? We raised funds, all we got we gave to that Grace man," she said.

"We'll talk to Ray Bowdoin," Milk said.

She nodded, began to walk, and then turned. "We pray for Della, all of us, every day we pray for her."

They watched her drive away and they walked slow back up the track toward the cruiser and the burned church.

"All these people prayin' for these girls," Milk said. "I really hope there's someone listenin'."

*

It was a little before midnight when Joe Ryan walked into the police station and asked to speak to Black. It weren't the way anyone thought he'd come—alone and through the front door.

Black appeared quick with Milk behind him.

Black ushered Joe into the back room while Milk locked the door and kept an eye on the four trucks sitting out front. The square was calm and sleeping but Milk knew how quick it could turn.

Joe sat, Black offered him something to drink but Joe waved him off.

"I heard Samson lawyered up," Joe said.

Black recounted Samson's version of events and didn't leave nothing out, even offered to let him listen to the tape just to prove he was showing his hand early and honest.

"You believe him?" Joe said.

"At the moment I ain't got reason not to."

Joe sighed, rubbed the muscles in his neck, and closed his eyes. His arms were big; his hands were scarred across each knuckle. The beard was thickening as each day passed.

"So I'm just supposed to leave it at that? Take your word, take his –"

"Ernie is sendin' someone over first thing in the mornin'. We'll go over to the Lumen house and search every inch; if Summer was there we'll know about it. To be honest it ain't much of a reason to search the place. We got so little, Joe."

"I appreciate you being straight with me."

"I appreciate you not comin' in heavy."

"There's still time."

"I know."

Black tried to put himself in Joe's shoes, found it weren't a nice place to be. Black's girls had been small when his wife took them. He'd tried to write them a couple times; RETURN TO SENDER was all that came back. He tried to imagine what it was like raising teen girls. A fuckin' nightmare was the way he saw it.

"How's Ava holdin' up?"

Joe looked down at his hands, fiddled with his wedding band, spinning it back and forth. "Ava's just about the strongest woman I ever met, but she's startin' to lose herself now. She was all right the first days . . . but it's so dark, this storm comin', and Summer being out there alone. The newspapers gettin' ready, talk of the Bird again. We're still searchin', do it in shifts so we can keep people here and watchin'.

"I remember when we found out it was twins, I was thinkin' maybe we'd get one of each, or maybe two boys, I could take 'em to ball games, take 'em fishin'. I didn't even think about two girls, I ain't even sure why." He cleared his throat. "I fucked up bad, missed out on more than you can imagine."

"Holman is a rough place."

Joe shrugged. "I ain't never been scared, not even when I was small, fear . . . it ain't somethin' I remember. But when I knew I'd miss it, first steps and first words . . . that smell, their hair when they'd come visit. I'd sit there, one on each knee."

Black smiled.

"They held hands all the time, you remember that?" Joe said. "When I got out Ava made that party, but I stayed outside awhile, just lookin' in, watchin' my girls holdin' hands, nervous faces 'cause they thought I weren't gonna show."

"You've changed a lot, Joe."

"I ain't, not really. It's all right though, doin' a job I hate, Ava pickin' up extra shifts, scrapin' to get by. They made it all right. Raine blames you, you know that?"

"I know that."

"Tell me this ain't linked to the Briar girls. Tell me this guy ain't got my girl."

Black looked down at the table between them.

"Five girls . . . the church, is that somethin' to do with it? All this talk about rituals and shit. Devil worship. When I was inside Ava was mad with it, the Panic, keepin' the girls safe from somethin' that maybe ain't even real."

"There's nothin' that says Summer's been taken. The Briar girls, they didn't pack bags. They weren't runnin'."

Joe nodded, his eyes heavy. "Could you have got him, that day, the Bird? Way people tell it . . ."

Black dropped his head a little. "Rumor ain't fact."

Joe nodded like he could see through.

"Can I ask you some more about Summer? I been tryin' to build a picture, I spoke with some of her teachers."

"You see her play at St. Luke's that time?"

Black nodded. He'd been there, it was a day no one would forget.

"I saw her that day. Really saw her."

"How?"

"Before it was talk, you know, just numbers and words, shit I'd never get. But watchin' her play, even though I ain't exactly sure what it was she was playin', that was beautiful. There were people cryin', not just those old coots you got that sit up front and cry every Sunday. I saw Dale Crashaw cryin', and Dale's mean as they come. So that's when I saw just how special my little girl is."

They heard noise outside. Black got to his feet quick, looked at Joe and fixed him with an even gaze. Joe stood and followed him out.

Milk was standing still, a hand on his gun but he hadn't drawn. He saw Tommy Ryan by the door.

"What's up?" Black said.

"I told Tommy to stay put, this ain't on us," Joe said.

"He's hammerin' on the door, said he needs to come in," Milk said.

"Let him in then," Joe said.

"Where's Samson?" Black said.

Milk nodded toward the back. "Safe."

"He ain't come for Samson. You reckon if we wanted Samson I would've walked in like this?"

Tommy banged the door again, getting pissed off now.

Black walked over quick and unlocked the door. Milk drew his gun and trained it in front.

Black half expected to get rushed, but then Tommy stepped aside and Raine was standing there, looking small beneath the station lights.

"What's goin' on?" Joe said.

Raine spoke. "There's somethin' I gotta tell you."

Raine sat opposite Black, with Joe standing by the far wall.

Milk was outside, at the top of the steps that led down to Samson.

"Summer had a boyfriend."

Black smiled and tried not to see Joe flinch.

"Well, I ain't exactly sure if he was her boyfriend but there was somebody she liked."

"That's okay, it's important we know this, Raine."

"She made me promise . . . I ain't sellin' her out. It's been long is all, so I'm gettin' worried. I thought maybe I could find her myself, but that ain't workin' out –"

"Don't matter that you didn't say. You were being loyal to your sister, ain't nobody that'd blame you for that," Black said.

Black poured her a glass of water. "Got anything stronger?" she said, and Joe shot her a look.

"She was nervous about askin' me," Raine said.

"What'd she ask you?"

"How to do shit."

Joe stared on, his gaze hard to read, his shoulders low and his hands jammed into his pockets. Raine twisted the ring she wore, the ring with the blue stone. Summer wore a matching one.

"How to do what?" Black said, willing her not to look at Joe, to stay with him and with Summer.

"Like how to get a boy to notice you."

"All right. And you know more about that sort of thing."

"I ain't a slut," she said, nose turning up as she glared at Black.

Black shook his head. "That's not what I meant, Raine. I just meant that Summer thought she could turn to you for that kinda thing."

"I guess. She ain't got experience of datin'. 'Cept this ain't what it was."

"What was it then?"

"She said the guy was older. Much older."

Black felt the tension.

"This boy –"

"Man," Raine said. "It weren't a boy."

"She didn't tell you his name?"

"She wouldn't. Said he'd get into shit."

"You must've wanted to find out."

"I thought she was lyin' at first. I thought maybe she'd made the whole thing up, read it in a book and wanted to live it or somethin'."

Black thought of Samson, with his funny ways and ten-dollar boots, that pallor of sickness, halo not horns. He thought of Summer Ryan, gifted and gold. No way it fit, however he tried to see it.

"What did you tell her?"

Raine glanced at her daddy.

"You want to step out for a while, Joe?" Black said.

Joe shook his head, managed to smile at Raine, which was an ask, but Black was grateful.

"I told her to smell nice, boys like perfume."

"That perfume we found in her bedroom –"

"It weren't mine. I know what Momma reckoned . . . she don't never believe me."

"You know where Summer got it?"

Raine shrugged. "I figured maybe this guy bought it for her. It looked fancy, expensive."

"What else did you tell her?"

"To wear some lipstick, 'cause that makes them think of your lips, which makes 'em think of kissin' your lips."

Black smiled. "That makes sense. That all?"

Raine looked down. "She . . ." Raine's voice shook a little. "She asked me what kinda underwear they like."

Joe moved fast, so fast he was out the door before Black could get to his feet.

Black heard Milk yell something but by the time he made it to the door Milk was on his ass, his nose a mess of blood.

Black followed the steps down quick and heard heavy thumps, fast and solid.

He found Joe outside Samson's door, hammering it with red fists, streaks of blood against the hard white.

27

Summer

It was worse with Olive Braymer, Briar girl number five. Olive lived with her momma in the unincorporated community of Wagarmont. She went regular to Northwood Church of Christ.

The Bird knocked her down with his van. I saw the photographs, the shards of glass and the pool of milk and the brown paper grocery bag. Before, I could reason it, I could sit in St. Luke's and pray that he was takin' them for some other reason, that maybe he was a collector of virtue. I saw them as Briar butterflies flutterin' together, while he sat there and marveled 'cause appreciation was enough for him.

But Olive Braymer, her momma reckoned she was a fighter. They found a spot of her blood, maybe she scraped her knee or bumped her head. Jesus, thinking of her hurt, limp beneath his wings as he drove her to a tomb.

"Y'all any closer to catchin' him?" I said.

Officer Milk turned like he'd just realized he weren't alone. I liked Milk 'cause he was so big but so calm with it.

"I'd like to say we are."

"But you'd be lyin.'"

He smiled. He sat on the bench by his momma's grave; the date on the stone gave it two years since she passed. The bench had been stained a week back, on a gray day where I watched Samson and his brush but didn't say nothin' to him 'cause he was concentratin' so hard. I see Raine in Samson, that fight to get what comes easy to others. Raine can read and write but it takes her longer. I reckoned maybe twins had to divvy up traits; if one is strong the other shies, if one is smart the other struggles.

I stood beside and stared at the stone and thought of his momma under all that dirt, maybe listenin' to us talk. What's a soul without a body.

I liked watchin' the grievers come and leave. I'd always go visit the grave they'd stopped by, I'd see who they were mourning and feel what they felt. The children were the worst: the Du Peret baby, his parents wore it so bad I could've cried for them; the Gambrell boy, his momma came alone and she died a little more every time; Mandy Deamer, the big guy that dropped to one knee and touched the stone.

So much hurt I couldn't feel my own blood no more.

"I pray for them," I said, 'cause it was true and it fit so right. I stood with my hands clasped together behind my back.

"Yeah," Milk said. "That's good. You should be careful, you and the other girls."

"I know."

He looked sad, maybe 'cause he was thinkin' about his momma. I imagined the day my parents ain't around and I wondered what would be missin' from my life.

"You reckon he'll quit soon, when he's got enough?" I said.

It was gettin' cold. That time where winter starts to move in and the trees are empty and you forget all the glimmers.

"Maybe. I hope ... Don't stay out late, don't go near the woods. Tell your friends."

"Yes, sir."

Della Palmer, Bonnie Hinds, Lissa Pinson, Coralee Simmons, and Olive Braymer. If they were dead I wondered what it'd say on their stones.

Taken too soon.

'Cause in the end we all get taken.

"Daddy told me not to come to church. And Chief Black said it too."

He looked up at me. He wore sunglasses but there weren't sun. "But you're still here."

I nodded.

He smiled.

At times the trouble was suffocating. You couldn't switch on the television or pick up a newspaper without hearin' of the fall, guilty disobedience in all its forms, like our world was spinnin' the wrong way. I read about the children in Fairfield County, saw them on Channel 17, their shadowed faces and their mechanical voices, speaking of rote horrors while their eager mommas prompted and cried. We were all desperate for an end, least for a little while.

I left Milk and walked into St. Luke's and watched him through the stained glass. I closed one eye and saw him red, all scarlet sins 'cause he was a man like the others. He dropped to one knee and laid a flower, a lone flower so white and heavenly that when he was gone I went and picked it up in my hand and flipped the petals off one after the other.

28

These People That Are Broke

They walked the half mile slow. They cut from dark streets into dark woods despite the early hour.

"You bring the knife?" Noah said.

" 'Course," Purv said, patting the backpack slung over his shoulder.

They padded across dry leaves and broken branches. Purv stumbled once, Noah grabbed hold of him. The breeze was too light to make it through the trees so nothing shook above them; all they could make out was the steady rush of the Red, going on like it always did, no matter the weather.

"My foot is cold," Purv said. He stopped for a moment, leaned on a wide trunk, and lifted his foot. His sneaker was old.

"There's a hole."

Noah stopped. "Maybe tape it, or pad the inside with newspaper. It'll hold awhile."

While he was leaning Purv lit a cigarette, then passed it to Noah and lit another for himself.

Purv had come by that morning early, found Noah in the kitchen eating a bag of Cheetos for breakfast. They'd shared them while they watched the news report and saw a pearly reporter standing in the center of the square, Mae scowling from the window behind.

"Has your grandmother seen the Buick yet?" Purv said.

"If she has she ain't said nothin'. I reckon I could convince her it ain't supposed to have four doors."

They walked on, twisting lines of smoke rising from each, only the glow of their cigarettes sharp enough to shape them.

They'd seen men by the end of Raine's street earlier, big men with reputations, exchanging looks and glancing up and around. Noah was glad they were searching too, that Joe had friends like that.

Purv kept his eyes on the ground, kneeled sudden, and sifted the leaves. "Thought I saw one," he said, then stood again.

They'd been searching for Alabama Pinks since they were small. They hadn't ever found one.

"There's a guy in Windale that'll pay fifty bucks for a single flower," Purv said.

Noah frowned 'cause Purv had been saying that for years.

"I'm serious. Ricky Brannon reckons his brother found a whole load in Hell's Gate. Made thousands."

"Ricky Brannon's full of shit," Noah said.

They walked on.

"I was thinkin', how come you ain't told Raine about dialysis?"

Noah shrugged. " 'Cause that's all she'll see."

They found her by the Red, sitting on the bank with her legs falling over.

Her eyes were red. She told them to go.

Noah settled beside her. She looked sad so he tried to take her hand in his but she batted it away and she told him she'd cut it off if he tried it again.

"I heard Black say they're searchin' the Lumen house today," Noah said.

"You reckon Samson Lumen is the Bird?" Purv said.

"No. Samson goes to church. The way folk tell it, the Bird is the devil," Noah said.

"You believe in the devil?" Raine said, looking over at him.

"If you believe in God it ain't much of a reach."

"I never said I believe in God," she said.

"What then?" Noah said.

"Maybe nothin'. If he wants me to look up he's gotta come down . . . prove himself."

"You have to believe," Noah said, staring. "You have to, Raine."

"Why?"

" 'Cause this can't be all there is. It ain't long enough . . . it ain't even close."

Purv picked up a small rock and tossed it in the water.

"What about the lady from the clinic? What are we gonna do?" Purv said.

"Watch her," Raine said.

"What if there ain't a link? Just a sad story."

"We'll watch her just in case. We'll keep searchin'. We'll follow up on all we got."

Raine stared at the water, at the turn and the rush.

The three sat together, wondering what had gone and what would come.

*

Black stood out front of the Lumen house, drinking coffee from a flask, a grim look on his face. They couldn't search the house. Deely had pulled Milt Kroll back from vacation. He'd been fishing the Caney Fork River and weren't happy but he was doing his job. Samson said they could go in but Samson's name weren't on the deed. It was a blow Black saw coming a mile off, which was why he requested a warrant, but Judge Delane weren't having none of it. The grounds were soft and everyone knew it.

They'd called in men from the Briar County Sheriff's Office. They were at the station now, watching the trucks out front and waiting.

Joe would likely make a move if Black didn't do something soon.

They could've charged Joe for knocking Milk down. They could've locked him up and with his record he'd serve decent time again, but Milk wouldn't allow that, not with the man's daughter still out there.

There were fields across from the house, long straight fields that used to be colored and worked.

Before long he was joined by Ernie Redell. Ernie had been sheriff for ten years, though Black had known him twenty. With a sharp mind and an easy charm, there'd been talk of

Ernie running for senator as long as Black could remember. Ernie always maintained he was doing what he loved, serving the people and all that, but Black had heard he was tiring of late. The Briar girls wrecked him. Now his smile took a breath longer to form, his voice had lost some of the oil.

They shook hands. Ernie turned and watched the house. The lights were on 'cause of the cloud, they'd set up a couple of floods too but the team were packing their shit. Deely had left it late to saunter over and halt the search, with Milt frowning from his Mercedes.

"Nice weather you're having," Ernie said.

Black didn't have the energy to smile.

"You all right, Black?"

"This one kinda crept up on me, now it ain't goin' the way I thought."

"I heard you got a situation brewing with the locals. Can't say I'm surprised, once I heard the girl was Joe Ryan's daughter. I don't envy you."

"Ain't many that do."

"You got much so far?"

"No."

"You want us to take him?"

"I can't see a way of movin' him without trouble."

"It'll calm soon enough."

Ernie reached over and patted Black on the shoulder.

"I got Burns and Urliss out knocking doors by our side of Hell's Gate. And I got men I can get over quick if you need more help in the square. Can't get a helicopter up in this weather, but soon as it breaks –"

"Yeah," Black said. "Soon as it breaks."

"You thinkin' about the Briar girls now?" Ernie said.

"I ain't stopped thinkin' about 'em."

"Bird huntin'. Five times and he played it near perfect. Makes you wonder."

"What?"

Ernie shrugged. "If his luck is running out. Where he went. Why he stopped for a while. Why church girls . . . Those same questions we been turnin'."

"You don't buy into that satanic shit," Black said. They'd had this same conversation over beers and whiskey a while back, though neither could recall the details.

"You can't deny the religious angle."

"You can. They're all young and pretty. That's what links them much as anything. It's harder to find girls that ain't believers in Briar."

Ernie ran a hand over his badge. "I saw Mae this morning, on Channel 14."

"I heard. We got a news van parked up now, saw it on the way over. Ain't sure what they want. Last thing I need is a bunch of idiots trailin' through the square."

"You never were much of a people person, Black."

"Give me a desert island and I'd be happy."

Ernie laughed.

Black watched him leave. Ernie flashed his lights as he passed, on the way outta Grace. Black loosened his collar, the panic creeping up outta nowhere.

He'd rolled the idea around in his head, that Samson and the Bird were one and the same. It fit nice, the religious angle, loner.

He allowed himself to think maybe it was over, they had the Bird and it was over.

The Lumen land ran to Hell's Gate, and there was a lot of it. Black walked around back. There was the jagged remains of a fence that ran maybe a hundred yards into the dark. Black turned his flashlight on and cast it over the area, over Merle's farmhouse next door and the barn.

He walked through deep grass, the roots damp. There were fruit trees planted.

He thought about the Briar girls, about Peach Palmer and the men she fucked. It hurt him, being needed that much, made him feel a hellish kinda unworthy, that there was someone lower on the chain than him, someone that craned their neck just to see the failure in his eyes.

He walked back and he sat heavy in the cruiser and closed his eyes 'cause he weren't making no progress.

He reached into the glove compartment and grabbed the bottle of whiskey. He drank it all down, too much and too fast. Then he reached for the bag he'd taken from Peach's drawer. He was sloppy and spilled as much on the seat as he got up his nose. Then he climbed outta the car and got up on the hood and heard it creak. He could just about make out the sunlight a long way in the distance. He reached for his gun, held it high, aimed it at the cloud and pulled the trigger.

*

They got Patty to serve crab potpie 'cause it'd been Savannah's favorite, but she didn't eat much at all. After, they sat beneath the glass roof in the orangery and her daddy sipped brandy from crystal while her mother held her hand.

She looked at the sky like she'd forgot how many stars could shine.

"Donald called and wanted to know if you're ready to proceed," her mother said.

"I'm not . . . I don't –"

"You'll feel better once it's done, sweetheart," her daddy said.

She glanced over at him. He was aging better than her mother; thick hair only touched with gray framing a handsome face.

"I said he wasn't right," he said. "I said it from the start but you've always been stubborn." He winked at her like that'd soften it. "Bobby's got that look in his eyes. I've seen it before in boys who have been through the system. Dally does pro bono at Grove and he says half the time he's dealing with these people."

"These people?" she said.

He caught it and smiled. "It's not Bobby's fault, and it's noble what he's doing, we can appreciate it, the church is lucky to have him. But you and him . . . and us too –"

"You know they brought charges against another man last week," her mother said. "He worked at that home where Bobby was and they only just caught up with him. You can't undo damage like that, sweetheart. Who knows what that does to a person. It breaks my heart, really it does, but we have to look out for our own. And you have a chance now –"

"What do you mean 'now'?" Savannah said, snatching her hand back.

"I just –"

"You couldn't have walked out before, when you had Michael to think about. You couldn't do that to him, you're a good person, sweetheart," her daddy said, easy like he didn't know how it sounded, or like the brandy was lulling. "But even now, when you smile, it's not the same smile my little girl used to have. You just look so sad."

She felt heat rise to her cheeks. She saw them, caring in their own way on their own terms, and for a moment she hated them. She didn't get angry; she didn't yell and curse.

"Sign the papers and come back to us, and you can start again," he said. "You're young and beautiful and I know you're not ready to think about dating –"

Savannah stood. "I still love him."

She caught her mother, the way she looked at her daddy, like she was fifteen and crying love for some boy at the club that'd danced with her.

"I still love Bobby."

She heard the sounds they made as she left them to their beautiful life, sounds of despair 'cause their daughter was lost and they didn't know how to right her.

*

"You look better," Black said.

Peach glared at him.

"I mean good. You look good, Peach."

She smiled, something fresh in it. "I feel better. Those folks I been speaking to, over at the program I was tellin' you about –"

"Pinegrove."

"They been helpin' me."

Black walked through the house and out into the backyard.

"I took it for granted. Just seeing the stars," he said, looking up.

She brought out two glasses of iced tea and set them down by the swing seat. They sat together close.

He sipped his drink, pulled a face and she laughed.

"Ain't no tequila, or vodka," he said.

"Ain't no rum neither."

She took his hand in hers, rubbed it light, and stared out.

Her yard was long; no back fence saw it run to the trees beyond. Black heard night songs and felt far from Grace.

"I was thinkin' . . . I been talkin', I been thinkin' like she's dead, but that don't mean she is."

Black looked down, didn't meet her eye.

"Same with those other girls. Maybe they're holed up someplace. Or maybe he's still got 'em. I know it won't be nice there, I ain't foolish enough to think that, but it . . . she might still be livin', might be breathin'. All the stats I read, it don't really mean nothin' when you ain't certain. That right, Black?"

He squeezed her hand.

"I like your dress," he said.

It was light and had flowers on it. Daisies. She had her hair pinned up and her lips painted.

"I been for a job. That diner on Route 11. You know it?"

He nodded.

"It's just waitressing."

"That's good, Peach."

"Yeah?" she said, looking over.

The moon was too big and too blue.

"I ain't seein' those . . ." she trailed off. She gripped his face and turned it toward her, holding it tight. "I'm stopping. Those things I do, I'm stopping."

"I'm glad," he said. "I worry . . . about that man. I listen out in case you call. I don't want nobody to hurt you, Peach."

She nodded.

"I hate it when you cry," he said.

"I know."

"Stop it then."

"I know what you see in me," she said. "I see it too. I hate it but I see it."

"I don't –"

"You reckon one day you'll see somethin' else, when I'm a better person."

"Why do you talk like that?" he said.

"Like what?"

"Like I'm good and you ain't."

"Everyone's lookin' to be more than they are."

He pulled her in.

"First I just wanted you to keep lookin' for my daughter," she said.

"I know."

"Now I just want you to keep lookin' for me."

"I see you," he said.

"You don't, Black. It ain't sex, like it was at the start. That's me, what I know to do, sex for money or sex for favors, there's somethin' at the end of it more than there should be. But now . . . I wait for you to call and to stop by, but not just 'cause you might've got someplace with Della."

She looked at him deep and he fought the urge to turn away.

"So, at Pinegrove, they said it helps, bein' honest about your feelings and facin' up. So that's what I'm doin'."

Later, when she was sleeping, he took the last of the old her from the drawer and sat out back beneath the broke blue that fell between swaying trees. He put the rock on the spoon and the spoon on the flame of the silver lighter his daddy had left for him.

"Enough now," he said, as he breathed deep. "Enough."

He slipped silent from her house and drove back to Grace. He left the cruiser parked in a copse a quarter mile from the Lumen house.

It was dark and it was silent and he sobered fast. He wouldn't leave nothing, he'd bare all the secrets till there weren't no lingering doubts left no matter the cost. Peach was right, it was time to stop hiding and face up.

He thought of Summer Ryan as he broke into the Lumen house. He swept each room quick and with care. The house was big but the rooms were empty, only a couple lived in 'cause maybe they couldn't afford to heat the old place.

He saw photos on the wall, the old man smiling that tight smile, eyes so hard he could've broke the lens. There weren't a trace of Samson, not in the frames or anyplace else. There was guest beds upstairs, sparse and dusty, the smell unkempt and cold. Wallpaper peeled and gold sconces hung loose. There was furniture, old and brown and heavy.

He found Samson's bedroom. There was a bed and a cross above it, a desk and some baseball cards in a neat stack on the small chest. He searched it careful and found nothing. Then he moved to the old man's room and did the same.

He wiped sweat from his head as the grandfather clock chimed loud. Black knew he couldn't use nothing he found, but Summer kept him moving, and when he saw the old staircase leading to the attic he climbed it quick and quiet.

The roof was stripped back and he could see white tarp that held out water but none of the night noises. He could see the cloud through gaps, its body so leaden folk were saying if it dropped it'd flatten the town dead.

He walked thin boards that ached and groaned and gave a little with each step. The timber was rotted and junk was piled. He searched awhile and was about to call it quits when he saw it: an old file cabinet in the far corner, a dust sheet covering one side.

When he got close he saw it had a lock but it was busted like it'd been jimmied. He opened it and took out the magazines. There was a decent stack, the kind Lucky Delfray sold at his gas station, sins of the flesh burning hot in Black's hand.

He shone his flashlight over them. He thought of the pastor, and of that fear in Samson. He closed his eyes and nodded, 'cause now it fit.

29

Summer

The devil is in the detail. I never really got that.

I watched Pastor Lumen preachin' before the stroke took him. I wondered about sanity, how it visits and how it stays or leaves.

I sat in St. Luke's and the hours passed like minutes and I watched Bobby as he did the things he did. People spoke to him and he smiled at them but I knew it weren't his real smile 'cause that one's so different. They fawned. I saw them carry him and he let them, with their wide eyes and their reverence and their faith so blind they couldn't see the nothin' in his soul when they asked for his blessing.

Samson was there more than any other. At first I reckoned he was prayin' for his daddy but there was somethin' more there, some kinda hurt that rode his body when he kneeled, shoulders hunched tight like his muscles was in spasm. Needin' the Lord that much, that lingering fear that maybe he ain't even listenin'.

"I reckon you should sing in the choir," Bobby said with a straight face.

"I reckon you should renounce the Lord."

Raine showed me how to paint my lips and make them look bigger and fuller like maybe I'd had some kinda allergic reaction.

"Maybe you've got a beautiful voice but you don't know it."

"I sing in the shower. Nowhere else."

He smiled, maybe wanted to say somethin' but held it 'cause on the face of it nothin' much had changed.

"How come you chose God?" I said.

"Is this the part where I say he chose me?"

"Maybe."

"I believe, Summer. Open yourself to that."

"Or put the blinkers on."

"You asked, I answered."

"I didn't mean nothin'."

"I know. Anyhow, most of the time that's true. You give somethin' thought and the thought becomes more."

"And other times?"

He reached up and wiped sweat from his head 'cause we were sittin' in sunlight.

"Other times I wonder if I'd do it again. If I had my time over would I walk the unforgiving path to offer others forgiveness."

"Were your parents religious?"

"I grew up in a children's home."

"Oh."

"I was too young to remember my life before, which I reckon is a blessing either way."

We didn't talk like this, where honesty takes a homeward turn. I reckoned maybe the truth lay nearer the start, that maybe the church gave Bobby a family so large.

"Savannah likes to picture me the orphan boy that didn't get anything for his birthday, but the truth lies a long way from that. I give my stories a lick of gloss when she delves 'cause her life . . . you know some of her family helped finance the Pensacola Railroad back in 1880? I've seen the photographs. It don't impress her, to trace a root so deep into history like that."

I nodded, saw Bobby, and wanted to reach out but didn't.

"That home, in Arnsdale, it's black and white in my memories." He didn't look at me when he spoke.

"Why do you like me?"

"I never said I liked you."

I smiled.

"I think about you all the time," I said. "Is that bad?"

"Thoughts aren't bad or good. They're just thoughts. Our mind is our own; it's the only place where true freedom exists."

I could feel the earth movin' beneath my feet and I was runnin' just to hold still.

"I can't sleep. I think about you then I can't sleep," I said.

"What do you think about?"

"You doin' things to me."

"What kinda things?" He didn't look at me, just kept his eyes on the church, the gravestones, and the long grass and the bell tower that rose so high.

"Things I read about. Things I heard about. Things I seen in movies. Things that make me so shamed I can't believe they're even right. If there's a line I ain't found it. I don't even know myself no more. What does that make me?"

He stood slow. He walked slow.

I got up and followed.

The church was shaded and empty and cool but I didn't feel it.

I watched Bobby, he moves with confidence, like he'd bowl over an army if they got in his way.

We walked over to the altar. The carved stone surround so intricate it must've taken a million years to finish.

I stood there, tryin' to be bold. He faced me and I looked down at my feet and my sandals were pink.

He has skin too flawless. I wanted to ask if he was real. Maybe if I touched him I'd leave a print that couldn't never be covered.

"In my dreams I do as I'm told. Why do you reckon that is? I can't command my own dreams. I wonder if that makes me weak or meek, and I wonder if there's even a difference."

He took my hand and led me into his office.

He locked the door and he dropped to his knees and I wondered about Epicurus and the vanity of desire.

I could go on. It's my story.

The devil is in the detail.

Maybe I do get that after all.

30

Painted Fences

Ray Bowdoin stood in front of Black, a little too close but Black wouldn't step back, not ever. Ray was tall and strong and might've been handsome till he lost his money and the standing it came with.

"I need to speak with Samson," Ray said.

"Ain't happening."

Ray stared at Black and Black stared back.

"I need –"

"And I said it ain't happening."

Ray tightened his jaw and Black smiled. There weren't much else in the world Black would've liked more than Ray Bowdoin coming at him but he knew it wouldn't happen 'cause Ray was tough but he weren't dumb, least not when he was sober. He tried to imagine him going off on Purv – mismatch didn't come close.

"I'm working on the Lumen house, spend half my time on that fuckin' roof. Samson cuts the checks while the old man is sick. I can't finish till I get paid."

Black watched him awhile, took in the buzz cut and the hundred-dollar boots and the sports coat. Still dressed like he was something, but Black knew how bad he was into the bank for, and rumor was he'd partnered with the Kitcheners and their people, lost their money too.

"You started work on the West End Mission yet? I got their people calling about it, like I ain't got nothin' better to do with my time," Black said.

"I need the money from the Lumen job, then I'll get on it." Ray swallowed. "Please, Black."

Black smiled. "I like that you had to say that, Ray."

Ray glared and Black glared till Ray dropped his eyes.

"He's downstairs, room three."

Ray glanced across at Trix and then at Noah. And then he smiled at Black and walked back to see Samson.

*

As days passed Joe Ryan called in more favors. There were six trucks now, parked outside the station. They took turns making runs to Mae's, bringing back trays of coffee and topping them with liquor in the evenings. There was a news van across the street, local, but Joe had heard the networks were on their way. A missing girl, a member of the church being held, and a sky where night had bled day away for near three weeks.

Yeah, the networks were coming.

Black had come back late the previous night. Joe had watched him careful, looking for signs of change, but Black was a decent enough poker player. There was still no word about charging Samson.

Tommy was drinking coffee and smoking, keeping half an eye on the pretty reporter as she ate her lunch.

Hank Frailey had set up more tables outside the Whiskey Barrel, a fat candle burned on each of them.

They looked up when they heard noise, then they saw Pastor Lumen in his glorified shopping cart, and maybe twenty others behind.

The pretty news reporter dropped her sandwich to the street and ran to the van, rounded her men and prepped.

Black came out fast, followed by Milk and Rusty. They took the steps two at a time and jogged across the grass, hoping to head them off.

Joe glanced up at the station, at the lights burning, and the flags and pillars. When he was seven years old he'd sat on those same steps and waited for his daddy to get out. He couldn't remember the charge now, one of the minors before the major.

The square had changed some since then, like the shine was all but dull now. Eight stores shuttered, the promise of more.

They were faring better than some; Joe had a cousin in Danton and they'd lost everything. Joe wondered about the consolidation of the mills, about those that gained at costs greater than dollars. He looked at his boys, at their tired faces drawn with worry for his daughter.

There was more yelling so he turned slow and watched the madness unfold.

Two hours later lines had been drawn. Pastor Lumen had stood back and watched his people fight for him and for Samson. Black held a hard line, which weren't all that easy with the old man glaring at him. The church people clustered tight, the braver throwing glances at Joe and his boys, who looked on silent. There were placards calling for Samson's release.

At one point Deely White glanced over at Austin Ray Chalmers and spit on the ground. Austin was over quick. Milk stepped in before Deely got his ass kicked, then got heckled for his troubles.

Next Deely's wife spit at Austin as he was walking away. It landed on the back of his pant leg. He pulled a gun, Tommy Ryan wrestled it from him. There were screams.

Then it was Roly Garner's turn. He took off his Stetson and threw it like a Frisbee toward the Ryan side. Black weren't exactly sure what he'd hoped to achieve, but he felt the reporter looking on with excitement when one of Joe's men lit it on fire.

Black sent men to a room at the back of the station to fetch the sandbags. They kept them in store for when the Red spilled. They laid them out in a line down the center of the green to keep the sides apart. It was low enough to climb over and only stretched as far as the street, but neither side was looking to mix much with the other so it held.

Black took Deely and his wife to one side, told them if there was any more riling he'd tell Milk to let it go, then Deely could take his chances with Austin Ray Chalmers. He watched the fight drain outta the pair of them.

Another news van rolled into the square at three o'clock, quickly followed by another and another. The networks had arrived.

Pastor Lumen saw his moment and got Roly to rig a microphone to a big speaker mounted on the back of Deely's truck. Pastor Lumen stooped low, swiped his good fist from right to left, then rose high and stirred the crowd. He was mad, the cloud had been sent by God himself 'cause something bad was going down in Grace, and the town wouldn't be rid of it till Samson Lumen was set free. He let out a low growl then stretched his arm up to the sky. Most joined him, then tilted their heads and closed their eyes and united in prayer. The pastor stared at Black and pointed and consecrated.

*

Noah, Raine, and Purv lay star shaped in the grass, heads together, eyes staring straight up. Purv smoked a fat cigar, trying his best to blow rings and frowning when they wouldn't hold.

"Why's it so quiet?" Noah said.

"The birds," Raine said.

After his shift Noah had found Raine waiting in his backyard. There weren't no talk of the other night, of what she said. Maybe she had nobody else to drive her, maybe there was truth to it, but he weren't nearly cool or cruel enough to call her out.

They'd taken the Buick, picked up Purv, and headed to the Dayette Women's Clinic.

It was early evening but still hot outta Grace, the streets cooking with rumors as the temperature soared north of a hundred degrees. Purv groused about sitting in the back. Every time they made a left turn he held tight to the seat in front and worried he'd slide right out the hole where the door used to be. Noah laughed till he was red faced.

They sat till she finished her shift then they followed her Taurus and Noah kept a couple cars back and felt like a real cop.

The lady with the fire-red hair lived in a small apartment above Adler's, a five and dime on Faust Road, three miles from the clinic. They'd watched her a couple of times now.

From what they got she had three kids, no man, and debt troubles. Raine had fished through her trash and seen red envelopes.

She left the kids alone whenever she went to pray with the West End Mission.

They agreed it was something, 'cause they saw that fire when the preacher spoke of the sanctity of life, but none could figure exactly what. Purv reckoned maybe she was keeping an eye on the holy rollers in case they were planning something, maybe to burn the clinic down.

On the drive back, Raine had told Noah to pull over beside one of the yellow fields on Winans Road. They'd followed her a long way through the rapeseed till they'd come to a lone apple tree, standing on a small mound of grass. Not fifty yards away Noah could see the sun setting, but they stayed on their side, like they belonged.

Raine lay back. She reached a hand up like she could tear a piece from the cloud.

"Is it dropping? I feel like I can't breathe here," Noah said.

"You ain't the only one," Purv said, coughing. "These Backwoods are fuckin' deadly."

"Where'd you get 'em?"

"Barrel. One of the cloud tourists weren't watching his bag. Black was in last night. Worked through a bottle of Jim Beam, sat alone in the corner outta sight. I wonder why he drinks like that?"

"Maybe he's haunted by a past case," Noah said.

"Fuckin' cliché," Raine fired back.

"Maybe he just likes the taste of whiskey," Purv said.

Purv stubbed the cigar out then buried the end in the dirt beside. As he leaned down his T-shirt rode up and Noah caught a glimpse of another nasty welt on his back. He glanced over at Raine, saw she'd seen it too.

"I was thinkin' maybe we should go and see Pastor Bobby," Purv said, quiet.

"Why?" Noah said.

"This cloud."

"What?"

"I know you'll say it's bullshit, but people keep sayin' God sent it down to Grace for whatever reason."

"You're right, that's bullshit."

"But what if it ain't? What if it is somethin' to do with God? We ain't exactly prepared."

"For what?" Noah said. He looked over at the sunset again, saw a swift land on the earth, glance into the darkness then take off.

"The end," Purv said, looking to Raine and then Noah, afraid they'd get on him. He brought a hand up and touched his hair. "You're supposed to tell all the bad shit you've done over the years. All the shit that God ain't gonna look on kindly. You tell him then he forgives you and lets you into heaven. Ain't that right?"

"That's the way they tell it," Raine said.

"Then we should go see Bobby 'cause it's better to be safe. If somethin' bad happens . . . is all I'm sayin."

"You don't even have to tell a pastor. You can just confess, right now. Sayin' it out loud is enough. God hears everything," Raine said.

"All right. Worst thing you've done," Noah said.

Purv looked down. "Those sunglasses Noah wears . . . I stole 'em from a blind man over in Windale."

Noah puffed out his cheeks.

"I tried to take his dog too –"

"Jesus," Raine said.

"It wouldn't come. Beautiful thing with a golden coat."

"Loyal too," Noah said.

"Anything else?" Raine said.

Purv went quiet.

"Spill it," Raine said. "You wanna go up when the end comes or not?"

He looked up and around like he thought somebody might've been listening. "And I think about killing him," he said, his eyes burning with pride or shame or maybe both.

Noah reached out and put a hand on his shoulder.

"You reckon God will understand that?" Purv said, looking up.

"Yeah," Noah said.

"Yeah," Raine said.

Purv nodded, like maybe he felt better, then he took another Backwoods out and lit it. "Anyone else goin'?"

"How long you got?" Raine said.

Purv smiled.

"Sometimes I hate my momma," she said.

Purv watched her, smoked and coughed and watched the shadow over her face. She took a Marlboro from her bag and he lit it for her and watched it glow.

She spoke in a dead tone. "I hate her for the way she looks at me, and the way she looks at my sister. I hate her for only seeing the difference between us." She blew smoke toward the cloud. "I ain't sure that's a sin, but it don't feel right. I know she had it tough, with my daddy and all." She swallowed and turned.

Noah felt the quiet after, like it was his turn. He wouldn't say they were lucky to have parents to hate. He worked out years back that he was better off alone. It weren't a hard truth no more, though he learned it those long nights when the nurses stopped by and drowned his momma's cries with drugs while he sat out back and stared up at her window. Those days were short, the nights long and winding. He didn't know what to say to her, didn't know how to look at her when she turned thin and gaunt and her new smile scared him 'cause it weren't even close to the same. One night a lady came and sat with her. She was old and trained and she spoke about closure and legacy as Noah listened from the door.

He didn't cry. Not during or after or ever. He was brave. He was fierce.

Before long Purv drifted off 'cause he didn't get much sleep at home.

Noah got to his feet when Raine did. They walked over to the apple tree. Last light dying ten feet from its roots.

"You reckon it's funny we ain't never spoke before, like at school or something?" he said.

"No. You and Purv are losers, no offense."

He frowned. "I ain't sure it's possible not to take offense."

She nodded.

She turned and crossed into bleeding sunset and when he saw her standing golden he drew breath.

"Sometimes I forget when I was small, when life weren't nothin' like it is now. These are supposed to be the good days, the easy time," she said. "If I look back and that's true then I wonder what kinda mess is waitin' on me."

"You'll be okay, Raine."

"You don't know shit, Noah."

"I know, I just, I see you –"

"What? What do you see?" She said it hard.

He kept his eyes down. "I see a nice house, like maybe those ones on the other side of Hell's Gate, in the nice part of Brookdale. They got the painted fences. And I see two kids, probably twins—boys though. Maybe you'll be good at baking cakes or somethin'."

He looked up and maybe he caught the tail of a smile before she turned away.

"Black reckons Samson didn't do nothin'."

She turned. "He say that?"

"Black's taken a few runs at him and Samson ain't wavered. It holds up, that he was just helpin' her carry her cello 'cause the case was broken."

"My momma checked. The case is broke. The handle snapped."

"So that part is true at least. That's somethin'."

"Is it? If Samson ain't got her, if he don't know where she is then we got nothin'. That's the way my daddy sees it. That's why he won't let Samson go. Walking her home is enough to get him in trouble. You should've seen my daddy's face, he was fit to be tied, and that was before all that about Summer fallin' for an older man."

"We'll keep lookin'. We'll find the Bird," he said.

"And then what?"

"We'll –"

"You ain't tough, Noah. That fight or flight, it can't be taught or forgot. Maybe you stand up to the big kids and take a hidin' for Purv, and that's decent doin' that, but you don't want what's comin'."

He looked down, away from her eyes.

"I feel it, my life is turnin', there's somethin' bad happening out there. You're all right. Maybe you and Purv got trouble at home but that ain't nothin'. You'll leave it behind. My fight ain't yours. And maybe you reckon you got a shot with me 'cause you'll treat me nice and that's what I need. But you don't even see, none of y'all do. I need my sister, she's all I need."

He stepped forward and she stepped back.

"I'll find her. I'll help you, don't matter what you say. Don't matter how brave or strong or fierce I am."

She stared at him.

"And we got the gun."

"You ever fired a gun, Noah?"

The apple was twenty yards away, on a mound of earth Raine had built up with her hands. Dirt and sweat colored her face as she stood beside Noah and told him how to sight. He put two bullets well wide, glanced back and saw Purv watching from the shadows.

"This gun ain't standard issue," Noah said, frowning. "Put a Koch in my hand and I'll make apple sauce."

Raine turned her back for a minute and he saw her shoulders shaking.

"Are you laughin'?" he said.

He saw her head shake and then she turned back, mouth tight like she was fighting a smile.

"It's too dark now," he said.

"Remember to breathe this time."

He fired and missed again.

He took a moment. "My father was a crack shot."

"You'll hit it."

"If I do will you let me take you out to dinner?"

"No."

"Please?"

"You won't hit it."

"Then you ain't got nothin' to worry about."

"All right," she said.

He dropped to a kneel, pulled the trigger, then heard the crack and watched the apple kick up from the dirt.

He turned to her and grinned wide, then he went to hug her and she threatened to shoot him.

31

Summer

We held our breath for the rest of winter and into spring. We watched the news every night and we waited. Momma took us to church every Sunday and Daddy and Tommy sat at the end of Jackson drinkin' coffee and watchin' out. According to the newspapers the whole of Briar County was watchin' out too. Maybe it was too hot for him to move again, that's what folk said when weeks stretched to months. Raine still snuck out after dark, went to the kinda parties where she came home stumbling, sometimes cryin' and bruised. She'd climb in bed with me and sleep pressed close and I'd watch her turn innocent just by closin' her eyes to the world.

As Grace returned to color there was less talk of the Briar girls 'cause it couldn't be maintained, that ain't how life works for those standin' off-center. And we were off-center; those girls weren't Grace girls and even though Hell's Gate ran to our town there was a feelin' we'd been missed, that the strike had sailed over and hit the dirt around us. 'Course we felt the damage but it was an aftershock and nothin' bolder.

There were posters up on the streetlights, just a pair of eyes 'cause that's what they ran with, said it was enough to remind us. I didn't forget but I saw the other girls goin' on, talkin' boys and prom and life beyond fear.

"Can I have a little wine?" Raine said.

Momma shot her a look.

Bobby and Daddy were out back, sittin' on the porch and drinkin' beer and talkin' football 'cause that was easy ground. Savannah was sat beside me, her French perfume so thick and familiar. The supper had been Momma's idea, to thank them for all they'd done. She served Royal Reds and Bobby said it was the best meal he'd had since he got to Grace, she smiled so wide I reckoned it must've hurt.

"How about gin?" Raine said.

"Raine," Daddy hollered through the open door.

We sat out back, side by side on the swings. Savannah kicked off her shoes, her bare feet in the yellow grass. I could hear Momma yellin' at Raine 'cause she was supposed to help clear the dishes but she was grousin' 'cause I got to head out 'stead of doin' my share.

"Me and Bobby have been married ten years today."

I glanced over. "Y'all should've said somethin', we could've done this another night."

"We don't make a fuss."

I imagined being married to Bobby but it didn't seem enough, the eyes of the law and the Lord, they couldn't see us like I did.

I wanted his soul. And maybe I wanted hers. I wanted their son to come back so I could see the kinda perfect they'd made.

"How come you care so much?" I said. "How come you're here?" I kept the edge from my voice 'cause I wouldn't never want to hurt her.

"Sometimes I don't think you get it. What you've got."

"I play the cello, like a shit load of other people. Maybe I do it better, or will do, whatever. What does it even matter?"

I swung again. The crickets were loud and constant and I was grateful. I couldn't see it like she did, to attach importance to something that weren't.

"Have you finished your paper?" she said soft.

"One time when I was in the library some Maidenville girls came in and laughed at me, and when I got home I saw Momma hadn't cut the tags from my dress."

"Summer –"

I pushed back and swung higher.

"Are you happy, Savannah?"

She watched me and smiled the saddest smile I ever saw.

We looked up as Tommy strolled out and Bobby stood and shook his hand. I wondered if she'd answer, but she was watchin' them close, or pretendin' to, so I reckoned maybe it was a question I could've answered myself.

After a while Bobby came over and I smiled and he grinned. He was carryin' a bottle of beer and looked a little drunk 'cause his eyes had a shine.

"You go any higher and you'll flip over the top."

"Can't be done, I tried," Raine called out the window.

Bobby stood there, glancin' up at the stars. I felt Savannah watchin' me watchin' him.

"Congratulations," I said.

He looked over blank.

"Ten years," Savannah said.

He smiled, then he turned back to the sky.

32

Beautiful Grace Girl

The weekend after the networks picked up the story, traffic backed up from the town line of Grace all the way to Windale. Cars slowed to a crawl as they cut into the dark. Horns blasted, kids stuck arms outta windows, old ladies climbed from rusting pickups and crossed themselves.

One of the younger Kinleys charged two bucks a car to park up on their flat field, which stopped a foot short of the dark wall of shadow.

Just before noon, Noah and Purv caught wind and made their way to the crowd. It took them an hour to get a small table in place, and a further thirty minutes for Purv to lift two crates of lemonade from the back of Ginny's convenience store. They sold out quick, even after raising the price to Maidenville levels.

"We need more," Noah said, sitting back on his fold-out chair and watching the long line twist into sunlight.

Purv looked up when a Chevy with Mississippi plates coughed and died right in front of them. An old guy got out and glanced up at the sky, fear in his eyes.

"Like a gift from God," Purv said, getting to his feet and making his way over. "I can fetch someone to take a look at the engine. It'll cost though."

They walked back toward town, Purv with a ten-dollar bill from the old guy and Noah with the roll they'd made from the lemonade.

"How'd we make out in the end?" Purv said, as Noah counted the bills.

"Nicely," Noah said, handing half to Purv, who gave it straight back.

"For tonight, take Raine someplace better than Mae's."

He smiled. "I ain't even sure she'll show."

They stuck to the streets 'cause it was too dark not to. They didn't use flashlights 'cause they were saving the batteries for Bird hunting in Hell's Gate.

They came back to chaos in the square. More reporters had arrived; they sat in news vans with dishes on the roofs and bright lettering splashed across the panels. Action and Eyewitness and NBC, like there was something going on more than a cloud in the sky.

The pickups were gone from outside the station 'cause Black moved them on, but they just double-parked at the corner of Jackson Ranch Road and came back on foot. There were more of them now, maybe fifteen, and they looked mean. An even match for the fifty Pastor Lumen had on his side. They mostly ignored each other, though when a camera trained on them Pastor Lumen would get to his feet and start raising holy hell, the effort taking a little out of him each time. Deely White hovered by the old man's lawn chair, sometimes cooling him with an oriental hand fan.

The church people lit lanterns and placed them around, a vigil for a man most hadn't ever spoke to.

Trix told Noah the lines was jammed with calls about the cloud now, most from old folk in town who were worried about checking out in the venomous dark, like God wouldn't be able to find their souls.

The Kinleys had found some hick with an old school bus over in Haskell. They'd paid him handsomely to stop by the church every morning and cart some of the older folks into the sunshine for the day.

Noah and Purv cut up Whatley and onto Sayer, walking slow toward Merle's Auto-Shop. It was small, maybe three cars wide, and made of sheet steel that'd once been red, white, and blue but had faded and browned with the seasons. There were trucks out front and tires piled ten high. Light burned inside.

"You reckon Merle will go help that guy?" Noah said.

"Yeah. Rip his eyes out though. Probably charge him a hundred before he opens the hood."

They walked across the concrete and heard angry voices, so ducked low behind a jacked-up Dodge.

They watched through the window.

"Who is it?" Purv said.

"Tommy Ryan."

Tommy was yelling something and Merle was looking down, eyes on his shoes. He said something back and Tommy got mad, reached for a .48 and held it high and level. Merle started pleading.

They watched on wide-eyed.

"Gambling debts," Purv said. "I bet it's over gambling debts."

"You reckon he'll shoot him?"

"Nah. He won't get paid if Merle's dead."

*

Raine stood in front of her closet and leafed through the clothes. She reached for a skirt and held it against herself, saw it was short and cast it to the floor. She pulled out another, then did the same.

She didn't date, that weren't what she did when she rode with the boys.

They didn't call on her, they didn't take her someplace beyond the dark lanes, where they'd park and the windows would steam as she panted.

When she was home her mind never strayed far from her sister. She listened out, hoped to get that feeling that she was close by again. It weren't easy to explain or understand. They both felt it—each other. One time Raine cut school and spent the day getting lit with Danny Tremane and one of his friends, then they'd driven to Hell's Gate and they'd done shit to her she couldn't or wouldn't recall. And after she'd got home, and she'd got in the tub and the room was spinning, she slipped beneath the water till Summer kicked the door, breathless and crying 'cause she'd cut out during sixth period and run the mile home to get her.

Raine walked down the hallway and into her sister's bedroom. She flipped the light on and opened the closet and found the dress, the same dress Summer had worn when she played cello in the church and made people cry then talked about like it weren't something special.

*

"It's beautiful," Noah said, as Purv slipped the peach linen jacket over his shoulders. "Where'd you get it?"

Purv smiled. "Ask me no questions –"

"They got that same jacket in the window of Dee's," Trix said.

"Not no more they don't," Purv said.

"It's women's, it has shoulder pads inside," Trix said.

Trix stopped by to check on Noah and stock the refrigerator. She tried to do it at least once a month.

Purv scowled at her. "Ain't you never seen *Miami Vice*? They wear this shit all the time down there."

Noah buttoned the jacket and then unbuttoned it. "That's right. And I ain't takin' fashion advice from you, Trix."

"Yeah," Purv said. "No offense, Trix, but you're old as shit. And your hair . . . kinda makes you look like a man."

"I need to talk to you, Noah," Trix said, turning serious. "Missy called me; she reckons you ain't been to dialysis again. Third time recently, is that right?"

"Missy is a liar," Purv said.

Trix shot him a look.

"I been busy," Noah said.

"Shit, Noah, are you dumb or somethin'? What do you reckon your momma would say?"

Noah shrugged.

"You know what she'd say."

"I'll go tomorrow," Noah said.

"I'll see that he does," Purv said.

"I'll check with Missy."

Noah took a breath and then turned and spun. "Ready?"

Purv nodded. "Almost. I'll go fetch a toothpick."

*

They sat in the yard, side by side. Ava poured them vodka straight.

"Bobby's still out every night," Savannah said. "He walks the streets and sometimes he drives up to Hell's Gate. He spoke with Pastor Milburn and the folk at St. George's."

Ava held cigarette smoke deep.

"I mean ... they said they'd pray for her. I know how that might sound but –"

"Thank you," Ava said. "And thank Bobby, not just for this, but for everything y'all have been doin' with Summer."

The Red ran close to their yard but they couldn't hear the rush 'cause the crickets still sang.

"I think of her out there and I feel sick," Ava said. She stared out like there was something to see. "It ain't real, that's what I say in the night when sleep don't come."

Savannah reached for her hand and held it tight.

"She used to talk about you, and Bobby, all the time. *Bobby said this and Savannah said that.* She'd come home full of it. Especially after that first time, said y'all had nice things and she asked Joe if maybe she could have the spare room for all her books, like a library she said."

"She's a sweet girl."

"And we was so glad she had you two, folk she could look up to. It's rare you know, young couple, Bobby being a pastor, it's somethin' special. She reckons you two are just about perfect."

"We're a long way from perfect."

Light dropped as the neighbor closed their drapes.

"I know about your little boy," Ava said.

"Michael."

"You don't have to talk. I'm just sorry, I wanted you to know that."

"I like to talk about him. I don't get to . . . Bobby." Savannah reached for her glass and drank and felt the burn in her chest. "I don't drink, not much. Bobby doesn't either. He did when Michael died. Then he stopped. He's strong, Bobby, he's a strong man in so many ways. But he doesn't talk."

"Maybe he talks to God." Ava said it soft.

"I need him though, down here I need him. Is that selfish?"

"It ain't selfish, Savannah."

Savannah drained her glass. "God, I'm sorry. I came here for you and I'm talking about me and my problems like they have a place."

Ava smiled. "What was Michael like?"

Savannah took a breath. "When he came, it wasn't like I thought. He was so fragile and foreign, difficult and perfect. He didn't sleep, not at night."

"I remember that with the girls."

"I didn't take to motherhood easy. I was just treading water those first months. I didn't feel the bond either, not right off, not like I was supposed to. Bobby did; he got up with Michael every night so I could sleep. I could tell it didn't bother him, that he was just so happy to have his family."

"But it got easier for you."

"There was one night Michael was screaming for hours, maybe he was teething. I looked in and saw Bobby was struggling, first time I ever saw him worried, like he was failing. So I sat at my cello and played *The Swan* and Michael quietened. I looked at Bobby and Bobby smiled and I'll never forget that moment."

They heard noise and they saw truck lights in the distance.

"That's the thing about Bobby, he was always searching for meaning, and I think he finally found it in Michael. His purpose, more than being a pastor, he thought he was there to raise Michael, to protect him."

Ava swallowed. "And he couldn't."

"No."

"Joe's feelin' that now. He's big and he's tough and he can't do nothin'. It kills him. He don't say it but it kills him. And Raine, she's strong but she's hurtin.'"

"It must have been tough, when Joe was in prison."

"It was. And we had all this . . . Pastor Lumen talkin' about the devil at the door. Raine, she reckons I'm so hard on her but . . ." Her voice wavered. "I love them so much. They're all I got, my girls and Joe."

"She'll come back, Ava. You have to believe that."

Savannah stood and Ava saw her out the side gate. She watched as Savannah strolled the dark streets back toward her lonely life and she felt despair so heavy and total.

And then she turned 'cause the light inside burned and she stared through the glass and saw her, standing golden like she'd never been gone.

She ran up the porch steps and into the kitchen, stopped still and rubbed her eyes. Ava knew the dress, she'd bought it for her; it was white and so pretty.

She stood there, shoulders back and neck straight, kissed by a grace that missed most. She was perfect. Her perfect girl.

"Summer," she said, though she weren't sure if the voice belonged 'cause it was distant.

And then Summer turned to face her but it weren't Summer after all, so Ava screamed at her to take off the dress, and she lashed out and ripped the strap and then she fell. And she glanced up and saw Raine make for the door.

And then she cried hard and long for her daughters, for both of them.

*

Raine walked quick. She glanced up at the street lamps as they blurred behind tears she wouldn't let fall 'cause she was stronger than her momma.

She didn't turn when she heard the truck draw alongside. Not even when the window opened and the two boys inside called her name. She tried to keep moving, to keep running from herself. But then she remembered the look in her momma's eyes, the look that told her not to run 'cause there weren't nothing to run toward. And so she stopped and faced them. They were older, maybe they used to go to her school, maybe she'd been with one of them before. They said they had booze and they asked if she wanted to have some fun.

She didn't, not really, but she climbed in anyway.

*

When she didn't show, Noah drove down every street in Grace searching, night stealing in through the open hole in the Buick. He summoned courage and knocked on her door, but the house was dark and no one came.

He thought of Della Palmer and the other Briar girls. Their photos were in the newspapers again, alongside the cloud and the square and Pastor Lumen.

The square was swelling when he reached it. There was a host of folk outside the Whiskey Barrel, standing with beer glasses in hand and looking out at the madness. Purv had it that people were drinking more now 'cause Hank Frailey opened the Whiskey Barrel early and folk turned blind to the hours that made day and the hours that made night.

Dark was its own time.

There were day-trippers from the counties and they made Grace a destination, the world of weird.

Noah dodged past a couple of drunks then found himself right by the sandbags. The church people were sitting together, talking and eating, some on china plates, civil like they were at a fancy picnic. Noah walked over to Joe's side, where he saw a couple of guys drinking beer and tending to a barbecue. They aimed stares at the tourists, and the Maidenville natives. One got a little near when he was backing up for a photo and Tommy Ryan shoved him hard. There was some hollering but Black was over quick, red eyed and a hand on his gun like he was about ready to shoot somebody.

At the back, way at the back, Noah saw Joe Ryan sitting alone. And in that instant Joe saw him, and he raised a hand and beckoned Noah over. Noah's first instinct was to turn and run. Joe scared him. But then he thought of Raine and took the long route round not wanting to walk through the cluster of bodies and beer and smoke.

"Sit," Joe said.

Noah sat.

Joe was smoking and he had a bottle of beer but he hadn't touched it. His shirt was tight across his arms, his biceps bulging.

"Where's Raine?"

Noah looked down and Joe smiled.

"You reckon I don't know who my daughter is hanging out with?"

"I was lookin' for her. I thought maybe she'd be here."

Joe shook his head. "Must be home with her momma. Why you gussied up? You taking her someplace?"

Noah swallowed.

"I said it's all right. Better you than those older boys I seen lurkin' by the house. At least you got a jacket on, though I reckon that might be a ladies' jacket."

Noah sighed.

"You lookin' after her?"

"Yes, sir. Though I reckon it might be workin' out the other way round."

Joe laughed, then dropped his cigarette and stubbed it. "Where you takin' her?"

"I was thinkin' Clyde's." Clyde's was one greasy step up the ladder from Mae's.

Joe reached into his pocket and handed Noah a twenty. "You make sure you take care of her while all this is goin' on. She needs her friends."

"Yes, sir."

Joe lit another cigarette, the flame glowing soft against his face. He had a thick beard and tired eyes.

"I used to know your daddy."

Noah looked up.

"He was tough."

Noah smiled.

"We was on opposite sides but I always liked him. He gave people a fair shake, I could appreciate that. You remember him?"

"Not enough."

Joe nodded slow. "Sad . . . what happened. I knew Jasper Stimson back when we was growin' up. Nasty son of a bitch, somethin' not right in his head." Joe blew smoke toward the lights. "Black still carries it."

"Was it his fault?" Noah said. He'd read all there was to read, heard a dozen tales but his momma never spoke of what happened that day in 1985.

Joe shrugged. "Best to lay fault at the door of the man who pulled the trigger, not the man who didn't."

Noah glanced up at the station, and then he stood.

"You know Summer?" Joe said.

"Not really. I mean, I saw her at school, and I was in church that time she played cello. But I ain't never spoke to her."

"All right."

"I reckon she'll turn up soon. I mean, for what it's worth, I think she'll be okay."

Joe nodded like he was getting tired of hearing it.

Noah decided to make a final stop by the Ryan house before he called it a night. He passed a couple of trucks on the way down Lott.

He left the Buick in the weeds and started up All Saints. He heard her before he saw her. A rustle, not far off, then a sound like coughing. He moved fast through the bushes, then along the wood till he came to the clearing and the bank of the Red.

He saw a shape by the water's edge.

"Raine?" he said, moving near.

"Fuck off, Noah."

She sat up, her limbs heavy and her hair loose. He could smell booze.

"You all right?"

"Just leave me alone."

He sat beside her for a long time. The Red moved slow that night.

"I miss the moon," he said.

"And the stars," she said.

"Yeah. And the stars."

She wore no shoes, he wondered where they were but didn't ask. She wore a nice dress; there was a tear in the strap.

There was a small mark on her cheek, red and fresh.

"You need me to call your momma?"

"No."

She leaned to the side, coming to rest with her head on his lap, her eyes facing the water. On another night they would've seen the mirrored stars.

"How come Purv tells you shit sometimes? Like we'll be walkin' and he'll tell you some fact, random, just random like that."

"If I'm strugglin' maybe, or if he reckons I'm nervous he'll tell me somethin' to distract me. My momma told him it works 'cause she used to do it."

"Just like you to get nervous. Does it work?"

"Sometimes."

"Tell me somethin'."

He cleared his throat. "Did you know the dragonfly breathes out of its anus?"

She shook her head, suitably horrified.

He looked down at her and noticed a shiny clip in her hair. It was cheap and pretty and brought a lump to his throat.

"Got anything better?" she said.

"Holdin' hands with someone you love can help ease pain and stress and fear. That's proved by science."

"I ain't holdin' your hand."

She rolled onto her back and stared up at him and her eyes were heavy with tears.

"I'm so sad."

He looked down at her and tried to smile. "I get it."

"You don't, Noah. You don't take nothin' serious."

"I do. It's just . . ."

"You wear that badge and people laugh at you, like you're a joke or somethin'. Don't that bother you?"

"Does it bother you?"

"I don't care. But you want to take me out, like you can see somethin' between us, and you're serious and that bothers me."

"Why?"

"I want more."

"More than what?"

"You." She said it quick but it hung long in the night air.

"Oh."

"More than dating some boy who wants to be a cop in the shithole town we grew up in."

"You don't know nothin' about me." He said it soft.

"I know you ain't goin' nowhere. Maybe you'll get your wish and you'll be a cop, and in fifty years you'll still be in this town, and that's enough for you. I want more, like my sister. I want more than I got."

"I won't be here in fifty years," he said.

"Wishful thinkin', Noah. I'll come look you up, see what's come of your life. Dollar says it ain't never gonna be more than nothin'."

She turned her head toward the water.

He breathed deep, feeling the cloud drop down another inch above their town. He tried to think of something else to say but found out of all the words there weren't none left to speak.

He watched her for a long time, the shape of her head and the way her hair caught the breeze as she closed her eyes and drifted away.

He sat there without noticing the pass of time, listening to the rhythm of her breaths and watching her chest rise and fall.

"And you know that jacket is for women," she said, her eyes still closed.

"I do," he said.

33

Summer

Sometimes the Red is a mirror of green 'cause it narrows to nothin' but a stream between the trees. We'd pass and I'd throw a stone just to watch the ripples.

As the town exhaled, I lived with the Briar girls. When I started out writing that paper, all they were was a slice of what I was livin' 'cause that was so real. The more I thought and saw and read . . . they were us—me and my sister. There weren't no difference. I went to their churches and stood in their yards and watched the pieces of their mommas through moonlit windows. The nature of man, the good and evil, that line that gets blurred by religion and love and war. The Briar girls were my altar and I knelt before them. I'd always reckoned there was safety in God and the church, but the Briar girls took that from me, turned my world and snipped the strings that tethered me to my practiced life.

I crept out and walked the Red and saw the fires burnin' and the kids with the spray cans. The devil is a concept, a theory that binds wrists and bows heads. I reckon I have too many thoughts, which is worse than having too few.

In my dreams I saw Della Palmer and Bonnie Hinds walkin' hand in hand, their faces fixed in Edvard Munch screams. I saw Lissa Pinson and Coralee Simmons and Olive Braymer at the foot of my bed, lookin' on silent as Bobby thrusted between my legs. It would come to nothin' and somethin'—my story of me and my time, and the Briar girls that shaped my life.

Raine was worse, the way she acted and the things she did, it was feverish and obvious and I wondered what it'd take to alter her course.

We sat at the table and said grace with our heads down and our minds swimmin'. We sat in front of the television and laughed at Roseanne and Dan, Becky, Darlene and D.J. We watched the twisted metal, the dark smoke and the haunted faces when Oklahoma was broken apart. Life happened around but I didn't live it, I was a passenger to all it entails 'cept for when I was with Bobby.

We talked more but never about Michael 'cause Michael was his and he wouldn't share him. I got that feelin' more and more, like an ache that comes with loss, so deep you ain't even sure where the pain is. I would lose him one day.

Sometimes I liked lookin' back. I'd close my eyes till I was livin' those same moments over.

I walked with Raine across the fields behind our house. They rise and fall so we held hands 'cause that's what we did when the world shook beneath our feet. We were twelve and reckoned we knew all there was to know.

"I was thinkin'," Raine said.

"Yeah?"

"That snow globe that Daddy brought you back from Biloxi last year. The one with that village made of tiny houses."

"Yeah."

"I really love that."

I squeezed her hand tight and she smiled that wide smile that's mine and not for the boys.

"You can have it," I said 'cause I knew she wanted it. Sometimes I'd catch her in my bedroom watchin' the snowflakes fall.

"You know why I love it?"

"Why?"

The air was thin with first frost and we wore our big coats. Sunset was happenin' and Raine pulled me down onto the hard earth, and we sat and watched the last fired colors.

"That time when we sat like this in the backyard at night, and the snow was fallin'. You remember that time, Sum?"

"Yeah, I remember."

She put her forehead against mine and grinned so I grinned too.

Then she pulled me up and we walked.

"You reckon the Red is frozen?" she said.

"Could be, the part by the Wilsons."

"You want to go walk on it?"

I nodded. "Yeah, I do."

When we got there we walked out careful, fingers linked, our boots on ice that locked the Red beneath.

"Momma said we'll go through."

"We won't," she said.

We moved slow and the moon rose, our breath smoked and pale light hit the ice through empty winter trees. The Red turned up ahead and we walked together and listened for cracks but there weren't any.

As we rounded the curve I saw them and stopped.

"What?" she said, and I pointed.

I looked at Raine and she was watchin' them and she squeezed my hand too tight.

"How come they're here?" she said quiet.

I shook my head 'cause I hadn't never seen them before. They sat on the ice, huddled, necks entwined and feathers so white.

"They're so pretty."

"They stay together for life," I said.

"Like us."

"Yeah," I said. "Like us."

We sat on the frozen Red River and watched the swans a long time 'cause we felt certain we wouldn't never see them again.

34

The Burning

Noah opened the door and saw Black standing there, grocery bag in his hand, the cruiser parked in the driveway. It was early and for a minute he thought he might've been in shit but Black smiled and asked if he could come in.

Noah watched Black take in the kitchen; the torn linoleum and the broke cabinet doors.

"Is your grandmother home?"

"Sleepin'," Noah said. "She sleeps a lot now."

Black glanced over at the television, at the Grace square and the flamelight vigil. He shook his head like he still couldn't believe it.

"How's Raine doin'?"

"She's scared," Noah said. "But she acts like she ain't."

"Right."

"You okay, Black?"

"Yeah. Tired, maybe, got a headache most days. You can't come in for a while, to the station. I know you worked somethin' out with Trix, 'cause you go on beggin' each year, and we like havin' you round, but with the square the way it is . . . I can't have you in there. It ain't safe."

"Okay."

"I ain't sure when Joe will come, and what he'll come with."

"I get it, it's all right."

Black nodded. "You headin' to church this mornin'?"

"Yeah. It'll be mad down there. They got cameras on Jackson Ranch Road now."

"Heard you and Purv were makin' money from the visitors."

Noah frowned.

"Some guy Purv took cash off, supposed to fetch Merle but didn't bother. Guy came to us lookin' for someone to help him, like we ain't got nothin' better to do. You tell Purv to quit stealin' from folk."

"He weren't really. We went down to Merle's but he was gettin' into it with Tommy Ryan."

"That right?" Black said.

"Purv reckoned it was over gambling debts."

"Probably," Black said. He stood for a minute like his mind was someplace else. "You had breakfast yet?"

Noah shook his head.

"I brought eggs." Black walked over to the cabinets and flipped through them till he found a saucepan.

Black made scrambled eggs and they sat and ate together.

"Can I ask you a question, Black?"

"You can ask."

"Have you ever been in a shoot-out?"

Black dabbed his mouth with a napkin. "I was a state trooper, with your father."

Noah nodded 'cause he knew that. He had clippings and photos, all that was written.

"A guy named Rick Fallon and his two boys held up the Sun Trust. We chased him for six miles before he dumped his truck and tailed it into the cornfields. I couldn't see shit, just kept hearin' bullets whistle by my ear."

"Did you shoot back at 'em?"

"I just aimed for the noise."

"Did you win?"

"I ain't sure there's winners in a gunfight. Maybe degrees of loss. Your father put Rick down in the end. He was a deadly shot."

Noah nodded, eyes a little wide.

"I got his boys. One of 'em was fifteen."

"Oh."

"You look like him . . . your father."

Noah smiled 'cause he couldn't check it. "He was tough, right?"

"He was."

Noah cleared his throat. "You reckon he would've liked me . . . I mean, the way I turned out? 'Cause sometimes I don't feel it."

"Feel what?"

"I just . . . we got cop blood in our family, right? I ain't even sure what I'm sayin'."

"He would've been proud, Noah."

"Yeah?"

Black nodded, and turned back to his plate.

Jackson Ranch Road was fit to burst. Cars were parked tight on the grass verge, people walked heel to toe toward St. Luke's. The visitors glanced up, the locals stared hard at them. Trouble rode close to the surface, threatening to rip through every time a Maidenville SUV double-parked in the square, and every time a Grace local couldn't find a seat in Mae's.

There'd been a couple fights, stopped before they got bad but the square was tight with folk now.

Noah saw a bank of cameras by the gate, and shiny reporters facing them. He'd seen them on television that morning, working religion and the devil and the Briar girls, trying to make out everyone in Grace was either crazy or headed that way. He overheard a sharp-suited guy with a microphone saying that folk were coming to ask God's forgiveness, to ask him to lift the darkness from above and bless them with sunlight. There were cheers as Dale Crashaw bowled straight into him and sent his mic to the floor. The suit looked startled, called out to Milk who ignored him, a slight smile on his face.

Noah slipped outta the line, cut across the gravestones, then into the church ahead of a couple of ladies he didn't recognize.

He saw Purv sitting near the back with Rusty and one of his boys, Noah couldn't remember which. The church was lit up like Christmas, extra candles and lights and new faces staring up at the arches like they were viewing God's own handiwork.

Noah liked Christmas since he was a kid, even found dialysis easier in the run-up too. They decorated a tree at Mayland, Missy dressed as an elf, Purv wrapped aluminium foil around his chair 'cause he reckoned it looked festive.

When he was young they'd arranged for Santa to come see him. He was struck dumb and could barely get his words out when asked what he wanted for Christmas. Purv had helped, though blurting out "*a functioning kidney*" had earned him a clip from Missy.

"Lucky you got a seat," Noah said, settling in beside Purv.

"I got here early since you didn't show."

"Sorry, late night."

Purv turned to face him, his lone eyebrow raised at one end.

Noah shook his head. "Long story."

"What you two yapping about?" Rusty said.

"Noah had a date with Raine Ryan."

"Shit, son," Rusty said, shaking his head. "Don't call on me when her daddy finds out."

"Joe knows and he was all right."

"Could be he thought you were a lady in that jacket you were wearin' in the square last night," Rusty said.

A hush fell when Bobby stood at the front. There were folk standing three deep against every wall, as well as the couple hundred jammed onto the benches.

Again Bobby asked them to pray for Summer, for her to come home safe. Again he asked them to pray for Raine, and Ava and Joe, to give them hope and strength through this difficult time. He spoke loud and his voice carried and Noah closed his eyes real tight.

Bobby didn't mention the cloud and Noah was glad of that. It weren't nothing to pray about, it weren't real like Summer and the Briar girls. He glanced up when he heard the door open.

He saw Ava and heard whispers, then he saw Bobby smile at her and motion to a spot near the front where Savannah kept a place.

Ava kept her head up, dressed nice but Noah saw the change. If the past month had been tough on Raine, it'd ruined her momma.

*

Long after the service, when the church was quiet 'cept for the hollow echo of prayer, Bobby stood alone and looked at the bench where Summer would sit. And then he heard steps and he saw Raine ghost into the building. A vision of her sister, she was a sore sight, and Bobby drew a long breath.

She reached a hand up and smoothed her hair, angling her head so he wouldn't notice the graze by her eye.

"Why do people kneel when they pray?" she said.

"There's a passage in the Bible, *O come, let us worship and bow down, let us kneel before the Lord our maker.*"

She took a step forward. "I'm worried Summer ain't comin' back," she said, bold, like it was a challenge. "I wore her dress last night. Momma bought it for her to wear that time she played cello here in the church. You remember that day, Pastor Bobby?"

"Sure, I remember that day. I reckon the whole town does. It's part of Grace folklore now."

"Momma's real grateful, how the two of you look out for Summer, 'cause with all the Bird and that she said it's hard to find folk you can trust."

Bobby fell silent a long time.

"I ain't really spoke to Savannah. She looks –"

Bobby smiled. "She's from Maidenville, what'd you expect."

Raine nodded.

"I'll tell you somethin' about Savannah," he said, walking over. "She plays the cello. I mean, you know that, but she used to play concerts, with an orchestra. It was her life, music. And then we had a son, and he died." He cleared his throat. "She didn't quit for good, she was just sad. So she didn't feel much like playing. And then Summer came along and Savannah started teaching her, and when I heard that music I realized how much I'd missed it, and how quiet our house was without it."

He turned and started to leave her.

"Can I ask you a question?"

"Of course."

She pointed to the rear of the church, to the side where the font sat. "What's that little door for?"

"Do you want to see?"

She looked down first and saw Grace lit below her, the street-lights bright despite the early hour and the summer sun that held the horizon.

"On a clear day you can see for miles," Bobby said. "That's Hell's Gate over there." He pointed.

She looked at the forest, part dark but all so wild and endless and she thought of what might be in there.

"Can I bring Summer up here sometime?"

"Yeah."

She watched the bustle of the square and the lights from Mae's and the news vans.

"How come those reporters are stickin' around?" she said.

"All this talk about God, I guess. Have you been up to Hallow Road?"

She nodded.

"The dark wall. I've never seen anythin' like it. If it happened someplace else I might be joinin' people in goin' to see it."

She brought a finger to her mouth and bit a nail. "Can I ask you somethin' about Samson?"

"Okay."

"I don't even know if you'll tell me what you think 'cause most just reckon I can't handle nothin', like I'm some kid that don't know how the world works and don't know what men think when they see a pretty girl."

"I don't think Samson did anythin' to your sister, Raine."

"But you ain't sure."

"Samson walked Summer home when it was raining, which might've been a simple act of kindness. And the rest we have to guess. Or we don't. We take the facts that are there in front of us and that's what we do. So when you go home tonight, and you're lyin' in bed, try and remember the facts. It's Black's job to worry about the rest, not yours, Raine. You just need to look after yourself. And try not to worry about your parents, because that's not your job either."

"It's easy for you to say all that –"

"I know."

She leaned over and she could see gravestones, and lanterns on the gate. She rubbed her eyes 'cause she was so tired she couldn't barely stand it.

"It'll all be okay, Raine. I know it don't feel like it now, but it will."

"How do you know that?" she countered, staring hard at him.

"It has to be. Summer is okay. I believe it."

"Belief ain't enough, Pastor Bobby."

He smiled like he was sad, like she'd just told him a truth too cruel.

"I heard you're out there lookin'."

"I heard you are too."

"You need to be careful, Raine."

"I got Noah with me. And Purv."

She thought of Noah and the lights blurred. She turned her head away from Bobby and wiped her tears and he acted like he didn't see, which she was grateful for. She hadn't never cried so much and she felt weaker for it.

Noah had sat with her a long time, till she felt better. She said things to him, horrible things about his place in her world.

He'd carried her home, along the Red, her face against his chest, his hand soft on the back of her knees. He didn't ask nothing and that was something big. He wore cologne, no doubt Purv had stole it for him. He'd made an effort, booked a table at Clyde's and worked up the courage to ask her out. He'd chosen his clothes, albeit women's, combed his hair and fought his nerves. For her.

"How's Noah doin'?" he said.

She shrugged. "I used to reckon he was retarded. Maybe I still think that."

He smiled. "He has it tough, with the dialysis."

"What?"

"Dialysis."

She stared at him.

"Noah is sick, Raine. I'm sorry, I thought you knew."

She swallowed and her throat hurt. She reached up and rubbed her head and she saw her hand was shaking.

"What does . . . he ain't sick. He can't be."

Bobby smiled sad.

"I mean, he'll get better, right? They do transplants, that's what they do when kids get sick like that."

"He's had three already, Raine. They won't do another."

She nodded, and she felt hot, and the sweat was stinging her eyes as she ran from the roof down the winding stairs.

She burst from the old church and ran so fast and hard her chest was burning by the time she made it to his house. She hammered the door and Noah's grandmother answered, her eyes were layered with confusion but she knew where her grandson was, 'cause he didn't ever miss D-day, not since he was a little child.

Raine rode the Transit bus alone, from the lights of the square past the bustle on Hallow Road. She closed her eyes as she crossed the border, and she opened them to dying day. She sat above the wheel and the bumps rattled her tired bones.

When she got to Mayland she stood awhile and watched the nurses and the doctors as they moved in groups and smiled and laughed.

She walked into the bright reception and looked at the map of the hospital and saw where she needed to get. But then she walked back out and followed the flowers a long way till she came to the window.

Night fell and stars rose and she stood there for hours, watching Noah sitting in his chair in front of the television, tubes in his arm and a police badge hanging from a string around his neck.

*

The reporters beat Black to the scene, though a couple of engines were in place and the fire chief was doing his best to keep them back.

Trix had taken the call, thought it was another hoax, but radioed Rusty who was nearest. Rusty had been over in Windale, talking to the pastor at the New Hope Baptist Church. The guy was old and sour but said he'd be vigilant and tell parents not to let their girls outta their sight.

"Shit," Black said, as he climbed out. Rusty stood beside the cruiser, close enough to feel the heat. The house belonged to Radley Coke, though he'd moved to a nursing home several years back.

The flames glowed bright, the smoke rose toward the cloud, and cameras fired off shots of it all.

"They'll put it out quick," Rusty said, hooking his thumbs into his waistband and rocking back and forth on his heels like he was enjoying the show.

"Stop that," Black said.

"Who do you reckon?" Rusty said.

"Crazies. Rollers. Scaring the devil away. Could be the other side though, welcoming him to town."

"Led by the Circle of Black Knights?"

"Yeah, them, or mescaline."

Rusty laughed.

They spun when they heard a high whine and saw Pastor Lumen scooting toward them.

"How the fuck did he get here?" Black said.

"Deely White's truck is over there," Rusty said.

Pastor Lumen parked in front of the cameras, reached for one of his medals, and held it out in front.

"The lake of fire. Unquenchable," Pastor Lumen said, as cameras trained on him.

They got money shots of the crippled preacher under the dark sky, the fire framing him in hellish red. Photographs that'd run on all the front pages come morning.

Black turned back to the house.

They heard Pastor Lumen spewing, so took a step nearer the heat. The flames licked and crackled.

"Hell of a summer we're havin'," Rusty said.

Black heard the radio and ran over to the cruiser.

"What is it?" Rusty said.

"Another fire. One of the Dennisons' barns."

Black started the engine.

"Shit," Rusty said. "Grace is burnin'."

35

Summer

That day the rain was so loud I thought maybe somethin' broke up there. I watched it from the trees and Samson stood dripping beside me. He stands awkward, he's such a funny shape I ain't sure there's anywhere he'd fit.

We talked for a long time 'cause I didn't have nowhere to go and I reckon Samson didn't neither. I'd see him at the church, always lookin' at me like he wanted to talk but couldn't manage it.

"You ever want to move out on your own, Sam?" I said, 'cause he said sometimes he still felt like a kid, like he hadn't never left school.

"My daddy said I don't earn enough for that. He keeps my books, gives me what I need."

I nodded. "He's sick though."

"Mr. White looks after the money now, he . . . I ain't sure I'd know how to do it."

I wondered about Samson, about nature and perception and all that's between.

"It's nice that your daddy cares like that," I said.

We heard a snap and saw a flycatcher, it was gray and lookin' down from the treetop.

"People reckon he's hard," Samson said.

I couldn't imagine no one harder but I just smiled.

"Momma said it's 'cause he cares, about all of us and where we're headed. I didn't want to let him down, I just . . . you ever feel there's somethin' dark inside you, Summer?"

"Yeah."

"Momma said it's temptation, to do somethin' you know ain't right. How come it feels right, though?"

I shrugged. "You seen that apple, in paintings, gotta be the sweetest-lookin' thing I ever saw. Wouldn't be no test otherwise."

"I thought I was strong."

"Everybody does. The truth comes hard at you, Sam. I bet even your momma did shit she knew weren't right."

I worried I'd stepped far but Samson grinned.

"She used to pick flowers, and she used to get me to pick 'em, flowers you ain't supposed to pick," Samson said. "But then that don't seem much, not really."

"Right and wrong and shades of gray."

He reached into his pocket and took out a pink flower. "I brought one for you, thought I'd see you at church maybe. I was thinkin' about how you like the colored glass."

I took it from him careful.

"That dark," he said. "You reckon God will give me a chance to make it light again?"

"Sure, Sam." I stepped out and felt the rain but it weren't the cleansing kind. "I didn't reckon it'd be so hard."

"What?" he said.

"Everything."

I turned and walked and he called me back, and he told me to hold that flower up to the light when I got home.

Sometimes the dark turns on me till I switch on my lamp and reach for a book. I move into their world, no matter if it's '20s West Egg or '30s Maycomb, it's all so much warmer and brighter. It's like headin' home again.

The Swan by Camille Saint-Saëns. That's my favorite piece of music I ever heard and ever played. There's notes in there that can stop my heart.

One day I played it for Savannah and watched her eyes close like usual but I could tell somethin' was different 'cause she scrunched them pained tight.

She got up and took Michael's photograph in her hand. She walked to the window and she bent double. She cried till there weren't nothin' left of her but a perfect shell with a perfect crack down the center. I watched her insides trickle out and I kept playin' 'cause I reckoned maybe she needed what I gave her.

And then Bobby was in the room and he was holdin' her so I closed my eyes and I went to the place where the real swans were. Their grace and Raine's eyes as she took them in. I saw them with their necks entwined and I knew what bliss was and how far I existed from it.

I could take my life.

It's all right to say that if it's true but if it's just a cry for help then you're really fucked 'cause a part of you clings to all of this.

When my mood digs me down in the dirt, till I'm so deep the sky ain't nothin' but the earth, that's when I'm the girl who could slip from this lifetime. And if I did what would happen is nothin' much at all 'cause hearts would still break and the world would circle like I'd never been a part of it.

He held her so close they became one, but his eyes fixed hard at the sky and I knew he'd moved far from her and from me and from Grace.

If I didn't have Bobby, or even Savannah, 'cause I needed her too, then I had the kinda nothin' that made me the sum of my parents' parts, a chemical reaction that went wrong somewhere vital.

We can't all be well.

I was so sad.

So sad.

So sad.

"It's freezin'," I said to Raine. My teeth were chatterin' like a wind-up set.

Raine's hand shook as she held the cigarette out in front of her. We were eleven and snow fell light around us.

I lit a match and brought it up to the end of the cigarette and Raine sucked hard on it.

She coughed and spluttered.

"How is it?" I said.

She looked up at me and her eyes watered but she nodded as she spit in the snow.

"You try," she said.

I brought the filter to my lips and sucked.

"Now breathe it down," Raine said. She was excited 'cause she wanted me to cough too.

She stood and stared at me, her head cocked to the side.

"Blow it out," she said.

I tried.

Raine looked at me with her perfect eyes wide, a smile formin'. "Where's the smoke?"

I shrugged.

"Could still be inside," she said, pattin' my back hard.

Nothin' came.

"You've eaten it," she said, startin' to laugh.

I blew and blew, wheezin' all I could.

"Oh, Jesus," I said. "What's gonna happen to me?"

Raine laughed so hard. "It'll come out at some point. Just try not to breathe round Daddy."

I pushed her. She fell back and sat in the grass. She laughed even harder as she pulled me down too. Cold seeped through our pants.

"You reckon we'll see another special star?" Raine said, lookin' toward the sky.

"Yeah, if we keep lookin'."

She pulled a bottle of Seagram's from her coat.

"Momma will be pissed if she smells gin on your breath."

"Momma's always pissed." She drank and smacked her lips and then grimaced. "Tasty."

She offered me the bottle and I took it and drank. "Christ," I said.

"I know, good, right."

"Hmm."

"You reckon we'll ever get married?"

I nodded. She took my hand and held it.

"Imagine us married, livin' on the same street. Our kids could play together. We might get twins of our own."

"Shit," I said.

She laughed.

There's a sweetness to Raine that'd ruin you.

"It's comin' down now," she said.

I looked up at the snowflakes swirlin' round and down and dizzying.

That was one of those moments too pure and perfect, the memory I'll forget, the still at my funeral.

36

Those Smitten Church Girls

They sat in a half-empty diner off Colombus Highway. It was small and the windows were steamed and they sold whole hams to take home.

Savannah smiled at the waitress as she brought over two cups of coffee.

They sat in silence awhile and watched the traffic beginning to stack 'cause there were men working the road.

"I heard it's gettin' real bad in Grace," Peach said.

"Yes. I know Summer Ryan, I teach her cello."

"And the cloud."

"And the cloud. Though it hardly seems worth the fuss."

"They're sayin' it's bad, that somethin' bad is comin'."

The waitress hovered and asked if they wanted pie and they said no so she left them.

"Della's birthday today," Peach said.

Savannah reached across and squeezed her hand. She'd met Peach at the center in Pinegrove.

"I walked the route she took to church this mornin'. I do it most days, before the heat gets up. There's a cypress grove, by the backwater. The trees by the line, the roots ain't covered no more so they just sweep the ground and they look like snakes, or arms or somethin'. The wildflowers are pretty though."

Savannah watched her speak, the way her mouth moved, and she wondered who Peach had been with in her life. The men that would visit. She wondered if there was pleasure, if there was ever pleasure.

"I hope he didn't hurt her," Peach said, and she stirred her coffee and didn't cry. "Sometimes I want it over, but I ain't ready to pay that price. I can't stay here much longer, this place where I'm at between wonderin' and closing off. Would it be easier if I got to bury her and say good-bye? . . . I ain't sure of nothin'."

"You do well, Peach."

"They thought she was trash," Peach said. "At first, those cops that stopped by and knew what I did to get money, they saw Della as nothin' but my daughter 'stead of the girl she was. Didn't matter she was smart, or she went to church or that she was a sweetheart."

"That must have been so difficult for you."

"I stopped by the station weekly. Ernie was kind but the other cops, they fixed me with stares that lay someplace between pity and disgust, the Bible Belt looped over my head and ready to hang me. They had it figured, those shiny cops all sharp judgment."

"But it changed."

Peach nodded. "After the other girls, girls from the better families. Maybe they looked at Della and started to see her. That piece they wrote in the *Herald*, they spoke to Della's teacher and she said nice things. I ain't got much pride, Savannah, but I'm proud of my daughter and I needed them to see her too."

"Who?"

"Everyone. I wouldn't let them look at her and see my mistakes, I'd die before I let that happen. We're all more than the bad things we do."

Savannah felt the words.

"I ain't been sleepin'," Peach said. "Funny, now I ain't got the worry of who's showin' at my door."

"Do you know why?"

"Sometimes I see him outside, sittin' in his car."

"The man you're seeing?"

"Yeah. But he don't come in, he just sits there watchin' the window. So I kneel down and I pray." She laughed soft as she spoke.

"Why?"

"I don't know. I want him to see somethin' else, maybe it'll throw him 'cause it ain't what he's expectin'. You reckon maybe I'm a bit mad, Savannah?"

"I think everyone is a bit mad, Peach."

They watched a big man pass and he shot a glance over both of them then settled at the counter and reached for a newspaper. He had a scar by his eye and he turned his head embarrassed when Savannah glanced at him. She wondered about scars, visible and not. She wondered how little people saw when they looked at her.

"I want him to come knock at the door and take me someplace."

"But he doesn't."

"I reckon maybe he's shamed, 'cause people know me after what happened, know all about me and what I do. He's good though. He hurts, for the things he's done, he tortures himself so bad. Maybe that's why I love him, 'cause he feels for others like that." Peach sipped her coffee and rubbed her eyes. Her nails were painted and broke.

"You could just ask him. Just ask where you stand."

"I couldn't lose him. I'd take this, whatever it is, I'd take it over nothin'. Does that make me weak?"

"You're not weak, Peach. Far from it."

"I don't expect the fairy tale, what you and Bobby got."

"That's not –"

Peach caught herself, eyes sad, and this time she reached across. "I'm sorry, I didn't mean that . . . Michael."

Savannah smiled.

"I just meant you and Bobby . . . he's a good man. I saw that. He came in once, to the West End Mission."

"Did he?" Savannah said.

"One Sunday. He sat at the back during the service. Pastor Roberts made a show of him, got him to stand up, and Bobby was shy. Then after, Bobby was talkin' about the Christian Youth drive. He's got a way about him."

"He works hard. He visits churches all over the state."

"Della was smitten, had those big puppy dog eyes for him, like all the church girls."

*

Noah and Raine left the Buick parked on Hallow Road but far from the crowd.

People stood thick at the border at all hours now.

They passed a couple ice cream trucks, and a guy selling coffee from the back of his pickup. He had an old urn and a couple bottles of milk in a cooler, and a wife with a hard face and a stack of bills in her hand.

Crowds stood against the dark wall, stuck a hand through the shadow before finding the courage to follow it, like it was a gateway to someplace forbidden.

There was awe among the visitors, talk about God and light. They took turns taking photos. Some knelt in prayer. A small line held hands and dipped their heads, chanting soft enough to keep their words from traveling to the onlookers. Noah heard they'd tripped down from Viker Hill or maybe someplace just as bleak and devout.

There were folk laughing, some on lawn chairs with sandwiches, settling in for a day of cloud gazing.

A wild-eyed black man stood alone. In his hands he held a sign: THE SKY IS FALLING DOWN.

The man glanced up at Noah and nodded. Noah nodded back.

The world was flat and Grace hung over the edge.

They walked side by side, Noah in the light of Windale, Raine in the dark of Grace. They moved slow, the ground uneven beneath their feet.

"I saw some guy with Arizona plates," Noah said.

"I saw Colorado."

"Jesus."

"You reckon maybe we would've liked all this shit goin' on a while back, before?"

"Maybe. I know Purv's enjoyin' it, he's making a fast buck every day now."

They walked on.

"I see you watchin' me sometimes," Raine said.

"Yeah."

"It's all right, all the boys watch me."

"How come you're being nice to me now?"

"I ain't."

He tried to take her hand. "Fuck off," she said.

"That's better," he said.

They'd been to three houses the night before, watched the lady with the fire-red hair, and also a honky-tonk way out in Midway. They'd staked half the night; Purv and Raine drifting off sometimes, Noah staying sharp. At one point he'd seen a flicker of light from a basement window in a house by the old Monroe railroad. He'd crept out alone and sidled up to the window then dropped to his hands and knees, peered through and caught sight of the guy, Chester Mulharney, whacking it to some grainy videotape.

They heard yelling and they turned but couldn't see nothing 'cause they'd walked far along the line.

"Probably a Kinley shakin' down the wrong guy," Raine said.

They struggled on, the ground turning to dips and waves and lumps of earth baked hard as rocks. He'd skipped dialysis again, 'cause Raine needed him, 'cause the days were passing fast.

He felt tired. Missy called and he didn't answer. Trix stopped by and he didn't come to the door. He'd get back on track. As long as he didn't leave too long between each session.

"You reckon Summer's dead?" she said without warning. "You reckon the Bird took her like he took those Briar girls?"

He stopped and turned to face her. He pulled her forward, into the sunlight, and she squinted back, eyes burning like she was daring him to lie.

"She'll come back. She will come back. I promise."

He knew it was a moment that'd last and haunt and keep pace till it was over. A moment taken from a summer when a funny kinda cloud shaded their lives, a summer when he made a promise he couldn't possibly keep no matter how much he asked and how much he prayed.

He tried to take her hand again but she slipped it from him.

"My sister holds my hand."

"Oh."

"Can we bring her here one day? Even if the cloud has gone," she said.

"All right."

"All right."

"You reckon Summer will like me?" he said.

"No."

When they got back he bought her a cone, though she tried to stop him. Raine held it and licked the edges, trying to keep pace with the melt. They reached the Buick and climbed up onto the dented hood, leaning back against the windshield and staring straight up.

"Imagine if there ain't no sky above the cloud. Imagine if it's just gone," he said.

"What will be there then, when it moves out the way?"

"Just space. It will be like we're livin' in outer space. The stars will shine so bright that we won't even need the sun no more."

"Imagine the cloud takes gravity with it too, and we can just float round. Imagine when we drive back into town, we'll get to the border and the Buick will just take off."

"We'd have to tie it somehow. Tie everything. Otherwise folk would just float away too, everything would just float away."

"Maybe that wouldn't be so bad," she said.

"I want to go up there. Into space. Since I was a kid and Purv stole a rocket from that toy store that used to be next to Ginny's. We tied it to a firework and lit it by the Red. It fell just as the fuse sparked, aimed right back at us. We hightailed it, I was laughin' so hard and Purv was screamin' real high like a girl."

She smiled.

"My momma said I could be an astronaut if I worked hard at school. I believed her. Funny how it slips as each year passes," he said.

"What?"

"Hope, maybe. Belief. That there's better out there. Better than what I got, which ain't all that much really."

"I didn't mean it, what I said the other night."

He shrugged like it weren't nothing. "We don't think about that, me and Purv."

" 'Cause you're brave and you're fierce."

"We are. Don't stop me wishin' though."

"For what?"

"I sit in the station, watchin' the real cops and maybe for a moment I feel like one of 'em. I step outta my life and into theirs. I got this need to be somebody else so bad it hurts."

"But you can just be you, Noah. Don't matter what you end up doin' or where you end up livin'. You can just be you."

"I don't want to be me."

"Why not?" she said, her voice quiet.

He looked up at the sky and didn't say nothing.

"I know," she said. "I saw you . . . at Mayland."

He swallowed. "I saw you too."

"It'll be all right," she said.

"It will, just not for me," he said.

*

Black sat beside Bobby on the wood bench in the cemetery. Lights burned in the church and dropped color through the stained glass.

Black sipped his beer slowly. He'd bought a six-pack from Ginny's then came to sit awhile. He'd been surprised to find Bobby there, even more when he'd taken a beer for himself.

"How come you ain't home?" Black said. "It's gettin' late."

"I'm not sure really. I sit out here sometimes. Makes me feel closer to death."

"Closer to God then."

"Maybe."

Black glanced over at him. Bobby looked beat, like a man that didn't ever rest no more. Black could relate.

"Do any pastors ever give up, just walk away from it and join the rest of us down here?" Black said.

"That what you reckon? I exist on a higher plane?"

"Maybe you're less flawed. I was brought up like that, respect the church and all."

"I knew this guy . . . a pastor over in Hattiesburg. He seemed to love it, I mean, he was a decent speaker, warm and compassionate and funny."

"What happened?"

Bobby ran his finger around the can. "He woke one mornin' and stopped believin'. Suddenly it was all lies, all nonsense. Just like that. He carries all this guilt with him. For wastin' his life, for wastin' people's time."

"You ever worry that'll happen to you?"

Bobby nodded.

"I get that, kinda like losin' your mind."

"Or findin' it."

Black smiled.

"I used to come out here after church, when I was a kid. I used to read the gravestones. I'd look for the oldest, then the youngest," Black said. "I still do it now. I got a thing about the messages on the stones."

"How do you mean?"

"It's hard to get it right. People try and say too much, flower it up. It bugs me."

"So what's the perfect script?"

"Somethin' that means somethin' to someone."

"How do you mean?"

"Just somethin' so simple, but it gets you right here," Black said, tapping his chest with his fist.

"Like Mitch Wild?" Bobby said. "I'm always drawn to that stone."

Black nodded. He could make out the grave from where he sat, the marble shined 'cause Noah tended it often, the script proud against lantern light. *Brave and fierce in his service to the people of Grace.*

"They got that one just about perfect," Black said as he lit a cigarette. "You ever hear of the Boyington Oak?"

Bobby shook his head.

"It's an oak tree in a cemetery over in Mobile. So there was this guy named Charles Boyington, he was a printer, lived in Mobile in the 1830s. He was also a gambler. One time he was seen with another guy, Nathaniel Frost, who folk reckoned owed money to Charles. Later they found Frost's body, all stabbed up and robbed, near the cemetery on Church Street."

Black passed Bobby another beer.

"Now Charles Boyington was the obvious suspect. He was executed and buried in that same graveyard. Before they hanged him Charles kept sayin' a mighty oak would spring up from his heart and prove he was innocent."

"Did it?"

Black nodded. "Grew right out his grave. Now that's gotta beat a headstone, right?"

Bobby smiled.

Black set his beer down and rubbed his eyes. "Fuckin' cloud."

"I can hear Pastor Lumen from here some nights. When he's got the microphone. I tried talking to him –"

Black waved him off. "He don't listen to no one. Never has, never will. We were all glad when you and Savannah came to town. I mean, I ain't wishin' the man ill or nothin', but he's always had a cruel tongue. I got the press here, the dark sky and the girls."

"I helped search, went to Joe and walked with his men," Bobby said, staring down at the dirt. "I think of Summer out there and it kills me."

"He's preyin' on church girls, you know that?"

"I do."

"That's the kinda world this is now. I wonder if things will get better in the future. Religion . . . makes you wonder about it. The gains and the losses."

"What do you believe, Black?"

"I got a cross tacked up in my kitchen."

Bobby nodded.

"How do you do it?" Black said. "That compassion, for people that ain't good, a lot of them, askin' forgiveness when you know they'll do it again."

"It's not on me to forgive. How many faces do people have, Black? I don't have the empathy I need anymore. I see people round me, people close to me, and I see what they want to see. But it don't make it real. I died years back, the part that goes on does only that."

"Your boy?"

Bobby nodded. "If I stop believing then where's Michael now?"

"Blame is a game you ain't never gonna win, Bobby."

Bobby saw lights in the sky. "This guy you're lookin' for."

"The Bird."

"I really hope you stop him soon."

Noah lay in his bed but sleep didn't come.

Raine didn't need his problems 'cause she had her own.

They'd driven back to her place after, the Buick bumping along the track roads in the kinda silence that made Noah wonder if they were the last people left out there, the rest just sucked down and swallowed by air too heavy now, sky too dark and too sad.

He'd watched her walk up her street then blend into shadow without a glance back in his direction.

He rubbed his eyes till there were colors, then he sat up quick when he heard tapping on his window.

Raine's face pressed against the glass, the world behind her cut to a single cloud. He opened the window and she climbed from the flat roof into his bedroom.

She kicked off her sneakers.

She told him to lie down, then she lay beside him, her head on his chest, rising and falling with each of his breaths.

She moved up and kissed him hard.

She sat up and took off her T-shirt and bra.

He looked away.

She reached for his hand and brought it to her breast.

"Why are you doin' this?" he said.

"Pity."

"I'll take it."

She smiled.

"I think I love you," he said.

"Shut up," she said.

*

It was as the square slowly woke, as weary eyes opened to morning dark, and as the two warring sides of the green readied for another long day, that the network vans came to life. Reporters got into position, makeup was hastily applied, and cameramen roused from makeshift beds.

Joe got to his feet and walked over, leaving Tommy sleeping on the bench beside. He asked one of the reporters what was going on and might've got nothing if it weren't for the look on his face.

Joe kept even as he was told.

Before long the news ravaged the town like wildfire.

Another girl had gone missing.

37

Summer

I lay my head on Bobby's golden chest and listened to the mechanical function of his heart, and I wondered about love and the intricacies and imbalance of emotion. I thought about the Greeks and agape and eros, how maybe there's too much play in that particular four-letter word.

At the start, before I knew, Bobby's soul was a winter garden and my body was the first color of spring. I didn't know death so leaden, so endless, and so despairing.

I wondered about sex and its forms; fingers and tongues and fevered tears. And afterwards, when the action had reaction and he saw me with empty eyes.

I had sat in the library and looked up that boys' home in Arnsdale where Bobby was raised. There was lots of pieces, more than I could read, all tellin' the kinda tales that scored out divine providence. They shuttered it in 1984 and brought charges against the soulless; those dead-eyed men that took silent to the stand 'cause remorse, even feigned, was a trait too human.

"Will you hurt me?" I said.

He stared at me and I smiled.

"Is that my role, Bobby? Impressionable innocent."

"Yes."

"I think Savannah suspects somethin'."

"I know," he said.

"You know?"

"I can't see her hurt."

"Will you just stop things one day when I ain't expectin' it? I reckon it's best if I don't see it comin'."

He nodded.

"That'll be a bad day."

"Yes, not just for you."

"You'll have to do it 'cause I wouldn't never leave you, Bobby."

"I know, Summer."

I squeezed his hand so tight the blood stopped flowin'.

"Your interview is tomorrow," Bobby said.

"I know."

"Are you nervous?"

I shook my head 'cause I knew I weren't going.

"I played Fauré, the Élégie. There was people there, Savannah's friends from the school in Maidenville, and they stood there and stared and after they clapped."

You can mourn somethin' that weren't never yours, like those teenyboppers that cut themselves when one of the pretty boys tires of sainthood. It still hurt though, right then, what could've been, it still hurt.

"Did you finish your paper?" he said.

"They're out there," I said.

"The Briar girls?"

"I see them buried in shallow graves, coughin' dirt and clawing at wood."

"Summer."

"You reckon he raped them?"

"Summer."

"He must've. That's what they do, the monsters that live so deep that when they surface it's all or nothin'. Perfect pleasure is perfect pain. Why's the line so fine, Bobby? God made it that way. It's another apple."

"Summer."

"What?" I said, sharp, turnin' up to face him.

"Why are you cryin'?"

"Sometimes there ain't nothin' else to do but cry."

He stroked my shoulder gentle.

"People crane their necks so far back to look at you," I said.

"They don't see me."

"Do you still think about the Briar girls?"

"I pray for them."

"What am I to you?" I said.

"Life is a line. The things we do might alter the route but the end is still the end and nothin' will change that."

"And you stay fixed on the end."

"Yes."

He kissed the top of my head and I was glad my hair smelled of oranges that day.

"But that doesn't mean I don't care," he said.

"I know," I said.

"I don't want to hurt you, Summer."

"But you will."

"I will."

"I look at you and you look sad, Bobby."

"I am sad."

"Do you want to have another child one day?"

"No."

"No."

"If there is a heaven, and if I go there, I'll find my boy and he'll see I lived only for him."

I wondered about honesty in all its forms—blunt and brutal and beautiful.

That night I walked past the Kinley field with the devil sign and I thought of the Briar girls immortalized. Bobby reckons people's biggest fear is being forgot. We all know this life ain't eternal, what we leave behind outlives us by a distance that can't be measured.

I could break from myself, that's the way I saw it when I decided to do it alone. I could be that question mark for a while. Who ain't never thought of their own funeral? Who ain't turned on by the outpouring of grief and the size of the hole left behind?

Maybe I wanted Bobby to feel it, a stretch of that ache I lived with since I first met him. Maybe I did, but that seems too neat now, too oh-I-get-it, 'cause truth was he'd lived enough hurt for all of us.

There ain't a reason for everythin', some things just were and are and will be.

We are passengers trapped.

If you trust, if you truly believe, then you're immortal.

I couldn't take a wrong turn; I gave myself to the Lord and dared him to intervene. I packed my bag and wrote my note and said I was sorry but sorrow is wasteful. There ain't no mistakes, there ain't room for them.

38

The Nature of Addiction

Black and Milk drove toward the King place. Black flashed the lights the whole way and blipped the siren twice when they ran up behind a tractor and the old man behind the wheel didn't pull aside quick enough.

"Another girl missin'," Milk said.

"It's early, we only got the bones so far."

"They're connected. He's back, the Bird. Ain't no doubt now." Milk wiped the sweat from his head.

Ernie had called; he was putting a team together but asked Black to head over 'cause he was nearer.

Black cranked the A/C the second they crossed the town line and the sun hit.

A thick crowd watched them pass as Black put his foot down, saw the needle climb and the horizon close.

The Kings lived in Sundown, a dust and weed town a couple miles west of Grace. Black almost overshot the turn into Stockdale, had to wrench the wheel hard enough to leave him worrying they were headed into Still Creek.

The King house was quiet. Black knew the press were heading out, though they didn't know the roads like he did. There weren't no signs in Sundown.

"Hotter than Hades," Milk said, squinting.

Black took a moment. The house was small but the Kings' land sprawled. He caught site of a combine maybe a quarter mile out, looked like it'd been left a while ago 'cause the birds were on it.

The screen door opened before they got near. A kid ran out, barefoot and smiling, his momma not far behind.

Jessie-Pearle King thanked them for coming and offered to make a pitcher of iced tea. It was so hot in the house Black almost took her up on it. There was a fan in the corner, he made the mistake of glancing at it 'cause the next thing he knew Jessie-Pearle was plugging it into the wall and aiming it at them. He knew folk rationed, kept the bills down, maybe an hour at nightfall to help the kids get off to sleep.

"Amber's a good girl," Jessie-Pearle said straight off. "I know, believe me, I know what you must be thinkin' but you should know she ain't the sort to stay out. She's got a boyfriend but he's a neighbor's kid and just about as worried as we are. She didn't have a fight with her friends. I know what to do, I know where you'll look. I called round the other parents. I spoke with Pastor Brazell."

"Amber goes to church?" Milk said.

"Every Sunday, Brook Hill Baptist, with me and her brother. And I know what that means . . . with the Bird still out there."

"Is Amber's father –"

"Out lookin'. He's drivin' the streets."

"Any neighbors who might know somethin', or want to help? We're short of men at the moment," Black said.

"I know about the circus in Grace. I seen the news."

"Have you got a recent photograph we can –"

She passed them a stack: Amber smiling, Amber playin' softball, Amber eating a hot dog.

They ran through the stocks: what time they last saw her, where she was headed, when she was due back. While Milk took details Black went up to her bedroom and saw much as he'd expected. Time was short, they'd move on the assumption she'd been taken and they'd set up blockades, all points. It was Ernie's show but Black was deep.

When Black headed down the stairs he heard Milk finishing up so he didn't sit again, just stood looking out across yellow plains, the sun so fierce three wildfires had been called in in the last week alone.

Milk smiled at the kid, who smiled back but pressed close to his momma.

"Chief Black, I need you to do somethin' for me."

Black met her eye.

"I need you to skip the part where you look for an angle that ain't there, where you look at us and our lives, and Amber and hers. I need you to trust me on this." She wiped a tear as she spoke. "Someone has done somethin' to her. She didn't run. Every road you go down that don't lead to a fresh kinda hell is wasted time. I know how that sounds, but I need you to get that."

Black glanced at Milk. Milk glanced back.

When Ernie and his men got there they headed out.

Jessie-Pearle stood among the crowd in the front yard, the sun hot on her shoulders as her world slipped from her grasp.

Black and Milk drove most of the way back in silence, both watching the sky. They saw the cloud from far off, hanging heavy above Grace like some cursed creature. Black eased off the gas as they drove down Hallow Road. The group had swelled with the news.

Both flinched a little as the cruiser was swallowed by the dark wall.

"It's gettin' harder to come back," Black said, switching the lights on.

"It is."

"It ain't home. It ain't . . . I don't even know what it is. A month and the world has shifted."

Milk ran a hand over his .22.

"Got all these fuckin' vultures circlin'. Got the church on one side, Joe and his men on the other. We got a guy locked up for somethin' he likely had nothin' to do with, can't be released 'cause he'd be strung up before he got the chance to open his mouth. We got Summer missin', and the more time passes the more I reckon she ain't comin' back."

Milk rolled down the window. The square smelled of fire and trouble. An SUV with Maidenville plates was blocking the entrance to the lot.

"Hell," Black said, keeping his hand on the horn. He flashed the lights a couple times and ran the siren.

Black gazed in the mirror and saw Joe Ryan staring back at him, more concern in his eyes than anything else. Black would go speak to him, tell him about Amber and hope that'd mean he'd lower the price on Samson's head.

He took his hand off the horn, pressed it twice more, and cursed.

Milk opened the door, pulled his gun before Black could work out what was going on, and fired at the SUV. He put a bullet just above the wheel arch. There were a couple screams that came from the church side, a couple cheers from Joe's men.

Milk got back in as a guy emerged from Mae's and ran over to the truck. His face was ash when he saw the hole. He raised his hands to the sky and near shit his pants when Black pressed the horn again.

*

Pastor Lumen was waiting on Black. Black would've cursed at Trix but she looked like she weren't in no kinda mood for it.

Pastor Lumen wore his finest suit and his collar.

"What do you want?" Black said.

Pastor Lumen took the hostility in his stride. "I want you to let my boy go."

"Ain't happening. Anything else?"

"I heard the rumblings, is it right? Is there another child missin'?"

Black nodded and the old man shook his head sad.

"Samson is innocent."

"Yeah."

"You're bowin' to criminals, Chief Black. How do you reckon that makes you look?"

It was a question Black asked himself every morning when he got to the station. "It ain't about how I look."

"It is. It's about faith, and not in God, in you, Chief Black. This town ain't what it was when I was a boy, even when you was a boy. They call it the Panic but it's so much more. It's the slow slide to a world without conscience. People are angry."

"People are always angry. There ain't jobs, money. Country's boomin' and they ain't felt none of it."

"I hold sway, still."

"With fear," Black said. "When I was a kid I was scared of you."

"Much of it is show. But we need fear. You need it, fear of you, fear of the law. I need it and the church needs it, the fear of burnin'. Do you still lie awake at night?"

Black stared at him.

"I know about the nature of your addictions, Chief Black. I know this will tip you, another girl gone. I know how you'll reason with the pain and the guilt you feel."

Black closed his eyes to the old man.

"You came to me when there was no one else," Pastor Lumen said.

"It didn't help. Askin' like that, forgiveness means nothin' down here."

"So you go on, you roll over, you stand and fight. You mourn the death of your partner and you drink till you die. If that's an offering . . . your only purpose now is to assuage your guilt."

"It's not. I am tired of my place on this earth, that's all."

"That's all. You're holdin' my boy and –"

"Why do you care? I see how you look at Samson. That day at the river, when Mary called us –"

"I'd rather you didn't speak my late wife's name."

"I ain't never seen a boy so scared of his father. What did you do to him? Clothes all wet like that."

"He was swimmin' in the Red, we told him not to."

Black smiled. "Swimmin' in all his clothes?"

"Samson is a boy who needs guidance. The devil works hard to claim him."

"He ain't a boy now. You don't care about him, I see that clear."

"He carries my name."

"So it's vanity. Ain't that a sin?"

Pastor Lumen smiled with something like pity in his eyes. "Let him go."

"You can't protect him. Blood will be spilled."

Pastor Lumen stood. "Blood is always spilled in times of trouble. This cloud, I believe it's time. I believe the reckoning is comin'. How will you measure up, Chief Black?"

Black spent the next hours liaising with Ernie, tipping the news vans, and making sure the whole county was watching for Amber King.

It was gone midnight by the time he left the station. He stood on the top step, looking out over the square. The lights were still burning in Mae's, business was brisk till the early hours and Mae took on a couple Beauregard girls to help out.

There were rowdy folk outside the Whiskey Barrel, mostly outsiders, though Black caught a glimpse of Merle.

The church people had laid down their placards for the night. Some lay back on the grass and stared straight up at the cloud, their mouths open as if they still couldn't quite believe what was going down in Grace.

Joe's people were sleeping in lawn chairs, leaned right back with their guns on the ground beside them.

Black walked down the steps and over to Joe, who was sat on the far bench, smoking a cigarette and looking out.

Black settled beside him, pulled his gun out, and lay it between them.

"Ava always wonders why you do that," Joe said, exhaling heavy.

"The gun?"

"Yeah. She reckons maybe you're tryin' to show people you're packin' or maybe you're tryin' to show you don't mean 'em no harm."

Black laughed.

"But I said to her she's readin' too much into it. She does that. Lot of people do that. They're always tryin' to see shit that ain't there, or work out why. Why this, why that."

"Maybe tell her it's 'cause the damn thing digs into my hip."

"I would but she won't believe it."

"You heard about the King girl?" Black said, taking a cigarette when Joe offered one.

"I heard."

"State cops are comin' down."

"That's quick. No messin' this time."

Black nodded and took the hit.

"I know the Kings. I ran with Jimmy when I was fifteen. We tried to hold up the liquor store in Dawson, you remember it?" Joe said.

"I remember."

"Stole his old man's car and we parked it right out front, didn't even hide the plates or nothin'. There was an old guy that owned that store, I don't remember his name, but when I told him to open the register he said no. He was calm, even though I was wavin' a SIG about. It was a replica, didn't even fire it was so cheap. So I told him again, and he said no again. I asked why and he said he didn't want to get into it."

Black laughed.

"What kinda shit is that? '*Didn't want to get into it.*' "

"What did you do?" Black said, holding the smoke deep and feeling his lungs burn.

"I left."

"Just like that?"

"Just like that. I just got this feelin' it was gonna go bad. Like this voice in the back of my head sayin' '*not this time, don't push it this time.*' So we walked out nice and calm and that's when I noticed the old man had a .22 in his hands, and it'd been pointin' right back at me. His hand was low on the counter so I hadn't noticed. He would've shot me, ain't no doubting."

One of Joe's men glanced over, Black met his eye and he looked away. They didn't have a problem with Black, not really, they probably wanted to get home and get on but knew Joe would've done the same for each of them.

"What if the King girl is connected to Summer?" Black said.

"What if she is?"

"Then Samson didn't have nothin' to do with it."

"You had time, Black. You got about as much an idea where to look as I have. Samson Lumen is the only lead. The *only* lead, you get that? I can find out if he knows somethin'. I can look him in the eye and ask him what happened to my daughter and he won't be able to tell no lies."

They settled back into near silence, only the muttering of a few cameramen leaning against a news van reaching them.

"Fuckin' carnival time here," Joe said. "I was thinkin' about this cloud . . . the day it came."

Black glanced at him but Joe didn't say nothing else.

Black smoked to the end, dropped his cigarette to the grass, and stood. "That feelin' you got, with the old man. That feelin' that told you not to push. I got that same feelin' now. If you push me on this I think somethin' bad will happen."

"Shit, Black. Somethin' bad already happened. Look around. Can't you see that? I think about Summer, if she's dead –"

"You shouldn't –"

"If she's dead did I do all I could for her? That's a question you need to ask yourself too, Black."

*

Black sat in his high-back chair and stared at the wall. With a trembling hand he cut her photograph out of the newspaper and rose and stuck Amber King's pretty face beside the others. Briar girl number six. Or maybe number seven.

He drank a bottle of Old Crow, the whole thing chugged like it weren't nothing that could do him bad. His muscles were so tight he took Vicodin, laid the pills out in a long line like soldiers ready to die for him. He injected, between his toes where the skin had healed and healed. And then he wondered why he weren't dead, why it took so fuckin' much to take a man down. But he did swim, far across golden fields that shined up at him like the jeweled streets Pastor Lumen told of when he was a boy.

That night was eternal. In his dreams he called on the churches, made hard pleas that fell on deaf ears. *Keep the girls away from church till it's over, till he's caught.* He saw Eliza, at the shiny Baptist church on Route 84, and she was calling on him but he couldn't move 'cause he was so weighted now. He surfaced only once, and that was when the shrill jar of the telephone cut his dreams. It rang off and on for maybe minutes or hours.

And then he woke to gentle knocking that he thought might've been in his mind. He sat up and knocked over the table with the bottles and the pills.

He got to the kitchen and stumbled at the sink, ran the faucet and splashed cold water on his face. There was a mirror in the hallway and he didn't look in it.

He might've been all right, might've put it down to a blip on a long road that didn't have no destination. But then he opened the door, and he saw the mess that was her face.

"Jesus, Peach," he said. "Jesus, God."

"I tried to call you," she said.

39

Summer

Geraldo, that episode where they list the warnin' signs your kid might be driftin' toward Satanism. Abrupt emotional changes and rejection of parental values. I reckon being a teenager hadn't never been more dangerous.

In the spring of 1995 people began switchin' sides. All that interest in the devil, that Panic that ran roughshod, the FBI chalked much of the testimony to kids being led places they ain't never been, false memories seeded and watered till morality itself was on trial. Devils were folk, stats were molded with frightening finesse.

That shift changed everythin' and nothin'. The Briar girls were still gone, whoever done it was still out there.

When I left my house that night, bag weighin' heavy on my shoulder 'cause I packed more than I reckoned I'd need, I felt close to Della Palmer and the others, like I was walkin' in their godly shoes, headin' someplace I couldn't never come back from.

When I walked, I closed my eyes for a moment, and I told God what was comin' and I dared him to intervene. I wondered what Bobby would say, and what Savannah would say, but it didn't matter, not then and maybe not ever.

I noticed the van right off. It was creepin', rollin' slow on low revs. I didn't glance back 'cause I knew who it was and who was comin'. I was chosen; Fuseli's sleeper laid out, my throat bared white while the stallion looked on. The fear didn't come then 'cause maybe I too was content in my nightmare.

I reached the end of Lott and heard the engine loud, and then it died sudden as a car pulled over from Hutchinson Avenue.

He drove an old station wagon. Maybe it was blue but I can't recall the details 'cause salvation bowled me right off my feet.

I got in quick and watched the van pass me by, my soul unclaimed.

It was as I breathed deep and as he eased into first without sayin' nothin' that I realized what a cold hand destiny deals with. The vision, the appointed time, you can't outrun none of it.

There ain't no *Scooby-Doo* moment in my story.

The bad guy ain't wearin' a disguise.

What y'all hope ain't gonna happen . . . it's gonna happen.

40

The Hard Death

Black drove to the Marsh house an hour off dawn. The roof of the farmhouse had caved three storms back so Merle lived in the barn behind. He drew the cruiser close to the building and left the lights rolling blue and red. He'd driven Peach to the hospital, stayed long enough for the doc to say it was just bruising. Anger coursed hot in his veins.

He hammered the door a couple times. "Merle, open the door."

Merle appeared a couple minutes later, unshaved and grousin' about the hour like he knew what it was.

"Took your time," Black said.

Merle glanced at the sky and shook his head. "Fuckin' devil droppin' down on us," he mumbled as Black followed him in.

There was a roll of old carpet underfoot, laid straight onto the dirt. Merle slept on a couch. When it rained he pulled a sheet of tarp over himself 'cause the roof weren't tight.

"Fuckin' mess in the square," Merle said. "Got them reporters. Those news girls though –"

"Had a late night?"

Merle shrugged. "Ray Bowdoin, poker, guy's a fuckin' animal. Willie burned him with a straight and Ray tipped the table over, walked out without settlin'. Willie chased him down, I told him not to."

"How bad?"

Merle shrugged. "Weren't just the beatin', Ray put a cigarette out on his eye, nastiest shit I ever saw. Willie ain't gonna talk, case you get any ideas."

Black nodded.

"Heard you got into it with Tommy Ryan the other day."

Merle looked around and then down and then shook his head. "Not me."

"Where were you the day Della Palmer went missin'?" Black said.

Merle looked up with a stare so red Black could feel the hangover worse than his own.

"Do I look like the kinda man that keeps a diary?"

Black had the information already and knew it wouldn't take long for Merle to roll. He'd been inside a couple times before, the longest stretch fifteen bruising months. Merle was approaching seventy years old.

"You were fishin' Wheeler Lake with Tommy Ryan."

Merle's eyes widened and he half stood, his hands shaking bad. "Yeah. Yes, I was. Wheeler Lake, with Tommy. That's right."

Black sighed. "The Kinley girl, Anna, she got a flat that mornin'. You changed the tire for her, up by Gaston Lee Road."

"Not that day. Couldn't have been."

"She paid you cash, then her daddy came by the shop and asked for a receipt. They're careful like that, the Kinleys. All that money to protect, don't wanna go the way of Bob Butler, all that he lost to the IRS."

"They got that date wrong," Merle said, his voice flat. He looked around the barn, maybe for a way outta the mess he was getting in.

"I thought that. So I got Milk to call Arlene."

"That bitch'd say anything to see me in shit."

Arlene was married to Merle for a while. She got half the garage in the settlement, kept the books straight enough to make sure she earned from it.

Merle sat again, sighed, bit his black thumbnail, and weighed his options.

"I'll lock you up, Merle. I don't want to, got enough on at the moment. I'll bus you to county jail, let you sweat there for a few weeks. Ernie will put you in with the drunks and pushers. Perverting the course, you'll serve a decent stretch."

Merle closed his eyes.

Black glanced up at the rafters and saw the cloud through the gaps. "How much do you owe Tommy?"

"Too much."

*

They left the cruiser in the bushes and hiked in. They carried flashlights but didn't use them.

Tommy Ryan had cleared a track from the edge of Route 43, a quarter mile to his place. Black had checked the registry and the land had belonged to Tommy's great-grandfather. Rumor had it he won it from a Kinley in a poker game.

"I'm gonna try a rain dance," Milk said, glancing up.

"I'll ready my camera," Black said.

They walked along a tract of woodland that ran parallel to Tommy's land then cut in by a clearing. Milk shined his flashlight out and they saw the house fall into view.

The timber was stained a rich brown, the porch wrapped the front. They watched awhile but stood in the kinda silence that told them they wouldn't be bothered. They'd left the Ryans in the square where they were settling in for another evening of waiting and watching.

"How come you sat on this?" Milk said.

Black shrugged. "Alibi checked out, that lady at Pinegrove. Then Noah said he saw Tommy gettin' into it with Merle so I thought I'd roll the dice."

"We gotta find somethin' soon. Press are chewin' us for this. The eyes of the country are trained on Grace and all they can see is some fuckin' freak show playin' out on the green. The crazies from the church and the fuckin' rednecks, eyeballin' each other over sandbags while they pass round snacks like they're at the movies."

Black laughed and kept watch while Milk worked on the lock. It didn't take him long, maybe 'cause Tommy weren't all that worried about break-ins.

They closed the door behind. One room, large and neat, the wood stripped and buffed and a deep rug on the floor. There was a fireplace, a small kitchen, and a door off to the left.

The roof arched at the far end.

"Ain't gonna take long to search," Milk said.

They didn't have a warrant. Paperwork never held them up. Black wanted to take a look, to do the groundwork before he tipped his hand. Tommy was at a rodeo that Della Palmer went to. Tommy went to the Baptist church on Route 84. Tommy lied about being with Merle. Tommy was close to Summer Ryan. Tommy was tall—maybe knew Hell's Gate better than any man alive. Put it all together and there weren't a doubt he was interesting.

They found a stash of guns under a false floor beneath the couch. There was a closet that held a lot of hunting gear. Black noticed a lock-up beside the generator so guessed he kept more in there.

There were photos of the twins, from when they were babies to recent.

"You reckon Tommy Ryan is the Bird?"

Black sighed, shook his head, and rubbed his neck.

"Fuckin' surprise that'd be, if he was livin' in Grace this whole time."

Milk disappeared into the bedroom while Black went through the kitchen cupboards. "Black."

Black walked into the bedroom. Milk held up a necklace, gold and delicate, a couple letters on it. SR.

"What do you reckon?"

Black felt the heat rise to his cheeks. The past weeks, the past year, all the girls, Peach Palmer. He thought about Tommy and Merle and the lies. He ran a hand over his gun and took a deep breath.

"I reckon I'm tired of being lied to. Whatever it means, I'll find out right now."

And then he was out the door, and he was moving fast through Hell's Gate, back toward the cruiser. And Milk was calling out and telling him to calm down, but Black was so mad he didn't break stride.

Black ran the cruiser up onto the sidewalk and left the lights burning full as he got out. Milk followed, eyeing the bustling square and looking for Austin Ray and Joe in case Black did something foolish.

Black moved fast. He saw the church folk staring. They had lanterns; the flames dancing hypnotic, spiked into dying grass. There were people spilling from Mae's holding greasy paper and eating hot dogs and fries and drinking Cokes. Big guys, with baseball caps pulled low, bearded and tired.

There were a couple reporters, their backs to the crowd as they recorded evening pieces and spoke of the rumors stealing through the town, that the devil himself was living in Hell's Gate and the cops weren't brave enough to go get him.

Milk jogged to keep up, his eyes darting.

Black saw Tommy standing by the benches, his eyes low and scouting, a cigarette hanging from his lips.

Black picked up to a fast run and charged Tommy hard, sent him sprawling over and landed on him heavy.

Milk drew, people screamed, and cameras trained.

Rusty was looking out and grabbed some men and before long there was chaos in the square. Joe made to help his brother but Milk was ready. He stepped forward, gun raised and aimed. Joe raised a hand, glanced over at Tommy who was down with Black kneeling on his chest.

Joe's men angled to draw so Rusty fired a shot toward the cloud and the chaos was drowned by a taut silence that stretched a mile wide.

"Get off me," Tommy said, his eyes burning.

"You lied to me, Tommy. I was holdin' off, watchin' and waitin' but now I'm tired and I'm right on the edge so I could shoot you soon as ask you any more questions."

"Black," Joe said.

"Shut the fuck up," Milk said, raising the barrel to Joe's head.

"I ain't got time for games, Tommy. I don't give a fuck about all these people watchin', let 'em film it. Y'all reckon I ain't got it no more but I'll blow a clean hole in your skull. I got you connected, I got Briar girls to find and you're my link. And that might be bullshit, but you called it on by leadin' me on this dance."

Milk glanced around, met Pastor Lumen's good eye, and thought he saw something of a smile on the old man's face. The reckoning, like he'd called it.

"Where were you the day Della went missin'? Where were you the night Summer ran?"

Tommy was breathing hard, flat down on his back, looking past Black and up at the sky.

"Tell him," Joe said.

They went into the station 'cause Tommy wouldn't talk outside. The cameras flashed as they walked up the steps and the story ran on the evening news.

Black led him into the back office. Tommy said he didn't want a lawyer and Black reckoned he knew the system well enough. So his heart slowed and the exhaustion swept over him like a blanket pulled up high and heavy on his bones. He didn't know what was coming but Tommy looked about as beat as he did.

Trix brought in two cups of coffee, set them down, then closed the door behind.

Black pulled out the necklace and set it on the table.

Tommy looked at it, then at Black, then the fight left him and he slumped low.

"It's Savannah," Tommy said.

"What is?"

"Who I was with. It's Savannah Ritter."

"Pastor Bobby's wife, Savannah?"

"Yeah."

Black closed his eyes for a long time. "Shit, Tommy."

"High cotton like to slum it sometimes."

"I gotta worry about fallout from this now?"

"She broke it off. First time I been dropped."

"I have to speak to her."

"I know."

Black rubbed his eyes. "How'd you meet her?"

"Pinegrove, I got dragged there by Greta. I mean, I saw Savannah round town before but didn't ever speak to her."

"Right."

"So Greta was doin' her thing, workin' the desk, and I went out for a smoke and saw Savannah and she was sittin' in the sun, upset, maybe she'd been cryin'."

"Saw your chance and took it."

Tommy shook his head. "Weren't like that, not with her. You talked to her before?"

"Yeah."

"Then you know. She ain't the type that'll fall for what I got, the way I do it, tell them they're pretty and all that." He cleared his throat. "She's had it rough."

"She told you about her boy?"

"Not right off. But . . . she's sad, Black."

"So you were there for her?"

"I listened. Didn't think nothin' of it but she showed at my place late one night and said she couldn't take it no more, being alone like that. I was just, I was there and there weren't more to it."

Blacked nodded like he was sad. "I get it. And I nearly killed you for it. In front of all those cameras." Black sighed. "A pastor's wife. No wonder Grace is dark and burnin'."

When Tommy left Black reached for the bottle of Crown in his desk drawer. He was done in all ways, the girls kept falling and he'd run outta leads. There weren't nowhere left to turn.

He drank all that he found and then slipped out the back of the station, the bustle and the noise so deafening he couldn't barely stand it no more.

*

"That how you do it? Leave a message on my machine," Peach said.

He sat on the porch and watched the cloud.

Her eyes were still swollen. There was a cut on her forehead.

"I can't keep doin' this, Black. Whatever it is we got, I can't keep doin' it."

"So don't," he said, cold and dead. His sleeve was rolled, tracks marched down his arm.

She settled on the porch beside him and stared at the sky. "They weren't kiddin'."

He followed her eye. "I like it now. I want it to stay."

She took his hand in hers and grasped it tight. "They said I ain't strong enough for this. At Pinegrove, they say I need time to look after myself."

He watched the treetops. "You know where the door is."

"Why are you like this? Why don't you care about nothin'? I know, about your wife and your kids, and about your partner –"

He turned sharp. "What do you know, Peach?"

"I know what you're doin'. All this, you don't sleep, you drink so much. You ain't got no life, Black. You want to die, is that it?"

He tried to reach for the bottle but it tipped from the porch and smashed on the stone path.

"Jesus, Black." She stared at him and he lay back, flat on the wood grain as he stared up at the cloud.

"It makes you realize how helpless we are," he said. "How we don't know shit, how there's always someone nastier in the wings, waitin' for their moment to shine. Who'd be a cop now, can't even dent the numbers. Ain't for me. I'm retired from life and all of everything."

She pulled him up and he leaned back against the siding.

"We were always using each other, Peach."

"Maybe, at the start maybe."

He looked at her and needed her far from him 'cause that was best for both of them. He'd make her see that now. He thought of what Pastor Lumen said, how well he knew him and how sick that made him feel.

"I can't find Della. I can't keep you safe. I can't be relied on for nothin' . . . Mitch. Noah looks at me like he can't understand what I was."

"Self-pity is ugly on you, Black."

She stood.

"Peach," he said.

She turned.

"I don't pity myself. I pity you."

She nodded and he closed his eyes tight to the world.

41

Summer

I didn't say nothin' as we passed through town. He hadn't locked the door. We came up to stop signs and I could've got out and run, I ain't even sure he would've chased me.

I weren't close with Samson, no matter what we spoke about; the unburdening was just that and nothin' deeper. I felt somethin' in that car, like I'd left the straight paths to walk in dark ways. I didn't tell him where I was headin' 'cause I knew that road was closed.

I wondered if Samson was the Bird 'cause I wondered that about everyone I met. The more I played it the more it fit, 'cause monsters . . . they ain't monsters half the time.

I saw him on the front pages, cuffed, white head bowed, and the haunt of death in his pink eyes, people screamin' at him like they could get through, like theirs was a voice he could hear. It'd go to trial 'cause the defense lawyers would climb over each other to take it there. They'd comb his childhood, find so much that was troublin', then roll insanity toward the God-fearin' jury and hope it'd bowl them over. Nobody wants blood on their hands, not even the blood of a devil 'cause it's still just as red.

I turned and looked at him and he glanced back at me.

"There's a new moon," he said quiet.

The engine was a rattle of noise. I reckoned maybe the belt was worn or slippin'. My daddy loves cars. When he got out he used to get me to stand on a stool and hold the hood up while he worked on the engine. After a little while my arm would shake and he'd raise the stay and I'd smile.

We turned down an old track road that ran between the Kinley cornfields. The beams shone out. The crops looked pretty; so bold and beautiful and yellow against the night sky.

Yellow is the color most visible to the human eye.

I wanted him to take me to them. The Briar girl ghosts. I had to see them.

"There's a new moon every twenty-nine and a half days," I said.

"I know that you're pregnant."

I glanced at him. Those words, spoke out like that.

"I clean the bathroom at St. Luke's. I don't mind doin' it, to help Bobby. I found the test in the trash."

He gripped the wheel tight. "The sink is blocked. I went to call the guy, the plumber in Windale, maybe I hit redial 'cause I got that clinic in Dayette."

They wouldn't see me again unless I got my parents to sign. I said I was gonna kill myself and maybe I meant it 'cause I got put through to Cara and she told me to come in.

"The light shines in the darkness, and the darkness has not overcome it."

Sometimes when I would lay in the bathtub I'd slip beneath the water and hold my breath till it hurt. I like that there's a point so clear, a line you cross over and there ain't room to turn back.

42

The Damned

"Quit smilin' all the time, you're starting to make me feel ill," Raine said.

"I ain't smilin'," Noah said, smiling.

Purv watched them and shook his head. "Stakeouts, man, so fuckin' boring."

They sat on Faust Road, half a block up from her apartment. She'd worked late at the clinic, maybe watched TV awhile 'cause they saw the glow before the light died.

"Dream kidney?" Purv said.

"All right, shoot," Noah said.

"Gandhi."

"Gandhi?"

"You go."

"Schwarzenegger."

"Steroids, ain't no tellin' the damage they done. Gandhi wins easy."

"He was borderline malnourished."

"Fuck that. Mahatma was lean, but muscle lean, you can tell he worked out. He was pure too, get a piece of him inside you and you're guaranteed to head up when your time comes."

Noah nodded. Purv always won.

"How about you, Raine?" Purv said.

Raine shrugged. "Elvis?"

Purv closed his eyes, shaking his head. "Spastic colon."

Noah straightened up when he saw her. Raine watched too, Purv leaned forward between the front seats. They watched silent as the lady with the fire-red hair slipped from her apartment and climbed into her '79 Taurus.

"Could be headed to church," Purv said.

"Not this late," Raine said.

Noah pulled out and kept the beams low.

"Stay back," Raine said.

"Relax, darlin', ain't my first rodeo," Noah said.

Raine sighed wearily.

They drove five miles out toward Roxburgh and the Briar County line before she turned down Chason Road.

Noah eased off the gas till the Taurus lights grew faint then disappeared down into the valley.

They rode over a hill then saw the Taurus pull over.

"Go past," Raine said. "She'll see us."

They drove a quarter mile before Noah found a spot he could turn around in.

"Shit, we can't lose her."

Noah floored the gas and watched the needle climb as they drove back through the woodland.

"There," Purv said, pointing.

They followed the Taurus back up to Highway 45 and saw her signal right.

"She's headed back," Noah said.

"Turn round, we need to see why she stopped," Raine said.

When they reached the spot in the valley Noah pulled the Buick to a stop and they sat awhile and saw nothing much beyond trees. Raine reached for her bag and flashlight and they moved out.

"There ain't nothin' here," Purv said.

Raine moved in front, cutting the light over the trees and the dirt.

Noah saw it first, bushes grown wild around, at the front of a track so dark he couldn't make out nothing at the end. He called them over and they stared at the mailbox, rusted, stuck deep in the earth, the red flag flipped up.

"Could be a house at the end of the track," Purv said.

Raine opened the mailbox and took an envelope out. It weren't sealed and there weren't no writing on it. She pulled the paper out and shone the flashlight.

"What is it?" Noah said.

Raine swallowed. "Names, addresses . . . the forms from the clinic." She glanced at him. "The girls, the girls who want to get rid of their babies."

They put the envelope back in the mailbox and hiked up the dark track, silent 'cept for their breath. It was warm and starry but cold fear fell over them. Raine held the gun in her hand and Purv held the hunting knife and Noah held the flashlight.

The church was burned. There was a sign, WEST END MISSION, and Raine remembered back when they saw it on the news and her momma asked what kinda person it took to light up a church like that.

"Della Palmer's church," Raine said.

*

Black saw candlelight so he walked toward the church, opened the heavy door and moved in from the sounds of the square.

"I heard you stopped by the station earlier," Black said as he saw her.

Savannah nodded and he walked over and sat on the bench beside her.

"That criminal crucified beside Jesus, he made it into heaven because he was sorry. That's what people struggle with," she said.

"Forgiveness is a powerful thing, Savannah."

"It is. Sometimes it lies outta reach."

Black wondered how much of his life had been spent in the old church, asking but never giving.

"Tommy called me. I meant to come see you, but I couldn't face it. What I did. I'm sorry, Black. I'm so sorry."

He shrugged. "All right, I'll let you into heaven."

She laughed and it came out sweet and so sad.

"I saw a lawyer in Maidenville. I've had the papers for a while but I see Bobby sometimes and I can't ever imagine being without him. Is that funny, after what I did?"

He looked up at the print, at Mary and the baby and the bird that didn't fly. "No, it ain't funny. Sometimes people need a break from themselves, sometimes it takes something God fuckin' awful to make you see what you got and what you ain't."

"Do you miss your children?"

"I miss the life I might've had. I ache for it like I got a chance of turning back the clock. If we don't learn from our mistakes . . . that's the waste, right?"

He heard her cry but he couldn't see her tears 'cause the shadow of the cross hid her so fully.

"This is your crossroads, Savannah."

"I don't know what to do."

"You know, deep down you know 'cause people always do."

"I love Bobby."

"That's all you need."

"Is it?"

"It has to be, 'cause there ain't nothin' else out there."

"Is that naive?"

"Maybe."

"I want to ask for a sign," she said. "I want God to tell me that he has Michael and that we'll be a family again. I think that's what Bobby wants."

"Bobby's searchin' for somethin' he knows he ain't never gonna find. You either take his hand and help him or you leave him to get on."

"I can't leave him alone. I can't. He's had an awful life, Black. The things they did to him in that home . . ."

Black reached across and took her hand. He held it tight and closed his eyes and he asked God to make it right, he asked God to end it all now. He didn't know what that meant for her and for him and the people of Grace. But he asked for light 'cause there hadn't been none for such a long time.

*

The stairs moved; each bowed and noisy and flaking paint. Purv stayed in the Buick on the street, by the side door. He reckoned it was time to call in Black but Raine had the feeling in her stomach and that heat in her eyes so Noah drove where she told him, back to Adler's and the lady with the fire-red hair.

He stood beside her and she knocked the door quiet, it opened on the chain.

The lady stood there, eyes tired till she locked on Raine and they widened.

"Dolores," Raine said. "I saw you at the clinic."

"How'd you know where I live?"

"I need to talk to you."

Dolores shook her head. "You have to call the clinic, I can't help you . . ." She began to close the door and Raine stuck her foot against the jamb.

"I know about the mailbox. The burned church, I know what's in the envelope."

There was a moment that stretched, where maybe Dolores was weighing things.

"And I know you broke into the clinic. We got cameras, I open up each mornin', I check the tapes," Dolores said.

Raine took it quick and shrugged it off. "Call the cops. I'm a minor, I reckon breakin' and enterin' ain't nothin' on what you been doin'.'"

Dolores looked at Noah, then at Raine, then she slipped the chain from the door and they followed her inside.

They sat 'cause she told them to, and she closed the door 'cause her kids were sleeping. A lamp burned soft light but she looked cold and beaten.

"What do you want?" Dolores said.

"My sister is missin'. Summer Ryan."

"We get a lot of calls, more than you can imagine."

"Yeah, we saw the files."

"'That's just the girls on the books, the ones that go through with it. We get calls, walk-ins, they leave a fake name 'cause they're scared and we don't see 'em again. Every day, every week. Girls like you."

"Briar girls?" Raine said.

Dolores swallowed and maybe her hands were trembling but she knitted her fingers tight.

"What did you do?" Raine said.

Dolores put her hand to her head and then rubbed her eyes. "They're closing the clinics, shuttering 'em. There's so many girls now. I knew someone would show. I didn't reckon it'd be a couple kids."

"What did you do?" Raine said again.

"What I thought was right, what I had to do. You can't go to the cops, I ain't got no one to care for my children."

"Tell us what you know. Is it him?"

"I ain't got money, my kids . . . their daddy ain't here. I been to that church since I was small, the Mission, before it burned and before we had to stand in fields just to reach up."

Noah glanced at the window, it was cracked behind the drapes and he could hear the idle of the Buick.

"I didn't tell nobody when I took the job." She ran a hand through her hair, her mouth set hard. "I was in trouble before, when I was young, I got a record," she said. "They gave me a shot 'cause nobody else wanted to work there. I thought . . . with God, I thought about it but I got kids of my own to care for. I tried to talk to the girls who came in, to help 'em see, but Cara said I ain't to do that."

The door opened and Raine almost reached for the bag before she saw it was a boy, maybe six or seven, hair jutting at sleep angles.

Dolores scooped him up and took him out.

Raine looked over at Noah and he tried a smile but they knew they were close now, that something was coming.

"He gets up, sometimes five or six times, has done ever since," Dolores said, as she sat. She had a drink, clear in the glass like vodka. "I was them, those girls, back when I was fourteen. I went to the clinic in Birmingham but I couldn't see it out. The Mission, they reached out and they saved me."

Raine nodded slow, staring at Dolores.

"The first time he called it was late but I was up 'cause even before I didn't sleep good. Just one of those people, 'the damned' my daddy said, body don't like to sleep." She smiled a small smile. "He said he was from the church, that he could help the girls, he could save 'em too. That's all I wanted."

"Who?" Raine said, inching closer, eyes locked tight on Dolores.

"And I thought about the babies, those children and my children. I reckoned I could handle things . . . it's murder. I saw a way to make it right, he said he'd talk to 'em, that he'd show 'em. He said it was clear, why I took that job, 'cause I was supposed to. God painted a path for me."

"Who is he?"

Dolores met her eye. "Newspapers call him the Bird."

Noah swallowed.

Dolores rubbed her neck, pinching the muscles hard. "I give him the names and he stops 'em burnin'. And maybe stops me burnin'."

"Jesus," Noah said quiet.

"What's he done with them?"

Dolores cried but palmed the tears hard. "I tried to stop right off, after Della, after she went missin', 'cause I knew it was him. And I knew Della, she was a good kid. They make mistakes, even the good kids. He called, in the night, he called me and said things about my children. But I . . . and then he showed up." She looked at Raine, her face ghost white, eyes sunk but the fear was sharp and clear. "At midnight he knocked the door and broke the chain and my son came out and saw."

"What did he say, the Bird?" Raine said.

Dolores shook her head fast. "Nothin'. He just stood there till I backed right up, and then he turned and left. He knows me, it can't be undone now; it's gone on too long."

"All the Briar girls, they were all on the lists, they were all pregnant," Noah said.

Dolores nodded.

"How come no one said, the newspapers?"

"No one knows 'cept me and him."

"What about their parents?"

"They either don't know or don't want to say. You know about the color of judgment; there ain't forgiveness, not for all things, not for the shame. I think about the girls, maybe they're safe and he's just holdin' 'em. But his eyes, his face . . ."

"What does he look like?" Noah said.

"The devil. He looks like the devil."

*

They left Dolores staring straight out the window like she was lost someplace far. They made no promises 'cause all knew they'd be hollow. Bets were off, they knew of the Bird, that he was real, and how he was choosing the girls. They'd found out what the cops couldn't, Black and Ernie Redell and all the state cops.

"We gotta call Black now," Purv said from the rear seat.

"Black will go in blazin'," Raine said.

"Still have to make the call, Raine," Noah said.

"We will, after we see him," she said.

They parked deep in the trees a hundred yards from the mail-box, then they settled back and took it in shifts to keep watch. No one slept though, they were too close to something bad.

An hour from first light the van pulled up. It was dark and rusted and the three watched in silent horror as it stopped in front of the mailbox.

Raine felt the rush of her heart.

"Can't see who it is," Noah said in a whisper.

"Missouri plates," Purv said.

It moved off fast and Noah pulled the Buick out and worried they'd lost it before he saw dim light a long way in front.

They followed for miles, till the sun began to break the night sky and they remembered to breathe again.

"At least we're headed back toward Grace," Noah said, glancing at the fuel gauge. "We're almost out."

They didn't talk about what it meant, what they'd found and who they were following. They didn't need to 'cause they all felt it.

It was as they neared Hallow Road, as they saw the cloud towering, that the van turned sharp from the road down the throat of the woodland.

They rolled right by, didn't even slow 'cause there weren't another way to do it. They weren't equipped, not even close.

"That's Deamer land," Purv said. "What do we do?"

"We tell Black, all of it, we tell him," Noah said.

"We'll get in shit. They'll know we broke into the clinic," Purv said.

"We'll say you weren't there," Noah said.

Purv stared out the window. "Won't matter . . . not once he hears."

"So we go in then. Through Hell's Gate," Raine said.

Noah gripped the wheel tight. "I ain't sure that's a good idea."

"I'll go on my own then," Raine said.

"You can't . . ."

Raine turned, eyes full. "You two have done enough. I'm grateful, serious, I ain't gonna forget it. But I'm goin' in, right now, 'cause my sister might be in there and she might be in trouble. I don't know what it means, what he's doin'. So you go, you tell Black now if you need to, whatever you reckon is right, but I ain't waitin' no longer. I got the gun, I know the woods."

Noah slowed as the road curved. He met Purv's eye in the mirror. "You comin'?"

"Come this far, ain't we?"

43

Summer

The room in that house. There was a lamp on a nightstand but it didn't have a shade so the bright was hard. There was a bed and there was canned food stacked in the corner. The roof was bowed like there was weight sagging it down in the center. The smell of damp got in my lungs and I wanted to cough but the fear got hold of me.

"I made you tea," Samson said. " 'Cause you said you liked to drink tea sometimes. I want you to be all right."

He handed me a cup and I set it down on the nightstand and he told me to sit on the bed so I did.

I looked at his hands and fingers.

There was flowers by the bed.

"Alabama Pinks. You ain't supposed to pick 'em," he said, following my eye. "They're endangered, Wildlife Service are supposed to watch out for 'em."

"Nobody knows where they grow," I said, my voice quiet.

"My momma did. She showed me once, there's a hidden spot in Hell's Gate. She loved these flowers. I picked 'em for her.

I brought them when she got sick and they made her smile so I reckoned it was all right, 'cause she needed them."

The bed didn't have no sheets, just a mattress that was stained and cold and wet.

"I can't let you do it. I can't let you take a life."

I heard it but I didn't, the sounds were far and mixed, a different voice like it didn't fit in that room on that night in Grace.

I looked down at the ring my daddy bought for me with a blue stone the very same color as my eyes.

"Summer."

I didn't like my name then, the way it sounded when he said it like it weren't nothin' but a collection of meaningless letters.

I looked up and somethin' died in his eyes.

"It ain't about the right to choose. Life or death ... we're made in God's image. You believe in redemption, Summer?"

"Yes."

He smiled. "I see it. What was meant for me. I see a way back for all of us."

In my mind I heard Bach and I saw Peter denying Jesus over and over. *Have mercy, my God, for the sake of my tears.*

I called it on by givin' myself over or sayin' I had. I let myself be guided to this place 'cause that's what fate does, it watches over you till you accept that your life weren't never yours at all.

44

Bird Hunt

They swung by the edge of the square and Noah slipped into the station and said morning to the auxiliaries. He carried a fat envelope of all they had and he left it on Black's desk 'cause that was the smart move. They'd go into Hell's Gate and hope Black beat them to the Deamer house and all that it held. Raine agreed to it, but she wouldn't wait on nothing; on plans and checks and whatever procedures had to be followed.

They picked up Purv 'cause he'd made a run into Ginny's, then they drove the Buick to Highway 125 'cause they wouldn't risk driving the Deamer tracks.

They pulled off where there weren't a road, just bumping along the grass and dirt and praying the wheels wouldn't come off.

Raine pulled the gun from her bag and she checked it was loaded. They had a couple bottles of water, a box of Minute Maid Juice Bars, a pack of Twinkies, and a bottle of Budweiser.

"Good haul," Noah said. "Nutritious."

Purv applied war paint to himself and Noah.

"Your turn, Raine."

She flipped him off.

"It's Deamer land. You wanna get shot?"

She sat on an oak root and Purv kneeled in the leaves and streaked her face with black and green and brown till all that was clear was the white of her eyes.

*

Jimmy King arrived to a sleeping square. He was beat; he spent his days out driving from place to place, looking for his daughter and the Bird and passing troopers doing the same. Sometimes he'd draw up and he'd see the way they looked at him from beneath their campaigns, like they were looking at a man who wouldn't ever see his little girl again.

He stood a moment, watched the sea of people dozing, placards and bottles and burger wrappers strewn.

Joe walked over and they shook hands.

"Got your call," Jimmy said.

"Still nothin' on Amber?"

"Gone like a ghost. They still holdin' that man for Summer?"

Joe nodded.

"Man messin' with children," Jimmy said, then he spit on the grass. "I'm here, whatever you need, Joe."

"I was waitin' on the storm but I'm starting to think it ain't comin'."

"So what are you thinkin'?" Jimmy said.

"You still handy with a rifle?"

*

They hiked for two straight hours, following Raine, who held the map and compass. They zigzagged in and outta Grace, passing from dark to early-morning light, from cool to climbing heat. They crossed a rusted water pipe that rose a foot over a backwater, arms out for balance. It was tough going and Raine checked Noah was all right a couple times.

They stopped and drank water and in the distance they saw the haze of woodsmoke rising from the forest. They were taught young about forest fires and how fast they could turn.

"It's dark smoke, flames gone out," Purv said.

Raine nodded and they moved on.

It was noon when they saw the first snare. The first sign they'd made it to Deamer land. Noah glanced around nervous, half expecting to have a sight trained on him.

They moved slow, past a couple trees with markings painted on them, a couple had the number nine carved deep in the trunks.

"What are they?" Noah said.

"Maybe to keep track of the border, let people know to turn back or they'll get shot," Purv said.

Raine moved on. She carried her bag on her back, only stopping for water. Her calves were red, burned by the sun behind. She wore a white T-shirt, mucky with dirt and sweat, her hair tied back and swinging.

They moved farther from the dark wall till they could make it out only when the trees thinned. They helped each other over a fallen tree, then up a steep track weaving through dense brush.

They reached another bank, though Raine didn't wait for them this time. Noah watched her climb, lose her footing once, then grab hold of a root and pull herself to the top. She ducked low, dropped to her stomach, and waved them down. Noah and Purv crouched, hearts racing.

They didn't dare move, unsure of what Raine had seen and not exactly keen to find out. It went this way a couple of times before. Raine would stop still and they'd feel the adventure drain right outta them, the fear that replaced it so heavy they couldn't feel their feet no more.

*

"Same old shit," Milk said, looking at the line of cars and the people spilling from them. There was a couple of buses too, shipping in folk from all over and making out nicely from it.

Trix had taken the call, diverted them as they were headed back from the King house where they'd been since early morning for no other reason than to tell Jessie-Pearle they were all on it.

Milk rolled the window down when the Kinley boy walked over, his pockets bulging with bills but his face stern and serious. Money flowed to the Kinleys like water ran the Red.

"You seen smoke?" Milk said.

The Kinley boy pointed east, toward Hell's Gate. "Twenty minutes back."

"Best check it out," Black said.

They drove half a mile across Kinley land till they pulled up close to Hell's Gate.

Ten minutes in they were nearing the Grace line, loping back toward the dark.

"Ain't got the flashlight," Milk said.

"I'll go," Black said, heading back while Milk leaned against a tree and stuck an arm through the dark wall.

It was as Black opened the door to the cruiser that he heard the shot. It cracked, an echo, maybe some birds flew high, he couldn't be sure 'cause he had his head down and was running, gun drawn.

*

"You hear that?" Noah said. "Sounded like a gunshot."

"Hunters," Purv said.

Fifteen minutes passed before Raine slowly slid down the bank and crept over to them. She wiped sweat from her face, war paint colored her hand.

"What is it?" Noah said.

"Might be a blind."

They kept to a whisper, huddled close.

"Anyone in it?"

"Can't tell. But I ain't keen on walkin' right in front of it. It don't look right, not like the kind my uncle builds. Looks too solid."

"Maybe it's for storage," Purv said.

"Way out here in the woods?" Raine said. "It don't feel right. We're at least a mile from the road . . ."

"I heard the Deamers are strange," Purv said. "Rituals and shit."

"Lot of bullshit said about the Deamers," Noah said.

"So what do we do now?" Purv said.

"Watch it awhile. We can hide out at the top, stay by the bank and keep low, see if anyone comes. Black will be headin' in soon."

*

Milk pulled Black down to the leaves.

"Where?" Black said.

Milk pointed to a hole in a tree, maybe a foot from where his head was.

They heard a burst of gunfire.

"Shit," Black said.

Black got up to a kneel, tried to peer round when a second shot whistled by his head and struck the oak behind him. He fell back.

"They got the jump on us," Milk said. "And they're in the Grace dark so it don't look good."

"Who?"

"Ain't sure. More than one I reckon."

Another burst of fire and they kept low.

"The Kinley boy will call Trix, that much noise. They'll send everyone we got. We just need to hole up till then."

Black nodded. "We're too open here. There's a drop over there." He nodded toward a cluster of bushes. "We get behind it and we got a better chance."

Milk moved first, careful, raising his gun and keeping low. Black followed. Another shot just left of them, hit that same oak. Milk fired back and Black's ears were ringing.

"Shit, Milk," was all he could manage when another shot kicked the leaves up near his foot.

"Did you get a look?"

Milk shook his head, sweat dripping from his nose.

Black breathed hard; he'd caught his head on a branch and blood was rolling down into his eyes. There weren't no room for anger, the fear all consuming.

"You all right?" Milk said.

Black waved him off. "I reckon there's four of 'em."

"Bad odds, Black."

"Bad odds."

Black dabbed the blood away with his sleeve, watched it turn red, then looked up at the sky. The line of shadow rose so high. They listened to forest noise till they calmed.

"I'm thinkin' it ain't leavin' now, this cloud," Milk said. "I'm thinkin' we'll have to move the town."

"Move it?"

"The whole town. Rebuild, maybe in Windale. "

"How about Maidenville?"

Milk smiled. "You reckon they'll have us?"

Another shot struck the same oak, an inch from the last.

"Jesus," Milk said.

"It'll be all right."

Milk closed his eyes.

"Go," Black said. "I'll cover."

Milk shook his head.

"You got family," Black said, and then he stood quick and pushed Milk and started firing.

*

Joe watched them leave. Three cruisers, lights flashing and sirens blazing, a couple news vans in pursuit too.

His crew moved so fast the church side didn't know what was going down.

Joe held a gun but kept it by his side. He didn't want to raise on nobody unless he had to.

There was a couple deputies, they dropped their guns easy. They were Ernie's and not about to get shot over Grace mess.

"Time's up," Joe said.

Trix looked nervous but Joe knew she weren't the kind to lie down. He sent Austin Ray Chalmers over to cuff her, which he did gently, then sat her down on her chair behind the desk. They locked the door behind them.

"Keys," Joe said.

"Joe," Trix said. "This ain't helpin', you'll get yourself into real trouble. Black's doin' all he can, believe me. Please, Joe. Think about Raine, she needs you now."

Joe nodded at Tommy, who trained his gun on one of Ernie's boys.

"Keys," Joe said.

*

They moved slow, each step measured and quiet. They heard more gunshots in the distance.

They helped each other up the bank then lay flat on their stomachs. The heat was cloying and brutal, a hundred degrees easy. They were twenty feet from the blind and Raine was right that it didn't fit. The sights were too small, like they'd been added for effect. Brown paint had been splashed over it, and leaves piled at the base of each wall.

"See the door?" Noah whispered.

Raine nodded.

The door was steel.

Purv glanced at them. "If they find us here –"

"We got a gun," Noah said.

"Yeah, and what do you reckon the Deamers got?"

They sat quiet, nothing to watch but a couple white-tails passing by. Purv opened the beer silently, passed it to Raine and she sipped slowly.

As she went to pass it back Noah held out a hand and they fell dead silent.

They heard steps, heavy steps, and they saw birds fly up and out, making way.

It was a minute or so before they saw him.

He was giant big, wearing a suit of leaves and feathers and looking like some kinda monster. He walked slow, his shoulders hunched.

Noah hadn't never seen a bigger man in his life.

He had a rifle slung over his arm and a hunting knife on his belt and when he glanced in their direction they stopped breathing.

He pulled a set of keys from his pocket and unlocked the steel door. They watched him walk in, the relief giving way to blind terror when they heard a cry as the door clicked shut behind him.

Fear dropped so heavy over Purv that his hands began to shake, then his legs. He swallowed hard, then opened his mouth wide and gulped air down.

Raine made to get up but Noah grabbed hold of her wrist and pulled her down.

"He might be watchin' out the sight," Noah said.

Raine settled beside him, then reached for her bag and grabbed hold of the gun.

"The Bird," Purv said, his voice catching. "It's the fuckin' Bird."

Noah swallowed. "What do we do?"

"We wait," Purv said, pleading. "We wait for Black and the cops 'cause that's the only move there is. It ain't a joke, he'll kill us dead."

They looked up as the door opened again and the Bird reappeared.

Raine moved fast, too fast for Noah to stop her.

She ran across the leaves, the gun trained out in front of her.

Noah and Purv were up and following.

"Don't move," she said.

The Bird turned slow, dropped his gaze to Raine, and smiled.

He had a face full of scars, the worst running the whole way round his left eye, like someone had tried to take it out. Thick hair covered the backs of his hands. He glanced over at Purv and Noah, then back to Raine.

"Give me the keys," she said. "And drop the rifle. I'll shoot you, don't think I won't."

"I'm bulletproof," he said, his voice slow and so deep it didn't sound real.

"We'll find out," Raine said. "The keys, toss 'em over to the boys."

"You're pretty," he said. "An angel. You come to take me up?" He glanced at Noah, then back to Raine. "Or maybe you'll stay down and run with the heathens."

She took a step forward. "Give me the fuckin' keys."

"Why?"

"I want to see inside."

"You can look inside of me. Take out my rib; make me another of you I can keep awhile."

She gripped the gun tight and raised it higher, aiming at his face.

He dropped the keys and kicked them toward Noah.

"Over there," she said.

The Bird walked slow and settled back against an oak, still smiling at Raine.

"Unlock the door, Noah," she said.

Noah walked over to the hide, struggled for a moment with the lock then heard it give. Purv was standing still, his eyes locked on the Bird like he was watching a ghost.

The door swung open.

Noah peered into the dark and listened.

"You'll have nightmares, boy," the Bird said. "Eyes like yours. There's demons down there. They'll rob your soul before you get a taste of what's next."

Noah stared at the Bird.

"Go on, boy. Leave. Come back once you're prepared. The son of man is comin' at an hour you don't expect. But I'm ready. I been ready."

Noah wanted to run but he thought of Summer and beat back his nerves.

"We're fierce," Raine called. "We're fuckin' brave and we're fierce."

He heard fear there, but anger driving it back.

It was dark inside, the air so hot and heavy it dragged on him. There was a small table and a stack of rifles on a rack in the corner. He tried a light switch but it didn't work.

He heard the Bird laughing outside. He took another step, felt a board give beneath. He spun, sweating and panicked.

There was an old rug on the floor, dirty and stained. He dragged it back, knelt, pulled up a loose board, then another and another. And then he saw the steps.

Sunlight streamed through the door.

The steps were wood. He took them slow, ducking his head.

It was big down there, dug out high and wide. He held his father's badge tight, his thumb tracing the eagle.

The smell was strong; he brought a hand to his nose. He stood in the center of the room, fear kept his breaths quick and shallow. It took a while for his eyes to adjust and when they did he saw her. In the corner, curled away from him, on a low camp bed.

"Summer?" he said.

She spun, stood, and stared at him. She took a step, he heard the chain, clamped tight around her ankle. She wore a shirt, maybe the Bird's 'cause it swamped her. Her hair was dirty blond, greasy and long. She was barefoot and bleeding from a fresh cut on her knee.

"It's all right," he said. "We'll get you out."

She grabbed him tight, so tight he couldn't breathe.

"Where is he?" she said, trembling.

"Outside. Don't worry, we got a gun on him."

"He'll kill you." She cried, a quick painful cry that came out raw.

He tried to calm her; she wouldn't let go of him.

"Is there anyone else?" he said.

"There ain't no one else. It's just him."

He reached for the keys, knelt down, and undid the lock. Her skin was torn beneath the cuff.

She hung on him as they crossed the dirt floor. He held her as they climbed the steps. She squinted hard, a hand over her eyes.

She stopped for a moment, held her face in her hands and palmed her tears away.

"What's your name?" he said.

"Amber King." Her voice was dried out.

They walked out slow and careful. Raine looked over quick, then back to the Bird. He was still smiling, watching Amber and smiling.

"Don't look at him," Noah said.

Raine spit in his direction.

A flash of something lit his eyes.

"This is Amber," Noah said.

"Amber King," Purv said.

Amber nodded, her shoulders up and her head low. Noah took the chance to look at her in the light. Her lower lip was puffy, each eye blackened but healing. Her arms and legs were a mess of cuts and bruises. She was still holding Noah, a hand tight in his.

"There anybody else in there?" Raine said.

"No."

"There was," Amber said. "He said I weren't the first."

Amber doubled over, retched, and puked. Purv gave her a bottle of water.

Noah watched the Bird careful, the way he breathed nice and slow, the way he clenched his fists and looked Raine up and down.

"I don't like this," he said. "We need to get Amber back, get Black and Milk –"

"We will," Raine said.

Noah glanced at Purv.

"Y'all from Grace. Then you know about it. What's comin' down. Ain't God but somethin' purer. You heard the draggin' chains. Hydra's watchin' –"

"Did you take my sister?" A tear rolled down Raine's cheek, cutting a clean line in the paint.

"I took my own sister, hung her up and gave her over."

"Her name is Summer Ryan."

"Her name was Mandy Deamer."

Noah stared at him. "Mandy Deamer killed herself."

"My hand or hers, the thief comes only to steal and destroy." He laughed loud then he glanced at Amber. "You think you're a butterfly in the light." Then he turned back to Raine. "Tormenting storms mean she can't fly, her wings ain't strong enough." He laughed again.

Noah glanced at Purv.

The gun was shaking wild in Raine's hands.

"Summer Ryan. Did you take her? I ain't askin' again."

"Shoot me," he said. He beat his chest with a hard fist. "Shoot me where you think my heart beats. You'll see what bleeds outta me. Your sister came to me in the night. She asked me to show her the sights."

"He's crazy, Raine. Black will find out what he knows. Or your father, we'll get Joe to come here, and your uncle Tommy. Both of 'em, they'll make him talk."

"Send them. I like to be in company. I'll hollow out their fuckin' heads though." The Bird made a gun with his finger and thumb and aimed it at Noah.

And then he ran at Raine, and he was fast for a man his size.

The gunshot echoed.

The Bird dropped to one knee, his right ear gone, but then he was up and he reached out and grabbed hold of her.

The gun fell from her hand.

She screamed.

Noah moved fast, grabbed Raine, and threw her toward Purv and Amber.

The Bird roared, then went for the gun.

Noah beat him to it, picked it up quick and fired.

The bullet buried deep in his chest.

Noah fired again.

The Bird fell back to sitting, raised a hand to the hole, and grinned at Noah. Blood emptied from his lips.

Then Raine was on him, punching him and kicking him and screaming at him.

He was gone before they dragged her off.

*

"That was stupid, Black. Fuckin' stupid."

They sat silent. They'd heard more shots but they were far off.

"You should've run."

Milk shook his head. "Ain't what we do and you know it."

"Yeah."

"There was a time . . . I questioned you. I wondered, if a call came, I wondered if I weren't better with somebody else. Just 'cause –"

"It's all right."

"It ain't," Milk said.

In the distance they heard sirens.

Black listened out. "Three cars."

"They'll hear 'em too, make their move or leave."

"I know which I'm hoping on."

"It's over," Milk yelled.

Off to the right they saw the last smoke of a small fire.

Black rolled his sleeves back and felt the hot sun on his arms. He checked his gun.

It was a long while of nothing but forest noise before they heard the rustle of steps. Black hoped Rusty was leading. Ernie had sent his rookies, no way of telling what they'd do in a gunfight or who they'd end up firing at. Black caught sight of him. Rusty was crouched low, more or less hidden from sight. He locked eyes with Black.

Black held up four fingers, then signaled toward the dark. Rusty nodded.

Black and Milk moved together. Rusty and Ernie's men crept forward, guns aimed at the shadow. They repeated the procedure a couple of times till Rusty was near enough to cover.

"Took your time," Milk said.

Rusty flipped him off but Black could tell he was worried. They were tight, the three of them.

They moved back a couple of steps, keeping the trees between them and the shadow.

"Any ideas?" Rusty said.

Milk shrugged. "Crazies."

Ernie's men fanned out.

"Maybe they've gone," Rusty said.

"Why? What was it all about?" Milk said. "Somethin' ain't right. The fire. The way they were shootin' and the cover they got they could've finished us off no trouble."

Black looked around, counting the men. Ten in total.

"How many officers back at the station?"

"A couple, and Trix," Rusty said.

"Hell –" Black said, breaking into a run.

*

Samson was praying when they came for him. Joe Ryan picked him up by his throat, clean off the ground, then dropped him onto the bed.

"What's goin' on?" he said, frantic.

Joe slapped him with an open hand, just hard enough for his ears to ring and his face to sting.

"Black asked you about Summer," Joe said.

Samson backed to the corner of the bed, knees up and holding them.

"You didn't tell him everything," Joe said.

He could hear Trix yelling upstairs.

"I'm sorry. I'm sorry. I pray for her, I ask God where she is now."

"There ain't a God. It's just me and you."

Tommy passed Joe the gun, then stepped outside, closed the door, and stood watch.

Joe gripped Samson's face and forced the barrel into his mouth. Samson coughed and gagged but Joe held strong.

"You walked my daughter home. You hung round her at church, followed her like some fuckin' puppy dog. Ava said she didn't see you at that place till recent, till Summer started goin' regular."

Samson tried to shake his head but Joe gripped tight. "I'll kill you, right now I'll end you."

Joe pulled the gun from Samson's mouth and slapped him again.

Samson cried helpless tears as he fell to the floor.

"You start talkin' or I'll start shootin'."

"Please," Samson sobbed.

Joe raised the gun.

Samson closed his eyes. "It weren't her . . . it was him."

Joe kept the gun on him. "Who?"

"Bobby," Samson said, eyes still locked like his mind was someplace far.

"What the fuck are you sayin'?"

"Leviticus. It's an abomination. I'll burn. It was Bobby I watched. It was Bobby I dreamed of."

Joe lowered the gun and he wiped the sweat from his head, the understanding was heavy and weighed on his eyes.

"You a queer?"

"They said it's a choice, at Pinegrove, that's what they said. But it ain't, 'cause who'd choose it? Momma said there's a way back, I just had to find it. I tried to fix things but I can't, Joe. I made it all worse. I thought if I saved a life it'd mean somethin'."

Joe turned his back and left Samson broke on the floor.

"You don't understand, Joe. I'm tryin' to tell you," Samson said between breaths. And then the door closed and Samson rose, and he hammered on it hard and dropped to his knees.

"What did he say?" Tommy said as they climbed the stairs.

Joe thought about Samson and Pastor Lumen, the shame and the pain.

"Nothin'," Joe said. "He didn't do nothin'."

*

Noah carried Amber the last hundred yards. She was weak and tired and hurt. Raine led. She was lost to them, silent, her eyes fixed on the forest floor and nothing else. Purv gave Amber all the water they had.

Noah lay Amber down across the backseat easy 'cause the door was gone. He didn't know if she was sick or in shock or just fucked up after what she'd been through. They'd got her though—she'd made it. Raine got in the back with her, lay Amber's head on her lap and stroked her hair.

Noah started the engine. For a moment it stuttered and he held his breath, then it caught and he gunned it, the wheels struggling for grip on the dirt. They didn't have the gas to get her to Mayland so he headed back toward the square. Black would know what to do. He'd have to, 'cause Noah felt like he didn't know nothing no more.

*

Black kept his foot to the floor, watching the needle climb as the sky darkened. He could see Rusty and the other cruisers in his rear-view, lights and sirens all the way. He passed the Kinley boy and the tourists who watched and took photographs like they was part of the show. Milk kept his gun in his hand, must've checked it was loaded at least a half dozen times. Black radioed Trix again and again but she didn't answer.

They drove down Hallow Road, overtook a couple of sedans, and switched the high beams on.

As they were turning into the square a Buick came from the Jackson side and nearly ran right into them. Black hit the brakes hard.

"What the fuck –" Milk said.

They followed behind as the Buick mounted the sidewalk and pulled right up at the bottom of the stone steps. Black climbed out and ran over, followed by Milk, both had guns drawn. The cameras were aimed at them, the reporters wide eyed.

Black saw Noah get out and then the girl in the back jumped on him, nearly knocking him off his feet. She held him tight. She wore a long shirt and her feet were bare and her legs were cut up. They couldn't see her face but they knew who she was.

"Amber King . . ." Milk said.

They were vaguely aware of a man pushing through the cluster of people, and then he called her name.

"Daddy," Amber said.

And then she fell into him and they dropped to their knees and they were crying, and the flash of cameras lit the whole square.

Black looked up and saw Joe Ryan at the top of the steps. Then he saw Raine get out of the car, and she looked up and met his eye. She walked up the stairs like she was in some kinda daze, her limbs loose and her head swaying.

She leaned close and said something to her daddy, and he grabbed hold of her tight.

Black looked at Noah and his heart dropped into his boots.

Noah was real pale, and then Black saw his eyes roll as he fell to the street.

45

Summer

There was a cross on the wall and a lock on the door but Samson left it open.

I bit down on my fist. My teeth broke the skin and blood filled my mouth but the taste of blood never bothered me all that much.

Samson had plans for me, plans colored pure with salvation 'cause that's all he saw.

My mind was a riverboat and it sailed the Red. I could see the girls side by side on the bank and staring up at a fallin' star, and one of the girls reckoned it was a firework.

I thought of Grace and the people of the town and what they were doin' that night. When I closed my eyes I saw Bobby and Savannah in their house, in their separate rooms with their shared grief. And I saw that photo in the *Maidenville Herald* of them before they lost him.

"I can't let you go. I won't," he said, eyes hot.

"You can't keep me here."

"I have to. I saw it; there ain't always a choice. I got a chance to save you and your child. I'll keep you safe. That's my way back, Summer. *Deliver them out of the hand of the wicked.* God will see me, he'll see what I done before and what I'll do now. Sometimes sayin' sorry ain't nearly enough."

"It ain't for you to decide."

"I can't stand idle. I won't."

I sat awhile and tried to calm but I saw the effort and the care and I couldn't stop my legs from shakin'. It was real and I was scared.

"Are you the Bird?" I said, my voice holdin' as my mind ran to the Briar girls.

He stared at me, confused. "How could you think that?"

"I . . . I just –"

"I don't have interest in girls like that. I'm not some monster. I want to save you, Summer. You and your child. Why can't you see that?"

He stood awhile, eyes down and closed like he was pained. And then he asked me to pray with him. He kneeled beside the bed and bowed his white head.

I could hold back. I could leave myself and I could float and see Samson shepherding my lost soul toward the light, numb till I heard that first cry. But that cry would've been Bobby's 'cause there weren't no way back for him after.

Or I could steal the part of my sister that makes her burn, that fire too wild to harness, and I could take what was mine.

I felt it then, maybe I felt Raine and I felt my daddy. Maybe I felt the girl they saw and the girl I was and I really saw the difference between the two. It weren't anger; it was something neater and cooler, that realization that I had it in me to act.

I reached for the hot tea and I turned and threw it in Samson's face, and I saw that divine contentment melt from it. His cheek, the skin blisterin' devil red on that pure white.

And then I ran.

I ran from that room in that house and I ran across the dirt and into the street.

There were too many stars that night, that's what I thought. He'd made it too pretty for me.

I saw the van straight off.

That same van from earlier, watchin', sittin' idle with dipped lights, waitin' on me 'cause the want was so strong. My choices, my decision; the ends were one and the same 'cause our only shared destiny is a physical death.

I stopped still in the middle of the road.

And then I turned and there was a truck. It was comin' fast but I saw it slow, the writing on the hood: BOWDOIN CONSTRUCTION.

That moment when it hit, I ain't sure how to tell it.

That divide that cut, that light and dark that people go on about.

The street was hot but I was shiverin'.

The moon was blue but I lay dyin'.

I saw the van roll away into the dark and I wondered which girl he'd call on next. The Bird didn't claim me but I was claimed.

I heard Samson's voice and he was cryin' but not from the pain, just maybe from the loss.

I heard Ray Bowdoin, and I heard the slappin' and the slurrin' and the threatenin' 'cause he was lit and he couldn't go down for it. And he told Samson he'd been in the attic and seen what was hid in the file cabinet.

Maybe it went on quick or maybe it was hours. Maybe I felt my clothes come off and my ring come off but by then there weren't nothin' left anyway.

It played like an opera and I was Violetta, resigned and broke, driftin' through nightmares and daydreams till the end found me.

She can't be alone 'cause there's no one to hold her hand.

My sister, I thought. I'd miss my sister most.

46

Motherfuckin' Badass Cowboy

Samson Lumen walked outta the police station at dawn. He chose to leave the back way, head down and moving fast, fear hotter than it'd ever been.

When word reached the pastor and the church people there were nods and handshakes and nothing more.

Black arrested Joe and Tommy Ryan, and Austin Ray Chalmers, then let them free. Charges could be brought later.

Black didn't know what the next days would bring for Joe, but no way he could face them from behind bars. Black guessed Jimmy King was one of the shooters in the woods; he was a sniper in the army for a dozen years and could hit a nickel from a quarter mile. He also guessed Jimmy left Hell's Gate via one of the slips and beat them back to the square. He knew Jimmy could've shot them dead but that weren't ever the aim. Joe had waited long enough, it was always coming. Black was just glad no one was hurt, and that Amber King was still alive.

If the circus was bad the day before, it grew outta control following the photos of Noah and Amber in front of the station.

The image of them and the flag behind, and that sky so tough.

The circus moved from the square to the wall on Hallow Road. They aimed cameras at Hell's Gate and spoke of the grisly discovery inside. The crowds were reeling 'cause all that talk and all those rumors had turned to facts so hard people could barely face them.

Black stood in the hanging shade of the trees watching the team work. He was so beat he saw in tunnels like there were hands cupped around his eyes.

The FBI arrived in heavy numbers 'cause there might've been more girls, girls from outta state. They left black sedans and tech vans parked at the edge of Hell's Gate while they cleared a road. The area was sectioned off a mile in every direction. There was another team up at the main house, sifting it on their hands and knees.

"You been in?" Milk said.

Black nodded.

"Must've taken him a long time, digging it out so deep."

Black nodded.

"Anything else?"

"Not yet. It's early. They'll take their time, could be a grave-yard under our feet for all we know."

"You thinkin' . . . Summer?"

"Yeah. I am."

"She left that note, Black."

"She did."

"But you still reckon –"

"Yeah. What he said to Raine, he could've been lyin' but . . ." he trailed to silence.

Black and Milk walked out of the shade. Milk wore sunglasses, Black just squinted. It was a quarter mile to the Deamer house, one of them. There were three in total, wood lodges built up and out. They'd cleared a large part of Hell's Gate, flattened the land and planted grass. There was an old slide, red with rust, and a couple chicken coops that stunk bad but didn't have any birds in them.

They heard the low rumble of a helicopter in the distance. They couldn't get close 'cause the cloud weren't far and covered some of the Deamer land, the dogleg that crossed the border.

There was a narrow track that led to an access road that came out in a hidden spot off Highway 125. There was a couple of trucks dropped around the land. One had Virginia plates, another had a Georgia Tech bumper sticker. A lot to look into. The FBI had picked up Dolores Auvil from the West End Mission and she was talking. Whatever she had to say didn't change much of anything now.

"They ain't hustlin' like they're searchin' for live girls," Milk said.

Black sighed, nodded, and closed his eyes.

They heard noise. The digging had started at dawn, after the dogs had been brought in.

They wandered over slow 'cause neither really wanted to. They stopped short of the hole, fresh dirt piled beside and men all over. There was a red flag planted.

"What you got?" Milk said.

One of the agents turned, he was young, too young. "Girl."

"Summer Ryan?"

The agent shook his head. "This one's been dead a long time. Got a necklace, nameplate, *Della*."

Black nodded.

Milk reached a hand out and grabbed his shoulder.

"Let's get outta here for a while," Milk said.

They walked back to the cruiser and drove back into Grace.

Lights burned bright in homes, trucks passed by with low beams.

*

Noah sat alone in the dialysis ward. The Transit bus had been bad; he'd stood the whole journey 'cause folk had taken to riding it just to pass through the dark wall. There'd been reporters at Mayland when he got off. They'd seen him and started yelling and scrambling. A Briar County deputy kept them away.

Missy had sat with him and told him how stupid he was, how bad it could've been skipping dialysis. But she'd seen the news so she kept her tone soft and held his hand. She told him he was lucky and he smiled at that.

He watched the television and saw news reports on every channel, cutting from the square to Hallow Road to aerial shots of the edge of the Deamer land. They showed a photo of the Bird, grainy and faded but Noah felt cold when he saw it.

His name was Harvey Hail Deamer, and reporters had it he was sent to live with an aunt in Odessa shortly after his sister Mandy died.

There were missing girls in other states so they were trying to piece Harvey's movements over the years. Despite the talk, he was the only Deamer living on their land.

What happened to the rest was still being worked out.

The press cooked up old reports of Panic events, ran a timeline like it was even close to being linked. They showed a shot of Richie Reams from way back, then a shot of Franny Vestal and her devil house by the woods. Then they showed Mandy Deamer, and Noah stared at her smile and was glad he was a believer 'cause that was the only way it could be all right. Heaven. They were all in heaven now.

When he was done he left the ward and took the elevator to the third floor. He saw another deputy, who smiled and nodded and told Noah he'd done good.

"Can I go in?" Noah said.

"Sure," the deputy said.

Noah opened the door careful, in case she was sleeping.

Amber was sitting up in the bed, her parents either side.

Jessie-Pearle got straight up and lunged and nearly knocked Noah off his feet. She squeezed him so tight.

"Jesus, Mom," Amber said.

"Thank you," Jessie-Pearle said into Noah's ear, then kissed his cheek and held his face in her hands.

Jimmy King stood, locked Noah with a serious gaze, and nodded; his eyes were red. Noah extended a hand. Jimmy shook it then pulled him in and hugged him quick.

"You need anything, ever . . . you're family now."

Noah smiled and didn't know what to say.

Jessie-Pearle made eyes at her husband. "We're goin' down to get some coffee."

Noah waited till they were out the door then pulled a chair back and sat.

"I'm Noah, by the way."

Amber nodded, then closed her eyes tight. Noah took her hand. They sat like that till a nurse looked in and asked if she was all right and she said yeah like she was.

"Raine . . . her sister?" Amber said.

"I ain't sure." He hadn't seen her since her momma led her from the station.

"I would've died."

"You don't –"

"I just want you to know." Her voice cracked. "That man, he said he was waitin' on a full moon. He would've done it, like the other girls."

They sat quiet for a while, both realizing they were perfect strangers. Noah looked down at his father's badge. He thought of TV cops and all those bright colors and how long and far they lay from the outside.

"They want me to talk to a shrink," she said.

"Oh."

"They look at me different."

"Who?"

"My parents. They reckon they want to know, what went on down there, but they don't."

"All that shit he was sayin', that man."

"The cops want to know, about the other girls." She stared at the sheet covering her, her voice flat and quiet. "I ain't got nothin' to say. The things he said, it didn't make no sense."

"That's the way it's been, ain't nothin' neat 'cause life ain't like that. Questions ain't always answered. None of it matters now. He's gone and you're here."

"Yeah."

"You can come hang out, when you're feelin' better maybe. If you want to come to Grace, or maybe we can come see you."

She nodded.

"Is everything else okay?" he said, 'cause he knew.

She placed a hand on her stomach. "The baby is still there. My parents know but they ain't said nothin' 'cept that it'll be all right. That it'll all be all right."

"I'll let you get some rest."

He smiled and stood and turned toward the door.

"Noah."

He looked back.

"You're brave, you know that? Most boys ain't, they just think they are."

"You're brave too," he said.

She lay back.

The halls were quiet, the strip lighting bare. He was brave and he was fierce, and he stopped in the restroom, locked himself in a stall, and cried.

*

Purv walked along Jackson Ranch Road then cut into the square. The warring sides had packed their shit and headed home. There was a cold feel to Grace, not just 'cause it was dark. The sandbags still cut the grass in half; there was litter all over. Purv looked up at the station, stopped and sat awhile on the stone steps. He worried about Raine and about Summer. And he worried about Noah. Purv had failed them; he should've got the gun and shot the Bird himself. He was nearer but couldn't move, would've stood perfect still and watched the Bird claim them all.

He got up and walked over to St. Luke's and kept his pace slow 'cause he didn't really have no place to go.

He saw the gravestones and wondered if they'd have a space for Summer. She was small like Raine, just a kid.

He looked up at the church and the bell tower, the colored glass and the big fuckin' cross. He leaned down and picked up a rock. He hurled it and it hit the big wood door. He heard someone yell so he took off, running so fast the town lights streaked.

He stopped at the bottom of Dove Ridge, one of the pretty streets, hands on his knees and panting. He glanced over at the Beauregard house and saw them saying grace through the drapes, candles on the table and silver shining above the fireplace. And then he glanced at the porch, at the bottom of the steps, and that's when he saw it, perfect and calling. Pastor Lumen's scooter.

He walked over and saw the old man had left the keys in 'cause there weren't no one dumb enough to steal it. He thought of that shit Pastor Lumen had said about Noah, how he deserved to be sick, that shit about past sins.

Noah was low, Purv could already see his smile.

Purv handled it like a pro, hopping curbs and gunning the engine till it whined so loud he thought it'd blow.

He pulled a cigar from his pocket and lit it, then rode one-handed in the direction of Noah's place, like a motherfuckin' badass cowboy.

He didn't notice the car beside till the lights flashed blue and red.

Purv watched the new cop get out, the cop that was over from the Sheriff's Office till the shitstorm died.

"You need to call Black," Purv said, as the cop opened the cruiser door and pushed him into the back.

"Chief Black is busy, or ain't you seen the news? I'll cut you a break and let your parents deal with you."

"Seriously, I ain't fuckin' round. You need to call Black right now, he'll sort this," Purv said, fear in his voice.

"Scared of what your daddy will say? You should be. Stealin' from a pastor, shit, he'll probably give you a hidin'. You won't be able to sit for a week," the cop said, laughing.

*

Raine had spent the day lying in Summer's bed. She curled herself around the cover, buried her head beneath, and broke into cold sweats.

She heard her parents leave, the truck start and pull away and she knew they were going to stand out by Hell's Gate, on the other side, where moonlight still fell in swathes of empty color.

She heard the door, felt herself move out of the room and down the stairs like she weren't there, like she was just a bystander.

She opened the door to Black. He didn't wear his hat, just carried it like it no longer fit.

"Are your parents home?" He spoke soft and kind and she hated him for it.

"No."

He nodded and turned.

"What did you find?" she said.

He shook his head.

"I can't breathe, Black. She's mine, more than she's anyone else's. I got to know now."

"We found a truck, burned out."

"Where?"

"Edge of Deamer land . . . where Hell's Gate forks the Red."

"And?"

"I should speak to –"

"What did you find?" she said loud and hard.

He held up a clear bag and she saw the ring in it, Summer's ring with the blue stone that matched hers. Their daddy had brought them home when he got out. They didn't ever take them off. Not ever.

She closed the door and climbed the stairs. She reached over and picked up the photograph in the glitter frame and held it awhile.

It fell from her hand when she cried.

The glass smashed. She slipped the photo out, grasping it tight, and she saw something behind. It was a flower pressed flat, and as she held it up to the light she gasped 'cause the checkered bell cast a lantern-pink glow over the room. And she wondered where her sister had got an Alabama Pink from.

Her sister. She had to see the place where the cops found her ring. The place where the Bird had taken her.

She walked down the stairs and grabbed the keys to her momma's truck.

*

Purv sat by the window, and if he strained real hard then he thought he could make out the sound of crickets. The front door was locked. The back door was locked.

They were downstairs. He could hear the television and maybe it was *Jeopardy* or *Family Feud* or some other game show his momma liked the visual of. Smiling families.

He crept into their bedroom, picked up the telephone and dialed Noah.

"Where were you?" Noah said.

"Couldn't get away," Purv said.

"Oh."

Noah knew. Always did.

"You want me to come over?"

"No, it's all right," Purv said.

"I saw Amber King," Noah said. His voice was quiet.

"Yeah. How's she doin'?"

"She's healing, the cuts, they cleaned 'em up but she had this look in her eyes like the Bird took somethin' that can't be put back."

"Is the baby all right?"

"Yeah, the baby's all right."

"That's good."

Purv looked around his parents' bedroom. There was a cross tacked above the bed. They left the drapes open so streetlight fell in.

"I couldn't sleep," Purv said.

"Me neither."

"They reckon Olive Braymer fought back. They found a knife, had her prints, and a bad scar on the Bird's stomach. He weren't done, all that time, he was just healing up."

"Too bad she didn't kill him."

"That was fucked up. The whole thing. Raine, havin' to hear him say that stuff. Watchin' him get blown away like that. I mean, you see that shit in movies . . . you pulled the trigger, Noah. People are sayin' you're a hero just like your father."

He heard Noah laugh but knew there weren't nothing behind it.

"You reckon that means I could be a cop?" Noah said.

" 'Course it does."

"I was thinkin' about New Orleans."

"Yeah?"

"I reckon we should go soon."

"Me too."

"We got a letter from Social Services this mornin'. They want to come again. And my grandmother, with her mind gone like that. She's got friends to look out for her, the church. She ain't gonna miss me, probably won't know I'm gone."

"We'll go. We can find work. We'll take the Buick, get a new door, plan a careful route. The guy in Windale, the one I was tellin' you about, he can get us fake cards. Real good."

"I was thinkin' maybe we could ask Raine if she wants to come."

Purv smiled 'cause Noah sounded nervous.

"Purv?"

"Yeah, I reckon that's a good idea. Though she'd have to square it with Joe. Imagine havin' him on our tail for three hundred miles."

Noah laughed.

There was quiet for a long time.

"I was also thinkin' . . . I know we don't say it, but maybe we got a raw deal. Our lives . . ." Noah said.

Purv swallowed. "Yeah. Maybe, when you think about it."

"We got this though, now. We get to go through it . . . side by side. I ain't even sure what I'm sayin'. I'm tired, I guess. We don't cry, right?"

Purv held the receiver away for a minute 'cause his voice wouldn't hold. "We don't cry. We're brave and we're fierce."

"We are. We don't forget that."

Purv set the phone down.

He crossed the hallway quiet. He went into his bedroom and climbed on his nightstand and reached on top of his closet. He grabbed the hunting knife and lay down and waited.

His father came for him just before midnight, when the liquor made way for the anger.

Purv raised the knife, gripping it tight, holding it level with his father's face.

It was then he knew it was a mistake. The kinda mistake you don't recover from.

He dropped the knife, his arm twisted up behind his back till he felt his shoulder slip from the socket.

He fell forward, his face against the window.

For a moment he thought he saw Noah at the end of the yard. But then the sky flashed bright, and the yard lit, and there weren't no one there at all.

And as the storm finally dropped on the town of Grace, Purv had the life beaten all out of him.

47

When the Storm Comes

It was late but the first wave of thunder was loud enough to see
the people of Grace rise from their beds. Lights came on and
robes were pulled tight as kids pressed close to windows, their
anxious parents beside. They stopped frozen 'cause of the sight
in the sky. The cloud was twisting. Hopes of it fading quiet died.
Doors were locked and prayers were said. Those with shelters
made their way down with packs they'd readied. Some called
family, others called the police department.

The agents working the Deamer land moved out of Grace as the
sky crackled and flashed. A young agent, the same guy Black had
spoke to, craned his neck so far back he ended up on his ass. No
one laughed 'cause no one could turn from the cloud.

   At the end of the Deamer track, standing in a line behind the
tape, was Joe and Ava and Tommy and fifteen of their people.
A little way up were families of the Briar girls and their friends.
And standing alone at the end was Peach Palmer. She paced a
while 'cause she couldn't stand the waiting. And when the deputies turned she slipped under the tape and ran toward the woods
and the town beyond.

"Raine?" Tommy said.

"Home. Safe," Ava said.

They looked over at Grace lit under flashes of fire in the sky.

*

Raine kept the high beams on and her speed down till she got to Lott and then she floored it. She didn't pay mind to the storm 'cause she didn't much care if the whole sky fell onto Grace.

She kept to the back roads 'cause she reckoned Hallow Road would be tight with visitors and cameras and cops.

She tried to follow the Red but the tracks didn't hold a true line so she crossed from Windale to Grace and back, from rattling thunder to easy starlight.

A couple miles up from the spot where Richie Reams's cock had once washed up she saw a line of police tape reflecting back at her. She parked in the grass and looked out the windshield at the deep tracks in the mud where they'd come and taken the truck away.

There weren't rain yet but the wind had picked up fast and it whistled around her momma's truck, rocking it from side to side.

She climbed out and moved slow, her head bowed low and eyes locked on her feet as she walked the woods.

She carried a heavy flashlight and shined it a couple of feet out.

Her throat was sore and her arms were heavy but she kept moving, beyond the cut of the truck beams and into shadow. The wind whipped so loud she couldn't make out the sound of the Red but she knew it was near.

She came to a spot where black-burned roots and leaves spread wide and she knew that was where the truck had been.

The calm that took her was so sudden and total that she almost smiled, 'cause she couldn't feel it, not at all. She was close to certain her sister hadn't been there. She held out her hands wide and she heard nothing but the sweep of tree branches above as they moved together.

The wind rose and died and rose again but when it dropped away to nothing she shined the flashlight out far and drew a sharp breath, 'cause glowing back at her were the light eyes of a hundred Alabama Pinks.

When she was small she'd wondered if they were real, the flowers so rare a lifetime of searching weren't enough to find them. She reached down and picked one, and she shone her flashlight through the bell and watched the pink glow fall.

And now Summer had one, and Raine thought hard about where she'd seen another. When it came to her she turned and she ran the trail back to the truck.

*

Noah eased the Buick down Lott, the wind slamming it so hard he fought to keep the wheel straight. He'd tried to sleep, but he'd turned and rolled in shallow dreams. He'd woke sweating and thought maybe he was sick. But then his mind had run to Purv, so he'd picked up the telephone and tried calling him but the line was out.

He jammed the brake pedal when a trash can dropped from the sky and landed beside the hood. Then a cop car swerved in front and Black jumped out. Noah watched as he bent low and ran over, then climbed into the Buick.

Noah expected Black to yell but saw nothing but sad in his eyes.

"Where you headed?"

"Purv. I think somethin's happened, Black. I can't explain it; I should've waited. I usually wait out in his yard and watch the window. And I got that feelin' tonight. I was so tired . . . but I can't even sleep 'cause I keep seein' what happened with the Bird and people reckon I'm brave for what I did but I ain't. 'Cause brave people don't cry, Black. You know?"

Noah stared at the cruiser, rocking in the wind, blue and red.

"We found Summer's ring."

Noah closed his eyes and breathed out heavy.

"I told Raine. You should go see her. I'll go to Purv's place and check on him."

Noah nodded.

"You get there and leave the Buick at her place and we'll sort it out in the mornin'. And drive slow, it's gettin' worse out there and you got a door missin'."

Black made to get out.

"Black," Noah said.

Black turned.

"I was thinkin', after all this. I know you reckon it was your fault . . . my father. I know that, but at the end, when my momma was sick, she told me to stick by you. She said there weren't a better man out there."

Black stared out at the storm.

"I reckon just 'cause people lose their way, don't mean they can't find it again."

Black reached out and gripped Noah's shoulder tight, and then he turned and ran for the cruiser.

*

Raine followed Samson into the Lumen house. It was dark inside though a lamp burned. Samson was taller than she thought, broader and more like a man.

They stood in the living room and she stared at him and he looked scared. Maybe he'd been crying too. He kept glancing at the window and the sky.

"My daddy wanted me to say sorry for what I did," Raine said.

"It ain't nice out, you should be careful."

"He said I should say sorry to the pastor as well."

"He's in the hospital again."

All the light flickered and died.

She saw the shape of him, the halo of hair.

"I know it's you," she said. "The flower. Summer had an Alabama Pink. I only ever seen one other and you got it in a frame on the wall." She could just make it out, the bold pink. It fit now—Samson was the older man.

"He's come for me," he said, eyes on the window like he hadn't even been listening.

He had the softest voice.

"My daddy should've drowned me that day by the Red. Momma stopped him but she was wrong. It didn't leave me, that dark. It don't never leave no matter what you do. I see that man on the television. The Bird. I can hate him 'cause he's bad but then I think of what I did –"

"Are you afraid of dyin'?" Raine said.

Lightning flashed and she saw him for a moment before the shadow stole him away.

"Yes."

" 'Cause you'll burn."

"Yes."

Raine swallowed. "Do you know where my sister is?"

"Yes."

*

Black stared up at the house, then up at the cloud, which was twisting and flashing mad. There was light burning over at the neighbor's place, people pressed at the windows and watched him liked he'd come to save them.

He got out to wind that howled all around like crying wolves. The sheet flashes were forking now, he'd seen strikes on the drive. Trix had radioed, told him Peach had made it to the station and that gave him focus on a night when death was strolling the streets.

He bent so low he could almost taste the dirt as he ran up and onto the porch.

He banged the door with a tight fist and kept on till he was sure no one was coming, then he started kicking. It split easy at the cracks that'd been filled and filled again. He crouched low and entered through the torn hole.

He turned the light on and saw tired bare carpet and yellow paper on the walls.

"Purv," he called. "Ray."

He drew his gun, trained it out, and moved into the living room. There was a couple sofas that didn't match nothing and a mirror with a jagged crack down the edge. "Purv, you all right?"

He moved into the kitchen. It was old oak and clean. There was a painting on the wall, a cheap print of a southern scene, a farmer and a horse and a pitchfork.

"Caroline," he called.

There were flashes in the yard, then deep thunder. The rain would come.

The lights cut.

He climbed the stairs slow, kept the gun up 'cause he got that same feeling that Noah had.

The doors around were shut.

He opened one, saw it was the spare bed so tried the next. And then he saw him, Purv, his body small and twisted and laying beneath the window.

"Hell, Purv," he said. And he kneeled and turned him over as the sky flashed and he saw Purv's face so white. "Hell, Purv. Jesus."

He took out a handkerchief and gently wiped Purv's face 'cause there was blood dried over his eyes, and then Black choked up. He thought of Peach and Della and the Bird and those deep holes they were digging in Hell's Gate that held such horrors.

He stood and walked across the hallway and opened the last door. He saw Ray Bowdoin lying in the bed in a heavy sleep, an empty bottle of Lawson's on the pillow and a handgun on the nightstand like he was waiting on trouble. He wondered where Caroline was but reckoned she'd run 'cause she'd done that before.

Black stared at the wicker cross tacked to the wall, and then he raised his gun and he shot Ray Bowdoin in the head.

He took his handkerchief, and he reached for the handgun from the nightstand and placed it loose in the dead man's hand, and he ran back out to the cruiser and called it in.

The medics arrived. And then Milk got there, and he saw Purv and he saw Purv's father, and he nodded at Black and Black nodded back.

*

Savannah watched the divorce papers burn black in the fireplace. She crouched close and felt the flames hot on her skin.

She'd heard everything about the bad man in Hell's Gate, and how he'd taken the church girls from Briar County. She thought of Ava and Joe, and she thought of Raine. But mostly she thought of Summer. Her heart ached with the loss, with all that Summer was and all that she would miss.

Savannah felt it now, because of Summer the doubt was gone, she couldn't lose anything more. Leaving Bobby was running and she didn't have anyplace else to go. She would do it, stand by silent for the rest of her life if it meant staying close to him.

She left the house and the storm was loud and wind knocked her back. She wasn't afraid, she'd lived through worse.

When she reached the church she fell on the stone path and cut her knees and palms. She forced herself to crawl till she reached the heavy door and pushed it open.

The wind echoed high and she called his name but her voice swept to nothing. She looked around and saw the small door open.

She climbed the steps till she was high in the tower and then she heard him.

He knelt on the wood plinth and cried so hard and raw she stood still. His eyes were clenched tight, his body shook and his hands knotted tight in prayer. The sound came in waves, from someplace deep inside him, guttural like he was hurt too bad.

She watched him fall, his head pressed to the wood like he couldn't hold himself any longer. And then she crossed the beams and he heard her.

He wiped his eyes fast and hard and she dropped to kneel beside him.

"She's one of the Briar girls, that's what they're sayin'." He said it quiet but desperate.

She felt the pain.

"I saw a lawyer, in Maidenville," she said.

"I know."

She closed her eyes.

"I saw the papers."

"How did you find them?"

"I was lookin' for Michael's shoebox."

"Oh, Bobby."

The tower lit white as the sky blinked and they heard thunder roar loud.

"Will you leave me?" he said.

She fought back tears.

"My mother left me," he said.

"I know."

"Do you know why?"

She cried and shook her head.

"'Cause there weren't room for me." Bobby looked up past the clockface and saw the spinning air as the storm cloud fell.

"I wanted to die," he said.

"I love you. It's not lost," she said. "I thought maybe it was but now I see you, I see you kneeling right here. I've done things, I'm so sorry. I wanted to feel something. It's been so long since I felt anything. Tell me you understand, Bobby. Tell me."

"I understand."

She moved to face him, her knees pained.

"How do I save you, Bobby? Tell me what to do."

He shook his head.

"For by grace you have been saved through faith. You can find it again, Bobby. You can. I won't leave you."

He took her face in his hands. "Summer . . . I can't lose anyone else. I see it, she made me see it."

"You haven't lost me, Bobby. I'm not going anywhere."

"Everything bad. Anyone close to me, I ruin."

She shook her head hard. "That's not true."

"My path and where it began. Those men and that home."

She took his hand and held it to her chest. "I'm your home. I am, Bobby."

He dipped his head and closed his eyes. She pulled him close and kissed his head and held him tight.

*

Raine stood behind Samson on the porch of the Lumen house. Samson was shaking, she could see that, his whole body shaking like he was sick.

"Where is she?"

He turned and looked at her like he'd forgotten he weren't alone in the world. "The sun shall be turned to darkness and the moon to blood, before the day of the Lord comes, the great and magnificent day."

She looked into his eyes. She didn't know what was waiting on her, or where he was leading her.

"Is this him comin' for me?" Samson said, as the sky roared and he crouched and cupped his ears with his pale hands. "Which he, is that what you're thinkin', Raine? But you ain't 'cause you know. I won't go to heaven."

"Where's my sister?"

"I couldn't do it. What Ray said. I dumped the truck someplace they wouldn't know about. But not with her inside. Cremation like that, profane, that desecration. I was weak, when Ray came and saw me at the station. He told Black it was just about the money but he held a blade against my throat."

"We'll run to the truck."

He shook his head. "She's near. I couldn't move her. I couldn't do it."

"What did you do to her?"

"I tried to save a life before it was taken. Redemption, for her and for me."

Raine swallowed. She had the gun in her bag and she kept her hand on it. She'd kill him, after, not tell Black or her daddy. If Summer was hurt she'd shoot him dead.

"He talks about forgiveness but some things shouldn't be forgiven or they kill the hopes of many to absolve the few. Does that sound right?"

She stared out across the plains, at the tall crops folding and ripping from the ground and flying into the darkness. Lightning fell and burned the land.

"Take me to my sister," she said.

"Don't be afraid, Raine. You'll keep safe."

He stared at her, tears in his pink eyes.

He ran then.

She tried to follow but he was fast and clear on his land.

She fell when the blue light dropped from the sky and struck him dead in a flash of fire, like he was damned.

She got to her feet and moved close and saw his body, the white burned black and his eyes locked in eternal fear. And she screamed at him and against the wind drew her gun and threatened him but he'd always been a ghost.

So she spun and looked around 'cause he said Summer was near but there weren't nothing near.

Then she saw it. Merle's farmhouse with the caved roof standing ruined.

Raine felt it so strong she could barely stand. Wind hurtled in through the window she'd broke. She tried the lights but the power was out. She breathed short and quick. She looked around, blue flashes lighting the farmhouse kitchen.

"Summer," she called.

She moved through the kitchen slow, jumping as the wind rattled the glass. The smell grew stronger in the hallway. Raine coughed, fighting for breath. She entered the living room; it was grim and dark and she looked up where the roof bowed.

The carpet was wet beneath. She reached out, touching the painted wall, feeling it slick.

Another flash, she saw a picture above the fire, could've been a boat but it was lost to the dark.

She stared out as another bolt struck the ground outside and cratered the dirt. And then she heard it, another sound close behind her.

She spun.

There weren't nothing there.

She stepped back, heard the sound again, this time loud. It was creaking. Her mouth fell open but the scream didn't make it to her lips before the ground fell from under her.

At the dark wall a crowd of hundreds gathered and stared into Grace. Reporters stood in front of cameras trained at the sky, most struck mute by the sight playing out behind them. Rollers from White Mountain had shown, and they watched from their knees certain the end was close, that the Lord had come and the powers of the heavens were shaking.

Joe and Ava and Tommy rode in a truck down Hallow Road as people looked on and wondered what kinda mad it took to see people so keen to meet their end.

*

Raine lay flat and stared up from the flooded basement of the farmhouse. Her shoulder hurt and maybe her ankle was twisted 'cause the pain was so hot she felt sweat running into her eyes.

She coughed and choked, trying to find clear air through the dust that smoked up around.

She yelled out for help.

She pushed at the heavy wood on top of her but the pain stole her breath. She could see her bag but couldn't reach it.

"Summer," she called.

She ran her fingers along the cement and tried to push and kick but couldn't do nothing. The water was cold and black and a few inches deep like it'd been flooding in over months. There weren't calm to be found 'cause the pain was searing, but she closed her eyes tight and she searched for Noah and Purv, and her sister and the photograph, and the glass globe with the falling snowflakes.

She heard the wind and the storm, she heard the roof tear from the farmhouse and felt the first falling rain. The water rose quick and climbed her. She thrashed and she screamed and she fought.

*

Black made it back to the station and he rolled the cruiser into the lot as the rain hit hard on the windshield. He sat awhile and thought of what he had done, and he looked at his hands but there weren't room for no more blood on them.

When he opened the door he stopped still and let the rain push him down. And then he looked up and he saw her and she ran at him.

"Della," Peach said, and he nodded and tried to hold her as she dropped to her knees and beat on his chest.

He kneeled with her and smoothed wet hair from her face. "Did you know? Did you know about the baby?"

"I couldn't let 'em see it," she said, desperate.

"What?"

"Me in her."

Black swallowed and nodded and didn't say all that he could have. He held her tight as the rain washed her tears.

*

The Grace roads turned to rivers. The Red filled and began to spill over.

The rain fell with a weight that left people believing the glass in their windows would shatter and the storm would fight its way into their houses and claim them. They hid in closets, under beds and in basements. They huddled together and closed their eyes. Prayers were spoke loud 'cause maybe God couldn't hear over the thunder.

The crowd on Hallow Road grew to a thousand as word spread to the towns around. They stood dry; a stark line of rain fell ten feet in front. The winds had eased but the rain fell harder, and the cloud still drenched the land with its shadow.

Merle was the first to notice the break, the thin line of blue moonlight that cut through as the cloud began to crack. He hollered but no one looked 'cause maybe they reckoned he was lit.

Then he grabbed a newsman and pointed.

There were cries.

*

Noah stared through the windshield at moments of clear that swept with the blades. He saw light in the distance and it stretched from the sky to the ground. He didn't know what it was but he headed toward it 'cause he didn't know where else to go. The Buick struggled for grip but he kept his foot on the gas.

It was only when he passed the yellow fields and the Kinley house that he realized where he was headed.

The Lumen house.

The light had fallen by the Lumen house.

*

Light flooded the basement bright. The water had risen to Raine's neck and she lifted her head back, trying to breathe slow. The rain fell relentless and she was so cold nothing hurt no more.

The black water weighed heavy and it shifted the wood enough for her to reach a hand out and grab hold of her bag. She found the gun and raised it high and she fired till the clip was empty.

And then the water rose over her head. She fought hard 'cause she always had, it was what she did, she fought and she struggled and she got no place at all.

It was quiet beneath, light and quiet and she stared around the basement floor with wide eyes. She saw broken wood and cans of food and an old mattress, and papers that floated like water lilies. And then, in the far corner, she saw strands of gold hair fanned and beautiful.

She cried out for her sister till her lungs burned and hope died around her.

Maybe she saw Noah dive down, and maybe she felt his hands on her, but she closed her eyes tight and she asked God to take her.

*

She woke on the bank of the Red. She turned and saw Summer laying beside her.

They were eight years old.

Above they watched a distant star tumble through the night sky. This time Raine remembered what to do.

She turned to Summer and took her in her arms and held her tight as sobs broke her small body, 'cause she knew she was too late for her wish to come true.

48

Summer

I played my cello during the early service at St. Luke's one Sunday mornin'. I didn't want to, I didn't like the thought of people watchin' me 'cause there weren't no way they would've got it, what it meant.

I couldn't sleep the night before. I lay there thinkin' about everythin' and nothin'. I wondered about Descartes and impossible certainty, what I thought I knew but didn't never.

I made Savannah play piano alongside 'cause I said I wouldn't sit up there alone.

Momma bought me a new dress and she fussed with my hair while Raine kneeled in front and painted my lips. I saw Daddy watchin' us, and he wore this smile like maybe he knew somethin' we didn't. "My girls," he said.

As I waited for everyone to take their seats I let my eyes drift to the stained glass. I thought about sittin' there when I was small, when white was white and black was somethin' nearer to gray. I wanted to cry but held it. That feelin', when somethin' you reckon you've got a handle on rears up and faces you, makes you see it for the first time. Fifteen ain't old enough to hit reset.

I played *The Swan* by Camille Saint-Saëns 'cause Savannah said I could choose anythin'. I played it even though I knew it was tough for her and for Bobby. I knew it was their song and maybe Michael's but that didn't mean it weren't mine too, 'cause in the end we are all one and we are all the same.

I reckon maybe that was the only time I got it, what they saw and what they heard.

My fingers found the strings with a grace I ain't never sought before. My fiberglass bow glided over them in the way I guessed a pernambuco might. I closed my eyes and breathed deep, I let my shoulders drop and my mind run far from the church and the people and the earth that carried them.

I ain't sure what I believed, God or somethin' like him, but at that moment I felt if there weren't a roof on the old building the music would've soared high into the sky and maybe those in the heavens would've smiled down on me.

I didn't count notes, I didn't search them out, they found me.

I played away my decisions, good and bad. I played away my sister's hurt and my daddy's loss and my momma's misplaced pride. I played away Bobby's touch and whatever it meant to him and to me.

When I reached the final note I listened to it melt away into the kinda quiet that only visits once. I dipped my head and clutched my bow tight, scared to look up in case they saw it, that there weren't nothin' left of me to give to anyone. They had it all.

The silence stretched long and wide and maybe the birds fell quiet and the Red stopped flowin'. I felt somethin' shift in Grace that day. Nothin' big, nothin' no one would notice but me.

I heard the first clap and knew it belonged to my sister. I ain't sure how I knew, but I did. And that first clap was joined by a second, and then a hundred.

I opened my eyes and saw my parents stand, and then Savannah and Bobby, and then everyone else. I saw people cryin' that didn't never cry, people that'd lost their jobs and their place but their faith remained true. And for a moment they weren't even shamed neither, and maybe they did see me and maybe that was all right just that one time.

I looked down at my cello 'cause I didn't know where else to look, and then back up at the stained glass 'cause I knew a rainbow fell on the other side.

And then I saw Raine sittin' lone in the far corner, no longer clapping but cryin' too. I met her eye and she smiled wide 'cause they weren't those sad cries I heard when she thought the house was sleepin'.

Through her tears she nodded at me, and through tears of my own I nodded back.

49

The Light That Was Left

Noah sat alone in the dialysis ward. He glanced over at the nurses' station. There was a new nurse and she was nice but she kept to herself. He stared at the television set, then at the empty space where Purv usually sat.

Six months had passed since the storm.

Since Ray Bowdoin was killed and Samson Lumen was killed.

Folk said that maybe the Lord's work weren't as mysterious after all; cause and effect in its purest form. When Pastor Lumen learned of his son's actions he suffered another stroke, this one so bad he weren't likely to recover.

Raine had been taken to Mayland; she was close to death that night. If Noah hadn't heard those gunshots it might've been different. The newspapers said he was a hero all over again.

The morning that followed saw Noah get up early and walk down the stairs and straight out the front door to stand in the yard. He stopped still and stared up at a sky fired with all the colors, a sunrise so beautiful maybe it slowed time awhile.

He'd looked across the street and seen Bud Grierson and his wife standing side-by-side and watching too. And then he'd heard the Dumans' front door open and saw them follow.

The reporters had it that near every person in Grace woke early that morning, didn't even notice the damage the storm had done 'cause they couldn't see nothing but the dawn of new light.

Noah was about to holler for his grandmother when Black pulled the cruiser up front. And then Black told Noah about Purv and Noah had run to the Buick.

Black had stood there beneath that open heaven and watched him go.

The summer cloud had finally lifted from the town of Grace, but an even darker one remained.

*

Summer was buried in the grounds of St. Luke's, beneath an Okame cherry that flowered so pretty folk stopped for a moment to notice it.

Noah sat alone at the back during the service, watching Pastor Bobby talk, then listening to a recording of that same music Summer had played that day that everyone still spoke of, each note reaching a place inside of him that brought him closer to a girl he wished he'd known.

Halfway through, when Ava was breaking and Joe had his eyes closed tight, the plastic sheeting blew from the large hole in the slate roof of the old church, and sunlight spilled in as the music lifted up toward the sky.

Raine had left town with her parents shortly after. She hadn't spoken to him since that night; she hadn't spoken to nobody.

Black said they had kin someplace near the coast, so when Noah closed his eyes at night he saw her riding in the back of a truck down Route 65, passing the plains, her hand out the window like it was a bird.

*

There was a new painting on the wall. Maybe he recognized one of the fields, but then again it could've been anywhere.

He swallowed and his throat ran dry. He glanced at the blue machine and at the tubes and he breathed deep 'cause he had that feeling like he couldn't take it no more.

He pushed back in his chair, closed his eyes and sat there for a long time, counting slow in his mind like his momma had once told him but finding nothing helped at all.

"So there's this animal called a bearcat. And it smells like popcorn."

Noah opened his eyes and he saw Raine sitting on the chair beside him.

"A bearcat?"

She nodded.

"And it smells like popcorn?"

She nodded.

She crossed her legs beneath herself, tucked her hair back, and stared at the television set. He watched her for a while like she weren't real, and he thought maybe she looked a little different but he didn't know why.

"Will you come with me somewhere after this?" she said.

"Anywhere," he said.

*

It was a cold winter evening, though no one in Grace complained much about the weather no more. Though the sky was dark it was lit by the shine of a thousand stars.

Black walked up the winding pathway and into the cemetery behind St. Luke's.

He kneeled and laid a small bouquet beneath the headstone. He did that often.

Though he was sad he managed a smile when he read the perfectly simple inscription written at the base of her headstone.

Summer, my sister.

"You all right, Black," Purv said.

Black looked up, only just noticing he weren't alone.

"Yeah," he said, and then he stood. "You healing up okay?"

Purv shrugged. "Noah reckons I'm strong."

"Noah reckons a lot of shit."

Purv smiled. "I was just payin' my respects. I ain't sure why but I keep comin' here."

Black nodded.

"You look different, Black."

"How's that?"

"Maybe your eyes are clearer or somethin'."

Black frowned at him. Truth was he'd been to Pinegrove a couple times. The road was long and he didn't watch it close but maybe it weren't as dark as it once was.

"How come you're all gussied up?" Purv said.

"I ain't."

"And that cologne."

"I got a date, not that it's any of your business."

"With that lady stayin' at your place? Peach."

Black sighed.

"Small town."

"How's your mother doin'?"

Purv shrugged.

"You hear Amber King had her baby?" Purv said.

Black nodded. "I also heard what she called him."

"Noah ain't stopped smilin' about it."

They turned and began to head back toward the square. Purv walked with a limp now and probably always would.

As Black glanced back at the church and at the clock tower a light snow began to drift and fall.

He didn't notice the two figures that stood at the top, side by side, hand in hand.

ACKNOWLEDGEMENTS

Thank you:

As always to my beautiful wife Victoria. I'm really going to miss you when you turn forty and I trade you in. Seven more years of heaven though. Savour them.

My dad, for the endless plot discussions, and for not laughing when I pitched 'The Cloud Story'.

Joel Richardson, though you broke my heart I'll always be grateful for our time together. I miss you every day. Thank you for helping me tell this story, for changing what needed to be changed, and for being so funny and kind during a very long and difficult process.

Bec Farrell – we did it! Thank you for your faith, your brilliant edits, and for getting me here (despite all my kicking and screaming). You've got skills, Rebeccason. Christopherson.

All at Bonnier Zaffre, I love you guys and am acutely aware of how lucky I am to be working with you.

Katherine Armstrong, crime queen, and one of my fave people ever. I owe you a ridiculously big pizza.

The magical Emily Burns, for your belief, your energy, and your ability to bribe the national press.

My special agent, Cathryn Summerhayes. I found an old email where you said *'you'll be a published author one day, I promise'*. And now there's two books out there! Sometimes a thank you isn't enough, so I'll send booze.

Everyone at Curtis Brown, especially Katie McGowan and the awesome foreign rights team.

Nick Stearn, for the wonderful cover. That kiss is long overdue. Stop pretending you have a cold whenever I come in.

Siobhan O'Neill, for the early reads and amazing levels of support. I miss Jack (and you).

Kate Parkin and Mark Smith, for being the total opposite of scary publishing boss people.

Jeff Jamieson, for being so funny and charming (whilst bullying the local booksellers).

TeamTwenty7 – love y'all. G.J. you deal your drugs, we ain't judgin'.

Dominick Montalto, for the masterful copy-edit.

Suzanne Gale, the most lovely and talented cellist.

Mum, Toby, Julie and Dave, who go above and beyond in their support of me and my writing.

Claire and Tim, for the penis consultation.

Caroline Ambrose. #TeamBNA.

To the readers and reviewers that took *Tall Oaks* to their hearts. Manny loves you all.

Liz Barnsley, for taking the matches away, for seeing Summer as I saw her, and for supporting me when you were going through such a difficult time. You'll never know how grateful I am.

If you enjoyed *All The Wicked Girls?* why not try
Chris Whitaker's debut novel

TALL OAKS

Shortlisted for CrimeFest Last Laugh Award 2017

Longlisted for CWA John Creasey (New Blood) Dagger 2017

Tall Oaks is an idyllic small town, until the disappearance of a
young child throws the tight-knit community into crisis.

Jess Monroe, the boy's distraught mother, is simultaneously
leading the search and battling her own grief and
self-destructive behaviour. Her neighbours watch on,
their sympathy masking a string of dark secrets.

This is a small town where nothing is as it seems, and everyone
has something to hide. And as the investigation draws towards
a climax, prepare for a devastating final twist . . .

AVAILABILE IN PAPERBACK AND EBOOK NOW

Want to read
NEW BOOKS
before anyone else?

Like getting
FREE BOOKS?

Enjoy sharing your
OPINIONS?

Discover

READERS FIRST
Read. Love. Share.

Get your first free book just by signing up at
readersfirst.co.uk